CAN'T GET ENOUGH OF THE DUKE

ALSO BY LENORA BELL

WALLFLOWERS VS. ROGUES

Love Is a Rogue

The Devil's Own Duke

Duke Most Wicked

SCHOOL FOR DUKES

What a Difference a Duke Makes

For the Duke's Eyes Only

One Fine Duke

DISGRACEFUL DUKES

How the Duke Was Won

If I Only Had a Duke

Blame It on the Duke

THUNDERBOLT CLUB

You're the Duke That I Want

CAN'T GET ENOUGH OF THE DUKE

A Novel

LENORA BELL

An Imprint of HarperCollinsPublishers

hc.com

FIRST EDITION

Interior text design by Diahann Sturge-Campbell

Library of Congress Cataloging-in-Publication Data has been applied for.

ISBN 978-0-06-331692-8

26 27 28 29 30 LBC 5 4 3 2 1

For Amelia. Let's do this.

Author Note

The book within this book, *The Dragon and the Blue Star*, was loosely inspired by Sara Coleridge's *Phantasmion: A Fairy Tale*. Published in 1837, this strange, beautiful, and often dark tale is considered by many to be the first literary fantasy novel written in English. Maybe she never had fantasy cosplayers attend her book readings . . . but I like to imagine that she did.

Prologue

Deckard Payne, Duke of Warburton, knelt on the cold ground beside the fallen cavalryman.

"I'm not going to survive, am I?" Lieutenant John Crewe's eyes were the wild, dark green of a forest so thick it lived in perpetual night.

"You'll survive," Dex said grimly, ripping a length of cloth from his shirt and pressing it into his friend's chest wound.

Dark crimson quickly saturated white linen, the lifeblood of yet another young man feeding the Belgian soil. Dex had a sudden, wrenching vision of this field in the future. A thicket of tortured vines springing up from the blood, bearing sorrowful red roses. An accursed place, fed by death.

Dex's heavy cavalry regiment were armed with longswords and two holster pistols each, but it wasn't enough against the French lancers. Help had arrived and the enemy was in retreat, but not before more than half of his regiment had been mowed down by the long oak weapon with the cruel iron blade.

Sending men into battle with mismatched weaponry. *His fault.*

Crewe's blood soaking his hands. *His fault.*

"I'll carry you to the field hospital." He attempted to slide his arms under Crewe's shoulders.

"No," Crewe gasped. "There's no use carrying me anywhere. I'm dying."

"I won't let you die."

"Warburton." Crewe's breathing was shallow and erratic.

Dex gripped his hand. "I'm here."

"My daughter . . ."

"Yes?"

Crewe had often spoken of his young daughter during the long nights of the military campaign. She was the light of his life. He'd shown Dex a miniature portrait in a gold frame. Pale red curls framing an oval face with a sharply pointed chin. Prominent freckles. Lively, dancing green eyes.

"She'll be all alone in the world when I die," he whispered hoarsely. Fierce love lit his face. "I have her letters." He placed a trembling hand over his breast coat pocket. "Promise me . . ." His voice faded. He was losing too much blood.

"Anything."

"Promise me you'll find Analise. Become her guardian . . . protect her . . . see her future secured."

Dex removed the bloodied packet of letters from Crewe's coat and slipped it into an inner pocket. "You have my word."

"Thank you." Crewe's eyes drifted shut. It wouldn't be long now.

"Warburton," a voice shouted from behind them. "On guard!"

Dex lifted his head in time to see a lone French lancer galloping toward them. Swearing, he jumped and swiftly dove as far away from Crewe as the long lines of his body would allow, drawing the lancer from the prone figure, then rolled to his feet in an instant. The lancer flew by, thrown off by his feint. For a brief moment, dizziness descended as his blood pounded in his ears.

The world seemed to go hazy, then completely still, and the sights and smells and sounds of battle faded to a faint buzz. *Watch yourself, Dex. Don't let them down.* His eyes snapped open, bright daylight flooding his vision, illuminating the clouds of dirt thrown up by the Frenchman's horse as it wheeled around to find him again. Quickly, Dex's arm shot up and his fingers, obeying an automatic authority that came from somewhere beyond conscious thought, pulled his pistol's trigger.

The man jerked backward, a ribbon of scarlet arcing from his shoulder. The lance clattered to the ground, but still the man advanced, drawing his saber and raising it above his plumed helmet. His face was wild. He was upon Dex before he could unsheathe his sword, the useless pistol falling to the ground as the saber point caught his ear and drew a horrible line to his chin, then another one, and another.

The white heat of pain. The sickening sensation of air hitting opened flesh. The man yelling French oaths as he continued to slash at Dex's face, managing a hideous delicacy with the heavy blade.

Dex wrestled his sword out and blindly brought it upward at an awkward angle, feeling the hilt slam into something solid. The horse reared high above him, and the injured lancer flew backward, still screaming.

Through the blood streaming into his eyes, a pair of massive iron-shod hooves above him . . . a sudden all-encompassing pain, harder and more explosive than the pain before. Then nothing.

Nothing at all.

THEY SAID HE'D drifted in and out of consciousness for more than two months, the pain of his injuries rendering him incapable of coherent response. Dex remembered floating above himself, looking down at his ungainly body splayed across the small hospital cot, head swathed in bandages.

They'd moved him at some point to a hospital in England. He remembered a kindly old nurse who held his hand and sang songs about summer and daffodils. He remembered his promise to Crewe. *Find Analise. Become her guardian. Protect her. See her future secured.* Poor Crewe. Anger and sadness choked him. His friend was dead, leaving behind an orphaned daughter. It was the weight of this promise that had finally forced his spirit back into his body. He couldn't die here. He must fulfill his promise.

"How are we feeling today, Your Grace?" the kindly nurse asked, bustling into the room with her arms full of fresh bed linens and a smile on her age-lined face.

He grunted. How did she think he was feeling? His limbs wouldn't yet fully obey his commands. One side of his face was a nightmarish crisscrossing of scars. It hurt too much to talk. But he was one of the lucky ones. He was alive when so many had died.

A physician had embroidered his face with a sharp needle and thick thread, stitching his wounds together. Now that they were healing into scars, his face throbbed, stung, and itched.

Whenever he attempted to speak, all that emerged was a harsh croaking sound. This time he was determined to force words from his lips. "Nurse," he began in a guttural whisper. "There were . . . letters in my coat."

"Got your voice back? How wonderful. Don't fret. We have your letters safe and sound. I'm glad you're feeling well enough to read them. I'll fetch them for you." She placed the folded linens on a chair and bustled from the room.

Dex struggled to a seated position and painstakingly slid his legs off the bed, cursing his weakened state. Bracing his hands on the bed frame, he attempted to stand, only to thud back down, his entire body screaming in protest.

"Damn!" He gritted his teeth and tried again.

"Your Grace!" The nurse rushed into the room. "Where do you think you're going?"

"To the gardens. I want air."

"At least let me help you." She lifted one of his arms and draped it over her sturdy shoulders. "One . . . two . . ."

"I don't require help—" Dex's knees buckled and he stopped talking, leaning on the nurse.

"Slowly now, Your Grace. One step at a time. We can always go back to the bed."

"Not . . . going . . . back to bed." Too much time had already been wasted. Months. He must find Crewe's daughter.

The nurse helped him outside and down a pathway to a small, walled garden. She settled him on a stone bench beneath an oak tree. Removing the packet of letters from her apron pocket, she handed it to him. "I'll bring you some tea, Your Grace."

She left him alone. The sunlight on his face was like a language he'd known in childhood but no longer spoke. A robin hopped over the grass, its shrill voice mocking him. The flowers planted along the garden walk were like splotches of mold, the bright colors assaulting his eyes.

He unknotted the green silk ribbon tied around the letters. Bloodstained silk for his bloodstained mind.

The address on the letters was from Miss Pincheon's Finishing School for Young Ladies in London. He'd dispatch a representative to the school immediately to relay her father's last wishes to Miss Crewe and pay her tuition fees.

He lifted the topmost letter.

Dearest Papa,

I do wish that horrid despot Bonaparte would decide to take up goat farming instead of running around attempting to conquer the world. I search the papers every day for news of your company. I want to understand your trials, the dark and dangerous times, even though your letters are full of bravery and good humor.

Miss Pincheon doesn't much care for me. She says I put on Airs and Graces and fears that I have been dreadfully spoiled, being a motherless child with a doting father. She says I am a right impudent spitfire of a hellion. Perhaps it is so but, oh, Papa! I try so hard to be good, to do you credit, but I find lessons in etiquette and decorum to be tedious in the extreme. I long for the day when you are returned to me and I might leave this dreary institution.

We shall set up house in London, with an elegant equipage, and you shall take me riding on Rotten Row and I shall be shown to advantage in my riding habit. We shall attend balls and drink champagne and dance until our feet ache. You will glare most forbiddingly at my suitors, making them tremble in their polished boots. And when I find my true love, we shall live merrily ever after, we three . . . and the large, happy family that comes along.

I find my lessons so tiresome that I've taken to composing fantastical tales as a means of escape. I intend to finish an entire novel! Writing my tale of princesses, dragons, and Destiny is ever so much more diverting than embroidering Proverbs. I've enclosed the first chapter and I hope it will help you wile away some of the long, dreary nights until we are reunited.

I miss you dreadfully . . .

Your loving daughter,
Analise

The words blurred on the page. All that youthful exuberance and optimism extinguished. Miss Crewe's father had never returned to her.

His fault.

He turned the page and found the first chapter of her novel in progress. *The Dragon and the Blue Star* was the fanciful title.

Amsonia's royal luck had well and truly run out. Her father, missing. Her purse of gold, her sapphire diadem—all left behind in the haste she'd made to escape before she too was lost in the dark red mist that had settled so mysteriously over Vyranthrall.

The luck that had seen her as far by foot as the village of Fennsweald, the luck that had pointed her in the direction of their mage, who could, in turn, point her toward a certain dragon that knew all and saw all—that luck had evaporated in the face of the mage's beady eyes and bone-dry air of skepticism. She certainly would never have consulted him if she hadn't been desperate. She must find her father.

The smell of the mage's chambers filled her flaring

nostrils with the reek of animal hides, spilled wine, and acrid smoke, causing her to feel queasy and ill at ease. He peered out from under voluminous gray eyebrows, sweeping her travel-stained garments and poor, weary face with an assessing glance.

"Help you find and free your supposedly royal father, for naught but your fabulous tales of future recompense? If you can't pay me this very day in gold, girlie," he said, a rapacious smirtle stretching his leathery cheeks, "you are of no value to me whatsoever! The Dragon Qavox would tell you the same, then swallow you whole."

His back was already turned and his hands busily weighing out portions of a noxious powder into small cloth parcels. Blindly she turned from him and tripped over a low footstool, her hands clutching at a haphazard stack of parchment papers in a foolhardy attempt at staying upright. Dazed by disappointment, her teary eyes slowly focused on the foremost parchment.

Bright green and brown shapes swam in the air and, written in blood red, the words "Here Liveth the Dread Dragon Qavox and His Most Coveted Cache of Jewyls" materialized. A flash of insight and determination (from whence, she knew not!) bade her keep the yellowed map curled within her fist and told her to run, run, run down the narrow stairs without looking back . . .

Dex didn't even notice when the nurse brought him tea, so engrossed was he in the princess's plight. The tea sat, growing cold, as he read every one of Analise's letters and the chapters from her novel, turning the thin pages swiftly, eager to find out what happened next. She'd only reached the halfway point of the novel when her father died. Dex would never learn whether the evil mist could be defeated, or whether the Dread Dragon Qavox (a helpful key instructed the reader to pronounce the name *Havox*) was a prince who had been cursed, as he suspected.

A brave young princess. A father swallowed by an evil mist. A schoolgirl whose father was torn away from her by war. But in her story he could be rescued, the curse lifted.

Beneath the stack of letters was the miniature portrait Crewe had shown Dex. Analise wore an emerald necklace and eardrops that Crewe had mentioned belonged to her mother, who had died giving birth to the girl. Her hands were folded demurely, her posture correct, but her green eyes sparked with impish high spirits.

If Dex still possessed a heart, it would have ached for this innocent young lady tucked safely away in her finishing school in London, writing fantastical tales for her father on the battlefield. Imagining that her love was strong enough to conquer any evil, lift any curse, and bring her father safely back home to her.

Dex knew how the story really ended.

The father taken by the red mist. Transmuted into memory in an instant by an inexplicable act of horror.

Analise's life had been ruined two months ago. Her sweet hopes and dreams for her father's return and her debut Season in London had been dashed to death. She would never see her father again.

Dex swiped the back of his hand over his eyes, his stomach lurching.

He couldn't take away her suffering, but he could do what he'd solemnly promised to do: Become her guardian. Protect her. Pave her way in the world.

He must leave the hospital today.

He had a promise to keep.

Chapter One

"'Tis indeed the very dragon that can help ye find yer kinfolk, milady! He be nae ordinary type o' dragon, that he nae." The hobgoblin dragged a line through the forest on the map with a gnarled forefinger. "But ye best be asking for an escort from Ogress Barlayhurl. These woods have a hungry way about them, that they do."

—*The Dragon and the Blue Star* by Analise Crewe

Several years later . . .

Analise Crewe had proven a damnably difficult young lady to find.

When his man of business had arrived at the finishing school, the headmistress had informed him that Miss Crewe, unable to pay her tuition, had left the school by night with one small valise, observed only by a guard, telling no one her destination.

She'd simply vanished. A young lady all alone in the world. Where had she gone? Every day that passed made Dex imagine worse and worse fates. He and his agents searched high and low—every distant relation of Crewe's, every possible connection with one of Analise's schoolmates—to no avail.

If only he'd regained consciousness earlier, he might have found her safe and sound at the finishing school. He would never stop trying to find her.

He'd done everything in his power: interviewed her schoolmates, placed advertisements with her portrait in all the newspapers, visited every boarding house for ladies in London. He'd left word at every pawnshop in London about the emerald jewelry she'd been wearing in the miniature portrait, offering to purchase it at three times the price in exchange for information about the seller. It was this latter line of inquiry that had finally yielded fruit. Just this morning he'd received notice from a pawnbroker that he might have a match on the emerald necklace. It was the best lead Dex had encountered yet. He wasn't going to entrust it to an agent.

The pawnshop was cramped and grubby and smelled of mildewed old clothing and acrid metal polish. "Are you Mr. Henry Arkwright?"

"Who's askin'?" The man behind the counter had a face that was permanently flushed a violent purple and deeply wizened, looking for all the world like a prune brought to life by a magician with a questionable sense of humor.

"The Duke of Warburton. You answered my notice about a particular emerald jewelry set."

"Oh, well now, a duke, is it?" He pantomimed a facetious bow, his florid face wrinkled and winking. "We don't usually entertain the Fancy in these parts lest it's for the bawdy house down the way."

Dex's throat closed and he had to fight to draw breath. If Miss Crewe had fallen into such dire straits that she'd been forced to sell her body he'd never forgive himself. Never.

"Do you have the jewelry?"

"That depends. Do you have my forty quid?"

"I'll make it fifty if you show it to me in the next two minutes."

That lit a fire under the man. He jumped up from his stool with an unexpected vigor and unlocked a glass case behind the counter. "Been keeping them safe, yer lordship. Wouldn't let no one buy them. Sure and it's the pieces you're searching for—the clasp of the necklace is engraved with the initials A.C., like your notice said would be there."

The necklace was composed of delicate strands of gold chain interspersed with bands of emeralds, the matching earrings featuring emerald drops hung by the same intricate gold chain. They looked like the ones Analise had worn in the miniature portrait, but he must be certain he wasn't being swindled. He borrowed Arkwright's loupe and studied the engraving. If it had been done recently, the patina would be brighter, but everything had the dull finish of age. The scrolling initials stood for Albertine Crewe, Analise's French mother.

Dex gave the loupe back to Arkwright. "Who sold these to you?"

"Well now, that might be difficult to remember . . . I'm an old man and my memory isn't what it used to be . . . Perhaps if you upped your reward to—"

Losing patience, Dex grabbed him by the collar, twisting until the man clutched at his neck with both hands. "Does this refresh your memory?"

"No need for . . . violence," Arkwright grumbled, scrabbling at Dex's fingers.

Dex released his hold. "Well? The seller. I want every detail you remember."

"It was a girl. About eighteen years old, I'd say. A redheaded wee slip of a thing. Had a very fast and confusing way of talking. Gave me her whole life history, she did. Her father was a cavalryman went missing in the war and on and on about how she was going to find him and this was her mother's jewelry and she'd be back to retrieve them just as soon as she sold some sort of novel she was writing."

Finally! It must be Miss Crewe. "How long ago was this?"

"The ear drops came in weeks ago. The necklace only two days past. You're lucky I saw your advertisement before I sold them."

"Did she say where she was living?"

Arkwright closed his lips mutinously and stared pointedly at Dex's coat pocket. "You promised thrice the price of the jewelry."

Dex laid the required amount of banknotes on the counter, pocketing the jewelry.

"Miss Flanagan's boarding house—down Old Nichols Street and turn right on . . ."

Dex was out the door before he'd finished the sentence.

Ana Crewe was surrounded by tempting books yet marooned on an uncomfortable oak chair with nothing to read. Every time she made even the slightest twitch, the officious clerk occupying the desk outside of Mr. Norwood's office fixed her with such a glare that she instantly froze.

She longed to run to the shelves lining the room and caress the spines of the illustrious novels published by Norwood & Pennington. The reception chamber smelled of woody ink, earthy leather, and her most cherished ambition: becoming a published author.

Her former employer, Lady Muriel Claridge, had sent Ana's manuscript to her publisher. Lady Claridge had been the author of a successful series of domestic romances set in the fictitious village of Clovercote. Ladies across Britain had written her letters almost weekly, gushing about how much they loved her novels, begging her to write a book featuring their favorite side character, or asking questions about contentious plot points.

Ana recognized the blue velvet bags embroidered with the gold publishing house insignia occupying one of the bookshelves. Lady Claridge had received one of those elegant bags by special delivery upon the publication of each new novel. Inside the bag was a personal note from Mr. Norwood, her editor, a bottle of port wine, and a small gift—usually gold jewelry.

Ana dreamed of the day when she would receive one of those velvet bags. The attached note on thick cream-colored stationery written with flourishing blue ink would read: *Dear Miss Crewe, we at Norwood & Pennington are delighted by the unprecedented success of* The Dragon and the Blue Star. *We await your new manuscript with eagerness. Yours devotedly, Theobald Norwood.*

Mr. Norwood had kept Ana's manuscript for nearly a year with no word as to its suitability for publication. She'd inquired at the publishing house every day since she arrived in London two months ago. Finally, she'd been granted an audience. She'd waited forever for this meeting. What was a few more hours? An eternity when her entire future was at stake.

This meeting could change the entire course of her life, or it could leave her friendless and alone in London, with no means of paying her rent.

The door to Mr. Norwood's office opened slightly, and the clerk leapt to his feet.

Ana perched on the edge of the chair. Finally she'd be face-to-face with the great man himself.

"Mr. Norwood will see you now, Miss Crewe," the clerk intoned, holding the door wider.

Ana fairly flew into the office, ignoring the pins and needles in her legs. "Mr. Norwood, it's an honor to meet you, sir!" He was smaller than she'd pictured him to be, balding, with a sour expression as though he'd been sucking on a lemon before she arrived.

He studied her for a moment. "You are Miss Analise Crewe?"

"Yes sir."

"When Lady Claridge sent me your manuscript, she wrote that you were her trusted companion and amanuensis. I assumed you would be older. What is your age?"

"Eighteen, sir."

He folded his hands on his desk. "I read the first few chapters of your novel this morning, Miss Crewe."

"You only read it this morning?"

"Do you see this towering pile of manuscripts, my girl? We receive hundreds of inquiries every month. Yours only rose to the top because of Lady Claridge's personal recommendation. I assumed your work would be similar in style and substance to your mentor's elegant and gentlewomanly tales, yet what did I find? Faery queens, talking dragons, princesses setting off on ludicrous quests. Pah!"

She wrapped her fingers tightly together in front of her in an unwitting attitude of prayer, willing herself to ignore a growing sense of dread. "Lady Claridge read my novel and said that it was quite different and delightful."

"Different, yes. Delightful? She must have been blinded by affection."

The breath left her chest in a rush, leaving her momentarily silent. Disbelief was giving way to dismal recognition of a new, unpleasant reality. She raised her face, focusing her eyes on his. "You didn't like it?"

"The writing had a measure of charm, I will grant you, yet the novel doesn't fit into any of the categories of literature that we publish, particularly the genres well suited to a woman's sensibilities. It's not a children's morality tale, nor is it a comedy of manners, nor even a volume of poetry, such as is fitting for the refined reader of today."

"The Brothers Grimm had great success with their fairy tales only recently."

"Jacob and Wilhelm Grimm are scholars, well educated and well endowed with that most masculine of traits, a rich intelligence. You are very young, far too fanciful, and, of course, through no fault of your own, female; what gentlewomanly traits you may possess through birth are surely outweighed by your current lack of both social standing and spouse. I always have my staff do research into the circumstances of potential authors. Imagine my consternation to learn that after Lady Claridge's passing, you arrived in London only to take lodgings at a boarding house with a most unsavory reputation and unfavorable address."

Miss Flanagan's Boarding House for Young Ladies had been the only door open to her, the only lodging she'd been able to afford. She'd pawned the last of her mother's jewelry but it wasn't enough for the back rent she owed.

She'd managed to convince herself that Mr. Norwood would offer her a contract then and there. Lady Claridge had praised her fantastical novel, but perhaps she had done so only out of pity mixed with affection?

She hadn't come all this way, trudging through the streets every day for two hours to inquire at the publishing house, only to come away empty-handed. Mr. Norwood must be forced to take her seriously.

"Oh that"—she waved a hand through the air dismissively—"it's all a huge misunderstanding. You see I arrived in London earlier than anticipated, with very limited funds of my own, but my . . . my fiancé is arriving very soon, and I'll be moved to luxurious lodgings in Mayfair."

Mr. Norwood's brow wrinkled. "You're engaged to be married?"

She attempted to keep her face from betraying the lie. "I am."

"And this purported fiancé's name?"

"Er . . . we've sworn to keep our arrangement secret for now. He hasn't told his family yet. They are a very ancient lineage and perhaps will attempt to dissuade him against the marriage. However, he is steadfast in his love for me. We are to be married as soon as he arrives in London."

"I see."

His tone said that he didn't believe her. She forged ahead regardless. In for a penny, in for a pound. "And if you don't like my fantastical novel, I have another manuscript that's nearing completion." She desperately searched her mind for a solution. What would pique his interest? "Before she passed, Lady Claridge gave me a detailed outline for her next Clovercote novel and bade me write the book and take up her mantle."

It wasn't completely a lie. Lady Claridge had dictated the outline to her, but only because she thought she would live to write the novel.

His eyes narrowed. "If that's so, why didn't she write to me about it?"

"It all happened so fast. She slipped away before her time. I was devastated by her passing."

"As were we all. Her readership was one of the most devoted in all of England."

Horrid man. Prejudiced against her writing, her sex, her very self. Small-minded—and greedy. It wasn't literature or the artistry behind it that he cared for; it was only the money Lady Claridge had made for the publishing house.

Her mind, made agile by stress and desperation, leapt at the thought. Perhaps she could use his avarice to her advantage? "Wouldn't another Clovercote novel, outlined by her ladyship and written by her companion, appeal to that very readership?" She held her breath and watched the machinery of his mind turn over this new idea.

"There could be some merit to that." He steepled his fingers, staring out the window past her head. "Another Clovercote novel . . . who is the heroine?"

"Miss Adora Dansey, the young niece of Sir Alfred Dansey. She played a small role in *The Bells of Clovercote*, if you recall?"

He nodded in assent. "And the hero?"

"Lord Stuart Alexander Fortescue, an earl. He's a new character. Very dashing."

"And this outline that Lady Claridge dictated to you, may I see it?"

"I don't have it with me."

"It sounds promising, though I'm not certain you are the authoress to complete her work. You are untried, unpublished, and unmarried."

"Soon to be married, don't forget."

"I suppose Lord Claridge could introduce you to society as his late aunt's protégée."

Over her dead body! Upon Lady Claridge's death, her nephew, Lord Thomas Claridge, had inherited his aunt's estate. Apparently, he'd considered Ana part of his inheritance as well. The day after the good Lady's funeral, he'd made his intentions plain: she was to be his. There was to be no dissent. He'd been deep in his cups, and in the aftermath of their altercation had passed out unconscious on her bed. She'd fled Cornwall in the dead of night with only the clothes on her back and a small, precious bundle containing her father's letters from the war and her mother's jewelry.

"I wouldn't require Lord Claridge's patronage."

"I beg to differ. His patronage is the only way you'll be viewed with any respect from the literary community that embraced Lady Claridge."

"I meant to say that I would have the patronage of someone far more elevated. My fiancé. Upon hearing his name you'll understand why I speak the way I do."

Mr. Norwood drummed his fingers on the desktop. "*If* you reveal this illustrious fiancé of yours, *if* you move to a respectable address in Mayfair, and *if* you produce the outline and at least half of the manuscript within the month, then, and only then, will I be willing to entertain the idea of granting you a publishing contract, Miss Crewe."

"I understand completely, Mr. Norwood. All three terms will be met most expediently. You won't be sorry, sir. As an intimate of Lady Claridge's, I'm precisely the person to continue her series. I'll be honoring her memory while bringing a fresh new perspective to her romantic tales of love lost and—"

"Of course," he broke in with a predatory smile, "if you don't produce said fiancé and said manuscript, you will promise to grant Norwood & Pennington sole ownership of Lady Claridge's outline for her next novel, and we shall have full authority to hire someone else to finish the work."

Ana took a deep breath. Where on earth was she supposed to find a titled fiancé, and how could she finish half a manuscript in a matter of weeks?

She had no choice. She mustn't waste this chance to achieve her dream of being published. *I'm sorry Princess Amsonia*, she thought sadly, *you'll never reach any readers.*

"In the meantime, Miss Crewe, I'm a very busy man . . ." He picked up his pen and began signing letters. She'd been dismissed.

"You'll be hearing from me, Mr. Norwood." She attempted to sweep from the room as she imagined a future noblewoman might, only succeeding in nearly knocking a statue of Plato off a pedestal. She caught it just in time, but Mr. Norwood didn't even glance up from his desk.

He was so sure she was lying.

She *was* lying. Had she lost leave of her senses? What had possessed her to tell such spurious untruths? She hadn't wanted him to win. She'd always been like that, rushing into battle armed only with her overactive imagination and the certainty that everything would turn out right in the end.

But life had proven that an optimistic outlook and a wide smile didn't always turn the world in your favor.

Her father was still missing, presumed dead, though she refused to believe it. She clung to the hope that his body had never been recovered. That he was still out there somewhere, searching for her.

Oh, Papa. What have I done? What am I going to do?

The clerk smirked at her as she passed his desk, as if he'd been listening at the door and overheard her humiliation and desperate lies.

"Mr. Norwood said I could take one of your gift bags," she said in a rush, snatching one off the table and darting for the door.

"Miss Crewe!" the clerk shouted, but she was already out the door and down the steps.

Heart stampeding, she ran down the street, dodging passersby, half expecting the clerk to pursue her. She didn't think they'd brand her a thief, because of her connection with Lady Claridge, but it had been a dangerous thing to do.

She hadn't left with her dignity intact, but at least she now possessed one of Norwood & Pennington's congratulatory gifts.

Not that it would pay her rent.

Chapter Two

The Ogress Barlayhurl commanded her fleet of hedgehogs to carry the Princess to Mount Runemor, then took her leave through the brush. Amsonia was borne aloft toward the dragon's lair on a teeming mass of spiny backs, enduring the pricks bravely. "I know not what awaits me on this journey," she murmured to the beasties, "but I hope to meet more helpful souls like you along the way . . ."

—*The Dragon and the Blue Star* by Analise Crewe

Ana closed the front door of the boarding house gingerly. If only she could make it to the stairs undetected. She tiptoed down the hall, wincing with every floorboard creak and groan.

"Miss Crewe, is that you?"

She leaned her brow against the wall, the worn wool flocking of the paper covering pressing gently into her skin like the buds on a willow tree in spring. She let herself stay still for a moment as the inevitable sank in. Nothing for it but to face the dragoness in her lair. If only Ana could weave an enchantment that would wipe the concept of rent clean from her mind!

"Yes, Miss Flanagan."

Her landlady reclined on an overstuffed settee in the front

parlor, bodice askew, hair piled in messy curls, lips painted scarlet, and a string of threadbare pearls around her neck. "Miss Crewe, you do know what day o' t' month it is?"

"The first day," Ana said brightly, praying for a miracle that wouldn't arrive.

"Rent day, it is!" blared Miss Flanagan, emitting a soporific mist of gin. "Where's me dough? Pay up or you'll be out on yer ear, an' no mistake. I'll hear no more o' yer excuses, luv."

Ana handed over the last of her coins.

Miss Flanagan tested the weight of the bag. "This can only be half. I'm not in the habit o' giving away free housing, y'know." She gave Ana as sly a look as she could muster with her gin-lubricated facial muscles. "'Ow about some more of that jewelry you arrived with? That necklace was a beauty! I could see my way to letting you stay a few months if you had some o' that t' pass along."

Ana flinched, thinking of the empty jewelry box upstairs in her room. "I have no more to sell. You'll have the balance of my rent by next month, with interest, I swear. I met today with Mr. Norwood of Norwood & Pennington and he's keen to publish my manuscript after I make certain revisions."

"Yer living in a fantasy world, girlie mine. It's time for you to face the facts o' the matter. Your best asset hain't yer quill, 'tis what's beneath yer cloak." She eyed Ana's slight form. "That's where t' profit is, and plenty of it, just ask me sister Maggie."

According to Miss Flanagan, Maggie ran a well-attended house of ill repute somewhere near the docks. Ana had never met the woman but had received an unwanted offer of employment from her via her marginally more respectable sister. As Ana's funds had diminished along with her prospects, Miss Flanagan had applied more and more pressure in that direction, extolling the money to be made in that old-fashioned profession. Leaving out, Ana felt sure, the odious hardships that must surely accompany it—and, no doubt, the cripplingly large cut the elder Flanagan would extract from any of her wages.

"I've made myself clear on the subject. I won't work for your sister."

"Miss High and Mighty, eh? Too good to be a working girl. Well, I'll let you in on a secret." She leaned closer, burping blithely, and Ana fought the urge to back away from her gin-heavy breath. "Beauty don't last forever. I was far prettier'n you in me own day. A celebrated beauty, that I was. I didn't turn me nose up at earning a living on my back, and look at what it got me? It got me this 'ere house. Left t' me by a generous lord, it was. And now I earn me living fair 'n square. All thanks to Maggie."

By charging exorbitant rates and funneling vulnerable young girls from the countryside into her sister's bawdy house. There was a reason Miss Flanagan was an inebriate. She drank to forget. She drank to survive.

"You've done very well for yourself, Miss Flanagan, and I do appreciate your continued leniency as to the matter of my rent. I swear to you that you'll have it, with interest, just as soon as—"

"No more promises. No more daydreams. Maggie always says a bird in the 'and is worth two in the bush. All is business and business is all, she says. She's found a protector for you, and a very fine gentleman he is, too. Very interested, he is, in young gels who ain't seen much of the world. Titled and wealthy. 'E's not reckoned to be handsome, but he's not one of the cruel ones, neither, although Maggie don't turn them away. Think of it, girlie, you could be living in a fine apartment in Mayfair, dinin' on pheasant and dressin' in silk. Wouldn't you like that, now, luv?"

For the briefest of moments, Ana almost entertained the notion. She was so tired of scraping by and living on the perilous edge of poverty. Maggie, by all accounts, would be a ruthless boss, but Ana had fallen so far that she felt hitting the bottom at last might at least feel like stability. At least she'd have the address in Mayfair. Perhaps her earnings might enable her to hire an actor to portray her fiancé? Ridiculous. One hint that Ana was a kept woman and Mr. Norwood would spit in her face.

Miss Flanagan never really listened to anyone else, she carried on as if she were standing on a ship's deck, running full sail, shouting into the wind. The only way Ana would escape this distasteful conversation was trickery. She removed the publisher's velvet gift bag from the inner pocket of her cloak. "I brought you a present, Miss Flanagan," she interrupted.

Miss Flanagan paused, belligerently set on her current line of discourse but eyeing the rich blue velvet and gold embroidery with interest. "I won't be distracted by presents, not this time. I want me rent in full, or yer—"

"Oh, then, if you don't want to know what precious treasures are inside this . . ." Ana shrugged her shoulders, making a show of sliding the bag back into her cloak.

"Hold a moment . . ." Miss Flanagan fluttered an unsteady hand. "What's inside, then?"

"Only a very expensive bottle of port and a gold bracelet. But you said you didn't want any presents, so I'll just keep it for myself."

Miss Flannigan lips fell slack. Greed was one of the primary motivating factors of her life, second only to alcohol and the procurement thereof. She snapped her fingers at Ana. "Let's see it."

Ana held out the bag and Miss Flanagan snatched it from her

fingers speedily, opening the gold tasseled string and peering inside. "You're a right beauty, ain't ye?" Extracting the bottle, she cradled it in her arms like a baby. With great effort, she managed to uncork the bottle and inhale deeply from its stem, her reddened nostrils flaring. Her expression turned dreamy. "That do smell lovely."

Ana made herself stay still, as much as she longed to run for the door. It was almost safe. The hare was almost in the trap, all that remained was to set the final bait. "Have a nip, why don't you?"

Miss Flanagan poured a measure of spirits into a cup and took a sip. "Cheeky li'il baggage, thinking you can butter me up wi' expensive spirits."

"And jewelry, of course . . ." Ana reminded her, dangling the gleaming chain from her fingers. Miss Flanagan, sipping port with one hand, reached the other bony wrist out for Ana to fasten the clasp, then brought it to her painted mouth. She bit the chain.

"Real gold. But thin-like. Won't fetch much at t' pawnshop."

"Enough to buy me another week." Ana let herself ease toward the exit and was halfway through the doorframe, her freedom in sight, when a loud knock sounded at the front door of the house.

Miss Flanagan startled, her hand flying to smooth her hair. "Who can that be? Martha," she bellowed. "The door!"

There was no response. Her maid-of-all-work, a timid, overworked girl with a lean, hungry look in her eyes, was often too busy scrubbing grates and washing the laundry to answer the door.

"Useless girl," Miss Flanagan grumbled.

More pounding on the door.

"That'll be the butcher or the greengrocer, after me again. I'm not here." She shrank into the sofa. "Go and tell 'em I'm not here."

Ana sighed and turned back toward the entrance. She'd wanted to be in her garret room by now. She had half a novel to pluck out of thin air, after all.

DEX RAPPED ON the boarding house door again. Still no answer. He stepped back to observe the tall facade of the house. Tattered curtains were pulled shut except on the highest level where a round window winked out at the rooftops. The stone was soot-stained and streaked with pigeon droppings, giving the house a derelict air. Could Lieutenant John Crewe's daughter really be living in a place like this?

He tried the door but it was locked. He knocked again, louder this time.

A maid finally answered the door. "Good day, sir. How may I help you?"

She was a tiny thing, reaching only to his collar. Her cultured accent didn't fit with her station. Pale red hair tied back in a bun with tendrils escaping framed an oval face. Brilliant green eyes stared at him suspiciously. Could it be . . . ?

"Sir?" she asked again. "May I help you?"

"Can it be you?" he marveled.

"I'm sorry, sir?"

"It *is* you. Good God." Crewe's daughter reduced to accepting employment as a serving maid in a down-at-the-heels boarding house. His stomach churned. "Miss Analise Crewe."

She regarded him warily. "And who might you be?"

"Warburton, at your service." He inclined his head. "I've had a devil of a time finding you, Miss Crewe," he growled. *Soften your tones. She's a young lady. Easily frightened.*

It was dusk and he wore a tall hat and a high collar, shielding some of his scars from her gaze. "I'm your guardian," he said more gently. He wouldn't attempt to smile. That never went well. His scars prevented one side of his mouth from lifting properly and the effect was more grimace than smile.

She gazed at his scarred face and her expression flashed from wariness to terror.

He was that hideous. One young lady had fainted upon the sight of his scars at a ball. The last ball he'd ever attended. His friends had told him that her corset strings must have been laced too tight and his visage wasn't enough to make a woman swoon with fright . . . but this woman, the one he'd been searching for these long years had the same horrified look on her face.

"I won't be any man's property," she said defiantly.

She attempted to close the door in his face. He stuck out his foot and blocked it from closing. He pried the door from her grasp and flung it wide. "You're coming home with me. I made your father a—"

She wasn't listening. With horror in her eyes and fear stamped across her face, she gathered up her skirts and rushed down the steps past him, making a mad dash into the street, narrowly avoiding being hit by a passing carriage.

Dex stood, nonplussed, watching her flee. What the devil? "Miss Crewe," he called after her. "Come back!"

She'd taken one look at his face and bolted like a frightened deer fleeing from a wolf.

She wasn't going to evade him again. Not this time.

He tossed his hat to the steps and set off after her, chasing coppery red curls and a slight figure down the darkening London street.

Chapter Three

The mouth of the Iniquitous Monster's cave opened in a baleful "O" before her, scarring the granite face of Mount Runemor. From deep within curled a plume of sulfurous smoke, accompanied by the tinkling of a million metal objects being trod on by a body of unimaginable size. This was the Dragon's home, and he was, apparently, awake . . .

—*The Dragon and the Blue Star* by Analise Crewe

He was gaining on her.

Ana knew these streets well, but the man thundered after her on long, powerful limbs and she didn't stand a chance unless she found a way to evade him and hide. She feinted to the right and ducked behind a passing man, hoping to lose her pursuer, but when she reemerged, he was right there behind her, closer than ever. He must be the nobleman Miss Flanagan's sister had promised her to, a huge, menacing hunter intent on capturing her.

He would never have her.

She knew a shortcut, a narrow lane that veered off up ahead, its entrance nearly covered with vines. If she could reach it before he saw her . . .

She summoned a burst of speed, legs aching and lungs bursting, and was through the vine-covered entranceway and halfway down the alley when a hand clamped around her arm.

She struggled and twisted but he held her easily.

"Stop running," he commanded.

She stilled, panting from the exertion of running. She shouldn't have chosen this deserted alleyway. There were no people in sight. He held her trapped easily, there was nowhere to run.

The light was growing dim and he was wrapped in shadows. He wore all black. One side of his face was crisscrossed with a webbing of raised purplish scars.

A nobleman of high rank, Miss Flanagan had said, not considered handsome, but not cruel. The iron grip on her arm felt cruel enough.

He'd called himself Warburton. One word to define him. Throwing his title around, as if she should be grateful to him for attempting to purchase her, make her his property. His name rang a bell in her mind. A warning bell, no doubt. She'd probably read about his exploits in the scandal sheets.

"I'll be no man's doxy," she cried fiercely.

"No one's trying to make you a d—"

She stamped on his foot with the heel of her boot.

"Oof," he grunted, but his grip on her arm never loosened. She fought and scratched but he held her immobile, his huge arms around hers, holding her tight against his chest.

She stomped on his shiny black boots a second time but it didn't seem to even make a dent.

"Are you quite finished? Will you allow me to explain?" he growled.

"I won't! I won't be purchased like a sack of flour. I will defend myself to the death!"

A disbelieving guffaw. He dared laugh at her? She'd show him.

"Release me," she said passionately. "You're hurting me."

He instantly loosened his grip. His mistake.

She twisted one arm free and plucked the pencil from her hair. She'd intended to jab him in the eye but his face was so far away and the sharp point of the pencil impacted somewhere closer to his nose. She dragged it downward, adding another scar to his collection.

He caught her wrist, gave one firm little twist, and the pencil clattered to the paving stones.

What had Miss Flanagan said when she'd been inebriated one afternoon and regaled Ana with tales from her past? When you had to defend yourself from unwanted advances, it was best to go for the eyes, or the kidneys, or soft, fleshy parts. If that didn't work, knee him in the bollocks.

She brought her knee up suddenly. He grunted.

"You missed," he said, his voice rough, his lips far too close. "You'll have to work on your timing and aim."

This wasn't an ordinary man. This was a scarred warrior who could break her arm with a flick of his wrist.

"You don't want me," she said desperately. "I'm a redheaded spitfire of a hellion with unfortunate freckles. I don't have much padding and, believe me, I'm not biddable. I should make a terrible mistress. I'd embarrass you greatly. Wouldn't you rather have a willing woman? I'm certain a more voluptuous and experienced lady would be delighted to be kept by you."

"I believe you're exactly the redheaded spitfire of a hellion that I've been searching for these several years. Analise Crewe, daughter of the late Lieutenant John Crewe."

"I don't want a guardian, or a keeper, or protector or whatever you choose to call it. Do you hear me? I will fight to the death!"

Fight to the death. She was her father's daughter and make no mistake.

She pummeled him with her tiny fists, shouting that she wouldn't be owned by any man. He deserved her punches, her hatred, her fear, and more. He was the reason her father was dead and she was alone in this world. The reason she'd been forced to seek shelter in that derelict guesthouse. She thought he was attempting to purchase her body for his pleasure.

The sickening thought flashed through his mind that perhaps she'd been so used before.

Goddamn it. He hated himself. He was too late.

Hit me harder, he thought. He stood stock-still as she beat him until she was exhausted and panting.

"Leave me be," she gasped. "Let me go in peace."

"Miss Crewe, if you'll be still for one moment, I'll explain myself. Your father—"

She kneed him in the groin again, and this time she connected. Pain twisted in his gut and stars danced before his eyes.

Enough.

With one easy motion he pinned both of her wrists behind her back, pushing her up against the vine-covered brick behind them. "Hold still and listen to me now. I'm not trying to purchase you. I'm the Duke of Warburton. I made your father a battlefield promise that I would protect you. I've been searching for you ever since the war ended. You're an extremely difficult young lady to find."

She went quiet in his arms. Finally.

She was so small and fragile, the bones of her shoulders visible beneath the cloak. Delicate, diminutive, and . . . fiery. Like a stick of dynamite with a lit fuse. She was gloriously alive and vibrant even half-starved and frightened to death.

He transferred both of her wrists to one of his hands, using his other hand to dig through his waistcoat pocket. "Look." He held out her miniature. "He gave me this portrait of you. And a packet of your letters. I made a promise to become your guardian. The paperwork is complete. You are my ward."

She didn't much resemble the girl in the portrait anymore. In his mind's eyes, she'd stayed fifteen, a young girl with her hair in precise ringlets, tied with a schoolgirl's white bow above her head. A girl with an emphatically pointed chin, laughing green eyes, wearing an emerald necklace and eardrops that were far too adult for her age.

The woman he held pressed against the wall was nothing like the portrait.

Her face was still oval but her green eyes flashed with hatred, not humor.

She was slim, but shapely. He couldn't help noticing the shapely part because her cloak had parted and her bodice had been pushed askew in their struggle.

No portrait artist could have captured her effect in person. The vibrant green of her eyes, the sunlight-on-old-copper of her hair, which had tumbled loose when she pulled the pencil free, falling in tangled curls around her neck and bosom.

The pencil that could have blinded him.

He still held her wrists. He didn't fancy another jab from whatever other weapons she concealed on her person. He'd keep her immobile until she trusted him. He was acutely aware of how they must look to any passersby. He had her pressed up against a wall. Covering her with his body. It was a good thing the alley was deserted.

"You fought bravely, Miss Crewe. Just as your father did."

Her breath caught, she stared into his eyes, attempting to read the truth of his words.

"You knew my father?"

"I was his commanding officer."

"Warburton." Understanding began to dawn. "Papa mentioned you in his letters to me but . . ." Confusion flooded her eyes. "You don't seem like the man he described. He said you had an easy laugh and you were . . ."

"Handsome? Carefree? I'm not that man. Not anymore." Now he was scarred. Hideous. Ill-tempered. "If I release your wrists, will you run away again?"

"Tell me about my father. Describe him to me."

"He had your eyes. Steadfast, deep green. He and I played whist in our tents and drank to your health every night. He gave me a packet of your letters to know you by. I read the chapters of the fantastical novel you were writing. What was it called, again? Something about a dragon?"

She relaxed in his arms, the fight leaving her body. A sob caught in her throat. "Papa gave you my letters. You were with him the day he was injured?"

"He was gravely wounded. A lance injury. I was tending to him when I was attacked by a French cavalryman."

"Then you didn't actually see him die?" Fervent hope flooded her face.

"I did not."

"His body was never recovered."

"Many were not." The mass graves hastily dug in villages along the way, death rendering the fallen nameless, and forever lost.

"There's a chance he's still alive, then. I knew it!"

"Miss Crewe, I . . ." The words clogged his throat. He knew this kind of blind hope that kept someone going day after day. He suddenly wanted to release her wrists and hug her to his chest, soothe her hair, press his lips to her delicate lids until the wild grief left her eyes. "There's no hope of that."

"You can't know that!" She twisted in his grasp again, trying to break free.

"Pardon me, miss, is this bloke bothering you?"

Two men had come up behind them without Dex noticing—that's how focused he'd been on her pain, her false hope. He dropped her wrists and turned fully to face them. She made use of the interruption to scoot out from behind him, but the arrivals kept her effectively hemmed in. "This is none of your concern," Dex said with cold menace. "Move along."

"Wasn't talking to you," one of them, a mean-looking fellow with his cap pulled low, said. "You'll be safer with us, luv. We'll see you home." He leered lasciviously into his necktie and came closer, sidling neatly into the slight gap between Miss Crewe and Dex, blocking her from view with his bony shoulders in their too-small jacket.

His equally unsavory and much broader friend moved toward her other side. The smell of stale ale and bacon grease rose from them in waves.

Miss Crewe chose the lesser of two evils.

Darting quickly around the man, she linked her arm through Dex's. "Oh, that won't be necessary, gentlemen. My brother and I were only having a bit of an argument!"

Dex side-eyed her in bemusement. Brother, was it?

"He doesn't like the bonnet I chose at the milliner's, imagine. A lovely satin poke with a stuffed dove on a velvet nest, carrying a sprig of satin blossoms in its little mouth. Ever so fetching! He says it makes me look like a shopgirl. Can you credit it? Men will never understand fashion. Now I want to give you gentlemen a word of advice, if you have sisters, or sweethearts, or wives, never, ever give them your true opinion of what they're wearing. If one of them asks you, 'Does this new pelisse flatter my figure?' you respond with an enthusiastic 'yes' even if the exact opposite is true."

Was she planning to vanquish them with chatter? Oddly, her plan appeared to be working. The steady stream of nonsense and the incongruously bright smile on her face was giving them pause, a slight glaze of confusion dulling their intent gazes.

"When he said I looked like a shopgirl, I said to him," Miss Crewe continued, as if she were chatting with a schoolfriend, "Why brother dear, I am perfectly capable of choosing my own millinery, thank you very much, please stick to your own. Why, the one he chose for me to wear was a dull gray muslin with nary an ostrich feather or a stitch of silk on it! I do believe he wants me to look like a convent sister."

"You could never look like a nun," the wider one grunted, "you're prettier'an a posy. Now why don't you leave him and come along with us, eh?"

Dex didn't like the way they were staring fixedly at Miss Crewe's exposed decolletage, jaws slackened above stained cravats. She'd defused the situation somewhat, and he admired her quick thinking, but it was time to finish this.

His way.

Chapter Four

"Burn me alive if you must! Flay me with thine iron talons, swallow me and let me be pickled in thine own hellish brine! But I stand before you to beseech you, O Great Qavox," Amsonia cried loudly, to drown out the knocking of her knees, "help me find my father and banish the red mist that hath marred the beautiful land of Vyranthrall!"

—*The Dragon and the Blue Star* by Analise Crewe

With the swiftness borne of military training, Warburton had disengaged her grasping hand and was standing in front of her in a boxer's stance.

In that brief second, he seemed to grow even taller, completely blocking her from the men's sight with his vastly squared shoulders, his head thrown back deliberately to catch the streetlamp glow. The light played menacingly along the maze of scars, capturing their gaze and knocking the lasciviousness off their faces, as surely as if he'd wiped it off with his fists.

"I am," he said slowly, as if explaining a simple arithmetic lesson to a couple of school urchins, "the goddamned Duke of Warburton. You've heard of me. Everyone's heard of me. I'm a hero of war. The list of men I've killed is long." He flexed his fists. "But I'll add two more to that ledger if I'm provoked. Do you see this signet ring?" He raised his fist.

The duo's eyes duly took it in, mounting fear writ large on their sorry brows. "I'll imprint it so hard into your skin you'll go through life with a dragon telling tales on your face, letting everyone know that Deckard Payne, Duke of Warburton, owns you until the end of your days. If I were you, and I wanted my cheeks to remain dragon-free? I'd disappear. Now."

He towered over the men, fist raised, signet ring glinting.

Ana shivered. This must have been what he was like on the battlefield, a lethal warrior, a vengeful god from Greek mythology, prepared to kill to defend her honor.

She'd never been able to picture her gentle, book-loving father riding into battle with sword raised, on a gigantic charger. But if he'd had this fearsome giant leading his regiment, he'd have felt invincible.

The men, hardened street denizens that they were, looked like knock-kneed schoolboys next to him. It was obvious that they felt like schoolboys, too. Their body language had shifted to that of puppies backing away in shameful terror from a threatening cat.

"Now, now, no need for threats, guvnor, we was only inquiring as to the lady's welfare." The big one's hands were splayed out in a placating gesture, while the other was already inching away, wormlike.

"We didn't mean no harm. Only coming to the aid of a lady, that's all." Touching their caps, they backed up a bit more, before turning and lurching off around the corner, coats flapping behind them.

The duke remained in his confrontational stance. Ana moved

out from his shadow and looked up at his face, reading the strength and purpose beneath the scars.

"Warburton." She touched his arm softly. "They're gone."

From a distance, her quiet voice reached him. He was far away, standing on a smoky battlefield drenched in blood. He had been ready to fight, to end them. To protect her honor.

With a visible effort, he shook himself back into the present and let the tension fall from his shoulders. "I'm sorry you had to hear that. Come, let's not linger here. My carriage awaits." He reached behind her head and she flinched, but he was only drawing up the hood of her cloak. "Keep your hair covered. Speak to no one."

"Wait." She bent over, searching the ground. "My pencil. It was brand-new."

"Leave it. I'll buy you a hundred more. If you promise not to stab me with them, that is."

She shrugged. "A girl has a right to defend herself against what she thought was a craven attempt to purchase her person. Why didn't you explain yourself immediately?"

"I tried to—you wouldn't listen. You lashed out like a cornered alley cat."

"Miss Flanagan, my landlady, has a sister who runs a house of ill repute. She's been attempting to recruit me. Just before you arrived, she said that her sister had a nobleman in mind for me. And then you arrived at the door, saying you were my guardian. What was I to think? I assumed that I was in grave danger."

"You're in grave danger if you stay in that boarding house. You're coming home with me." He took her arm and steered her back down the alley.

Her father had asked a duke to be her guardian.

Her world had changed in an instant.

"You don't have to hold me so tightly. I'm not going to run away again."

His only response, a dismissive grunt, his face shadowed and set into hard lines.

He had his prize. He wouldn't let her get away.

His carriage waited near the boarding house in the gathering gloom, as huge and glowering as its owner, waiting to swallow her whole.

His family crest painted in blood red on the door, the dragon rampant over the shield, its claws outstretched, a stylized plume of flames licking the air.

The sight of it gave her the shivers. The Dread Dragon Qavox, just as she'd imagined him. A coachman opened the door for her but she hesitated, shivers still chasing up and down her spine. "Where are you taking me?"

"To my townhouse, where you'll be safe. You're never to step foot in that boarding house again."

"But I must collect my things, meager as they may be. My most treasured possessions are the letters my father wrote to me during the war and a jewelry box of my mother's, even though it's empty now."

"On that score . . ." He reached inside his coat and when he withdrew his hand, gold sparkled in the dim light. "I used this jewelry to trace your existence. I purchased it back for you."

"My mother's necklace!"

"And the ear drops." He gave them to her and she held them marveling at how fate had returned her most precious possessions. A tear trickled down her cheek. "Thank you, Your Grace."

"I'll send someone round to collect your things and settle your debts tomorrow. Now get in the carriage, Miss Crewe."

The coachman waited impassively, holding the door open, waiting for her to climb in.

"Oh, very well." She was exhausted, suddenly, and it didn't seem worth it to fight for the chance to go back to that dreary, dingy boarding house and the inebriated Miss Flanagan—the woman who'd attempted to sell her to her sister.

Ana imagined the look on her face when a duke's servant in splendid livery arrived to settle her debts and collect her meager possessions. She'd think that Ana had found her own protector.

He lifted her into the carriage by her waist, and she landed on the carriage seat with a thud, breathless from the relentless grip of his huge hands.

He climbed in and took a seat opposite her, his forbidding expression mirrored in the downcast sky, the driving rain that began to fall as they departed.

He'd said he'd searched for her for years. How strange to think that all this time this man who, if he were to be believed, wanted to shower her with pencils and, presumably, other material comforts as well, had cared for her welfare.

Knowing that her father had been thinking of her, had made provisions for her future, made her heart sting and ache. "I have so many questions, Your Grace. I want to know every detail of the day my father was injured. He could still be alive." It was the slimmest of hopes, but she'd clung to it like a lifeline since the news of him being missing had reached her.

"There will be time for questions later, when you're warm, fed, and safely installed at my townhouse. I'll engage a chaperone for you tomorrow. Tonight I'll sleep elsewhere for propriety's sake."

How neatly he avoided her questions and gave orders instead. His commanding tone made her want to challenge him. "I don't require a chaperone, Your Grace. I've been living by my own wits and means these past years."

"You will have a chaperone. There will be no further discussion on the subject."

No questions and no discussion. His words were edicts delivered tersely and with finality. His eyes were shadowy in the dark interior of the carriage. They sat facing each other but he'd angled his body so that the scarred side of his face was hidden.

She'd seen the scars in the lamplight. A raised red and purple crosshatching on his left cheek and jaw. It made her think of what her father might look like when she found him, having suffered some terrible head wound that rendered his mind unable to recall his past.

The duke stared moodily out the window at the passing city with a stern, unyielding expression. Commanding nose, angular jawline. Several deep scratches down his unscarred cheek. That was from her pencil.

"You're bleeding." She held out a clean handkerchief.

He ignored her offering, wiping the blood away roughly with the sleeve of his black wool coat. "I wonder why." Sardonic tone, one thick eyebrow raised.

"I told you; I thought I was in danger."

She still might be. He wore the signet ring of the Duke of Warburton and his carriage was emblazoned with the same crest. She believed it was he, but she only had his word to take for the promise extracted by her father. Had she made a terrible mistake? Was she even now on her way to some dungeon?

Don't be foolish. Why would he make up a story like that? And he had returned her mother's necklace and ear drops. Why would he want her? A man like him—a duke, a war hero, wealthy and powerful—had no need to snatch down-on-their-luck lasses from dilapidated boarding houses for sport.

Still . . . he was a stranger to her. And she was alone with him in a carriage. She'd never been able to stop her imagination from running rampant. It was one of the reasons she'd believed she could write a good novel. And look how that had turned out. She'd labored so long over *The Dragon and the Blue Star*, editing and re-editing each scene to make the words sing, the metaphors sparkle. She'd thought it was a good story. Now, no one would ever read it. Except, the man sitting across from her had read the chapters she'd sent to her father. She wanted to ask him if he'd liked them but at the moment wasn't prepared to listen to another man pronounce judgment on her fanciful musings.

She shivered. She was only wearing a thin cloak and she'd stepped in several puddles as she ran from him. Her feet felt icy cold, the wet seams of her stockings chafing against her skin. The events of the last day were mounting, stretching her so tightly she felt as if she might leap out of her skin. Scream. Sob. Wail for the shattering of her few remaining dreams and the uncertainties glaring her in the face.

She flinched as he abruptly leaned toward her. He wrapped a soft, woolen blanket around her shoulders then retreated to his seat again, leaving her enveloped in warmth.

"Don't be fearful," he said gruffly. "I mean you no harm."

"I'm in a carriage with a strange man."

"I'm not a stranger. I'm your legal guardian. The paperwork was completed years ago."

"Requiring no signature from me, apparently."

That was the way of the world, and she knew it. What had her father been thinking, handing her future over to this grim, silent man? She was his possession as surely as if he'd purchased her from a bawd.

"No, your signature was not required, nor your approval or your participation in any way. But from this moment forward you will live as a wealthy heiress."

She snorted. "I'm not wealthy."

"But I am. And as your guardian I'll ensure you never want for anything ever again."

"What I *want*, Your Grace," she said, emphasizing the honorific with proud defiance, "is to not be beholden to you. Or to any man. I will find my own means of supporting myself and my own way forward in the world."

"Oh? Is that why you're staying at that veritable palace of respectability?"

Her cheeks flushed and she was glad he couldn't see it. "It was all I could afford, true, but I will soon be earning better money."

Doubt was evident on his face, even in the shadows of the carriage. "And what exactly is it that you will do for this money, Miss Crewe?"

"Don't look at me like that," she bristled, "as if I might be engaged in unsavory activities. Didn't I just fight you off when I thought you intended to ravish me?"

"Only because I allowed you to."

"Ah, so you *allowed* me to stab you with a pencil? That was part of your plan?"

"That was a surprise, I'll admit. I didn't know you carried a weapon in your coiffure."

"Admit that I had you on the defensive."

"I could have inactivated you at any moment. Should have done so sooner." He wiped more blood from his cheek. "If you'd managed to stab me in the eye, we might not be having such a civil conversation."

"You call this civil? I find you extremely domineering and uncommunicative. You rapped upon the door of the boarding house so forcefully it almost broke off its hinges, exhibited monstrous manners and employed no pleasantries, chased me down the street, cornered me against an alley wall, pressed your enormous body against me, making me feel trapped and . . . and small." She finished, suddenly unsure. He'd made her feel small and helpless.

But once she'd known who he was and that he was there to help her, there'd also been a strange and exhilarating sense of excitement. Especially as he vanquished those loutish men in the alleyway. Her body had responded to his words, thrilling with the knowledge that he was willing to defend her with his fists.

She wouldn't tell him that part.

"You *are* small. Too small. You could do with a hot meal. You're half-starved."

Food. Her treacherous belly clamored at the thought, emitting a long growl. Embarrassingly, he heard it, glancing down at her midsection. She wrapped the blanket tighter around her shoulders.

"Are you listening to me, Your Grace? I'm telling you what you did was wrong, so that the next time you try to rescue an unsuspecting girl, you won't terrorize her half to death."

"Believe me, I didn't choose to rescue you. I made an oath."

"If I'm such a burden, stop the carriage right now. Reimburse me for the pencil and I'll be on my merry way." Braver than she felt.

"I've just told you that you are now an heiress with a substantial dowry who will live in my house. Your days of being preyed upon by unscrupulous landladies are over. I'll personally pay a visit to Miss Flanagan and ensure she never attempts to recruit another desperate young lady for her sister."

"I hardly think you can change the tide of the world. Young girls with no money have targets on their backs."

"I have my ways."

No doubt he did. She remembered the terrifying look on his face as he stared down the men in the alleyway.

"Do you know how long I've been searching for you, Miss Crewe?"

"Obviously not. I had no idea anyone cared to track my whereabouts."

"I know you wouldn't have chosen a battle-scarred beast of a guardian. But I'm all you have."

"Why do you look so angry? You don't want to be my guardian?"

"I'm not angry with you, Miss Crewe. I'm angry because I couldn't fulfill my promise to your father sooner. I was unconscious, and when I awoke, you'd already left the finishing school."

"I couldn't stay there. Miss Pincheon hated me. When my father went missing, he'd only paid for one more month of my tuition. She told me that I'd be forced to become a scullery maid at the school if I stayed on."

"Another visit to pay, then," he said darkly, fists clenching. "She told you a lie. Your father had paid your tuition for a full year. She must have pocketed the remainder of the funds. Where did you go when you left the school?"

"The celebrated authoress, Lady Claridge, had visited our academy several months previously, doing research for one of her novels. She read one of my stories and told me that I had promise as a writer. We struck up a correspondence and when she heard of my plight, she offered to employ me as her companion and secretary. I traveled with her to her estate in the wilds of Cornwall and lived there with her. I became her faithful companion, secretary, and amanuensis. It was enjoyable work."

"You were in Cornwall this entire time? Did she not read the papers? I placed advertisements seeking you."

"She required utter peace and quiet for writing her novels. She didn't want the outside world to intrude. She was very reclusive. I was the only one allowed to read her novels before they went to her publisher. She didn't want them tainted by the outside world. She said that if she read the scandal sheets, or even books by other authors, those things might seep into her writing without her knowledge and the books wouldn't be wholly her brain children, as she called them. She was very eccentric, you see. But I loved her. She was like a grandmother to me. She passed away two months ago of sudden heart failure."

"I'm sorry for your loss."

"Thank you." Ana thought of Lady Claridge's kindly blue eyes and nearly burst into tears, stopping herself by remembering that she couldn't show any weakness. This man sitting across from her held her future in his battle-scarred hands. If she were to maintain even a modicum of control over her life, she must appear to be strong and capable.

"And so you returned to London?"

"I had no choice. Lady Claridge's nephew, Lord Thomas Claridge, inherited her estate and he . . ."

She tried desperately not to think about it, but the memory crouched in her mind like a vulture, waiting to pick her apart.

Lord Claridge, weaving unsteadily on his feet after drinking half a bottle of brandy, chasing her down the hallway into her bedchamber, grabbing her by the hair, thrusting his hand down her bodice.

You're a sly wee thing. Looks like I could break you in half. You're going to scream nicely, aren't you?

"What did he do to you?" Warburton's voice was like tempered steel, his gaze boring into her.

You're mine, Analise. I own you.

"He attempted to . . . He didn't succeed. I-I struck him in a delicate area."

Dex grimaced. "I recognize that maneuver. You do have a gift for close combat."

Despite herself, she smiled. The brief flash of unexpected good humor fortified her. "I was able to lock him out of my chamber. Waited until he drank himself into a stupor. Left in the middle of the night under cover of darkness and fled to London."

The stillness as she crept down the hall, his lordship's snores echoing from his chamber. Her heart beating loudly in her ears. The terror. Fear roughly scouring away her good humor, her hope.

She stirred restlessly, waiting for the duke to say something, anything. Waiting for confirmation that she'd been in the right, that taking matters into her own hands to remove herself from the nightmare wasn't too far outside the bounds of proper societal norms for him.

His silence deafened her.

"You've gone even more quiet and thundersome."

"I'm making a list."

"All of the ways I'm no longer an innocent young lady, fit for polite society?"

"A list of everyone who has wronged you." He slammed his fist against the padded carriage wall. "You shall be avenged."

His voice, his air of total authority. The way his dark brows knit together over cold silver eyes. He was the Dragon from her book, a creature of great power and purpose. The lines etched into his cheek, like claw marks.

She wrote about epic clashes and deadly curses. The duke had lived it. He had killed to survive. He bore the scars of battle. He had a wounded heart.

"You're safe now, Miss Crewe. Do you hear me?" He leaned forward and his knees grazed hers. He held her gaze in a cold iron grip. "Nothing bad will ever happen to you again. Not on my watch."

Chapter Five

From the far-off upper shadows of the cave, between two massive crystalline stalactites that dropped like inverted cathedral spires before her, the great golden eyes blinked quickly in succession, then narrowed in what might have passed for amusement.

"I'm afraid that you have been rather misinformed," came the sonorous rumble. "I care little for humans and less for their silly mishaps. But you intrigue me. I think I'm inclined to keep you as my pet . . ."

—*The Dragon and the Blue Star* by Analise Crewe

Your Grace!" a startled butler exclaimed as Warburton brought Ana inside his townhouse. "We expected you to be halfway to Drakefell Castle by now."

"I took an unexpected detour. I've brought you a young lady, McArdle."

"A young lady, Your Grace?" The long-faced butler stared at Ana with consternation.

"Miss Analise Crewe, my ward. I believe I mentioned my search for her."

"How do you do?" Ana asked.

McArdle frowned. "I've no guest chambers prepared."

"Don't make a fuss about me," Ana said. "My last chamber was a drafty old garret with mice in the walls."

McArdle's frown deepened. "You'll find no mice in the walls here, Miss Crewe."

"She may wait in my chambers until you prepare the guest room of her choice. She might be staying here quite some time. I'll stay at the Thunderbolt Club tonight. You." He skewered Ana with a stern expression. "Eat a hearty meal. That's an order."

He spun on his heel and strode away.

"Does he always give such barking commands?" Ana asked McArdle when the door had slammed shut behind Warburton.

"He's a duke." The butler inspected her bedraggled cloak and mud-stained boots with distaste. "What am I to do with you, Miss Crewe? His Grace was meant to be gone to Drakefell Castle, and we were in the process of closing the house and joining him there. Mrs. Hedges, the housekeeper, has taken some leave to visit her sister." He squinted at her through glinting round spectacles. "I don't know the first thing about young ladies."

He pronounced the words as if young ladies were a species of rare tropical disease that might be catching.

"I'll be no trouble at all. You'll see. I can sleep in any old corner. I don't take up too much space."

Another aggrieved sniff. "How did you come to be the duke's ward?"

He didn't think she looked the part and heaven knows she didn't. Until an hour ago she'd been subsisting on stale buns, butter or moldy crusts of cheese, and water. She hadn't bathed in an actual tub in weeks. She knew she didn't smell sweet and ladylike, and she didn't have the patience to act with decorum, either. She was suddenly bone-weary, and the mention of a hearty meal had her salivating.

"It's a long story. Shall I tell it to you over the meal I was ordered to eat? Don't go to any trouble. Some bread and cheese will suffice. Perhaps a haunch of cold beef and some mead?"

He gathered himself up and stared down his nose, even though he was only a few inches taller than she. "We do not dine like plowmen in this house, Miss Crewe. You shall have a proper meal delivered to your room after one of the maids has seen to your necessities. Follow me," he intoned.

She followed him on limbs gone shaky from hunger and the dregs of the fear that had made her attack the duke. Had she really stabbed his cheek with her pencil? She was quite proud of that. Perhaps she could use that somewhere in the Clovercote novel. In the outline, Adora is threatened by Sir Archer Falconer, a shadowy character who had served as a minor villain in an earlier novel. After he stole a kiss, she fainted away and was rescued by Lord Fortescue.

Perhaps Ana could change the storyline? Instead of fainting, Adora could stab Sir Archer with a pencil . . . and then she should save Lord Fortescue from a burning building, or something like that. Something valiant and uncharacteristic. Although Mr. Norwood wouldn't approve if she strayed too far from the outline.

"The duke's chambers are the only ones currently with a proper fire. You'll only be here long enough for your chamber to be prepared. Sit on that chair." He pointed to a leather-cushioned armchair in front of the fireplace. "And don't touch anything." He wheeled away on efficient legs, coattails swinging briskly.

Ana removed her boots and propped her stockinged feet up on the grate in front of the crackling fire. As blessed heat seeped into her tired limbs, she marveled at the strange turn this day had taken. This morning she'd awoken in a garret room where the wind whistled through the cracks around the windows and a miserly portion of coal barely dispelled the cold and gloom. And now here she was in a duke's private chambers.

Don't touch anything.

People certainly liked to give a lot of orders around here. She'd never been skilled at following rules. Who was this man her father had chosen to be her guardian? All she'd gleaned thus far was that he was a duke, he was lethal, he didn't like to talk much, and he was wealthy beyond anything she'd ever imagined. This was an opportunity to explore while he was away, look for clues about the life he led in London. She must know more about this man and his plans for her life before she agreed to live in his home and accept his largesse.

The rooms were appropriately dark-paneled and crimson-velvet curtained. A pair of black leather riding gloves had been tossed on a chair, the leather buttery soft. She laid her hand over one of the gloves, covering only a small percentage of the surface area. His hands were truly massive, just like the rest of him. During the ride here he'd taken up most of the carriage.

That moment when his knees had touched hers, when he'd leaned close to her . . .

Nothing bad will ever happen to you again. Not on my watch.

Thinking of that moment made her feel hot, as though she were still sitting in front of the fire. The thunderous knitting of his brows, the rigid set of his broad shoulders. The way he planted his feet, trunk-like thighs balanced and ready. The clenching of gigantic fists. He'd been her avenging warrior and she'd liked it. It gave her a thrill when he faced down those men in the alleyway, when he told her that nothing bad would ever happen to her again.

She'd love to believe him. Believe that this imperious nobleman could fix her life, like a broken carriage wheel. Set her back on a path to carefree happiness. Pull aside the heavy dark curtains that had descended over her heart when her father went missing and allow the sun to shine again.

She'd love to believe it, but she'd learned a thing or two during the long years after the war. She'd learned that orphaned girls, friendless and alone, shouldn't dream too large. That the life she'd envisioned for herself had been a fiction that fell apart at the lightest touch, like the pages of a very old book. She'd learned that a smile and a cheerful disposition weren't enough to get by in this world.

Fairy godmothers died, and their evil nephews attempted to force themselves on you.

This duke who thought he knew how to put her life back together . . . he could be a villain in disguise. Villains often appeared decent in the beginning and then showed their true stripes halfway through the novel.

She couldn't trust him. Not yet. Maybe never. For that reason, she must learn as much as she could about his character before engaging with him any further.

She walked around his rooms, careful not to disarrange anything. The oil paintings on the walls portrayed horses, not ancestors. The books lining the shelves near his desk were serious dukely books: Greek classics, collections of political speeches, Milton's poetry, and the complete works of Shakespeare, all bound in gleaming leather and projecting an air of importance into the room. Not a contemporary or fictional novel to be found. The desk had the usual inkwell and quills, official-looking papers, and ledgers.

She liked finding the small details about people that made them unique. But she had a feeling the duke hadn't personally chosen anything in these chambers except for the books and the horse paintings.

A crystal decanter filled with something amber glowed invitingly on a sideboard. Perhaps a small sip of whatever spirits the duke consumed of an evening would warm her more fully. She pulled the stopper from the decanter and sniffed. She wasn't a connoisseur of spirits but this smelled delectable—like burnt sugar and apricots. She poured a small amount into a glass and tried a sip. It didn't taste quite as good as it smelled, and it burned going down, but it did leave a nice warm glow in her belly.

With his expensive brandy giving her courage, she decided to venture into the bedchamber next door. It was mostly bed—a huge affair set high off the ground, as though the duke should be enthroned as he slept, the mattress dipping slightly in the middle as if the weight of his huge, muscled body had left an indelible imprint.

No silk negligees left in his armoire, or any other evidence of a mistress. Everything costly and of the highest quality—silk bed coverings in a deep gold shade, soft white linens, silver washbasin—but nothing that really told her anything about his intimate life. His cologne smelled of ambergris and bergamot.

Was there nothing illicit for her to find? Nothing that might give her a clue as to his vices, his pleasures, or perhaps, more importantly, his weaknesses?

A folded sheet of paper on the bedside table caught her eye. It was a list of names: Kitty, Janet, Tessie, Laurel. Ah, now this was interesting. Conquests? Potential wives? Sisters, even?

A mystery for her to solve.

She sipped more brandy as she tiptoed around his room, careful to leave no trace of her exploration. A black silk dressing gown hung on a wardrobe hook. She lifted it free and held it to her nose. Yes, it smelled like him. The earthy musk of the ambergris, the refreshing citrus tang.

An image of him wearing nothing but black silk, drinking brandy, propped up in bed reading Shakespeare popped into her mind. She shivered, hugging the dressing gown closer.

"Ahem."

She spun around, heart pounding. *Please don't let it be the duke.*

"I thought I told you not to touch anything, Miss Crewe."

Only McArdle, with a censorious frown.

"I was just having a look around."

He sighed heavily. "Follow me, Miss Crewe."

Ana grabbed her boots from the rug in front of the fireplace and hurried after the butler. It wasn't until they were halfway down a long hallway that she realized she was still clutching the duke's silk dressing gown in one hand.

"No trouble at all, says she," McArdle muttered under his breath as he glided ahead of her. "Ha!"

"What the devil happened to you?" asked Dane, Duke of Rydell, when Dex entered the Thunderbolt Club. "You're even more battered and bruised than usual."

Dex groaned and flung himself into a chair. He'd run away from his house so fast that he hadn't even changed his ripped coat or wiped the blood from the scratch across his cheek. "Miss Analise Crewe. That's what happened," he said glumly.

"The young lady you've been searching for?"

"The very one." Dex accepted a tumbler of brandy. "I found her."

"Excellent news! You've been searching for her forever. Where was she?"

"The rookeries."

Dane gave him an incredulous look. "I hope you removed her swiftly."

"I attempted to. She had other ideas."

"What's she like?"

"Small of stature but grand in energy. Self-described as a red-headed spitfire of a hellion." He smiled slightly, thinking about how she'd attempted to dissuade him from wanting to make her his mistress. "Delicate and tough, like the progeny of a bare-knuckle boxer and a goldfinch. Crewe was a mild-mannered man, though stalwart and deadly in a battle. She must have gotten the spitfire from her mother's side."

Dane laughed, studying his fresh injuries. "Don't tell me she did that to you?"

A servant handed him a cloth and Dex wiped his cheek. "Thought I was a bounder attempting to steal her virtue. Wouldn't let me get a word in edgewise to explain myself. Fought like a cornered alley cat."

"Wish I could have seen that. Hey, Somersby," he called to their dark-haired, strong-jawed friend who was slumped in a corner, nursing an entire bottle. "Warburton was trounced by a young lady this evening."

Somersby raised his bottle in their direction. "Young ladies. Can't live with 'em, can't live without 'em, am I right, gents?" He swallowed an unhealthy amount of whiskey and then slumped over the table, propping his chin on a deck of cards.

"Somersby's drowning his sorrows," said Dane. "His latest opera singer jilted him for a marquess."

"Think I'll do some drowning myself." Dex finished his brandy and the waiter quickly poured him another.

Dane joined him in another drink. "You probably didn't explain yourself to Miss Crewe, you just grunted and attempted to stuff her in your carriage."

"I did try to explain myself." Though he hadn't done a very good job of it. Silence was a habit he'd learned in the hospital that became more and more difficult to break. It was the protective shroud he wrapped around himself, the invisible armor he wore. "She mistook me for a gentleman sent by a brothel keeper to take her as his mistress."

"Then I'm glad she attacked you."

"She fought valiantly, if ineffectually." He shuddered. "If I hadn't arrived in time and she'd fallen into the clutches of the brothel madam . . ."

"But you did. And she's safe now."

"She's at my house. I can't return until I find a suitable chaperone. I was supposed to be halfway to Drakefell by now. I'm stuck in London instead. I was thinking of asking my aunt Glynis to chaperone Miss Crewe. She used to make me quake in my half boots when I was a child. I promised Lieutenant Crewe that I would see his daughter safely settled and I damn well will."

"You mean to find her a husband?"

"I suppose that's the usual meaning of seeing a young lady settled." He tried to imagine Miss Crewe on the marriage mart, viewing every suitor with mistrust, all raised fists, fiery curls, and flashing eyes. "Although she's not exactly your typical docile debutante."

"What I don't understand is how she escaped your attention for so many years."

"She took a position as secretary and companion to Lady Claridge, the celebrated authoress. They remained sequestered at an estate in Cornwall until Lady Claridge died and her nephew inherited the house and was, I gather, attempting to inherit Miss Crewe, as well. She fled Cornwall with only the clothes on her back and a few family keepsakes. She's been fending for herself ever since."

He was the worst guardian in the world. He'd failed her miserably. Small wonder the girl had taken one look at him and run for her life. She was wary, and understandably so. While he'd been searching for her, she'd been accosted by a reprobate, forced to flee at midnight, and propositioned by a bawd. Fury tensed his body into hard knots. He'd make certain the finishing school mistress, Lord Claridge, and the boarding house owner and her sister received their just rewards.

"What's she like? Other than sharp of tooth and nail."

"Sharp of everything. A pointy little chin, razor wit, talks non-stop. Just turned eighteen. Redheaded. Freckles. A blur of motion. She doesn't trust me fully yet. I'll have to convince her of my respectability and good intentions if I want to escape that sharp pencil and tongue of hers."

She put on a brave face with her jokes and her good-natured chatter, but she wasn't the same innocent, trusting girl who had written those letters to her father. Life had taught her hard lessons.

"I would offer my wife as a chaperone," said Dane, "but we're going on holiday next week. Perhaps one of the other ladies in our group?"

"No offense, but I don't think they're stern and unimpeachable enough. If I recall, your Sandrine was chaperoned by two elderly ladies whose permissiveness resulted in all manner of mischief."

"Ah, I do recall," Dane said fondly. "Bless their inattentiveness."

"I'm certainly not allowing my ward to sneak out and attend masked balls and meet the likes of you in hedge mazes."

"You'd better trim away any rose trellises near her window, then. I'm told that's how Sandrine made her escape."

"Good God."

"And definitely don't allow her to join the Pink Ladies."

"Are those ladies still terrorizing society?"

"Afraid so."

"I'm her guardian," Dex growled. "She will not be debauched in pleasure gardens on my watch."

"Even if she freely chooses debauchery?"

"She's my responsibility. I swore to her father I would see her safely and comfortably settled. She'll marry a worthy man within the year."

He would see to it that no one ever made her eyes cloud over, or her shoulders tremble ever again. Life had thrown her cruel twists and turns, but from this moment forth she would be safe and protected.

Chapter Six

Day upon day piled up like the mounds of treasure that surrounded her. Qavox brought her nicely charred field game and great clumps of greens and vegetables, obviously stolen from some poor peasant's fields. She slept on two golden thrones pushed together, covered in furs and the decaying raiment of long ago queens . . .

—*The Dragon and the Blue Star* by Analise Crewe

Ana awoke to find sun streaming in the windows and a maid setting a tray down next to her bed. Disoriented, she rubbed her eyes. "What time is it?"

"It's half past noon, milady."

Past noon! She should be writing the Clovercote novel. She was losing precious time. She also needed to find a noble fiancé, and quickly. She didn't have to marry the man, only introduce him to Mr. Norwood and stay engaged until the novel was at the printing press.

Wait a moment—whose bed was this and why were the sheets so soft? For that matter, why was there a maid in her room?

It all came rushing back. The duke darkening the doorway.

Her desperate escape. His huge body pressing her against a wall, his hand holding her wrists with a crushing grip.

Exploring his rooms . . . the stolen black silk dressing gown. There it was, hanging over a chair, a shadowy reminder of the gruff guardian who'd rescued her twice already.

"I've brought you some drinking chocolate, milady. Shall I pour some for you?"

The rich spicy scent of the chocolate made her mouth water. "Yes, please. Pour it at the table by the fire."

"Very good, milady."

Ana hopped out of bed, wearing only her shift, and stretched her arms and yawned. She couldn't remember the last time she'd slept so late. Her knuckles were faintly bruised from the punches she'd thrown, but other than that, she felt well rested and ready to tackle anything, even something so large and grimly silent as the Duke of Warburton.

Her gown was no longer hanging on the hook where she had left it. Her boots were nowhere to be seen, nor her cloak. "Do you know where my things are?"

"In the washing, I believe."

"How am I to go about my day?"

"I'm sorry, milady." The maid's lower lip trembled and her hand shook as she poured the chocolate.

"Never mind," Ana said brightly, smiling at the nervous girl. "I'll simply have to wear this." She lifted the duke's dressing gown and slipped her arms into the gigantic sleeves. She knotted the belt. It reached to her ankles, brushing against the carpet. She lifted her arms and the sleeves, which were ten times too long, flapped like crow's wings. "Does it suit me?"

The maid hid a smile by ducking her head. "It's rather too big, I'd say, milady."

"It's the duke's."

"Oh." The maid lifted her head with a frightened wide stare. "Should you be wearing that, milady?"

Ana rolled up the sleeves and cinched the belt tighter. "It appears to be my only choice. Is His Grace at home?"

"No, milady," the maid replied. She was young, no more than seventeen, with a heart-shaped face, brown eyes, and a gentle, timid air.

Ana settled onto the comfortable chair and held her toes toward the fire. Delicious.

The maid stood there uncertainly, awaiting further orders, her nose twitching slightly, as if inhaling the scent of the chocolate. Ana paused with her cup halfway to her lips. "Would you like some chocolate?"

"Oh no, I couldn't, milady. I must see to my other duties. They're short on chambermaids, you see, and I shouldn't be serving a grand Lady what with me being new, and all." She scurried toward the door.

"Do I look like a grand Lady to you?" Ana wiggled her bare toes and grinned.

The maid smothered a smile. "You talk like a lady."

"I used to be one and then my circumstances changed."

"Once a lady, always a lady. You're the duke's ward, they say, and that makes you very grand, indeed."

"Perhaps, but only yesterday I was living in a boarding house in the rookeries and eating bread and butter for my tea, so the transformation to grandness hasn't occurred yet and you needn't be the least bit intimidated. Come." Ana nodded at the chair opposite her. "Have a few sips of chocolate. No one need be the wiser."

The maid hesitated, glancing longingly at the silver chocolate pot, and then at the door.

"What's your name?"

"Tessie, milady."

Ana startled. Tessie had been one of the names on the duke's list. Was it a coincidence or could Tessie help her discern the meaning of the list? "Tessie, you look as if you could do with putting up your feet for a moment and having a nourishing cup of chocolate. You won't come to any trouble, I'll see to that. It will be our secret."

"I couldn't . . ." Tessie repeated, but she stayed still and watchful as Ana poured a second cup of chocolate and held it toward her.

Pulled by the scent of the chocolate, Tessie timidly advanced until she was perched on the very edge of the chair across from Ana, ready to bolt at any moment.

She took the smallest of sips from the cup of drinking chocolate Ana handed her, and then closed her eyes, inhaling deeply. "It's even better than I imagined."

"Have one of these currant buns. They're delicious if you dip them into the chocolate."

Tessie accepted a bun and couldn't stop herself from eating it in two large bites.

"Tell me about yourself, Tessie."

"Me? There's not much to tell."

"Do you have brothers or sisters?"

"I'm an orphan girl, milady."

"Why, so am I!"

"You, miss?" said Tessie in disbelief, obviously questioning if fancy ladies in luxurious beds could possibly share such a woeful status with herself.

"Truly. Except"—Ana sipped her chocolate, noting the flavors of cinnamon and some spice she couldn't name—"it's only a temporary status in my case. My father, Lieutenant John Crewe, went missing in the war, and everyone presumes him dead. But I know the truth. I know that he suffered a grave injury but was nursed back to health in a small village in Belgium. He can't remember his identity, you see. I'm going to find him."

Tessie's eyes widened. "Will you go to Belgium, milady?"

"If I must."

"I've only seen London."

"How long have you been employed here?"

"Only two months."

"And how have you found your position?"

"Ever so much better than the last. My wages are paid on time and no one beats me."

A low standard. "And the duke, have you observed him?"

"Only bits and bobs. He doesn't spend much time here. He's usually at Drakefell Castle in Surrey. He only comes to London for racing his horses, and the like."

As they talked, Ana slipped more buns onto Tessie's plate. "What do the staff think of him?"

"He does have strict rules to follow, but he's fair, he is."

"Now tell me what you truly think. I swear to you I'll repeat it to no one. I want your candid opinion."

Tessie hesitated. "I shouldn't say, milady."

"You shouldn't, but I swear I won't tell anyone. I need to know about him because I only last night found out he was my guardian and I'm unacquainted with him. Is he a good man, do you think?" Ana poured Tessie more chocolate. "What do the other servants say about him?"

"Well . . ." Tessie gulped more chocolate. It was probably the first time she'd tasted such a delicacy. "Mrs. Hedges says that he needs a wife, because he's all rough and ill-tempered and he frightens everyone. She says a wife will gentle him. He has wounds from the war that pain him. Sometimes he'll wake in the middle of the night with the most awful yelling, as if he's back on the battlefield, and those nights he'll—"

"Exactly what is going on here?" McArdle was at the door; arms crossed and face thunderous. Drat. He'd interrupted them before Ana could broach the subject of the list of names.

Tessie leapt to her feet, knocking her chocolate to the floor, where it made a stain on the carpet. "I'm sorry, sir." She burst into tears and dropped to her knees, scrubbing at the chocolate with her apron.

Ana set her cup down. "I invited Tessie to sit with me. It's entirely my doing and she's not to be punished for it."

"Return to the kitchens at once," McArdle ordered. "Scullery maids taking tea with young ladies. This house has gone all topsy-turvy."

"I thought you said that you had no maid to help me. I choose Tessie. She's my lady's maid while I'm here at this house."

"Preposterous. A scullery maid cannot and will not serve as a lady's maid."

"The duke said that I might choose my own chamber, and I daresay he would approve of me choosing my own maid as well."

"Ha." McArdle sniffed. "We'll see about that."

"The first order of business is having Tessie find my gown."

His nose wrinkled. “It was stained.”

Mud and blood from yesterday’s fight. “Then what am I to wear?”

“We’ve sent someone to collect your things from the boarding house. Until they arrive, you will stay in this room.” He gave his order and left.

“You’ve made an enemy, Miss Crewe.”

“I’m sorry, Tessie. I didn’t even ask if you wanted to be my maid, I was that irate with him. Should you like to be my maid?”

“More than anything, milady, but I don’t know how to dress hair and fasten elegant gowns.”

“Never mind, we’ll figure it out together. We’ll have to wait until my things arrive.”

“I’ll just go and fetch a cloth to mop up this chocolate, milady.” Tessie bobbed a clumsy curtsy and ran from the room.

Ana would make certain she wasn’t punished. She could use a friend and ally in this house filled with the duke’s absence and the disapproval of McArdle.

She had no clothing to wear. She couldn’t very well leave the house in her shift and a dressing gown. She was a prisoner here, as surely as if the duke had turned the key in the lock.

She helped Tessie clean up the spilled chocolate and then inspected the chamber she’d been assigned by McArdle, excitedly flinging the curtains wide only to find the decidedly uninspiring backside of the carriage house.

“This will never do. There’s no view.”

“There are some trees.”

“Even though I was living in a garret I had a glorious view, out over the rooftops of the city. It helped me write.”

"Are you a writer, milady?" Tessie asked, looking awed by the prospect.

"I am. I've written one novel already, although a publisher told me it was no good and I should write another. If I stay here for any length of time I must have a tolerable writing desk, a supply of fresh paper, quills, and ink." The duke had said he'd buy her one hundred pencils. He should be willing to supply other sorts of writing implements. "I must finish half a novel in a little over a fortnight."

"How exciting! What will it be about?"

"Have you heard of the Clovercote books by Lady Claridge? No? They're romances."

"Romances," Tessie said dreamily. "I'd love to have time to read romances."

"I'm going to write a Clovercote romance."

"You are?"

"And you shall be my early reader. Should you like that? I'll make sure you have time to read and tell me your thoughts."

"Would I ever!"

"I'll begin writing my novel as soon as I have a suitable desk. Do you know of any chambers on this floor with a view and a writing desk?"

"Loads of these rooms have grates need cleaning—I've been in almost all of them! There is one room, at the end of the hallway. It has a view of the square and the grandest desk you ever did see. It's shut up and no one uses it, but I think you would like it." Tessie blushed a bit at her own presumption, but obviously felt strongly enough on this point to persevere. "I could take you there so's you could see for yourself?"

"Perfect! Lead the way."

"But . . . milady"—she glanced doubtfully at the dressing gown sweeping the floor around Ana's feet—"you're not clothed."

"No one will see us, we're only going on an exploratory mission to find the perfect writing room." She cinched the belt of the duke's dressing gown even tighter, rolled the sleeves higher, and followed Tessie out of the room.

A DISTRAUGHT, QUIVERING McArdle met Dex at the door. "Your Grace, I'm so relieved you've returned."

"What's wrong?"

"I must say, with apologies to Your Grace, that Miss Crewe is a most disruptive type of ward."

"How much disrupting can she have achieved in one morning?"

"I caught her sharing her breakfast with the new scullery maid, and when I informed her that scullery maids were not to take meals with ladies of the house, she informed me that she'd chosen the girl as her lady's maid, which won't do at all. The maid is untrained and barely able to perform her current functions."

Dex's lip twitched. The thought of the petite firebrand upending the apparently delicate inner structure of his household so easily was not, upon reflection, difficult to believe.

"My ward has perhaps grown unaccustomed to the ways of polite society. You'll be pleased to learn that my aunt Glynis has agreed to come and live here as Miss Crewe's chaperone." She was a rigid disciplinarian and wouldn't mince words when it came to instructing Miss Crewe in all things proper and decorous.

"That is good news, indeed. But it doesn't make the current situation any less objectionable."

"The current situation?"

"I assigned Miss Crewe the turquoise chamber, which I accounted to be the largest and most well-appointed, with a vanity mirror and large dressing chamber for the new wardrobe you will be furnishing her with."

Dex hadn't thought of that, but of course the lady would require new fashionable clothing if she was to be launched into society. "Very correct of you, I'm sure."

"And yet Miss Crewe rejected my choice."

"What was the reason given?"

"It doesn't have a writing desk and she's writing some manner of . . ." McArdle sniffed disdainfully. "Romantic novel."

Dex recalled the pawnshop broker mentioning something about her writing a novel. Perhaps she was finishing the book he'd read several chapters of in the letters to her father. "So? Simply have a desk moved in."

"You would think that solution would suffice, but apparently the desk must be positioned in front of a window with a view, because her previous desk, though rickety and scuffed, had a view of London's rooftops that sparked creativity."

"Then find her another room." Dex was growing impatient. "I have important business to attend to." He meant to visit the boarding house and the bawdy house and fulfill his promise to ensure the unscrupulous Flanagan sisters stopped recruiting young, destitute ladies newly arrived from the countryside.

"Yes, Your Grace, I attempted to do so, but she chose a new chamber on her own." An ominous pause. A trembling of his upper lip. "*That chamber.*"

There was only one room in his house that could be so described. "That chamber is always kept locked."

"The lock must have broken, because she is inside, Your Grace.

She and the scullery maid. And she enlisted several of the footmen to help her redecorate. It's utter chaos, Your Grace! I've been unable to dislodge her."

As though Miss Crewe were something stuck between his teeth.

Staid and stuffy, meet redheaded hellion.

"I've already had a clash of wills with Miss Crewe, McArdle." And he hadn't emerged unscathed. "Never fear, I shall win this round."

He stalked upstairs and down the hall. He was willing to be lenient about fraternizing with serving girls, but breaking into locked rooms that were kept locked for good reason was going too far.

The door was cracked open. He flung it wide.

The scene that greeted him was chaos personified, to McArdle's credit as descriptor. A footman, holding steady a brocade-backed chair. A chair definitely not designed for the task at hand, which was acting as step ladder for a young lady to climb. The lady in question was wearing a heavy black silk garment that swallowed her up, the sleeves hanging loosely about her raised arms, the belt wrapped twice around her waist, the bottom hem skimming the seat of the chair, except for the part caught on the mahogany chair back, exposing a length of creamy leg that the footman was valiantly trying to ignore.

She was busily trying to remove the voluminous dustcovers housing a gilt mirror that lined most of the wall. Curtains that had long been closed to the day had been thrown wide, and a column of sunlight was making the dust motes dance, lending a celestial glow to her ruddy curls.

Why in God's name was she wearing his dressing gown?

The footman caught sight of him and his face blanched. He let go of the chair and backed away. The young scullery maid took one look at Dex standing in the doorway, let out a high-pitched squeak, and scurried around him and out of the room. The footman hastily followed.

"I've got it!" Miss Crewe shouted merrily, wrapping the dustcover first around her hands and then around her torso, end over end. She wobbled on the chair, wrapped in the dustcover.

"Miss Crewe," he said coldly. "Just what do you think you're doing?"

There was a muffled reply from inside the dust covering. She wriggled around to face him, the chair wobbling, and then she lost her balance.

Chapter Seven

"Help me," pleaded Amsonia, as she did every night. "Help me or let me loose to find my family." And as he did every night, Qavox cocked his horrible head above her in the shadows, and said absolutely nothing at all . . .

—*The Dragon and the Blue Star* by Analise Crewe

"Oof," Ana exclaimed as her body connected with something rock solid. Not the floor.

The duke.

Once again he held her tight against his enormous, muscular body. She wriggled one hand free and peeked out of the dust covering, giving him a cheery smile. "Why, good morning, Your Grace. And how are you this fine day?"

His eyebrows met, giving him the glowering look of a minotaur she'd once seen, painted on the side of an ancient Greek vase in Lady Claridge's library.

He set her feet down on the carpet and began unwrapping her. She tumbled out, breathless, laughing heartily. "Thank you for catching me. I'm afraid I became rather tangled." Where were Tessie and the footmen? It appeared she was all alone with the duke. And he didn't look happy to see her. He helped her to her feet, still silent, though his eyes spoke volumes. His gaze swept from her unruly hair to her bare feet. She snatched up the dust covering and wrapped it around her torso.

His eyes narrowed. "Why are you wearing my dressing gown?"

"I didn't have anything else to wear, did I? My things haven't arrived yet from the boarding house, and I wanted to get started on airing out my new chamber. I love this room. It's perfect for my—"

"You may choose any room but this one." His face was immobile and determined, the face of a statue carved from Pentelic marble.

"But why? I love this rosy wall covering, and this mirror." She twirled in front of it. "Whoever saw such a large looking glass? I'll have the footmen move the desk closer to the windows so that I might gaze out while I write."

"Did you not hear me?"

"I heard you, but you didn't answer my question. Why can't I choose this room?"

"You can't. And that's final."

"But why? I don't understand. Did—did someone die here?" She clapped her hands, the thought rather delighting her. "Is there a ghost? Maybe it hides by day in these patterned wall coverings! Ooh, I read about such a thing once, a spirit that materialized at night from a painted design featuring great boughs of cherry blossoms and an ornamental urn. Popped right out of the urn and scared the bedroom's occupant straight to death, so that there were then two ghosts in the room, and so on until the room's spirits outnumbered the cherry blossoms!"

He was still as stone, waiting for a chink in the wall of chatter she was erecting.

"Or perhaps . . ." She glanced around the room, her gaze alighting on the large wardrobe she hadn't explored yet. She was in a fanciful mood that set her eyes sparkling. "Or . . . are you hiding something in here?" She danced toward the wardrobe.

"Do not open that."

"I knew it!" she cried. "I've stumbled upon a secret collection of scandalous novels. Your Grace, how delightfully rakish of you." She turned her back to him and fumbled with the lock.

"You'll have no luck with that. It's kept locked. For a reason."

She shrugged merrily. "It's a wonder what a hairpin can do." She turned back, hairpin in hand, waving it at him, before flinging open the wardrobe. Rows of lace sleeves and gossamer silk skirts greeted her surprised face. She turned to the duke, an unasked question on her lips, momentarily silenced by the sight.

He had already turned away, wincing. "Allow me to say it one last time: you cannot have this chamber. Now kindly remove yourself and choose another."

"Why?"

"Because I wish it to be so."

Which she assumed was the standard response to so many things in a duke's life. Because he wished it to be so, it was. Because he was wealthy and titled and male and the world must do his bidding.

"But doors are meant to be unlocked," she exclaimed. "Chambers to be lived in. Curtains to be opened to allow the sunlight in."

He crossed his arms over the vast bulk of his chest. He held out his hand. "Come with me, Miss Crewe. I shan't ask again. I shall bundle you back up into that dustcloth and forcibly carry you out of here."

She ran to the open window, putting distance between them.

"But only look at this spectacular view, Your Grace. Why, just this morning I observed an attempted pickpocketing and lovers quarreling in the park. And there is a family across the street, I don't suppose you know their names? They have a remarkable number of children. I count nine in all, and the eldest daughter must be making her debut this year because there is an inordinate amount of fuss over her wardrobe. I'm quite attached to her after only an hour of observation. I've decided that her name is Cygnette, because of the lovely curve of her neck, and that she will be the diamond of the Season. It's wonderful fodder for the novel I'm writing."

He paused, halfway to her, brows knitted together. "Which novel, the one with the dragon?"

"Oh, didn't I tell you? I visited Norwood & Pennington yesterday, before I met you, and Mr. Norwood didn't want to publish my fantastical novel, but he said I might attempt to take up Lady Claridge's mantle as the authoress of a new Clovercote tale. I have a detailed outline dictated by my mentor before she passed. I promised Mr. Norwood that I would submit half of the novel in a fortnight's time. Hence, I require the best writing desk in the house."

"You may have the desk, but not the room."

Immobile. Unmalleable. He truly was carved of stone.

"But why?" she asked, hands on her hips, exasperated now.

He didn't bother to answer this time. He advanced on her, eyes stormy, with the obvious intent of bundling her back into the window covering.

"I'm leaving, I'm leaving." She rolled her eyes and exited the room as gracefully as one could in an overlarge dressing gown that dragged upon the floor, nearly tripping her with every step. "But don't think this is over," she whispered softly.

"I heard that, Miss Crewe," the duke said tersely as he locked the door and pocketed the key. "Now, go and make yourself presentable. Your possessions will have arrived by now. My aunt Glynis—Lady Glynis to you—is coming soon. She's to be your chaperone. She can't find you looking like a . . ." He waved his hand at her.

"Hellion, Your Grace? I did warn you about my character," she said archly.

He grunted. "Be in my study in precisely half an hour." He spun on his heel and stalked away.

Tessie was waiting for her in the old room. "Was he very angry, milady? I never should have suggested that room, they do keep it locked except for cleaning! I only thought you would like the view ever so much, but I shouldn't have taken you there."

"Don't fret, Tessie. Why such a fuss over one room? It's ridiculous. And high time for a change! The duke is keeping secrets, Tessie, and I aim to uncover them."

"I should think that's not advisable, milady. You might come to trouble that way."

"I've already come to trouble. The duke thinks I require a chaperone, though I don't see the need for it. I'm to go and meet Lady Glynis in a half hour. I was told to make myself presentable."

"Your trunk arrived, milady. I've already hung your gowns."

"Thank you, Tessie. Which shall I wear, do you think?"

"The dove gray gown with the white lace collar."

Tessie helped her dress, fastening the buttons at the back.

"Will I do?" Ana asked.

"What about your hair?"

"What about it?"

"If I were a lady's maid I'd help you tame them curls with hot tongs."

"That sounds like I might be scorched. I've never done anything with my hair except twist it into a knot at the back of my head and pray too many curls don't escape."

"At least a ribbon, perhaps?" Tessie found a pink ribbon in Ana's trunk and looped it around her head, tying it in a bow at her ear. "That does look nice."

"Thank you, Tessie. You're a wonder."

Tessie's cheeks reddened. "I'll do my best, milady. But honestly, wouldn't you want a real lady's maid? One with training, like?"

Ana shook her head. "I want you, Tessie. Now, do you know where the duke's study is?"

"I'll take you there."

When they arrived, Ana knocked on the door. The duke's gravelly bass voice bade her enter. She glanced back at Tessie, whose eyes were wide with fear. "Go on, milady."

Ana took a deep breath and entered the room. A tall, thin woman with iron gray hair and iron gray eyes regarded Ana steadily. Her immaculate posture matched that of the duke at her side, who was also staring straight at Ana with a concentration that made her feel slightly breathless.

"This is the girl?" Lady Glynis asked.

"This is my ward, Miss Analise Crewe. Miss Crewe, this is my aunt, Lady Glynis."

"How do you do?" Ana made a curtsy.

"Humph." Lady Glynis narrowed her eyes. "That wasn't a proper curtsy at all. And what are you wearing?"

"A . . . gown?"

"It's drab and does nothing for your complexion. Come here, girl."

Ana approached her in the same way a plaintiff might approach a judge seated high on their throne, gavel in hand.

She grabbed Ana's chin and tilted her face toward the light. "Freckles. How unfortunate. Equally unfortunate, the color of your hair—not red, not blonde. I'll admit your eyes are a pleasing green. Open your mouth."

Caught off guard, Ana did as she was told. Lady Glynis inspected her with growing disdain. "Crooked teeth. You'll have to smile with your mouth closed."

"I beg your pardon?"

"Keep your mouth closed and smile demurely."

"I'll have to open my mouth to speak."

"You'll speak as little as possible."

Ana glanced at the duke. He was reading a ledger on his desk, oblivious to the fact that she was being evaluated like a broodmare in a stable.

"Hold out your hands."

When she didn't obey, Lady Glynis lifted one of Ana's hands. "Ragged nails. Do you chew them? A disgusting habit. I'll coat them with rapeseed oil, the bitterness will soon cure you of that. You're altogether too slight and small of stature, you'll have to wear heeled slippers and lift your chin. We can perhaps add some padding to your gowns to give you more of a feminine shape. Now then, are you proficient on the pianoforte?"

"I play very poorly."

"How many languages do you speak?"

"Just the one. I did learn French but I'm afraid it's mostly slipped away."

"Do you draw or paint?"

"Badly."

"Well? What are your accomplishments?"

"I'm writing a novel for publication."

Lady Glynis shuddered delicately, her thin lips turning down. "Don't ever mention that in public. Warburton will dower you generously, of course, otherwise we have no hope."

"Pardon me, but no hope of what?"

"Making a success of yourself on the marriage mart. You must be a credit to this family. I can't very well sponsor a girl who will shame us."

"I've no wish to debut in society, nor to find a husband." She'd told Mr. Norwood she had a titled fiancé, but surely a titled guardian would do just as well? Once she wrote a brilliant half of a Clovercote novel, she could then inform him that she had the patronage of a duke. She didn't require a fiancé now. But how was she to write the novel if she was to be readied for a debut? No, she must wriggle out of it somehow.

"Then why am I here?" Lady Glynis turned to the duke. "Warburton, this young lady has no wish for a husband, therefore she has no need of a chaperone. I'll bid you good day."

Warburton slammed the ledger closed. "Not this again. Miss Crewe, I'm becoming rather tired of your contrary nature. We discussed the need for you to be settled."

"I don't recall a discussion. I recall you barking orders and ignoring my plans for my future."

"Well!" Lady Glynis shook her head disapprovingly. "She has neither the docile temperament nor classic beauty to be a success. Perhaps you should allow her to pursue her own future and wash your hands of her."

The duke closed his eyes, pinching the bridge of his nose with his thumb and forefinger as though he had a headache coming on. He turned to his aunt, opening his eyes. "Aunt, you will instruct Miss Crewe in the niceties of making her debut. She will enter society in a matter of weeks. She will make a respectable match and her future will be secured." He turned to Ana. "And you, Miss Crewe, will obey my aunt's every instruction. Is that clear?"

"Clear as a bell, Your Grace."

"Excellent. Your lessons will begin immediately—"

"However," Ana broke in, "I don't wish to attend the Season, therefore I won't follow instructions." She had a novel to write.

Lady Glynis rolled her eyes heavenward. "Nephew, I'm leaving. When you have your ward in hand, fetch me again. Until then, I bid you good luck." She left with a swish of heavy silk skirts and an indignant sniff.

"Do you always have to be so argumentative?" asked the duke.

"Did you see her evaluating my teeth? She forbade me to smile with my lips open."

"She's a paragon of propriety. With her by your side your celebrated entrée into society will be assured." He rose from the desk and stood in front of her, forcing her to tilt her chin to meet his gaze. "I'm weary of you thwarting my every attempt to help you, Miss Crewe. My aunt will chaperone you. I'll dower you generously. I will see you comfortably settled."

His unspoken words: he'd buy her a husband. Then she wouldn't be his problem anymore.

What was it about his size that made her tremble? She'd faced down larger men. She knew she was petite. A pint-size virago. A big life force in a small package. But she'd never been aware of her body in the way that he made her aware. She stared at his hands and remembered when he'd lifted her by the waist and plunked her into the carriage.

Something about him felled her like she was a sapling under a woodsman's axe. It was the sheer magnitude of his presence. The way he seemed always a hairsbreadth away from losing his temper and doing something outrageous.

Like now. He could be towering over her because he wanted to shake some sense into her, wanted to bend her to his will. Or he could be standing so near because he wanted to kiss her.

Kiss her? What a ridiculous thought. Where had that come from? "Your Grace, I'm far too busy to attend the Season. I have a novel to write, or have you forgotten?"

"I haven't forgotten. And I don't care if you write ten novels. Only do so after you are safely married."

"You have my future all planned out for me. A wealthy husband, a townhouse in London and a home in the countryside, no time to write frivolous novels or gallivant around the country on doomed missions to locate my missing father."

"No, you had your future planned in the letters you wrote. You wanted to attend balls, find your true love, set about creating a large and happy family. I'm only trying to give you what you envisioned."

"I wrote those letters when I was fifteen. I didn't know what I wanted, or who I was. I only knew what I was supposed to want. And, yes, I did long for a large family because I had never known one, but now I want other things. I want financial independence, the chance to travel and experience life like Lady Claridge did."

"Your patroness was protected by her status as a respectable widow while she was traveling."

"Then I shall invent a husband and kill him off quite handily.

Let's see . . . dear Reginald. He was a devoted husband. We married when we were young. He wrote me truly awful poetry. He had red hair, like mine. We were doomed to produce redheaded children, though it didn't bother us because we were quite jolly and content with our quiet life in the countryside. Until poor Reginald, poor sweet soul, was killed by a . . . runaway bull in the paddock. I'll wear a ring when I travel and tell stories of my dear departed Reginald." She sniffled. "See there? I've nearly made myself cry thinking about Reginald and what a devoted husband he was until he was gored by that bull."

The duke crossed his arms, glaring most ferociously. "Are you quite finished?"

Ana attempted to match his ferocity. If only she had a stepstool, she'd climb higher than he and glower down from a great height, show him how it felt. She jutted her chin, staring him down. "Just getting started, Your Grace."

SHE WAS BRAVE. She didn't back down easily. He respected that. "Don't you want to make your debut?"

"It won't work. I'm ill-suited to London society. I'll stand out like a sunflower in a rose bed. I'm hardly the modest, sheltered young lady society demands. I've had to learn hard truths about the world."

He winced. "And that is entirely my fault. I mean to make reparations. You may not be the daughter of a titled gentleman, and you may have had several years outside of society, but as a duke's ward, you'll attract the notice of all, especially when they learn about your dowry."

"In other words you're going to bribe someone to marry me."

"Don't view it as such. I'm giving you an appropriate sum that will signal your worth to a society that places much value on such things."

"I shall attract only fortune hunters then. And they'll know I'm not an innocent debutante. I'm not the girl Papa left at the finishing school. The girl who wore ribbons in her hair and had a head full of sentimental dreams."

"I read your letters. I know what those hopes were. I can't bring back your father, but I can see that the rest of your dreams come true."

"I'll bring my father back. If there's even the slimmest of chances that he may be alive, I must attempt to find him. If you are set on paying for my way in the world, I will accept those funds in order to place advertisements in the papers for any news of my father's whereabouts. I shall interview the men who fought alongside him, perhaps even travel to Belgium to search for news of him—"

"Those men are dead." He hadn't meant the words to be so cold, so harsh, but there was no other way to communicate the truth. "Your desperate hope that your father is still alive is dangerous. It could make you the target for unscrupulous charlatans."

There was no gentle, kind way to say this. She must abandon this false hope. "I'm very sorry, Miss Crewe, but there's no way your father survived his injuries."

"The official report says he's missing in action and his body was never recovered."

"It's true that he was never found. Many were not. We had to . . . dig shallow, hasty graves. Men were piled into them. We had no time to erect grave markers or make lists of names to send home." He winced at the memory. As long as he lived, that tumult of limbs and faces being steadily swallowed by dirt would never fade from his mind's eye.

"And yet you didn't actually see him die," she said stubbornly.

"I staunched his chest wound with a cloth. He'd lost too much blood. He's gone, Miss Crewe."

"You have no imagination, that's the problem. Some kind villager found him and dragged him to safety. Nursed him back to health. He lost his memory. He can't even recall his own name."

"Impossible."

"It's not," she insisted, her cheeks gone pink with emotion. "I'm going to find him and then I'll set about restoring his memory using the things he used to love. I'll read him his favorite poem—Coleridge's "The Rime of the Ancient Mariner"—we'll play a game of whist, and I'll feed him his favorite dessert—flummery."

"Flummery?"

"A lovely custard flavored with almonds and rosewater. I'll make it for you sometime. I must keep in practice so that I might produce it in an instant upon his return."

He raised his hand to touch her shoulder, then dropped it at his side. How could he make her see? "You can't cling to this mad hope. I'm telling you that he's gone. So many are gone. It's better to mourn him. Honor his memory by making him proud of you by marrying a gentleman he would have approved of."

She stifled a sob. "You don't know what's best for me," she said in a wobbly voice, biting her lip.

"I'm your guardian. He entrusted you to my care. I take my duty very seriously. I will see you happily settled."

"My debut will be no success. People will ask questions about why I didn't make my debut earlier. Where I've been."

"We'll tell them the truth—you were companion to Lady Claridge, there's nothing objectionable about that."

"It's true, there was nothing objectionable about it—until she was gone and unable to protect me from her nephew. She was such a kind lady, taking me in and allowing me to be her companion. She was like a family member to me. I learned so much from her. But her nephew . . ." A shadow crossed her face. "If I enter society too boldly, Lord Claridge is apt to spread vicious rumors to ruin me, all because I spurned his horrid advances."

Dex's jaw clenched. "Lord Claridge will never mention your name again."

"How can you be sure of that?"

"I have my methods."

"So you've said. You seem to believe that everyone dances to your tune. But you can't simply force me to marry. I can't be one of them—the beautiful carefree society ladies who've never had to navigate a problem more vexing than finding the perfect gown, or the perfect match. You're asking me to attend balls, and fetes, as if I haven't spent the last years of my life fending for myself. I tell you it won't work. They'll sense that I'm not one of them."

He'd often had the same thought. He wasn't one of them. The carefree, beautiful people. On the rare occasions when he appeared at social events, he felt like an outsider, a cloud of gloom that made everyone around him uneasy. He had no intention of marrying. At least not yet. He'd put off the begetting of an heir until the last possible moment.

"Your life should have been free from harsh realities. Your father, if he had lived, would have collected you from finishing school and launched you in society. The eligible bachelors would have vied for you."

"Vied for me—are you mad? I'm a redheaded spitfire with freckles and crooked teeth. You heard your aunt. I'm hardly a diamond of the first water."

His heart ached at the quiver in her voice. She didn't feel good enough, beautiful enough. Everything had been taken from her and she'd been left with nothing but her clever mind and her optimistic nature. He wanted to hold her in his arms, stroke her soft hair, and whisper that she was beautiful and that from here on out her life would be all silk and rose petals. He would give her the best of everything. Kiss her troubles away.

Hold her in his arms? Kiss her? Was he stark, raving mad? He took a step backward, away from the sight of her lush lips and startlingly green eyes.

"You have your whole life ahead of you," he said gruffly. "Trust me. This is for the best."

"You don't know what's best for me," she repeated.

"But your father did, and he tasked me with seeing you married."

"And what about you? Why aren't you married, if you're so keen on the idea?"

"I've no intention of marrying for quite some time. Perhaps never, though I'm expected to produce an heir. My brother, Roland, has several male offspring."

"You're not one of those grumpy dukes who don't believe in love, are you?"

"I believe in love." He swiped a hand angrily through the air. "I believe it squeezes every last drop of blood from your heart and leaves you hollow. Love isn't for the likes of me." Not for men who had spent so much time with Death that it was practically a member of the family. Not for those who bore deep scars, both inside and out.

All of his limbs were intact. He was luckier than many. It wasn't his arm or his leg that was missing. He didn't wake up in the middle of the night from a dream of running through a field and realize that his legs had been amputated.

"I thought I was in love once. Never again."

"What happened?"

"Never mind."

"*Never mind.* Two of the most infuriating words in the English language when used together. You never want to talk about your past, even if it might explain why you persist in interfering with my present."

"You're free with your words."

"And you keep yours locked so tightly it's a wonder your lips know how to part. You are all the g-r words. Grumpy, gruff, grim, grave, grunting, growling . . ." She counted them off on her fingers.

"And you don't appear to be that most appropriate of g-r words: grateful. You will attend the Season. That's an order."

"We'll see about that. May I be dismissed, Your Grace?" she asked with a decidedly sarcastic emphasis.

"You may. We'll speak of this again tomorrow."

She left, taking the light from the room with her. Suddenly it was quiet and gloomy again. He sat down at his desk, shaken to the core by his reaction to her. This longing to comfort her, to hold her and kiss away her tears must never happen again.

They were in close physical proximity, that was all. He was a man. She was a pretty woman. And . . . he admired her for standing up to him, for not being intimidated by his scars and his bluster. He couldn't blame her for defying him. Her life had been overturned and shattered, like an upended tea cart spilling its contents on a hard parquet floor, and she was scrambling to find some order in the chaos, attempting to salvage some control amongst the shards.

This wouldn't be easy. But it would be exponentially more difficult if he didn't control himself. He must never have a thought of that nature again.

She was his ward. Completely and utterly forbidden.

Restlessly, he paced the study, reliving their conversation. The vulnerability when she'd spoken of searching for her father. The mad hope that she would somehow find him.

In his nightmares, Dex saw dead men rise from the grave. Skeletons chatted with him, sitting at his bedside, talking heaps of bones and tattered clothing that once were men. Once were friends.

Lieutenant Crewe was dead. No amount of searching would bring him back.

If he were alive, he'd castigate Dex about the sorry job he was doing as guardian to his daughter. She'd nearly been forced into a brothel.

Analise entrapped. Forced to sell her body unwillingly. Analise with tears streaking her face, those big dreams of hers strangled and left for dead.

He pushed away the vile idea. He'd promised to avenge the wrongs that had been done to her and he had an excess of frustration to exorcise.

It was time to pay some not-at-all friendly visits.

Chapter Eight

The vermilion-clad regiment that he intercepted outside Mount Runemor were no match for the Dragon's might. He spat a lethal spray of deadly fire across the squadron attempting to overpower him from the rear, then pinned a fleeing soldier to the spot with a talon tip. "Who sent you?"

"The Red Wizard, Master of Vyranthrall!" came the reply. "You have captured something he desires!"

Qavox cocked his massive head, his eyes narrowing to slits. Amsonia? What did the Usurper want with her?

—*The Dragon and the Blue Star* by Analise Crewe

Lord Thomas Claridge was going to seed. His fair hair, thin and straggly, cheeks florid from drink, and blue eyes watery. Dex could barely make out his features through the red haze of rage cloaking his vision.

This was the man who had terrorized his ward. He was going to pay for that mistake. It wouldn't do to accost him in public. Dex had shadowed him all afternoon, from club to restaurant, and now to his townhouse. Best to deal with him inside his home.

He didn't even notice as Dex walked up behind him.

"Claridge," Dex said loudly.

His target turned. "Er . . . do I know you?"

Dex turned his cheek and Claridge saw his scars. A spasm of distaste on his lips, quickly replaced by an oily smile. "It's Warburton, is it not?"

"That's right."

"We've met on occasion."

"We have."

"Is there something I can do for you?"

"There is." Dex waited, knowing that silence was a weapon he wielded with skill.

"Look, if I owe you money at the gaming hells and I've forgotten, it's simply a mistake. I've come into an inheritance and I'm settling all my debts. You can talk to my man of—"

"I'll talk to you. Let's go inside." Dex took his arm and led him up his own steps.

Claridge looked worried now, searching his memory for some offense he could have given to the duke. He fumbled with his keys, his fingers trembling as he opened the lock. He hesitated once the door was open, and Dex knew he was calculating the odds of being able to dart inside and slam the door shut safely behind himself. It was a bet he would have undoubtedly lost, and Dex made sure he knew it by quickly reaching around him and shoving the door open.

Helped along by an unfriendly push from Dex, Claridge stumbled into the dim hall, which sported an air of neglect similar to his own. Dust covered the artifacts from his aunt's world travels, which populated the chamber. Spiderwebs clung to the taxidermied ibex standing proudly on a mount in one corner and hung in swathes from the carved wooden masks on the wall, connecting them to various statues arranged beneath. Dex strode inside and closed the door.

Claridge collected himself with obvious effort and assumed a jaunty air. "So, how can I be of service to you, old chap?"

"You can disappear from my sight, and the sight of all respectable society."

"Come again?" Claridge's voice wavered.

"You heard me. Your time fouling up the general atmosphere of London is over. For the time being. Until I tell you otherwise."

Claridge squared his shoulders, drawing himself up as tall as he could. The effect was ruined somewhat by the alcoholic undulations of his entire body, a drunken weaving that robbed him of any authority whatsoever.

"Now see here, Warburton. We've no common business to discuss, and you have no right to talk to me in this manner! Kindly remove yourself from my abode and I shall endeavor to ignore your confounding and, frankly"—he fixed bleary eyes on Dex and jabbed a finger ineffectually in the general area of his chest—"*blastedly* insulting conduct."

Dex caught his wrist in a fluid motion, bending it back with subtle pressure. "Claridge, we have more *business* in common than you realize, and you have every reason to listen to me."

"Ow— How so? What exactly have we got in common?"

"For a start, you want to stay alive, and I have a way of making that happen. You will stay at your estate in Cornwall for the period of one year, lest the sight of you bring discomfort to my ward, Analise Crewe. You will never, ever attempt to force yourself on another woman. I will find out if you do. I have my ways. I will receive reports from those close to you, who were frighteningly easy to bribe, I might add. You aren't exactly a popular man, Claridge. And, finally, when Norwood publishes the next Clovercote novel, you will heartily endorse it as a welcome continuation of your aunt's legacy."

"But my aunt's dead, damn you! I fail to see—" And then tardy clarity dawned on Claridge's blotchy countenance. "Miss Crewe. That presumptuous little baggage. She's still trying to take advantage of my dearest aunt's largesse? Redheaded spindly pinch-faced thing, pah!" He attempted to spit, but his lips were loosened by booze and fear and the spittle settled ineffectually on his own waistcoat.

Dex breathed in. Out. In. Out. Breaking every bone in Claridge's body in the man's own hallway would be a trifle difficult to explain, even for a man of his social standing. *Spindly*. He thought of Ana's deceptively slight frame and smiled.

"I'd have a care what you say next. I'm about three breaths away from knocking your head against the wall."

"You can't simply order me about, Warburton! If you hurt me, I'll have you brought up on assault charges! You don't own me, and I'll do what I want."

"Oh but I do! I literally own you. I've purchased all your debts. And they're large ones. Largest I've seen, racked up in such a short amount of time, it's almost impressive. How you managed to squander your 'dearest aunt's' legacy with such haste boggles the mind. I am now the sole person you owe money to. And I won't let you default on payment. Your estate, this townhouse, even your horses—they will fall to me unless you follow my every instruction."

It paid to have friends who were lawyers, who were justice seekers and knew their way around the rougher gaming hells. It had been easy enough to obtain a list of the man's staggering debts, easier still to purchase them from frustrated creditors.

He let go of Claridge's wrist, certain by the man's rapidly graying face that reality was sinking in. He gave him a gentle pat on the cheek.

"Don't take too long thinking about it, old man. The city's fairly clamoring to be rid of you. Do us all a favor and disappear."

He left Claridge palpitating in the foyer, whey-colored and gasping. He had a feeling the man wouldn't be a blight on the face of London for very much longer.

Another name crossed off the enemies list. On to the next.

The facade of Maggie Flanagan's brothel was anything but subtle. Dex regarded it with a sort of horrified amazement as he approached.

He'd visited plenty of bawdy houses in his wild youth, filling the role of the young blood about town to the hilt. He couldn't recall, however, having seen anything remotely like "La Maison de Mme D'Oiseaux," as the scarlet sign proclaimed in gold-edged script. Every inch of its surface was crowded with architectural frippery, cornices and arches and florets crowding one another along the front, gawdy colors of paint that clashed violently with the blazingly orange velvet drapes hung in the windows. It had obviously started its life as a much humbler business, but its plain bones fairly sagged now with added-on ornamentation.

She had been hard to find, this Maggie Flanagan, the woman who would have sold his ward's innocence for a pittance. He'd asked around at his club, but none of the younger set had heard of her or knew where her place of business was. It wasn't until his queries had been overheard by a group of older gentlemen that things fell into place. "Maggie Flanagan?" a white-whiskered colonel had said with a snort of recognition. "It's been ages since I've heard that name. She goes by something French now, something deucedly silly and fancified. Marguerite D'Oiseaux, I think it is? Outfit's totally different now. Used to be one of those plain-and-simple places you visited if you weren't feeling that particular about how you spent a quick quarter-hour. Girls were . . . an interesting lot."

"And where is this Marguerite D'Oiseaux's?" Dex had pressed, offering the talkative elder man a pour from his private decanter.

"Ahh thank you, this stuff's divine. It's near the Rose & Crown, off the docks, just look for the most overdone terrace on the block . . ."

An apt description, thought Dex, raising his hand to the bulbous knocker, made of two comely brass maidens pressing their lips together at the top and twining their bare legs together at the bottom. A brutish lug with a brick wall of a face, fully as tall as Dex, opened the door and grunted a welcome. After stating his intentions of meeting the famous Madame Marguerite D'Oiseaux, Dex was escorted into a salon so festooned with frills, drizzled with gilt, and dripping with draperies that he had the claustrophobic sensation of being on the inside of a ladies' armoire.

The doorman lumbered away, leaving him to perch his tall frame on a rickety gold-and-fuchsia-striped divan. He was offered libations by a buxom woman in an absolute mockery of a maid's uniform, with a décolletage so plunging he wondered if the seamstress had simply forgotten to add that part of the dress. He declined the drink and the smiling invitation that accompanied it.

A few minutes passed, then a door opened and into the room

came the Madame, gliding in on a cloud of feathers. She was of an indeterminate age, with a face so covered in paint and powder that it resembled a masquerade ball mask. She had faded blonde curls tucked into a turban. Her plum-colored dress was trimmed with undulating marabou feathers; so too were her bodice and sleeves, and a gauzy robe covered the whole eye-opening ensemble. She stopped in front of him, feathers still gently waving to and fro, and cocked her head to the side.

"Bonsoir, monsieur. Welcome to my humble house of business. How may I be of service?" Her voice was husky and low, her words almost indecipherable beneath a thick French accent.

"Maggie Flanagan?" he said pointedly, rising to his feet. He watched a muscle twitch in her right cheek, just over an artificial beauty mark.

"Ah, that name. From a lifetime ago, n'est-ce pas!" She laughed delicately, musically. The accent remained. "I am she. But you may call me Madame Marguerite. And you are—?"

"I am Deckard, Duke of Warburton." He said it loudly and forcefully, waiting for the usual fawning recognition, the thinly veiled fear that followed his famous name and infamous scarred visage. He wagered that not many men gave their real names in her establishment. But she seemed neither surprised nor excited.

"Well, Your Grace," she said, smiling slightly and raising her inscrutable face toward him. "What flavor of entertainment may Marguerite and her lovely birds provide for you this evening?" She raised her right hand, snapped her tinted nails twice, and a panel at the far end of the salon slid open. Female bodies began to pour through, lining up to the left and right of the Madame, who controlled their placement via subtle eyebrow lifts and quick nods of her chin.

As the room began to fill, he contemplated his options both internal and external. He had intended to confront Maggie Flanagan, easily extract a promise from her to forget she'd ever heard the name Analise Crewe. He'd expected (as indicated by her sister's sordid dwelling and Ana's rather scant exposition) a hard-bitten harridan riding roughshod over a house of tired women, someone who would cower and beg for his mercy. He had been misled. The composed woman in front of him, with her implacable mask and steady dark eyes, was something else entirely.

She was brazen and unafraid, but the girls in the room were obviously the opposite. They ranged in size and shape, but all had a unifying factor: a nervous eye trained on the Madame. The ones standing closest to her shuddered from her touch as she guided them closer to Dex. He felt the slow river of fury that always flowed within him start to roil. But for a quirk of fate, this was where Ana would have landed—paraded in front of strangers, shrinking from the beringed ivory hand of this cold woman, this carefully constructed poseur.

He noted bruises on some of the women, partially concealed by gloves, hems, or garters. One of the youngest-looking lasses had the faint shadow of a black eye and was visibly shaking in her chemise.

Madame Marguerite wasn't the only one who knew how to wear a mask.

"Well, well!" He made a show of surveying the assembled faces, letting his eyes travel the length of their bodies, every inch the lustful gent looking for his evening's pleasure. "A delightful mélange. You obviously have an eye for talent, Madame!"

She dropped her head in exaggeratedly humble acknowledgment, her obsidian eyes remaining fixed on his. "I have indeed been blessed. My little birds are honored that Your Grace admires their plumage. They come from the finest of nests, you know."

"How wonderful to hear you say so, Madame," he said, matching her tone, and began to walk slowly back and forth, hands clasped behind his back. "It is the fresh ones I am after, you know. Do you have any . . . newly out of the nest, you might say? I have a penchant for . . . fledglings."

The Madame clapped her hands and smiled a knowing smile. "Quelle chance! We have such a bird indeed, Your Grace." She turned her head abruptly to the side and whispered into the ear of the nearest girl, who quickly left the room with a palpable air of relief.

"I am indebted to you." He settled back down onto the divan. "And how long have you been in this line of work, Madame?"

"It is hardly work, Your Grace!" And her accent suddenly dropped away, stripping her voice bare. "I quite enjoy it." He looked quickly in her direction and saw a snarl of sheer depravity stretching her lip, violently wrinkling her skin, so that for a second the mask was gone and he knew he was seeing Maggie Flanagan in her true form, sans artifice. This was the monster who might have ruined his ward.

The door opened again, and a young girl was led reluctantly in. So young. So skinny. And so scared. She could barely keep her head up, it kept drooping toward her chest as if she wanted to curl into herself and away from reality. He schooled his face to display a correct amount of interest.

"Does she please you, Your Grace?" Again, Maggie's voice was minus accent, and again it filled him with rage. He could barely speak his part, so great was his disgust for the entire proceedings. But he was here to help. To right a wrong.

"Yes. Yes, she most definitely does."

Once in the room they'd been allotted for their supposed assignation (garish orange and purple flowers on the bedspread, plush velvet pillows masking the hard skeleton of the well-worn bed frame), he sat the poor thing down and stood in front of her. The young girl's head stayed down, even as she began automatically to unfasten her corset with shaking fingers.

"Don't," he said, and she raised her head disbelievingly, huge eyes taking in his scars and falling again immediately. *Damn it.* His face, agitating when he meant to calm. Once again.

"Please keep your clothing on. I don't wish to dally with you," he said as gently as possible. She started to shake in earnest.

"But Madame will—" and she broke off, a sob choking her throat.

"What will the Madame do?" he said, trying to keep the iron edge out of his voice.

"She said she'd—I have to—ah, it don't matter! I'm lost, lost!" Tears wet the wretched girl's face, her hands twisted over and over in her lap.

"What's your name?"

"Daisy, Your Grace." She choked out the words.

"Daisy," he repeated soothingly. "I promise you, the Madame will never hurt you again. I am here. Where are you from, Daisy? How did you get—here?" He gestured around the room, taking in the magenta fleur-de-lis–patterned flocking, the stained floor, the tarnished cage of the brass bed.

"My parents died of a fever, Your Lordship. I didn't have nowhere to go. I heard as there was work in London and I spent every last farthing to get here. I stayed at Miss Flanagan's boarding house, saw an advertisement for it posted at Hyde Park. She said I didn't have to pay her upfront-like, but could pay as soon as I found work. Only I couldn't find no honest work, could I?"

He saw it all so clearly, the same plan that had almost snared Ana, stretching out in all directions like the web of a malicious spider. The poor girls arriving from the countryside and immediately beat down by the hard truth of the city. Then a glimmer of hope, the promise of lodging and safety—and the sticky strands of the web catching them, surrounding them, bringing them here to this horrid place, to be used until they'd lost their usefulness.

"That's how I ended up here," she continued. "Oh but please don't tell Madame I told you! She beats them that don't please her. I can't— I can't bear it! I held out long as I could. You were to be my first. I don't know what to do!"

"Daisy, I'm here to help you. I know you have no reason to trust me, but you must believe that this city holds people who care, who want to help you. I am one, and there are others."

"You want to help me? But how?"

The idea, borne of the revulsion and rage he had experienced downstairs in Maggie Flanagan's tarted-up salon was now a full-fledged plan. "Daisy, are there other young girls here with the same story as yours?"

"Several, Your Lordship, but some 'as gotten more used to it, I suppose."

"What about the girl with the black eye?"

"That's Susan, m'lord. She's a particular friend of mine, we arrived almost the same time. She has no family, same as me."

"Would you trust me enough to come with me this very evening? I would convey you to the residence of a friend of mine, the

Duchess of Harland. She runs a home where girls like you can get back on their feet. She will train you for a new job, give you lessons in defending yourself."

Daisy's lower lip quivered. "Madame won't let me walk out of here."

"She will if I offer her a princely sum of money for your exclusive use."

He saw hope beginning to replace the abject fearfulness that had been her distinguishing feature before.

"I suppose . . . I suppose if I trusted you and left with you it couldn't be much worse than what I'm meant to endure here."

Dex nodded. "I know it's a lot to ask. I give you my word as a gentleman that no harm will come to you. And my friends and I will come back for Susan, and any of your friends who are being mistreated here, if they wish to leave."

"W-why are you helping us?" she asked, looking up with bewildered but brightening eyes.

Flashing green eyes and small fists battering his chest. *I'll be no man's doxy.* Miss Crewe's brave words echoed through his mind. If he'd been even one day later . . . if the avaricious Madame had trapped her here . . .

He swallowed, choking back the wave of revulsion and anger that swamped him. "Because I know an innocent young lady who was once headed toward the very same sad fate."

Chapter Nine

He had spent so many centuries alone that he'd almost forgotten where his heart was, but watching the princess explore the cave, so small, so determined to find her way out, reminded him of its location. Something was stirring in his chest, something that had almost disappeared. Qavox thrashed his tail restlessly against a heap of jewels. Why could he not offer her a small amount of assistance? He was a dragon, after all. He could do whatever he chose.

—*The Dragon and the Blue Star* by Analise Crewe

No, no, again! You must start over," Lady Glynis exclaimed. "Have you truly never curtsied? How is that possible, a young woman of your previous station as a gentleman's daughter?" Disbelief animated her normally stern demeanor.

Ana shifted her shoulders, biting her tongue in frustration. She had practiced this simple movement for the better part of an hour and seemed no closer to mastering it than ever. She found that as soon as she sank into the correct attitude, she wanted to spring right back up, the better to observe the world around her.

She found the deferential posture incredibly boring. Eyes that were cast down couldn't take in the details that fed her soul, triggering the flights of fancy that made up her very being. She supposed she'd curtsied plenty as a youth, but nobody had judged her with the steely concentration of Lady Glynis. Her father had certainly never spoken up, if he'd found her grace or comportment lacking.

She'd never paid much attention to any of the etiquette lessons forced upon her by governesses and schoolmistresses. Those were hours for daydreaming about the future, for making up versions of her life, paths she might go down. She'd become a celebrated authoress. She'd marry a handsome lord and host London's most celebrated literary salon.

The only lessons that truly held her interest were any related to writing and reading. Her tutors had never emphasized the subjects overmuch, but their desultory approach had suited her perfectly. She was given leave to play in her father's library, steep herself in the classics, explore newer voices in poetry and prose. Her particular favorite was Mary Darby Robinson, whose poems spoke so movingly to the ever-changing roles of women within society, weaving the romantic and the political with skill and poignancy.

She bowed her head and sank down once more—but missed her mark and kept on sinking, dwindling into a petite heap of skirts upon the floor. Lady Glynis gave an exasperated sigh. "You're not even trying."

Ana endured another lecture forbidding her to express her real opinions, directing her to cast her eyes down modestly, and, above all, to hide her crooked teeth and knobby elbows.

Four hours later, she collapsed into a chair in her new chamber. "The drill sergeant has left the building," she said to Tessie, who giggled as she helped Ana unlace the tight gown and slip into a day dress that was far more comfortable.

"They should have sent Lady Glynis to face Napoleon. She would have lectured him on etiquette until he surrendered if only to stop her from droning on."

"You're a naughty pupil, milady."

"I'm an unwilling pupil."

"But why don't you want to attend a ball and dance with handsome gents? I've never even dared dream of such things."

Because what was the point? Every moment she wasn't writing her book, she wasn't coming any closer to achieving her dream. "I know I should be grateful. I have this contrary streak in me, something that chafes against rules and orders. I can't hold my tongue. It got me into ever so much trouble at school. I was always being sent to my room without supper or being held up as an example of what not to do for the other girls."

"I think you're lovely, I do. Don't change to please someone else. Even if he is your guardian."

"I'm only pretending to change. It's easier than arguing with my stoic guardian and his imperious aunt. Besides, it gives me more time to write."

"I'm looking forward to reading your novel, so you'd better keep writing."

"Thank you for the encouragement. I should like to write two chapters this afternoon."

"I have faith in you. I'll leave you to your work."

When Tessie was gone, Ana finally settled in at her desk. She was occupying a room with only a partial view of the square. If she angled herself just so, she could still see Cygnette's house, though she didn't have nearly as expansive a vantage point.

None of the servants would tell her why she wasn't allowed to occupy the forbidden room with the odd assortment of female garments, including one that had looked remarkably like a wedding gown, in the wardrobe. They pretended not to hear, or said something along the lines of "It's locked up by the Duke's orders, ma'am," then pressed their lips together and refused to offer anything more on the subject. Perhaps they were the garments of the woman he'd thought himself in love with. But then, why were they still hanging there?

And she didn't even know where to begin to find out anything more about that intriguing list of names she'd found on the duke's bedstand. Tessie had professed no knowledge of why she might be included, suggesting that it was a common enough name. Ana had recited the names to McArdle with the hopes that he could shed light on it (maybe it was a hiring list of potential staff, if Tessie had been included, maybe before she was hired?) but he'd dismissed her inquiry with a look of such withering scorn that even she'd felt the need to retreat. Another dead end.

Warburton was still a mystery. A glowering presence she sensed more than saw. When he was in the house, the servants walked more softly, held their breath, not wanting to disturb him. Everything in the household revolved around his wants and needs. The cook spent hours every morning creating a menu to tempt him to eat.

She refused to make him the center of her existence. She tried not to think about him or remember their encounters and conversations in great detail. Tried and failed. He was larger than life, his pronouncements made enigmatic and meaningful by their brevity. He certainly wasn't giving her more than a passing thought. He'd fulfilled his duty, or at least he believed himself to be on the right track. He'd given her shelter, a chaperone, and she'd even been to a modiste for fittings for an extravagant new wardrobe.

Thoughts of the duke were a distraction from the urgent task at hand. She must write as if her life depended upon it. She didn't have the luxury of self-doubt or any time to revise. This first draft must force Mr. Norwood to fall in love with her prose. This was her one chance to prove she was worthy of publication. If valiant princesses and talking dragons wouldn't sell, she'd pour her heart into writing a comedy of manners worthy of Lady Claridge's pen.

One hour later she sat, sharpened quill in hand, watching the well-dressed people of Mayfair bustling about their business like industrious ants on an anthill. She only had two paragraphs to show for the hour.

Not good enough. She must write faster. Or perhaps she should reorganize the contents of her linen drawer? She'd already rearranged the books on her shelves by color, braided and re-braided her hair, and developed a sudden passion for the writing of the obscure English Renaissance author, poet, and playwright Lady Mary Wroth, whose work she encountered in a historical tome she'd found in the duke's library.

In short, she was doing anything but writing.

The trouble was that she'd come to the point in the novel when Lady Claridge's outline read the following: *After a lively parlor game, the dissolute Sir Archer Falconer steals an illicit kiss from Adora as forfeit. Adora swoons and is in grave peril until Lord Fortescue rescues her from the ruffian.*

She'd written the part about Adora stabbing Sir Archer with a sharp pencil. But that happened *after* the kiss, and it was the kiss that was giving her problems.

She'd never been kissed. What did it feel like? Lady Claridge always described kisses as producing fluttering sensations. Her heroines sometimes swooned directly after the act, as though the meeting of lips upon lips was something so overwhelming and momentous it might render one unconscious. Ana had always felt that her mentor's descriptions of the feelings associated with love were somewhat hyperbolic. She didn't want to merely copy the superlatives Lady Claridge had used. She wanted to describe the sensations afresh and therein lay the conundrum. How could she describe something she'd never felt?

She closed her eyes, imagining that she was Adora and the Adonis-like Lord Fortescue was rescuing her from ruin. The image that coalesced in the darkness behind her eyelids was Warburton with fists raised, towering over those ruffians in the alleyway. *I am the goddamned Duke of Warburton.*

And then he was holding her up against the brick wall, holding both of her wrists in one of his giant hands behind her back.

Warburton leaning forward in the dark carriage, wrapping the soft blanket around her shoulders, his fingers brushing her cheek. *Nothing bad will ever happen to you again. Not on my watch.*

The moment when she'd landed in his arms in the forbidden room. How he'd unwrapped her from the dustcloth and it had become something else, something . . . shivery and new. Was that what Lady Claridge was describing? That breathless feeling of danger, like she was only two steps from the edge of a cliff overlooking the ocean. A drop in the pit of her stomach. A desire to touch his scars, feel the ridged skin beneath her fingers. Every line a testimony of the battles he'd fought, the internal war that still raged within him.

That moment in his study when he'd stepped closer and she'd thought . . . she'd thought he might be about to kiss her. No, of course he hadn't been, but her overactive imagination had painted it.

What would it be like to be kissed by Warburton?

It wouldn't be like any kiss described in Lady Claridge's books, she knew that instinctively. It wouldn't be a chaste peck on the cheek, or a worshipful brush of his lips against hers. His kiss would overwhelm her, send her senses into an uproar, like storm waters breaking through a levee.

But what, exactly, would he do? While his lips were on hers, where would his hands be?

Inside her bodice. His large hands covering her breasts. The scandalous thought made her pulse race. She certainly couldn't write that in the book. Mr. Norwood would never publish such lusty details.

She could imply certain things, though, and the reader would fill in the rest. She dipped her quill in ink. *Warburton kissed the way he hunted—with precise aim and single-minded focus. Adora was his prey. Her lips his prize.*

No, that was too dramatic. And . . . goodness! She'd written *Warburton*.

She was becoming confused. Both her hero and her villain kept transforming into an ill-tempered, forbidding man who lived his life as if constantly negotiating for territory on a battlefield.

She'd even written a scene where Fortescue, the supposed hero, glowered and frowned and said things like "I shall bundle you back up into that dustcloth and forcibly carry you out of here!"

No reader would cheer for such a domineering, unfeeling hero.

She crossed the lines out and began again.

THE DOOR TO Miss Crewe's room was cracked open and Dex could hear her pen scratching across the paper. He knocked but there was no answer. He pushed the door wider. She sat at her desk, afternoon sun gilding her skin and running riot in her curls. She was luminous, all gold and copper, concentrating so fiercely on her work that she had no awareness of his presence at all.

Her quill sped across the paper. She paused, staring out the window, and then bent to her work again. She filled every inch of the room with bright, crackling energy, like a fire blazing away on a hearth, warming and illuminating everything around her.

He cleared his throat. She jumped, and turned, quill in the air. "Oh, Your Grace, I didn't hear you enter the room."

A fiery blush spread across her cheekbones. She hastily covered the page she'd been working on with another sheet of paper.

"I knocked but you didn't hear. Intent on finishing your novel?"

She grimaced. "More like my novel is intent on finishing me."

"It's not going well?"

"The tale I wrote to entertain my father and escape finishing school seemed to pour from my pen with ease. This one moves like treacle. I don't have any practical experience in the ways of society."

"You didn't have any practical experience of dragons or sword-fights."

"That was different. I imagined an entire world. It's not as if anyone could judge it and say I got it wrong—it was my creation. This book is much more difficult because I must do Lady Claridge justice. I have an intimate knowledge of her novels and yet it doesn't seem to help when I attempt to write my own words. I keep rewriting the same scene over and over. I must astonish Mr. Norwood with my elegant and erudite prose. In short, this book must be perfect."

"You're expecting rather a lot of yourself. It doesn't have to be perfect. It only has to capture the tone and style of Lady Claridge.

Then the editors at Norwood & Pennington will help develop and improve the manuscript."

"No." She shook her head stubbornly. "This first draft must be perfect. It's my only chance. I honestly thought it would be easy. After all, Lady Claridge dictated three whole novels to me. I'm steeped in her prose." She waved a sheaf of papers at him. "But writing an entire novel, even with a detailed outline, is much more difficult than I'd anticipated."

"How difficult can it be to churn out a romantic tale?"

"One would think it would be simple, I know. I have the outline—simply flesh it out, throw some meat on its bones, and have done with it. But it's so much more difficult than it looks."

"When I read your letters to your father, I also read the chapters of the fantastical novel you were writing. Truth be told, they were captivating. I read eagerly and was disappointed when I never found out what happened to the princess and the dragon."

She shot him a surprised glance, obviously struggling to absorb the compliment. "You enjoyed it? I-I wouldn't have thought it to your taste. Mr. Norwood said *The Dragon and the Blue Star* would never appeal to the sensibilities of the modern reader."

"He was wrong. My sensibilities were well engaged."

"But it doesn't matter if he's wrong. He's the publisher, and he won't publish it. A new Clovercote novel is the only one he will consider. It's been my long-cherished dream to become a published author. I want to hold my book in my hands. Smell fresh ink on the page and know that my imagination might open a door for a reader to walk through. I wouldn't even care if the critics hated the novel if it found its way into the hearts and minds of readers. I want all the joys and sorrows that come along with being an author, and that dream has only solidified since my father's disappearance. My father and Lady Claridge encouraged my dream, told me that I possessed creative talent, but now I'm not so sure. Perhaps it's an impossible fantasy."

He hated the dejected look on her face. She was usually so sunny and optimistic. "I'm certain your writing can't be as bad as all that. Here, let me have a look." He reached for the sheet she'd been working on.

"Not that one!" She placed her hand on the sheet, weighing it down on the desk.

"Why not?"

"The ink isn't dry yet."

"You'll have to relinquish your writing to others' eyes at some point."

"Here, you can read this one." She handed him a sheet, covering her face in her hands. "Don't judge me too harshly."

THE DUKE READ in silence, sitting in a chair near her desk, his face as impassive as ever. Only a slight quirk of his eyebrows betrayed any emotion. What did that quirking mean?

He finished and lowered the sheet.

"Well?"

"Ah . . ." His face contorted. "Ah, it's . . ."

"Are you laughing at me?"

"Of course not. I rarely laugh."

"That thing you're doing with your lips. You're manfully attempting not to laugh. Admit it!"

A strangled noise. More twitching of his jaw muscles.

"Well!" she cried, snatching the sheet from his hand and retreating to her desk. "At the very least, I've finally managed to elicit some mirth from you! That's worth something. I told you it wasn't any good. I truly don't know what I'm doing wrong."

"It's not you. You're a good writer, there's no doubt about that."

"If it's not me, then what is it?"

"It's the subject matter. You're approaching the kiss as if you're describing tactical moves on a chessboard. I'd wager it's your lack of life experience that's impeding your progress. Lady Claridge was a woman of advanced years, a widow who traveled the globe."

She bit her lip, taking in his analysis, weighing it with her head cocked to the side. "Meaning that I've never been kissed and therefore I have no business writing about such things? Was my kiss so unrealistic?"

"There were certain . . . logistical inconsistencies."

"Well, I don't know what happens during kissing. Whose hands go where, how the lips move—if they do move? Does the tongue move? *Is the tongue involved at all?*"

This last train of thought sent her into a slight panic. Had she spoken it aloud? To the *duke*? She must be suffering from writer's strain. Lady Claridge had often spoken of the condition, which always occurred around the date when her novels were due to the publisher.

"Sometimes the tongue is, ah, involved, yes." The duke cleared his throat. "And the hands go wherever they want, when the participants are amenable."

"That tells me very little! But I can see that you're trying to be helpful. You're a man of few words, and not up to describing the art of kissing to me. Perhaps you could write a brief description in your terse, manly language and I could embellish it?"

Or . . . he could kiss her. That would solve the problem of her lack of experience in the area. His lips weren't so very far away. His large hands rested on his knees. His thighs were spread, boots firmly planted on the floor. She could go to him, perch upon one of his knees . . .

She would never be so forward. And her stern, regimented guardian would never reciprocate even if she was mad enough to beg him to kiss her.

"I'll introduce you to some ladies of my acquaintance. Talking to them will be far more helpful than anything I might write. In fact, that's why I came to see you. My friend the Duchess of Osborne is hosting an art exhibition tomorrow evening. Should you wish to attend, I'll ask Aunt Glynis to accompany you there."

"An art exhibition? How exciting. I'd love to attend." The next best thing to actual kissing would be asking for descriptions from ladies who had been kissed.

"It will be your first appearance in society, but you'll be among my friends."

"So you'll be testing me."

"Aunt Glynis will be observing whether or not you conduct yourself with appropriate propriety."

"I was just now thinking that going to such a society event would afford me the opportunity to ask your lady friends to help me describe kissing. If I can't describe a brief kiss, how am I to portray Adora's scandalous adventures in the world of the ton? She has a proposal from a duke, she turns down a viscount, she is nearly kidnapped, two gentlemen fight a duel over her, she drinks champagne, flirts outrageously. She's spirited into a dark garden by a handsome rake and then rescued . . . unless . . ." Her mind careened down a new path. "Unless I actually *experience* those things? Myself. Practical experience to enrich the written world."

She knit her brow delicately, then nodded, making the decision. "Perhaps I do wish to attend the Season after all."

"Absolutely not."

"Now you don't want me to attend the Season?"

"I don't want you doing any of those things."

"Which ones?"

"Any of them," he thundered. "You are to attend balls and other events under Aunt Glynis's watchful eye. That is all."

She eyed him carefully, trying to assess just what it was that was rubbing him the wrong way. Surely a man with his keen eye and obvious intellect couldn't be naïve about the tawdry adventures of the upper ton? She may not have any intimate knowledge of the details, but even she knew the broad strokes.

"You're the one who asked your aunt to prepare me for a debut in society. Aren't scandal and intrigue key parts of any Season?"

"You may try a few sips of champagne. I may take you riding on Rotten Row but I will definitely handle the reins. Nobody will be permitted to fight a duel over you. And you certainly won't be in need of rescue."

"Won't I?"

"Not while I'm in attendance."

"Then I shall have to evade you."

"Hah. You may try, but you will fail. There will be no scandal, no intrigue, and no kissing of rakes in moonlit gardens. Do I make myself quite clear?"

At that moment he was so very dragon-like that she almost believed smoke might rise from his nostrils and if he opened his mouth, she would see razor-sharp teeth waiting to make a meal of her.

Amsonia had willed herself not to tremble in the presence of the Dread Dragon, and Ana must do the same. "It's all very clear to me, Your Grace." She raised her chin, meeting his gaze. "You don't want me to have any fun at all. You will make balls as entertaining as sitting across from you listening to your deafening silence at the dinner table."

"I'm sorry that my presence is so distasteful to you." He rose from his chair and gave her a perfunctory bow. "I'll trouble you no longer."

"Your Grace—" she started, meaning to apologize for offending him, but he was already gone. The room seemed colder after his abrupt departure. Their argument had made her blood pound and her heart speed. What did he want from her? First he alluded so tantalizingly to logistical inconsistencies in her description of kissing, then he ordered her never to be kissed, and then he took umbrage at her very accurate description of the dinners they had shared.

And then there was the matter of how every time she was near him, she thought about what it would be like to kiss the man. What was it about him that turned her thoughts so wanton? He was distant and silent most of the time. Yet he'd thought enough about her to invite her to attend the art exhibition. She was looking forward to it. Perhaps she'd spent too long in the company of the Dread Duke of Warburton. It was time to experience all that London society had to offer, and then write the most vivid, wildly romantic novel imaginable.

A novel that Mr. Norwood simply couldn't refuse to publish.

Chapter Ten

"Be damned to a thousand eternities of pain, thou Wretched Fiend!" she sobbed, struggling against the supple, scaly limb that surrounded her. To have made it all the way to sunlight! To have tasted fresh air upon her lips and then be corralled again in such a humiliating fashion—it was too much to bear. "Let me go! If thou won't help me, yet have no desire to kill me, why keep me here as a prisoner?"

—*The Dragon and the Blue Star* by Analise Crewe

It's hopeless," Aunt Glynis sighed, an air of injury creasing her brow. "She can't be readied for her debut at Lady Chetwynd-Ellerton's ball, at least not in a fortnight's time. I swear it cannot be done, even by me. My dear nephew, you have given me an impossible task. I'm throwing in the towel. Find another chaperone for that hoyden."

"You can't quit. I'm counting on you," Dex pleaded. "What has Miss Crewe done now? I'll have a talk with her."

"It won't have any effect. She's impervious to good sense. She's more whirlwind than young lady. She's been dragging me all over town to various and sundry locations of interest and pestering me with an inexhaustible stream of oddly specific questions about societal rituals. I tell you my nerves won't stand for it."

Dex sympathized. He hadn't had a moment of peace since Miss Crewe arrived in his home. Her warmth and vitality filled the entire structure, even when he wasn't physically near her. He could hear her laughing with the maids, smell her clean lavender scent in the hallways. He found her pencils in the oddest places. They reminded him how fiercely she'd fought to protect herself on their first meeting, how a woman half his size had almost bested him with the aid of that humble but dangerous writing implement. That made him smile despite himself. And smiling made his scars ache.

The nights were the worst part. She had somehow found entry into his dreams. They were rife with bright red-gold hair and soft pink lips, supple skin that pressed into his own, tangled limbs.

He dreamed she was pulling him from a dark cave into bright sunlight.

He dreamed he was unfurling a great roll of cloth, and when he'd reached the end of it she tumbled out. Perfectly naked. Looking up at him with lambent green eyes, her arms outstretched, murmuring, "How does kissing work?" and other inane but wildly pleasant questions that woke him right up, boiling hot and aching to go back to sleep so that he could show her.

They never spoke without arguing, yet in his dreams all they did was . . . entirely inappropriate and entirely forbidden things.

"I'm afraid I'm partially to blame for those harebrained ideas. I said something about her novel lacking the ring of practical experience and now she's determined to experience as many of the things her heroine experiences in real life."

"Well-bred young ladies should not be writing novels, and they certainly shouldn't be rehearsing them. She's altogether too eccentric and opinionated to be a success. My advice for you, my boy? Give up the notion of introducing her to society altogether. Find some impoverished lord to wed her, offer him a handsome settlement, and he'll take her off your hands."

Her words filled him with disgust. Why did the idea of Miss Crewe marrying a fortune hunter make him so ill? It must be because he knew her to be a romantic. She'd never be happy in a loveless marriage.

"She must have her chance to dance at balls, to be on display, to make her own choice from the potential suitor pool."

"Then I wash my hands of this whole affair. I will not chaperone her at a ball, for fear she might say or do something to damage this family's good reputation."

There was a loud knocking on the door. "Enter," said Dex.

McArdle burst into the room, bright spots of color on his cheeks, panting heavily. "Your Grace, Miss Crewe is causing a commotion in the ballroom. She's forcing the footmen to fight a duel and it's frightening the maids."

Aunt Glynis raised her eyebrows. "You see what I mean? I wash my hands, I tell you. You're on your own, my boy."

"Wait, Aunt, don't leave. There must be something I can do to induce you to continue?"

The good lady paused. Though a veritable pillar of society, she was not immune to bribery. He did some quick mental calculations. "Your townhouse—I've heard you speak of renovations?"

"Ah yes," she sighed, turning aggrieved eyes skyward. "The whole thing needs remodeling! Such a sorry state. But the cost—"

"Allow me to cover it."

"And the furnishings! In such desperate need of updating . . ."

Aunt Glynis was far too good to gloat, but she had him where she wanted and they both knew it.

"I'll cover them. Anything you want. Just stay."

"Anything I want? Any designer I choose?"

"Yes, of course. Just please stay. I need you."

She favored him with a regal smile of acquiescence. "Very well, nephew. I can see how much this means to you. I shall renovate your Miss Crewe, and you shall renovate my home."

"Take the afternoon and evening off. Go and begin arrangements for the renovations." He escorted his aunt out of the house, relieved he'd managed to find a way to keep her as chaperone.

And now to douse the next conflagration threatening his once tranquil home.

Dex found Miss Crewe in the ballroom commanding a crew of reluctant duelists, who were arranged in formation on the shining oak-and-walnut floor. She was barking orders and waving her arms in the air, like an orchestra conductor about to box the ears of a second violinist with lamentable timing.

"Seconds! Where are my seconds? You are to stand behind but to the side—here and here, so that you may observe your friend's actions and avenge as necessary. No, no—Mr. Appleby! You are the second to Mr. Smythe. You must not turn your back to him, however will you see the action?"

The poor Mr. Appleby shuffled shamefully around to face his assigned duelist, whose face wore a look of aggravated martyrdom. "Now you (yes, Mr. Smythe! You!) raise your pistol, Mr. Harkins same, yes that's it. That looks right. Hold them steady, you've only got one shot to defend your honor! Now, lower your arms, take aim and—"

"Miss Crewe!"

She jumped, spinning around guiltily.

"Are you really forcing my footmen to duel? You do realize that I actually need footmen who are alive and unmaimed to maintain my house?"

She gave a trill of laughter. "Only a mock duel! And infinitely necessary, so that I may describe the scene more fully in my novel. It was difficult to pinpoint the relationship between pistol and principle without seeing it in the flesh. The pistols aren't loaded, of course," she added, reassuringly.

"Of course." He turned to the footmen, who were frozen to the parquet in embarrassment. "You may go. Surrender your pistols to McArdle and continue about your day," he told them, as the four slunk by in procession. He caught a glimpse of ornate scrollwork on the handle of Harkins's gun, held cautiously away from the poor ex-duelist's body between thumb and forefinger. "Please tell me they weren't using my own personal dueling pistols."

"I meant to have them back in your study before you returned."

He glared at her in amazement.

"Miss Crewe, what am I to do with you? Aunt Glynis just threatened to quit her post."

A wide smile, swiftly replaced by mock concern. "How very sad."

"Don't look so pleased with yourself. I bribed her to stay. I'm now on the hook for a whole new apartment's worth of overpriced furniture and draperies."

"Did Aunt Glynis think of that? I'm surprised! I was certain she had no imagination whatsoever. She doesn't understand me, or my quest for knowledge. Her world is very narrow, especially where young ladies are concerned." She laid her hand on his arm. "I believe that worlds should be widened, not narrowed. Life holds so many possibilities, it's positively dizzying."

She was constantly in motion. Her hands making descriptive gestures as she spoke, flying high, punctuating her point, touching him to make sure he understood what she was saying. That soft touch of her fingers on his forearm and he had to steel himself, clenching his jaw in concentration. *Don't reciprocate. Don't reach for that hand.* Touching her anywhere, everywhere, was beginning to occupy an alarming quantity of his thoughts.

It put him off-balance, and he didn't like being off-balance. It was time to restore order to this household, and to his heart. It would be helpful if the daylight reflected in the chandeliers overhead stopped setting those shimmering blazes in her hair. Hard to set his world to rights with nature actively plotting against him.

"Perhaps my aunt lacks a certain . . . verve, but she has an impeccable reputation, which is what you badly need to cement your own respectability during your debut."

"I appreciate that she's attempting to make me palatable to society, but it will never work. I'm a redheaded—"

"Spitfire of a hellion . . . so you've said, and so I've observed."

"A hellion can't change her stripes."

"I wasn't aware hellions had stripes. Are you mixing your metaphors?"

"Tiger, then! Head-to-toe stripes. And this one's completely unable to change hers."

He had the feeling she'd be sticking out her tongue at him if his back was turned.

"But she can use her keen intellect to ascertain when it's in her best interests to obey her guardian."

The cavernous ballroom with its wide windows and high ceilings felt somehow small with her in it. No matter how far away from her he was, she seemed close by. It was her energy, her sparkling life force, creating an intimate pull on all his senses.

"I would be more willing to obey if said guardian allowed said hellion—*tiger,* a modicum of freedom now and then."

"You're no prisoner."

"Am I not? Lady Glynis wants me to put on a decorous, docile act. How would the gentleman who agreed to marry me feel if he thought he was engaging himself to a compliant paragon of propriety only to discover that my true nature is not at all to his liking, or society's? Pretending I'm something I'm not is a kind of prison."

Dex sighed. "Miss Crewe, no one wants you to be someone you're not. I only ask that you adhere to the basic rules that are in place for your protection."

"You do love your rules and regulations. Your entire household is run as if it were a military company."

"And you live your life at the mercy of every whim that enters that infernal head of yours."

She tossed the head in question back, the better to look up at him. Her eyes held a challenging gleam, her small chin jutting forward mutinously. He'd never felt taller, or paradoxically more vulnerable. Here was a duelist worthy of sparring with, using words as blades to get under his skin. How did she wield such power?

"If this were Greek mythology, you would be the deity known as Chaos."

"And if you were a Greek god," she rejoined immediately, "you'd be named Taciturnus."

"That's not an actual mythological figure."

She shook her head, impatience making her curls dance. "Then you're Zeus the Grim, hurling glowers and grunts like thunderbolts from the sky!"

"It's all for your own good. What I'm hurling at you is care and protection, you should be grateful."

"I'm sure Zeus told himself that very lie every night!" Her verbal rapier thrust made contact. He winced. She glowed in triumph. Dex took a deep breath to regroup.

"Will you just promise to behave? And stop destroying Aunt Glynis's nerves? She's gone home for some well-deserved rest."

"But aren't we meant to go to the gallery opening this evening?"

Damn. He'd forgotten about that. Why had he allowed his aunt to leave? "We'll have to cancel. You have no chaperone."

"But I was so looking forward to it! I've always wanted to visit a gallery and meet artists."

"You should have thought of that before you scared Aunt Glynis away."

"Then I do apologize, Your Grace." With a sudden change of demeanor, she gave an elegant dip of obeisance, bowing her head diffidently. So she did know how to curtsy! The little minx. "I, Analise Crewe, do solemnly promise to follow all your many rules this evening! Please do let me attend, I'll be ever so quiet and docile. You won't even know I'm there."

Somehow he doubted that was possible.

"You said yourself there will be respectable duchesses there."

"I said there would be duchesses. I'm not certain how respectable they are. My friends made . . . unusual matches. I suppose I could ask one of them to look after you tonight."

"Splendid! I'll be a model of propriety. I'll drift around like a silent ghost, taking mental notes for my novel."

He wasn't buying this new tractable facade. She'd gotten her way, and now she was all demure smiles. It should have been infuriating. But it was . . . invigorating. Gratifying. He liked seeing her smile. He particularly enjoyed being the reason she was smiling.

Damn. And there it was again—his own smile, testing the edges of his scars.

Chapter Eleven

"Be still, Princess! For the sake of my own peace and quiet, I have decided to let you out of the cave during the day, with me as your protector. But stray you not from my side! These hills are full of danger. A red pall hangs over the valley, sending tendrils our way. You will do as I say, and I will keep you from harm."

—*The Dragon and the Blue Star* by Analise Crewe

Warburton, how good of you to come." Thea, Duchess of Osborne, clasped Dex's hands warmly, then turned to Miss Crewe. "And this must be your ward?"

Dex nodded. "Allow me to present Miss Analise Crewe. Miss Crewe, this is Her Grace, the Duchess of Osborne."

"Pish. You know we're not formal at my art salon. You may call me Thea." She smiled engagingly at Miss Crewe.

"Then you must call me Ana. It was the name my father used, short for Analise."

"Very well, then, I shall use it with honor. And we shall be friends, Ana. I can feel it. You have the most inquisitive expression and those green eyes of yours fairly sparkle with high spirits and humor."

Dex regarded the two ladies beaming at each other. He'd suspected they would feel an immediate kinship, both being creative souls who foolishly loved to see the good in people. "Be warned, Thea, she's writing a novel and everything she experiences in society may end up in her pages. Watch what you say, else you might find yourself prominently featured."

"I'll be on my guard."

"She probably has a pencil concealed somewhere in that knot of curls," Dex couldn't help saying, eyeing her gold-red hair with trepidation. "To take notes with."

"Whatever makes you say that, Your Grace?" Miss Crewe countered with an air of innocence, contradicted by a quick pat to the part of her coiffure that did, indeed, hold such an implement.

Thea regarded them quizzically.

"When I first met my ward, there was a bit of a misunderstanding. She found the sight of me terrifying and attacked me with a pencil she had hidden in her coiffure," Dex explained. "I still have the scar." He touched the place on his cheek. The mark she'd left on him. The visible one, at least.

"I wasn't terrified of your appearance. I thought you had been sent by a brothel keeper."

"Truly?" Thea's eyes widened. "There's a very interesting story here, I feel certain."

"One that must never be spoken aloud," Dex reminded Miss Crewe with a frown. She was free with her mentions of brothels in public.

"Ana." Thea took her arm. "Is there, perchance, a brooding duke in your novel who gives stern commands?"

Miss Crewe's cheeks flushed a fetching shade of pink. "The

villain is rather ill-tempered and given to expressing himself with grunts and growls."

Thea giggled. "And the hero?"

"He converses most eloquently and with ease on topics ranging from his childhood to his taste in poetry. He's always complimenting the heroine and acquiescing to her every whim."

Dex snorted. "Sounds like a right ninny."

He ignored the pang that struck his chest when she'd all but described him as a villain. Was that truly how she saw him? He'd try to be more agreeable this evening. After all, it was her first foray into society. Observing her obvious delight in making new acquaintances was, dare he think it, heartwarming. The pale pink of the simple gown she wore matched the roses in her cheeks. Her hair caught the candlelight and matched its flame, and she gazed about her with bright eyes eager for new sights.

"Your salon is beautiful, Thea. Who are the artists represented this evening?"

"I specialize in displaying new works by female artists. And here's one of them right now! Lulu, my dear, come join us and meet Analise Crewe, Warburton's ward."

Lulu, the younger sister of Charlene, Duchess of Harland, approached them with a wide smile. With her red-tinged hair and wide hazel eyes, she could have been Miss Crewe's sister. She stared at his ward with astonishment writ across her face.

"Why, we're already acquainted," Miss Crewe said wonderingly. "You painted my portrait several years past."

Lulu clapped her hands with genuine joy. "It's you! My first real commission! My art instructress, Mrs. Hendricks, was taken suddenly ill and I stepped in and completed the work. You were a pleasure to paint. Do you still have the miniature portrait?"

"My father took it with him to war, and it was lost for several years." Miss Crewe's expressive face registered a momentary sadness, then brightened with effort. "That is, until Warburton returned it to me."

"It was Lieutenant Crewe's most treasured possession and a beautiful piece of work," said Dex. "I was extremely gratified to be able to reunite the painting with its subject."

"Then your father . . . ?" Lulu asked with a somber expression.

"He went missing after a terrible battle."

"I'm dreadfully sorry. He was such a kind gentleman. Did you know that he insisted on paying me twice the fee?"

"That doesn't surprise me, although I like to speak of him in the present tense, if you don't mind? He's missing, not confirmed to be dead."

"Ah, of course. An important distinction. He's a congenial man and I was so lucky to paint you. Such a rewarding experience—my first real earnings as an artist! You and your father gave me the confidence to continue with my art."

"I should love to display the portrait," Thea spoke decisively, obviously enchanted with the conversation. "Your first work should be hung with your other portraits. Would you mind parting with it for a short period, Ana?"

"I'd be honored. Lulu, how wonderful that you continued painting. I've often wondered about how you were getting on."

"She's unstoppable," Thea enthused. "First the portraits, then the landscapes, and now . . . well, you'll just have to wander the rooms and see where Lulu's boundless imagination has led her."

"I want to speak with you more, Ana, but I see one of my patronesses." Lulu curtsied to Dex and waved at Miss Crewe. "I'll be back soon!"

Dex offered Miss Crewe his arm. The portraiture lining the first room was lovely, even Dex could admit that. Lulu painted each subject honestly, without the fawning embellishments sometimes favored by portrait artists, and yet, that honesty made each person glow with unique personality and beauty.

Miss Crewe approached a larger portrait of a good-looking fair-haired man. "This one is extraordinary. See how the subject is garbed all in simple black and standing in a sparsely furnished room at dusk, but the austerity of his surroundings serves only to enhance the gentleman's beauty. Who is he?"

"Patrick Fellowes. Thea's brother-in-law. Shall we?" Dex attempted to steer her to the next portrait but she continued staring at Fellowes.

"He's really quite extraordinarily handsome, don't you think?"

Dex had never considered whether the lawyer and occasional business partner was handsome. "He's passably attractive, I suppose."

"'Passably?' '*Attractive*'? I've never heard fainter praise. He's a positive Adonis! Look at those golden locks, and his excellent proportions. Why, the ladies must break their fans flirting with him—if he's a bachelor, that is."

He stirred uncomfortably, wishing they were conversing on any other topic. "He's a widower with a young son."

"I thought I detected a note of sadness in those fine blue eyes." She seemed to savor the thought, like a cat satisfied by a saucer of cream. "It must make him even more appealing to the ladies. He looks precisely how I envision Lord Fortescue in my novel. Perhaps I should make my hero a widower. It could spark sympathy in the readers, give him a poignant dimension. Make their cheers even lustier when he wins Adora's hand and vanquishes the avaricious Sir Archer."

In other words, Patrick was a handsome widower, a perfect candidate to play the hero in her novel, while Dex was the scarred, taciturn villain unfit to win the sweet, intrepid heroine's hand. Right. That was the way of it, the truth. Then why did the truth sting? And why did he want to change her thinking on the subject? He was conscious of a need to diminish the annoyingly attractive young man in her wide green eyes.

"Mr. Fellowes is a scholarly man, a lawyer and historian. Even though he's brother to a duke, he eschews all titles and privileges, preferring an ascetic life. It's his brother, the Duke of Osborne, that does the dirty work of vanquishing villains."

"He wields the pen over the sword," she said dreamily. "I'm beginning to think I may need to rewrite my hero."

"For heaven's sake, you're putting the man on a pedestal before you even make his acquaintance. He spends his evenings with a thick lawyerly tome and his days in court. He's rebuffed all attempts at matchmaking."

"Why, Your Grace." Miss Crewe smiled widely and tapped his arm with her ivory fan. "You're not jealous of a painting, are you?" She searched his face. "You are!"

"Am not," he grumbled. "Let's move along."

"Enjoying my portrait?" a voice inquired from behind them.

They both turned. Dex nearly groaned aloud. "Patrick. Speak of the devil."

"It's you!" Miss Crewe said, her face lighting up. "In the flesh."

Patrick bowed. "Indeed. Warburton, will you introduce us?"

"Patrick, this is my ward, Miss Crewe. Miss Crewe, Patrick Fellowes."

"I apologize, Mr. Fellowes, but I might just call you Lord Fortescue! You see, you're the very image I have in mind while writing a character in my novel."

"Is that right? And how did you describe me?"

"Broad of shoulder, a noble nose, hair the color of wheat stalks on a summer's day. A peaceful expression, a serene smile, an obliging personality."

"That's me to a fault." He chuckled delightedly. "It's almost as if we were old friends, yet we've only just met and hardly know each other. Shall we take a turn around the room and remedy that situation, Miss Crewe?" He bowed and offered her a sturdy arm, which she took gladly, smiling into his appreciative face.

Dex fought a sudden urge to knock their arms apart.

How had he never noticed how handsome and charming Patrick was? He was a bachelor by choice, but perhaps all he had needed was to meet the right young lady. One who already appeared to idolize him though they had only just met. The way she was looking up at him, laughing at every word he uttered. His speech was easy and intelligent and . . . he already had a child. A family of two just waiting for an agreeable third.

"Stop glaring daggers at my brother's back." Dalton, Duke of Osborne, joined Dex at the refreshments table.

"I'm not glaring."

"You are. If looks could wound, he'd be writhing on the floor in agony. Your ward is quite safe with him. He's a lawyer, not a rake."

"He's too handsome."

"He's my brother, isn't he?"

The story of how the two brothers had been separated, raised in different countries, and reunited was a fascinating tale.

"Why hasn't he married already?"

"Too busy working. He's defending an accused murderess right now. He believes she's innocent. He's gaining quite the reputation for defending the unfortunate, those that might otherwise be written off by a judgmental society due to lack of connection."

A respected advocate with noble goals and the gift of a silver tongue. And damnably good-looking and charming and . . . why should Dex care about that? Wasn't his goal to marry her off, and quickly? It would be a brilliant match. It would fulfill all he felt he owed her father, ease the burden of his overdrawn conscience.

So why did he feel like murdering Patrick with his bare hands? The answer that followed was an unwelcome one. She'd been right. He was jealous. Which was ridiculous since he was complete unto himself, he needed no one. She was an obligation to meet, a promise to fulfill, and nothing more.

"Is there something between you and Miss Crewe?" Dalton asked.

Dex shook his head vehemently. "Nothing untoward."

"I observed you walking about the room and it appeared to me that she takes every pretext to touch you. And you can't seem to tear your gaze away from her, even during a conversation with your best friend."

Dex returned his gaze to Dalton with a mighty effort. "She's lost, lonely, and I'm the one who rescued her. I care about her safety and happiness."

"It's more than that, isn't it?"

"She's impossible to ignore. Yesterday she had my footmen

fighting mock duels in the ballroom, all in the name of research for a novel she's writing. My aunt threatened to quit the post of chaperone."

"I like her already," Dalton said. "She's shaken you out of the fog you've been buried in since I met you. Perhaps she'll be my sister-in-law. Thea would dearly love to see Patrick settled with a good woman."

Dex grunted, not trusting himself to comment. What he felt like doing was striding across the room and punching Patrick square in his noble nose.

THE DUKE'S GAZE followed her as she moved about the gallery with Patrick Fellowes. It made her stand up straighter, sway her hips as she walked to make her skirts swish around her limbs. For some unaccountable reason, she wanted him to think her attractive.

"Your guardian is protective of you," Patrick remarked. "He's been glaring at me this entire time."

"It took him years to find me—he's trying to make up for lost time by vanquishing my foes, dowering me generously, and finding a brilliant match for me so that my future is assured."

"Do you have many foes?"

"I've lived an . . . unconventional life since my father's disappearance."

"As have I. You may wonder about my accent—I was raised in New York by a man who kidnapped me as a young child. I didn't know of my noble and British origins until recently."

"Goodness! It sounds like the plot of a popular novel." That could be quite a twist to throw into her Clovercote book.

"They do say that sometimes life is stranger than anything you find in fiction."

"I'm told you have a child?"

"Van. He's a good boy, a bit wild but that's to be expected when his life was uprooted and transplanted to a foreign country. I haven't seen him for twenty minutes—I expect he's sword fighting with his friend Flor somewhere on the balconies."

"I'd very much like to meet him. I have little experience with children and I'm writing a younger brother in my novel and finding it difficult to know how a child of nine might express himself."

"Very exuberantly, if Van is the test case. He's always chattering on about military campaigns, ancient weaponry, or the latest innovations in faster carriages. He admires his unofficially adopted uncle Warburton because he's an expert in every topic that interests Van. I don't know where he came by his intense interest in warfare. I've always been peaceable myself, preferring to pursue justice in the courtroom instead of the battlefield."

Ana listened raptly, glad of the details for the child she was writing. "Thank you for that detail. I shall be able to write the younger brother character more fully now."

"Another thing—don't think it's only male children who are interested in such bloody topics. His friend Flor is similarly obsessed, if not more so."

"Is she?" While Ana enjoyed writing the character of Adora, Lady Claridge's outline described her as mostly passive, a young lady who swooned at the slightest provocation and giggled frequently. Perhaps she should make her more like Amsonia, the heroine of *The Dragon and the Blue Star*. She tried to imagine Adora wielding a sword, or perhaps a small, ladylike dagger?

"What are you thinking about so seriously, Miss Crewe?" Mr. Fellowes asked.

"I was wondering if I should alter the character of my heroine to make her less timid and demure."

"If you want your art to imitate life, I'd say that I haven't known you for more than a few minutes, Miss Crewe, but it strikes me that you are the opposite of timid, and as for demure, I've always found that to be an overrated virtue." He turned the full force of a dazzlingly white smile upon her and she blinked rapidly. My, he was handsome. Lord Fortescue made flesh.

"If my son and his friend don't emerge this evening, perhaps I may call upon you at some future date?" he asked. "So that you may speak with Van in person. For your novel research, of course."

"I should enjoy that. Thank you."

"Your guardian is fast friends with my elder brother." Mr. Fellowes nodded at the two tall, muscular men standing near the refreshments table.

"What do you think they're speaking of with such intense expressions?"

"Horseracing. Bareknuckle boxing. Building faster carriages. Retribution on their enemies. Much the same as Van and Flor, actually."

Ana laughed. She liked Patrick immensely. "Your conversation is so . . . conversational. You express yourself so easily."

"Is that an accomplishment?"

"It is if you've been spending too much time with the Duke of Warburton."

"I'm a lawyer. I make my living by my conversation. I'm not a member of the gentleman's club that Warburton and my brother frequent. Far too much danger and excitement for my rather staid tastes."

"Do they have an actual club?" One of the chapters in Lady

Claridge's outline was set in an exclusive London gentleman's club of which Fortescue and Falconer were members.

"The Thunderbolt Club."

"A gentleman's club?"

"If you can call them gentlemen. Although they do occasionally host a charitable event whose proceeds go to helping destitute young women, or other such worthy causes."

"I'm writing about just such a club in my book. Of course I've never had any practical experience, I can only imagine what goes on behind those exclusive walls."

"Perhaps Warburton will give you a tour of his club."

"Unlikely. He wants as little to do with me as possible." He'd reluctantly agreed to accompany her this evening only because he'd given Lady Glynis the evening off.

Lulu joined them. "Are you having a good time?"

"Your paintings are extraordinary," Ana replied.

"You haven't seen the final room yet. Come along!"

Patrick made a bow to Ana and Lulu. "I must search for my errant son."

The final room was small and lit by flickering torches set in silver filagree sconces. The paintings were different, more vibrant colors, indigo blues and vermilions that shimmered and pulsed against the walls.

Ana stood still in the center of the room, turning slowly, taking it all in. "I can't believe it."

"What?" asked Lulu.

"It's as though you reached inside my mind."

"You feel a kinship with my fantastical beasts, hobgoblins, and faeries?"

"You don't understand. I wrote a book about such creatures. This one." She pointed to a painting of a huge black-winged dragon in flight. "This looks exactly like the Dread Dragon Qavox."

"I love that name," Lulu cried. "I want to read your book. Has it been published?"

"I'm afraid not. In fact, a preeminent publisher informed me that no one would want to read it."

"He was wrong," a gruff, deep voice proclaimed.

Ana whirled around to find Warburton had entered the room while she'd been lost in Lulu's paintings.

"You only read the first few chapters," Ana replied.

"I should like to read the book in its entirety."

"The only copy is with Norwood & Pennington, stuck in the purgatory of their submissions pile."

"Then you must retrieve it," said Lulu. "You have an eager readership awaiting. Perhaps you might find another publisher. And I shall illustrate it for you!"

Ana couldn't allow herself to dream about her beloved book—the fantastical tale that had taken her five years to write—being bound in leather with Lulu's gorgeous illustrations to bring her words to life. It wasn't going to happen. If she were to be published, it would be the Clovercote novel. She'd be expanding upon Lady Claridge's legacy.

"It's a lovely idea, Lulu. I don't believe it will ever come to pass but I shall forever think of the book with your illustrated plates as embellishment."

"Perhaps it's a dream that might come true." Lulu squeezed her hand. "Don't give up hope, Ana. Oh—I must go and speak to Lord Thistlethwaite. He's promised to purchase one of my portraits." She danced off, leaving Ana alone with Warburton.

"I appreciate your stalwart defense of my novel, Your Grace, but I'm pouring my efforts into the Clovercote novel. Mr. Norwood is a professional with years of experience and if that's the book he wants, then that's the book he'll get."

"But the fantastical novel is the one your heart demanded you write."

She touched his arm lightly. "What a phrase. Perhaps there's poetry in your soul after all, my Duke."

My Duke. The phrase, tossed so lightly, struck him forcefully. Yes. He wanted that, wanted to be *hers*. He shook off the forbidden thought.

"I can't claim the line as my own. You wrote it in a letter to your father. You said that your heart demanded you write this tale."

"So I did! And you remembered it? You must have thoroughly absorbed my correspondence to Papa."

"He meant a great deal to me. And your letters meant even more to him."

She accepted the thought with a nod and continued walking along the line of paintings, deep in a reverent contemplation. She stopped at a woodland scene and peered at the background. "Goodness, Lulu has left little to the imagination in this one."

He joined her beside the painting, careful to maintain an appropriate distance. They were, after all, alone together in a dimly lit room. On first glance it appeared to be an innocent scene: a woodland, a small cottage with smoke curling from its chimney, a field dotted with wildflowers. On closer inspection, one could make out a satyr and a wood nymph frolicking in the wildflowers. The nymph wearing naught but the covering of her long, wavy golden hair.

"Er, perhaps we should move to the next painting," Dex said, a bit desperately.

"It's only a study of the human form and of the ways of pleasure. I find it illuminating."

She stared at the sensual scene. He stared at her. He couldn't help it. Was there a change in her breathing? Were her cheeks flushing, ever so slightly?

Art, it appeared, was a dangerous setting for them. Her passionate nature was engaged, igniting and engaging his own.

"It's time we left." He turned from the painting abruptly. Miss Crewe, with one last blushing look at the satyr and the nymph, followed reluctantly.

After brief goodbyes made to Thea and Lulu, who were each absorbed in conversation with patrons, Dex handed his ward into the carriage, then followed and closed the door. It seemed excessively quiet and intimate inside after the noise and activity of the salon. They were alone. Just the two of them.

This had been a mistake, bringing her here with no chaperone, no maid. Too close. She was much too close, sitting across from him, wrapped in a soft green silk cloak, wrapped in dreamy thoughts that painted a gentle smile on her lips.

"You and Patrick had an intimate conversation," he observed.

"I like him very much. He was telling me about your gentleman's club—the Thunderbolt Society?"

"The Thunderbolt Club."

"Might I visit it? I'd very much like to see the interior, so that I might describe the one in my novel more fully and accurately."

"It's not an appropriate place for debutantes."

"You're very good at saying no to my requests."

"I have your best interests at heart." Except when he was picturing her as a naked wood nymph, red hair falling in luscious waves over small, round breasts . . .

"But Patrick said it wasn't too disreputable, that you held charity events sometimes."

"Don't believe him."

"Perhaps I could accompany you in disguise! No one need know it's me. I'll go disguised as your groom. I'll tuck my hair up into a cap and wear trousers and I'll speak with a Cockney accent. I will observe very quietly. I won't cause any trouble. I should like to learn to sit a horse. I've never even observed a gentleman's stallion and yet I'm to describe several such horses for my book."

"I have an excellent manual on horse breeding at my house. You may study the drawings."

"That's no good. You know I prefer real experiences to secondhand observations. I'll be your silent shadow."

He snorted. "I very much doubt you're capable of being a silent shadow."

"I will in the name of research for my book."

"You're not visiting the Thunderbolt Club disguised as my groom."

"Not as your groom. Then perhaps . . . as your pretend paramour? I'd wear a lace veil to hide my face. A scandalous red velvet gown. I shall hover by your side, catering to your every whim, perhaps even perching upon your knee? You can pretend to be fascinated by me."

There would be no pretending. Now he was picturing her in lace and red velvet sitting on his lap. He shifted on the carriage seat, glad of the cover of his coat.

"While the other gentlemen are distracted by their own birds of paradise I shall take a look around, memorizing the description of the interior for my book."

"Pardon me, but most of the gentlemen at my club are happily married."

"Has that ever stopped a London lord from philandering?"

"Well . . . yes. It has in the case of my friends. It's not a philanderer's club, it's a horse club."

"Surely there are unmarried gentlemen?"

"Yes, some members are bachelors with reputations as rakes."

"I want to meet such a gentleman and observe him at close range. I'm finding it very difficult to draw a portrait of a rake, having never met a proper one. A London rake, specifically, which is a thing I have no personal knowledge of."

"You're not to consort with rakes. I used to be one and I know what goes on in a rake's mind."

"You used to be a rake?"

Her astonishment rankled. "I was a rake. And a bounder." Entitled. Arrogant. Unheeding of anything but his own pleasure and position in the world.

"Then I may consult you on the character of Sir Archer Falconer, the villainous rake who contrives to corner Miss Adora and steal a kiss. I must know the flattering ardent things he would say to lure her into abandoning caution . . . and her chaperone."

"You won't be observing any villains at close range." Except for him. And from now on the range would be much farther out. He intended never to be alone with her again.

There were so many things she absolutely wasn't going to learn from him . . . how to sit a horse, how to flirt with a rake. How to kiss.

Chapter Twelve

Fear and fascination pinned her to the spot. She was transfixed by the poison green triangle of his face, seen clearly for the first time in the light of day. It filled the space before her. The finely scaled snout with its delicately waving whiskers, the cavernous nostrils mounted by expressive ridges, the webbed ears arching back from its brow, and suddenly, as two sets of eyelids flicked open above and below, the golden eyes, whirling at the center in a molten starburst, hypnotizing her, stoking an answering conflagration deep within her.

—*The Dragon and the Blue Star* by Analise Crewe

Are you quite certain that my nephew invited us to his club today? He didn't say anything to me about it." Lady Glynis was always suspicious when it came to any pronouncement from Ana.

"He extended the invitation this morning before you came down for breakfast. They are hosting a tea for ladies."

"At a gentleman's club?"

"It's a charity event, I believe."

She had to get inside that club. Last night she'd stayed up past midnight writing a chapter set inside an art gallery. She'd used

Patrick Fellowes as a model for Lord Fortescue. The writing had flowed more easily than anything she'd previously attempted. She had now reached eighty pages and she was beginning to feel as though she might finish the book. The scene she'd written last night was worlds better than anything she'd written before. She didn't need Mr. Norwood to tell her that it was good. She knew it in her heart.

The next chapter was Lord Fortescue and Sir Archer Falconer conversing in their gentleman's club. This was her opportunity to visit such a club, and she was prepared to bend the truth in pursuit of her goal.

Lady Glynis buttered her toast liberally. "I have heard that the club hosts a charity ball every year at Rydell House."

"I think this might be related to that event. A planning meeting, most likely."

"Did he give the names of the other ladies in attendance?"

"No."

"Well, if he requested your presence I suppose we must attend. It could be a useful test of your manners and comportment."

"I'll be the very portrait of propriety."

Lady Glynis sniffed. "I highly doubt that, but if you do well today, I may consent to take you with me to Mrs. Frinch's musical luncheon, featuring performances on the pianoforte from all of this Season's leading debutantes."

Not if she could help it. That sounded tedious and not at all like a scene in her book. "I should love that," she said insincerely.

"Had enough?" Dalton asked.

Dex raised his bruised fists, ignoring the stabbing pain in his gut. "Just getting started."

"Getting thrashed, more like."

"I'll best you this round."

"Not likely," Dalton scoffed.

Boxing with his friend helped break up the hard core of rage within him.

He was angry with himself for bringing his company into danger. Angry at the men who controlled the governments who were so happy and eager to sacrifice other peoples' sons, other lives, but never their own, sitting so safely in their ivory towers. Angry at his former self for being so cocksure and unfeeling.

Seething, roiling fury festered inside him and this was one of the only ways he could release it safely. This and riding his horse or driving his carriage at breakneck speed.

Though today was different. It wasn't anger he sought to exorcise, it was something even more dangerous, something made up of contagious laughter, flashing green eyes, and damnable impertinence.

His wild uppercut missed its mark, and Dalton moved in for a clinch. Dex shook him off with an effort and they squared off again.

"Your mind is elsewhere."

"I thought I heard my ward's voice."

"I saw the way you looked at her last night. It wasn't very guardianly."

"More boxing, less talking."

Dalton obliged with a barrage of blows and Dex raised his fists to protect his face. When he attempted to counter with a right hook, he missed the mark and lurched to his knees, off-balance and unable to shake the thoughts of Analise. Damn it. He was her guardian. He'd promised to protect her, to find a worthy partner for her.

He rose, head down, fists raised. "Again," he said, spitting blood onto the sawdust.

A LIVERIED PORTER met Ana and Lady Glynis at the door. He stood stiffly, blocking their entrance. "May I help you find the location you seek, ladies? For this is not it."

Oh dear. Even the doorman at the duke's club was determined to keep her out. "We're here for the charity event," Ana said blithely.

"Ah . . ." The man looked confused. "There's no event I know of, but if you care to wait here I'll go in and—"

"The charity tea," Ana interrupted. "The one my guardian, the Duke of Warburton, is hosting today. I'm sure he's waiting for us to arrive."

"The Duke of Warburton is here, my lady, he's round back by the stables, but he's occupied with—"

"Then you shall take us to him." Ana did her best to imitate Lady Glynis's supercilious tones but the porter was unconvinced.

"Move aside," Aunt Glynis said. "I would speak to my nephew."

Her clipped tones had more of an effect. The porter hesitated, not wanting to engage with the formidable lady. Finally, he ushered them inside a dimly lit hallway.

They followed him into an airy club room with groupings of tables and chairs and a long bar at the back. Men glanced up from their card games and brandy glasses to give them curious and increasingly incredulous looks.

Ana catalogued it all in her mind: the men drinking and conversing, boots propped up on tables, smirks on their lips . . . the general air of rakish dissipation.

"Are you certain the event was today?" Lady Glynis asked, staring through the windows at the yard with its gleaming carriages and horses pawing the turf.

"Absolutely certain. Perhaps we're early?"

The porter led them out a set of French doors, onto a lawn, and around the corner of the building and then . . .

Ana stopped abruptly, confronted by the sight of Warburton and his friend the Duke of Osborne stripped to the waist and pummeling each other on a bare patch of earth near the stables.

Her hand flew to her mouth. She hadn't anticipated such a brutish reception. Sweat glistened on Warburton's broad, bare chest, sparkling in the dark hair that disappeared into his tight, white trousers. They hadn't seen Ana and Lady Glynis yet. The men circled each other like wild animals, all glaring eyes and raised fists.

She'd most definitely write this scene when she got home. The two men locked in a primal dance, fists raised, grunting with exertion. Osborne was probably a fine figure of a man but Ana only had eyes for her guardian. He was solid rippling muscle, gargantuan and powerful. Dripping with sweat. A huge, lethal creature poised and ready to strike . . . She couldn't catch her breath, her stays were too tight.

Then Warburton's arm shot out, his fist catching Osborne under the jaw. Osborne's head wrenched backward but he stood his ground in a wide, dominant stance and suddenly he countered, the sickening thud of his fist connecting with Warburton's jaw sending Ana running toward them.

"Your Grace!" she cried, attempting to catch him as he staggered. The weight of his body knocked her off-balance and they fell together in a heap.

And then the world narrowed to slick sweat, the heat of his skin contacting hers, his ragged breathing, his massive body pinning her down and knocking the breath from her.

"Miss Crewe," Lady Glynis admonished sharply. "Come here this instant!"

A silly suggestion as Ana wasn't currently able to move, being pinned to the ground by an enormous duke.

"Miss Crewe?" The duke raised himself onto one arm, staring down at her. "What in God's name are you doing here?"

"If . . . if you release me I'd be happy to explain," she said breathlessly, every part of her body that was in contact with the duke's tingling and humming with awareness.

Osborne laughed heartily. "This round's over, I'd say. I win again." He pulled a shirt over his head. "Lady Glynis, Miss Crewe, what a delightful surprise."

"I was told there was a charity event for ladies at this club today," Aunt Glynis said frostily. "Apparently I was misled."

Warburton rolled off Ana, leapt to his feet, and held out his hand to help her rise.

"You told me about the charity luncheon at breakfast, remember?" Ana asked, staring into the duke's eyes and willing him to back her up.

"I did, did I?" His eyes danced with humor as he threw a shirt over his head.

Don't put a shirt on. He should be like this always, a magnificent beast, his true nature.

He caught her staring. She blushed.

Aunt Glynis narrowed her eyes and tapped the point of her parasol on the stone path. "What's going on here?"

"A bout of boxing, Aunt. You know the Duke of Osborne."

"Well? Is there a charity event here today or not?"

"It's tomorrow. I mixed up the dates. Dreadfully sorry." He lied so smoothly.

"Then we'll leave immediately."

"But we only just arrived," Ana protested. "I want to see the stables. I must be able to describe a gentleman's mount in vivid detail."

"This is no place for a young lady."

Osborne approached the highly incensed chaperone. "Lady Glynis." He bowed over her hand, fair hair swooping over his brow. "I can't tell you how mortified I am that you had to witness this most distressing of sights. Allow me to make my heartfelt apologies."

Lady Glynis's countenance softened. "It was rather distressing."

"There, there," Osborne said soothingly, taking her hand and leading her toward the clubhouse. "I know just the thing. A restorative nip of fine brandy. I could use one myself. And I've been meaning to ask you how the renovation of your townhouse is coming along? Warburton told me all about it."

To Ana's great surprise, Lady Glynis allowed herself to be led away by the glib, handsome duke.

"Gracious," Ana exclaimed. "Mr. Fellowes isn't the only charmer in that family."

"He'll keep her occupied for a few minutes. Which is all you'll have in the stables. I'm only taking you there because I know that if I refuse, you'll attempt to enter the club a different way. At least you didn't wear your groom disguise."

"I'm in disguise as an innocent young debutante."

Warburton made a scoffing noise. "An impudent hellion, more like." He steered her down the path toward the stables.

"Miss Crewe, meet Odysseus. He arrived in London only last week."

"Hello there, Mr. Odysseus. Aren't you a magnificent beast! You match your name perfectly. I can picture you defeating mythical monsters with those enormous hooves of yours."

The horse flared its nostrils and regarded her suspiciously.

"Offer him this." Warburton handed her a carrot.

"I don't want to put my hand close to his teeth."

"He's still skittish from the journey but he won't bite you. Hold out your hand, let him sniff it first."

She held out her hand, unable to stop the slight trembling. The horse nosed at her hand and stamped his hooves.

"Was that an approving stamp?" Ana asked.

"Now the carrot."

To her surprise, Odysseus nibbled gently on the carrot, though when his teeth got too close to her fingers, she relinquished the entire vegetable to him and took a few steps backward.

"Isn't that nice," crooned the duke. "Aren't you a lucky fellow? Such a luxurious new home. You'll be well cared for here. This is the best stall, the sweetest hay, and I've brought you the prettiest young lady to feed you carrots."

A pang of something in her heart. Surely she wasn't jealous of a horse? He continued to murmur endearments, gently smoothing his hand down its flank. Making prolonged, deep eye contact. She wanted to be under his hands, hearing those words, feeling his gaze, strong and steady on hers.

Stop focusing on the duke and observe the horse. "What breed of horse is this?"

"He's a Yorkshire Trotter. An elegant and powerful breed.

He'll pull a carriage or I'll take him riding or hunting. We're going to be fast friends. Isn't that right, Odysseus?"

"He has very intelligent eyes."

"Doesn't he just? Horses are highly intelligent creatures. Odysseus has already displayed his acumen for recognizing me, responding to my commands, and even showing a sense of humor. What?" he asked, noticing the way she was staring at him.

"Do you realize that you are conversing more civilly with that horse than you've ever conversed with me? It would appear that all I need to do is become a horse to be favored with your confidences."

"I've always had a bond with horses."

"Tell me about your first horse."

He smiled, still stroking Odysseus's flank. "Shadow was his name. My father's head groom taught me how to ride. I was frightened at first and then I learned to love the freedom that riding gave me. I could leap onto a horse's back and ride away from all the responsibilities, the lessons in how to become a duke. My younger brother, Rupert, was frightened of horses but I've always felt an affinity for these proud, wild creatures that we tame to our purposes."

"You've never spoken of your brother before now. Does he live in London?"

"Sometimes. He's in Surrey at the moment."

"At your ancestral estate?"

"No. He has his own residence."

"Is he married? Does he have children?"

"Yes and no." He gave Odysseus another carrot, his face turned away from her.

She blew a curl away from her eyes. "You're back to monosyllables."

"And you should be back with Aunt Glynis." He took her arm so firmly that she had no choice but to accompany him out of the stables.

"Goodbye, Odysseus," she said over her shoulder. "I do hope we'll meet again."

As she and Lady Glynis were leaving, Ana turned back for one more glimpse of the duke. He was standing with his huge arms folded over his chest, one sardonic eyebrow raised, a purplish bruise visible on his cheek, and his usual unreadable, stoic expression stamped across his face.

This wasn't over. She must find a way to return. She wasn't nearly finished observing the gentleman's club. As they departed, Lady Glynis marching purposefully in front of her, Ana had an inspiration. Ever so subtly, she pulled a fan out of her pocket and let it drop by the wide French doors, grateful for the lady's haste in exiting. Congratulating herself on her own quick thinking, she followed out into the street. Her new delicately carved ivory fan with its bewitching scallops of lace? Why, she'd simply *have to* return for it later . . .

Chapter Thirteen

With a brave little shake of her head, Amsonia shimmied up the back of his foreleg and found an indentation just between his wings that was big enough to lie in. Her body and arms outstretched, she rested her cheek against Qavox's back. "I'm ready!" she called, and the dragon took flight.

—*The Dragon and the Blue Star* by Analise Crewe

Later that afternoon at the modiste's shop, Ana barely recognized the woman she saw in the glass. She lifted the skirts of the simple, elegant white muslin gown, turning this way and that, admiring her reflection. Green silk trim around the neckline and waist glowed like a polished apple in the light from the high glass atrium of the dressmaker's shop.

"Oh, miss, it's so lovely. You look like a princess," Tessie said, clasping her hands together.

"I've achieved quite the transformation," Madame Fontaine, the dressmaker agreed. "The color of the silk trim is perfect for bringing out the green in your eyes and for highlighting the gold in your hair. When the duke sees you in this, Miss Crewe . . ." She smiled saucily.

"He'll think that I'm an investment and he'd better have a handsome return in the form of several marriage proposals from eligible gentlemen."

"He'll be thinking he wants to take a bite out of you," the dressmaker said, her smile widening.

"What an odd thing to say." Ana wondered whether she should use that line in her book.

Madame Fontaine tugged the bodice down an inch. "You'll understand my meaning soon enough." She pinned the fabric in place. "You don't have much but what you do have is now accentuated to perfection."

"Oh, Miss Crewe," Tessie said, running to the shop window. "I see my old friend Elsie. Might I go and speak with her?"

"Of course. I'll be quite safe with Madame Fontaine. And Lady Glynis will be back any moment from her tea."

"Won't Elsie just die to see me wearing this smart maid's uniform. I won't be long." Tessie ran merrily for the door.

The dressmaker lifted the gown over Ana's head, careful not scratch her with the pins.

"I must make the final adjustments. It won't take but a moment. Stay behind the screen and I'll be back with the gown shortly."

Outside, the bustle of London. Hackneys carrying fares vying with private phaetons and carriages for room on the street, people streaming endlessly past the brightly lettered shop windows. The clop of horses' hooves, the call of vendors, the whole of the city thrumming with life. Ana shivered in her thin shift. It felt odd and exciting to be so exposed, just a wall separating her from the hub of all activity.

The bell above the shop door tinkled. The shop assistant answered the door and Ana heard deep tones. Another customer in the shop, a male one! Ana looked around wildly for something to take cover in, her imagination painting a shocking scene—the visitor, throwing open the door. Ana, in next to nothing at all, caught like a frightened doe in the hunter's sight.

Where was her pelisse? She'd removed it in the antechamber at the request of Madame Fontaine, who had wanted to see her complexion before choosing more fabrics, draping it over the back of the chair. With, it occurred to Ana suddenly, her most precious possession still in the pocket! Her mother's emerald necklace, one of the last links she had to her past. The clasp had come undone during the carriage ride to the club, and she'd slipped it into her pocket, fearing it was broken.

"Madame Fontaine," she whispered loudly. There was no answer. The pelisse was blue velvet, lined with real fur, an expensive garment that any common thief would be happy to run off with. She couldn't chance having it stolen and losing her mother's necklace again. How could she have been so careless?

She could still hear voices from the front room, the deep male tones briefly following the higher-pitched chatter of the shopkeeper. The door between the antechamber and the front room was slightly ajar, giving whoever was out there a clear view of the sumptuous pelisse if they were to glance in that direction.

What if he was criminally inclined? She could see it so clearly: this shady new arrival directing Madam Fontaine's attention toward a bolt of velvet high on the shelf, the shopkeeper climbing the ladder to retrieve it, the thief running through the door, gathering up the pelisse with one quick hand, then dashing out to the street. She must retrieve it from the chair and close the door, else it and the necklace would be gone for good.

Ana cautiously ducked out from the screen. Her pelisse was

still hanging on the back of the chair. She darted over and grabbed it but just as she was going to make her exit, the voices grew louder—the shopgirl was bringing the customer into the room. Ana fairly flew back to the screen, crouching behind it and muffling her excited breathing with her fist.

"I'll leave you here, Your Grace. I'm sure your ward will be finished with her fitting momentarily and will join you here."

"Thank you."

Gruff, growling tones. Warburton! Why was he here? He mustn't find her here in this state! She could sense him standing across the room, hear him drumming his fingers impatiently on a nearby tabletop. Then stop. Silence. Then footsteps coming closer to the screen. He'd *sensed* her, damn his preternaturally observant self!

"Hello? Who's there?"

She squeezed her eyes closed and accepted her fate. "It's Ana, Your Grace."

"Miss Crewe? Why are you hiding behind this screen?" He sounded equal parts exasperated and amused.

Slowly, heat burning her cheeks, she summoned all the dignity she could muster and poked her head around the side of the screen. "I heard a customer come into the shop. My mother's necklace was in the pocket of my pelisse, hanging on that chair. I thought you were a thief! I was going to retrieve my pelisse and save the jewelry."

"In nothing but a shift?"

"The dressmaker hadn't returned with my dress yet. What was I to do?"

"Call for the shopgirl and ask her to retrieve your pelisse?" the duke asked, eyebrows raised.

"I guess I . . . didn't think of that."

"Where is Aunt Glynis and your maid?"

"They had errands to run and friends to greet. They'll be back any moment."

"Then you'd better stay behind the screen before someone catches us like this."

"Why are *you* here?"

"To return this, which was conveniently forgotten at the club." He crossed the room, holding her fan in his outstretched arm. She was suddenly aware of the scant material of her shift, the way the air in the room was making her flesh prickle and her hairs stand on end. The air . . . or his presence.

"Thank you. I can't think how it slipped from my grasp."

"You wanted a pretext to visit again. I know what you're doing, Miss Crewe. I'm on to you. You require a chaperone at all times," he said gruffly. "There's no question."

The bell tinkled again. "Oh, I'd better go back behind the screen."

Two ladies had entered the shop. They hadn't seen them yet.

"We can't be seen together with you in this state. Hide!" He grabbed her by the elbow and dragged her behind the dressing screen. He barely fit in the small space. He flattened against the wall and pulled her toward him, her backside against his front. He snaked an arm around her waist to hold her in place. There wasn't even enough space for Ana to drape the pelisse around her shoulders to cover herself.

"Your Grace—"

"Shhh." His large hand closed over her mouth. "Don't make a sound."

Chapter Fourteen

As he dipped his wings and soared in widening circles, Qavox felt the small body curled into his back begin to violently shake. "Are you well, princess?" he asked, knowing she'd be able to hear him even over the whistling wind. He craned his head backward on its long neck and gave a snort of astonishment, sparks flying from his nostrils. She was laughing! The princess's face was aglow with excitement. "I am well, indeed!" she cried in return. "I am flying!"

—*The Dragon and the Blue Star* by Analise Crewe

The two ladies chattered on about ribbons and dress trimmings, making the shopgirl fetch dozens of samples.

Miss Crewe rested her head back against Dex's chest. His hand still covered her mouth. He held her by the waist, her generously curved bum soft against his thighs and his . . .

He couldn't move. Couldn't stop holding her. The risk of discovery was too great. He had to stay like this, his body responding to a female body pressed against his. He shifted his hips but there was nowhere to go. Surely she could feel his arousal.

She squirmed a little, moving against him, and it was all he could do to suppress the groan of pleasure that threatened to escape his lips. So small and soft in his arms, locked together behind the silk-covered screen while the two ladies chattered on about ribbons and dress trimmings only inches away from them.

He'd seen the way she stared at him back at the club when he'd been shirtless. No doubt she'd been cataloging his physique to write a description for her novel, but the sight of her gaze roaming his body, lips slightly parted and cheeks flushed, had been devastating to his self-control. He had felt her gaze like soft fingertips running over his skin.

She'd wanted him in that moment. He'd seen the physical signs. She'd approved of his body, ignored his scars; she'd looked at him with hunger in her eyes. And damn it, he wanted her, too.

Wanted to turn her, lift her hands and place them against the wall. Learn the curve of her cheek with his palm, test the weight of her hair, see if those curls would tangle around his fingers like vines and trap him forever.

He wanted to breathe in her scent, like wildflowers heavy with morning dew, flowers greedily soaking up the sun, opening further. Slip the thin shift down her shoulders, slowly, slowly, revealing the delicate collarbone, the hollow at the base of her throat, the pulse that beat there.

He wanted to kiss the back of her neck while he learned the sweet curves of her breasts. Breathe against her skin, waiting, drawing out the moment, until she arched her back and urged him to continue his exploration. He wanted to kiss, learn, taste every inch of her. Wanted to apply himself like perfume to the insides of her wrists, the soft hidden skin behind her ears.

Rip the thin silk shift until she was naked for him. The flush spreading along her cheeks, down her neck, over her breasts. He wanted to outfit her with his hands, his body, his lips. That's all the covering she needed.

Rip his clothes off, too. Slide his hands between her legs, nudge her thighs apart . . .

Fuck. Why weren't those ladies leaving? This was intolerable. This dangerous attraction between them. The way she sighed and nestled closer, so trustingly. How could she know that he was having the most bestial of fantasies? Rending the thin shift, taking her from behind, up against the wall.

His breathing ragged, he fought for control.

Why had he visited the dressmaker's? He hadn't needed to return the fan, he'd wanted to see her again, see her in clouds of tissue-thin silk. He'd gotten more than he'd imagined. Pressed up against her behind the screen.

This desire was inappropriate, forbidden. The urge to ravish was in direct opposition to his promise to protect. He stamped it out, cold water on the fire. He couldn't want her. He shouldn't want her. She was his duty. Not his desire.

But what was it about her that destroyed him so utterly? The bravery she'd shown as she fought him off in the alleyway, thinking he meant to purchase her. The layer of scar tissue she had over her heart because the life of ease and love she'd known had been stripped away so harshly and she'd had to grow up, to fend for herself, a lamb among wolves.

The conversation they'd had in the stables. How she missed her father so keenly. Orphaned and alone in this world, longing to belong, to publish her writing so that an audience would give her the approbation and love she craved.

There was that survivor's instinct in her, that wound that she covered over. He recognized a wounded soul when he saw one.

And he didn't only want to clothe her in silks and velvets and furs, and place jewels at her throat and her ears. He didn't only want to make her life safe and comfortable.

There was something so much more selfish and so much more perilous to this desire. He wanted her. Full stop. He wanted to take her, kiss her, ravage her. He wanted to taste her and make her his.

The challenge in her eyes, the current between them, like threads of silk. Pull one and the whole thing unraveled. And she would have a permanent mark through the fabric of her life. One more sin to confess to, one more grave error in judgment.

Ward. She was his ward.

Under his protection.

He could never act on this desire.

ANA'S BREATHING WAS erratic beneath his palm. She twisted her neck, attempting to see his face, but he moved his chin. His body was tense behind her, ready to spring. To escape her? To pull her closer. That's what she wanted. She wanted his hands on her. All over her.

The sight of him boxing. The violence barely contained by the gentlemanly rules of the sport. His hands were so huge, so powerful. He held her around the waist with one strong arm. What if . . . what if those hands covered her breasts?

Thinking about it made her breasts tingle and her nipples stiffen to aching points. A restlessness made her shift against him, push her bottom against his . . . that must be his . . . she'd seen the male member illustrated in medical texts consumed in her all-encompassing reading sprees, but it had always looked somewhat silly and inconsequential. Nothing like this.

Hard and long, pressed against her lower back. His fingers spread over her navel, and the tingling sensation spread from her belly to between her legs. She wanted to sink back against him. Be surrounded by him, surrender to him. What if he turned her around, lowered his lips to hers?

She twisted around until her breasts met the solid planes of his chest. She stared at his lips, the sensual curve of the upper lip. The glowering look in his eyes, the grip of his hand on her waist.

"Your Grace . . ." she whispered. *I want you to give me my first kiss.*

His face closer now. Lips nearly touching . . .

Silence. Only their breathing. Only this dimly lit space, this world unto them.

"Yes?"

"The . . . ladies are gone, I believe."

He immediately released his hold on her waist and without another word, left her alone behind the screen. Not a moment too soon. She heard the dressmaker greet the duke, and then she was behind the screen, arms filled with delicate silk and lace.

"Your guardian is waiting for you. Here." She lifted Ana's arms and then slipped the gown over her head. "Ah, it is perfect." She made some final adjustments, smoothing the gown over Ana's breasts and hips and tying the sash at the back. She led Ana out from behind the screen by the hand.

"What say you, Your Grace?"

He swallowed, his Adam's apple bobbing. A faint sheen of sweat on his brow. That dark hair falling like sin into his eyes.

"She looks well enough." His words were so nonchalant but his eyes told her another story. They lingered on her face, her body. Was he back behind the screen? Imagining the same thing she'd so fervently desired?

"Does not the color of the sash bring out the green of her eyes?" asked the dressmaker.

"It does." He cleared his throat. "I should be going, before Aunt Glynis returns."

"Stay a moment," Ana said. "Why not choose a new waistcoat?"

"Perhaps one to match your ward's sash?" the dressmaker asked.

"Absolutely not."

"This would look well on you," Ana said, fingering a bolt of light blue silk with a silvery sheen. "You're always wearing plain, severe clothing. Why not introduce a small sliver of frivolity?"

"I'll leave the frivolous colors to the pretty ladies."

"Your Grace," she said archly. "Was that a compliment?"

"You're a pretty girl, and you know it."

She didn't know it. She knew that men had wanted her. Had wanted to own her. She hadn't seen this in their eyes. This tortured reverence. This longing. And she wondered if he could read the same thing in her eyes.

There was a moment where they simply stood, staring into each other's eyes. The dressmaker busied herself with something at the counter.

"Warburton, I didn't think to find you here." Aunt Glynis cast a suspicious glance at them.

He abruptly stepped backward, putting distance between them. "I was returning Miss Crewe's fan, which she left at the club."

"You have blood on your collar. You're not fit to be seen in public."

He bowed. "Then I will leave you, ladies."

Back at her desk, writing by the light of a lamp because the house was dark and silent, Ana attempted to describe the scene she'd witnessed at the club.

Lord Fortescue and Sir Falconer, stripped to the waist, pummeling each other with their fists. Bareknuckle boxing was an acceptable sport for gentlemen to indulge in but there didn't seem to be anything gentlemanly about it. What Ana had witnessed had been raw, primal. Frightening. And she'd hurled herself forward, unheeding of her own safety, to catch the duke as he staggered and fell. What had possessed her? She'd been worried he might have been seriously injured, that was all.

That wasn't all.

The entire day had been most confusing. First the sight of him shirtless, shaking her to the core, sparking the most carnal of thoughts. And then the tenderness he'd shown to Odysseus and to her in the stables. How was she meant to reconcile the two? The rare glimpse into his mind, his heart, had destabilized her far more than his body pinning her to the ground. Was he a good, kind man beneath that harsh, forbidding exterior?

And then there had been the dressing room.

She was all aflutter, confusingly attracted to the man she'd thought of as an obstacle to her happiness.

She wasn't doing any writing. She chose a fresh sheet of paper and dipped her pen in ink.

Dearest Papa, she wrote. *I'm to attend my very first ball tomorrow! How I wish you were here to present me in society. The man you've chosen for my guardian sets my mind into a whirl, I hardly know whether I'm coming or going. He's infuriating, off-putting, arrogant, and domineering. And yet, at the same time, I sense that he cares about me. And not only because of the promise he made you on the battlefield. Oh, Papa. I wish I could have your wise counsel.*

Would she dance with the duke at the ball? She pictured them whirling around a dance floor, his expression stern, his huge arms holding her tightly so that she couldn't breathe properly . . .

She set down her pen and folded the paper. There was nowhere to mail this letter.

And no one to talk to about her confusing feelings regarding her by turns hot-and-cold guardian.

She was alone.

Lady Claridge had been her confidante, as well as her mentor. She'd expected to have more time with the woman who'd become a motherly figure in her life. Finishing her final Clovercote novel was a tribute to her memory.

Attending the ball would help Ana achieve that goal. It wasn't to be a romantic occasion.

She would be observing the ton, nothing more.

Chapter Fifteen

They'd spent most of the day exploring the countryside, swooping and diving and sending the tops of trees rattling as they passed. She gazed with interest about her. She'd never seen the country, having spent most of her life cloistered in the castle walls. It was breathtaking in its scope and splendor, gilded as it was by the setting sun.

"Oh, can't we fly a bit longer? Won't you take me to my family's castle?" she begged when the dragon began its way back toward Mount Runemor. "I am filled with a longing to view it, and we are so very close . . ."

—*The Dragon and the Blue Star* by Analise Crewe

Ana paused at the top of the grand staircase, suddenly terrified. The crowded ballroom below was an intimidating tumult of candlelit crystal, garlands of red roses, ladies in pearlescent silk gowns, and gentlemen in crisp black evening attire.

"His Grace, the Duke of Warburton, Lady Glynis, and Miss Analise Crewe," a liveried footman announced in a booming voice.

Every head in the room swiveled toward them, as if they were the main attraction at the Theatre Royale on Drury Lane, illuminated by gaslights so that every member of the audience could make out their features.

The duke placed her hand on his arm. "Ready?"

"Why are they all staring at us?" Ana asked in a whisper, her stomach doing flip-flops. She was here to observe society, not the other way around.

"That's generally the point of being introduced," said her chaperone. "Remember our lessons and you'll bring no shame on yourself or the duke. Keep conversation to a minimum. No flights of fancy. Smile demurely, showing no teeth. No slouching. I don't expect you to sparkle, only to remain free from scandal."

Not reassuring. Wide grins and flights of fancy were second nature to her. How could she pretend to be someone she was not? She may be wearing a ballgown, and have pink rosebuds threaded through her upswept hair, but she wasn't one of them. They would sense it. Or, worse, they would know it. If any of the assemblage knew her past—knew where she'd been living when the duke found her—there was sure to be scandal.

"Don't be frightened." Warburton gave her one of his rarer-than-diamonds half smiles. "Think what Princess Amsonia would do if she was facing a horde of banshees or basilisks, or what have you?"

"Princess Amsonia would have a magic spell, or an amulet, or at the very least, a sharp dagger."

"You have me." His scarred face was unexpectedly gentle.

The space of only a few breaths. Enough time for the towering duke at her side to become something new . . . a sort of armor. The brooding beast promising his protection.

"But what if . . ." She gulped. How could she not have thought of this possibility before now? "What if Lord Claridge should be here?"

"He won't be here."

"How can you be sure of that?"

"I paid him a visit."

"What manner of visit?"

"One that extracted a promise from him to stay in Cornwall for the period of at least one year. He will also be writing a hearty endorsement of your Clovercote novel, should it be published."

"Warburton. What did you do?"

"Never mind. Suffice to know that he won't be here. Now then. It's time."

Halfway down the stairs she nearly tripped on her skirts but he expertly righted her. She leaned into his solid strength, his commanding presence.

The throng parted for them, everyone staring intently, the whispers swelling after they passed: *Warburton has a ward? Who is she? Haven't seen the duke in years. Those scars of his . . . she must be frightened half to death, poor wee thing. He'll dower her handsomely, no doubt.*

"Why is everyone so fascinated by us?" Ana asked the duke in a low voice.

"They're fascinated by you. Wondering who you are . . . and how you came to be my ward."

"Or perhaps they're wondering if you attended the ball not for me, but because you've finally decided to take a bride."

He snorted. "Highly unlikely."

Lady Glynis poked her in the back with her fan and Ana straightened her shoulders.

"They're whispering about your beauty," he said.

"Ha!" The loud cackle exploded from her mouth before she could retrieve it. Lady Glynis rapped her on the shoulder with a disapproving glance. "That's preposterous," Ana whispered.

"It's not. You look beautiful tonight. Your father would have been very proud."

A lump formed in her throat. Her dear father, adoration beaming from his eyes. She would have given anything to see his gentle smile again, to feel as special as he always made her feel. But he was gone, and any illusions she'd held about her own worth had departed with him. "It's only a mirage of beauty, created by this obscenely expensive gown and these borrowed emeralds. They wouldn't give me a second glance if they'd seen me on the street a mere fortnight ago."

He stopped walking abruptly and Lady Glynis nearly bumped into them. He turned to Ana, lifted her hand to his lips, staring into her eyes. "It's not the gown or the jewels." His eyes were the color of rain falling on weathered stone. "It's you, Analise."

The room went quiet, everything faded away. All she saw were his eyes, the steel of them, the certainty. The heavy, sweet scent of dew-drenched roses filled the air. The music swelled and it sounded like the song had been composed especially for them.

Beautiful, the strings sang, *he thinks you're beautiful.*

"Pardon me, Your Grace, Lady Glynis."

A man's voice destroyed the intimate moment. Ana turned to find a handsome, fair-haired young lord in an almost overwhelmingly abundant ivory cravat addressing them.

"Lord Darbyshire, is it not?" Warburton asked.

The man bowed. "At your service. I was wondering if I might beg the privilege of adding my name to Miss Crewe's dance card?"

The duke's eyes narrowed. "Darbyshire. You're Cavendish's firstborn?"

"I am."

"I hear you frequent the gaming hells."

"Er . . ." Lord Darbyshire ran a thumb under his tall collar, as if the air in the room had grown too warm. "No more than any young man does, that is I've visited the establishments but don't make a habit of it."

"If I visited Old Crocky's right now and asked how often you're there of an evening, and whether your bets are reckless and your cups deep, what manner of report would they give me?"

"Ah . . ." Another pluck at his collar, his cheeks turning pink now. "I might have made a mistake here or there, but that's all behind me now."

The duke's eyes were cold and hard. "Are you willing to sign a contract stating you will never gamble again?"

"I beg your pardon?"

"A contract. No gambling. I won't have you squandering my ward's fortune as well as your own."

"Oh, er, I think I see my cousin. I must greet him. I beg your pardon. Your Grace, Lady Glynis, Miss Crewe." Lord Darbyshire made a few hasty bows and rushed away.

"Good riddance," Lady Glynis said. "He's thoroughly unsuitable."

"Thank you very much, Your Grace," Ana said. "You chased away my first, and only, would-be suitor."

"He's nothing but a fortune hunter," growled the duke.

"So what if he is? He's fair to look upon, and we were only going to dance, not run away to Gretna Green."

"Miss Crewe!" Lady Glynis exclaimed. "You mustn't speak of such indelicate things."

"My ward is not going to dance with a known profligate and gambler."

"I'm not going to dance with anyone if you scare them away. Why did you buy me this new wardrobe and the etiquette lessons and all of it if you were only going to ruin my prospects?"

"He's not good enough," he said vehemently. "Trust me."

"Don't all the young lords gamble and drink? Isn't that their job in life?"

"He's not right for you."

"Didn't you drink and gamble at his age?"

"Enough." His large right hand raised in an unconsciously commanding gesture, the officer keeping his regiment in line.

"You are frustratingly domineering."

Lady Glynis cocked her head forbiddingly at Ana, her eyebrows arched emphatically. "He's your guardian, Miss Crewe. You must abide by his judgment and submit to him in all things."

Submit to him. Why did those words make her head spin and her palms feel clammy? "At least give me a chance to dance with someone."

"Only those suitors I deem appropriate."

"You should have written up a list of approved gentlemen before the ball."

"I promised your father that I would—"

"I know what you promised. And you've fulfilled it. You've restored my fortunes, launched me in society, and provided me with the most correct of chaperones. Your duty is done. You may leave now."

"Don't speak to him like that," warned her chaperone.

"Warburton, you remember my son, Lord Chetwynd-Ellerton?"

A woman's voice destroyed the intimate moment. The duke dropped Ana's hand. "Lady Chetwynd-Ellerton, of course."

The dowager countess and her son were a matched set, from their sloping cheeks to their solid ankles. There was nothing stimulating or sharp about them—they were stolid and dull as old doorknobs.

"And Lady Glynis, I haven't seen you in an age. How are your prize roses?"

"Tolerably well, though it's been unseasonably cold already."

"Miss Crewe." Lord Chetwynd-Ellerton made a bow. "Might I have the privilege of being your first dance partner?"

The duke nodded. "She would be delighted."

Ana glared at him. She wasn't allowed to make her own choice, apparently.

"They're just now beginning to form for the quadrille," the earl observed.

Lady Glynis pulled her aside briefly to whisper in her ear. "Lord Chetwynd-Ellerton has a large fortune and dozens of properties. He'd be a brilliant match."

Ana glanced back at the duke as the earl led her to the dance floor. It would be difficult to remember the sequence of steps and make polite conversation with her partner, as well as take mental notes for her novel, but she'd manage.

Halfway through the dance she realized she needn't have worried. Her partner required no conversational response other than a nod of the head every now and then. Every time they met in the dance, he advanced a bit further along the scintillating topic of his personal snuffbox collection, sprinkled with equally stirring observations on the weather (which, he posited, might indeed become more rainy than not at a date not too far in the future).

He may have a vast fortune and many grand estates, but his conversation was as sparkling as a bowl of porridge. Ana suppressed a yawn as he droned on and on. The duke had followed her command and left her alone. He'd left the ballroom entirely. Where had he gone? There were sure to be dark billiard rooms for the gentlemen to gather in, where they could hide and drink brandy. She mused appreciatively on that delicious beverage, the spicy caramel warmth of it sliding down her throat. She was developing quite a taste for the stuff.

"Do you like brandy, my lord?"

"Rarely touch the tipple." He looked as if he found the question shocking. "Find it makes my mind dull."

She pondered this skeptically. How could his mind possibly become any duller? Mutinously she raised her chin. "I do like a glass of brandy of an evening."

The look he gave her was one of surprised disdain. "Ladies don't drink brandy. They sip sherry, or a ratafia."

"This lady does."

"How unfortunate."

She wasn't likely to write a character like Lord Chetwynd-Ellerton—he'd bore a reader to tears. She must find someone more exciting to dance and flirt with.

She caught sight of a gentleman with a veritable thicket of chestnut curls atop a square-jawed visage. Had she seen him at the Thunderbolt Club? He was holding a crowd of young females captive with an obviously stirring tale that required many broad gestures, the better to display his well-muscled arms in their well-cut jacket sleeves. "Who's that gentleman there, who is causing such a commotion among the ladies?"

"That's Sir Michael Somersby. He's accounted to be quite the rake."

Perfect! Her very first rake. She must find a way to dance with him, if only to see what seductive techniques he employed.

"I do hope you're not thinking of dancing with him," the earl said disapprovingly. "His reputation is dreadful and may well taint yours."

"If he asks me, I must dance."

"No, then you feign an ankle injury, or a fainting spell, or a trip to the retiring room, or anything that will keep you away from him."

Ana wished she'd thought of feigning an ankle injury to keep from dancing with Lord Snuff Boxington.

The interminable dance finally concluded and Ana curtsied, eager to escape.

Lord Chetwynd-Ellerton was similarly disenchanted. She had obviously not fit his idea of a safe, suitable dancing partner. He left with the briefest of bows and she sighed with impatience and relief. Now to find a dangerous rake to dance with.

"How did it go?" Lady Glynis appeared at her side with alarming speed. "What did you speak of?"

"I could scarcely get a word in, but Lord Chetwynd-Ellerton spoke of the merits of ivory versus metal for housing his tobacco leaves at the greatest of length."

"And you didn't say anything to discourage him? I thought I detected a cold note as he made his bow."

"I don't think so."

Lady Glynis regarded her suspiciously. "You're shockingly frank of conversation. I do hope you said nothing to offend him. He's really the best match you could hope for."

"Analise, can that really be you?"

Ana turned to find Lady Lydia Seddington, her former nemesis at Miss Pincheon's finishing school. "Lady Lydia." Blast. She should have known her former schoolmates might be here. Lady Lydia and her group of fashionably garbed friends flocked to Ana's side.

Lady Glynis, seeing her charge swallowed up by a group of unobjectionable young ladies of noble birth, decided to take the opportunity to go and speak with Lady Chetwynd-Ellerton.

"What happened to you?" Lady Lydia asked. "Why did you disappear from school so suddenly?"

"My father went missing in Belgium, and I accepted work as companion and secretary to Lady Claridge."

"The authoress?"

"Yes."

"You were *working*," one of the ladies said, giving her friend a significant look.

Working was a cardinal sin in their eyes. To have been forced to accept employment was tantamount to declaring spinsterhood.

"And how did you come to be Warburton's ward?" Lady Lydia asked, linking her elbow with Ana's in a show of friendship that she'd never exhibited at school.

"My father requested it of him. On the battlefield."

One of the girls clasped her hands together in front of her pink silk sash. "How thrilling!"

"His Grace is never seen at society events," Lady Lydia continued. Ana surmised that she cared nothing for renewing what had been a contentious school relationship. She was intent on news of an eligible duke.

"Tell us about him," Lady Lydia commanded. "Is he thinking of marriage finally? I could certainly ignore those scars if I had thirty thousand and a castle in Surrey."

"Yes, indeed, who cares if he's no longer a handsome young buck," one of the other ladies agreed. "He can take care of me any day."

Not handsome? How could they say such a thing. They hadn't seen him bare-chested, going a round in a boxing ring. They hadn't observed him in a dark alleyway, intimidating ruffians into fleeing like frightened schoolboys.

"Those scars of his, though . . ." One young lady, with wide blue eyes, shuddered delicately.

"His scars make him interesting," Ana said. They were a visible reminder of battles, of strife, suffering. Each one had a story, each one held his past and his future. She hoped he might open up to her someday and tell her those stories. It would bring her closer to her father.

And closer to the duke.

"If you say so," the young lady simpered.

"I don't give a fig about his scars," said Lady Lydia. "What does he like to converse about? Surely you know that."

"His speech is curt. He speaks in short, terse sentences." But his eyes. Those gave him away. She saw whole novels being written in the gazes he gave her. "He was a cavalry commander and now he's a member of the Thunderbolt Club, so I'm certain if you ask him about his stables he'll be gratified."

"Stables. Noted," said Lady Lydia. "Why hasn't he danced yet?"

"He told me that he never dances."

"Such a pity. Dukes are thin on the ground this year, and my mama says I must marry a duke or a marquess, nothing less will do."

"Ladies," a deep voice spoke. They all turned to look at the intruder. It was Lord Somersby—the rake!

"Lord Somersby." Lady Lydia swatted his arm with her fan. "What manner of mischief are you getting up to this evening?"

"I was watching your friend here dance with Chetwynd-Ellerton and thought that someone should save her from expiring of boredom." Lord Somersby bent over Ana's hand, kissing her knuckles lightly. "Introduce us, won't you, Lady Lydia?"

"If I must. Lord Somersby, this is Miss Analise Crewe. Warburton's new ward."

"Didn't I see you yesterday in the club?" he asked, staring into her eyes in a most impertinent manner.

Ana pulled her hand from his grasp. "I don't think so."

"I could have sworn I saw you."

The ladies gave her curious glances.

"Why should I be inside a gentleman's club?"

"That's precisely what I was wondering. I was also wondering if you would grace me with a dance?"

She didn't much care for Lord Somersby's mocking manner, but in the name of researching rakes, she was duty bound to accept his offer. She inclined her head and allowed him to take her arm and lead her into the exact middle of the floor.

"Do you like to be the center of attention, Lord Somersby?"

"Always," he said with a seductive smile. "Especially when I have such an enchanting creature on my arm."

She smiled, remembering to make it demure just in time. "I'm hardly enchanting."

"Have you looked in a mirror tonight? Your hair is the color of sunlight dancing on a field of marigolds, your eyes sparkle brighter than any emeralds, and your lips . . ." He paused, staring intently at her mouth. "I could write a sonnet about your lips."

"Then by all means, write it!" she cried, delighted. Finally she would make some progress on her novel. "This is wonderful dialogue."

"I beg your pardon?"

"I meant compliment. That is a wonderful compliment."

"There's more where that came from, my lady."

He twirled her by the waist, his hand pressing harder than it needed to. She found herself breathless, but mostly from the twirling. He was incredibly good-looking, and he was well aware of it.

A rake was a curious beast. He was very handsome, there was no disputing that, but he was vain to the point of staring at his reflection every time they passed the large mirror on the wall, gazing into his own eyes with apparent satisfaction. His waistcoat was embroidered with a pattern of orange-striped tigers, and he wore gold rings on nearly every finger.

"Why do you have tigers embroidered on your waistcoat, my lord?"

"All the better to devour you with, Miss Crewe," he said with a lascivious wink.

He did say the most shocking things. She should at least pretend to be scandalized. As he spun her in his arms, she noticed that the duke was back in the ballroom. He stood against the far wall with his friend Patrick. They were both watching Ana and Somersby dance.

His watchful gaze made her tilt her head back to laugh, even though Somersby's conversation was more outré than witty.

The duke's expression turned positively thunderous. She did enjoy needling him, making him growl. He looked as though he wanted to stalk onto the dance floor and rip her from Somersby's arms.

Lady Lydia wanted to convince the duke to dance with her. It would be easier to convince a mountain to become a valley.

Or a dragon to purr like a kitten.

PATRICK GAZED AMUSEDLY at his friend. "If you glower any harder, a crack will open up in the marble floor and swallow us all."

"I hate this."

"Then why did you come? You engaged a chaperone for her, who is terrifying, I might add."

"I came because . . ." He wanted to be near her. Feel the brush of her fingers against his arm. She was all he thought about. Her fresh lavender scent. The brightness of her hair. The lines of her neck. The curve of the inside of her elbow. He was committing her every feature to memory, storing it up for the time when she would leave his care. "I can't trust Aunt Glynis to properly vet the candidates. She's dancing with that damned Somersby. I'll warn him away from her after the dance."

He couldn't let her out of his sight again. Too many predators in this ballroom.

After she finished the dance with Somersby, he'd pull the man aside. Have a private conversation about how he was never to touch his ward again or he'd be staring at the inside of a coffin.

"I saw you two together at the art gallery. The way she's always touching you. She teases you, tries to get a rise out of you, wants you to smile and laugh and be loving with her."

"You're mistaken."

"Am I? I don't think so. But if I am wrong about you two, then tell me what it is that's gotten into you lately?"

"What do you mean?" Dex responded cagily. He hated that he was so transparent to his friends.

"You created quite the disturbance at a certain brothel the other day. Whatever made you choose to play the knight errant at Madame D'Oiseaux's, of all places?"

Dex set his jaw grimly, a wave of disgust rising at the mere mention of that horrible place. "I owed it to a mutual friend to set that vile termagant back a pace or two. She had it coming."

"Well, you've made an enemy there, old boy! Once word got out that you'd taken such a negative interest in her affairs, customers dropped off sharply. She'd built quite a little empire for herself. She's been telling all and sundry that she's after revenge."

"Revenge!" scoffed Dex. "What could she ever do to me? An abbess of the lowest order!"

"Maggie Flanagan is not without means, friend. Has a reputation as a cold-blooded viper, doesn't take kindly to anything or anyone standing in her way. She's raised enough of a fuss about your interference to raise some eyebrows. If I were you, I'd keep an ear out in her direction. It doesn't hurt to be wary!"

"I do appreciate you looking out for a friend, but I think we can both agree that I have some distinct advantages over that harpy. What is she going to do, smother me in feathers?" He chuckled a bit, grateful for the brief moment of levity in what had otherwise been a tense evening thus far.

His eyes searched involuntarily for the source of that tension.

She wore flowing white, soft and drapey, the green sash at her small waist, and she almost seemed to float, her feet barely touching the floor. She was youth, beauty, zest for life. She moved like flickering candlelight, illuminating those around her, bringing smiles to faces and light to eyes. Whatever she might be feeling for him, she would soon flit off like a butterfly seeking an easier perch.

He was so accustomed to living life in this closely structured, regimented way, and she'd set him off-balance. Once he'd fulfilled his promise, protected her entrance into public life, seen her safely and comfortably settled, his life could go back to the way he liked it: solitary and uneventful.

And yet . . . one touch from her gloved fingers and his body was tense with longing. He had to get himself under control. If anyone in this room could read his thoughts, there'd be a scandal of epic proportions.

He was a man of thirty-five and she a young lady. His ward, to protect, to honor, and to see settled. Her father always there in his mind. The anguish in his eyes. The blood staining her innocent letters. She wasn't his to kiss. She would have a perfect, beautiful life. She would fall in love with a handsome young unscarred buck and leave his house and be mistress there.

As if pulled to him by his thoughts of her, she danced over, twirling and laughing, even though the music had stopped.

"Your Grace." She curtsied prettily, her face flushed from dancing, curls escaping the confines of her hair ribbons.

"You're not to dance with Lord Somersby again. Didn't I warn you about him?"

Her fingers curled over his bicep. He flexed instinctively, wanting her to feel the steel of his muscles. Her toes tapped in time to the music. "I was warned. I simply chose not to heed that warning."

Her fingers innocently stroked his arm.

"Are you enjoying yourself, Miss Crewe?" Patrick asked.

"Immensely. It's my first ball. I'm taking notes."

"For your novel."

"Exactly. Lord Somersby told me that my hair was the color of a field of sun-dappled marigolds. Isn't that a good line?"

Too good. Dex wished he'd thought of it. He'd stood there like a blockhead, telling her she was beautiful. The only words that had come to mind. Nothing so poetic as comparing her hair to sun-dappled marigolds. He'd lost the ability to make courtly compliments.

"Everyone's in a flutter about your return to society, Your Grace. Some of my old schoolmates begged me to ask you to dance with them."

"I don't dance."

"Would it kill you to be gracious just once in your life?"

Patrick chuckled. "Well put, Miss Crewe. Everyone's always attempting to match me with ladies. I'm delighted to see Warburton take my place as one of the most eligible bachelors this Season."

"I'd sooner scar the good side of my face than mince around a dance floor. If you'll excuse me, I'll go and find Aunt Glynis. She can't have gone far."

"I'll stay with Miss Crewe and say delightful things that she will want to add to the dialogue in her novel." He bowed over Miss Crewe's hand with an irritatingly charming upward glance.

Dex marched away, purposefully stopping himself from turning back to see what they were up to. He couldn't find Aunt Glynis. Perhaps she'd gone to the retiring room.

Several mamas with marriageable daughters attempted to engage his attention but he repeated his intention not to dance, to their great distress. When he returned, Patrick was alone.

"Where's Miss Crewe?"

"She said she needed to splash some water on her face. She left for the retiring room ten minutes ago."

"And you haven't seen her return to the ballroom?"

"Don't worry, my friend. I'm sure she's all right."

He searched the room. "Somersby isn't here either, damn his eyes. And I never had that chat with him. What if he's with her in the gardens?"

"She seems like a young lady who doesn't suffer fools. Leave her be to explore her newfound freedom and society."

"I'll leave her be when she's in my line of sight and not potentially somewhere being accosted by a reprobate," Dex growled.

Chapter Sixteen

The night air rushed by the dragon's wings as he bore her through the darkness toward the castle. A gibbous moon waxed o'er her head, hinting at fullness to come. Nervousness and excitement knotted in her belly, and she thrilled to the glittering stars above. Beneath her limbs, the powerful beast, her very own lethal weapon to command . . .

—*The Dragon and the Blue Star* by Analise Crewe

Where was she? Dex was growing increasingly desperate.

He'd checked the retiring room, the gardens, the balconies, and the ballroom again. He prowled the hallways of Lady Chetwynd-Ellerton's house, imagining sickening scenarios: Ana hiding from the unwelcome advances of Somersby—who was still nowhere to be found. Dex had accounted him to be harmless before, but what if he'd developed a recent nasty streak after having been jilted by a young lady he'd pursued?

Where would a young lady like Ana go to hide? Of course! He should have thought of it sooner. She would run to her beloved books. He hurried to the library, opening the door so hard it slammed against the wall. "Ana, are you in here?"

Silence. A fire dying in the grate, firelight wavering over the gilded spines of books.

"Your Grace?" came a whisper from the vicinity of a large armchair occupying a reading nook.

"Ana?" He rushed behind the chair, relieved to find her sitting behind it, her back propped against the wall, knees hunched over her chest. "What are you doing in here?"

"Hiding."

"I'm going to murder Somersby in cold blood if he harmed you in any way."

He held out his hand and she took it, allowing him to help her to a standing position. "You're safe now. Tell me what happened."

"I'm not hiding from Sir Somersby. I'm hiding from Mr. Norwood."

"Who?"

"Mr. Norwood, of Norwood & Pennington, the publishers. I've no idea why he's here but he is and he can't see me."

"Ah . . . why can't he see you?"

"Because he *knows*."

"Knows what?"

"Where I was living when you found me. He had his staff research me before I met with him about my novel. If he tells anyone in this ballroom that I was living in the rookeries with the sister of a brothel madam, my debut in society will be short-lived indeed. I'll be cast out, made a laughingstock."

He placed a hand on her shoulder and held her gaze. "No one's casting you out or laughing at you. Not with me by your side."

"Even you can't save me if they learn the truth. Do you really want such a scandal on your hands? Lady Glynis would be mortified if I sullied your family name. I told you this wouldn't work.

It's not just that I'm not one of them—I'm tainted by the circumstances of my past. You may have silenced Lord Claridge, but you can't silence everyone. Someone who knew me in the rookeries will surface eventually. I never should have come here tonight. I've no idea why I thought I could ever be published by the most respected and exclusive publisher in England."

"Stop, Ana. Just stop talking." He realized he was using her first name, but it felt necessary in this instance. What she was saying was wrong. He would defend her against the gossips and he'd make damn sure she achieved her dream of publication. "You belong at this ball. You're my ward."

She closed her eyes, her voice shrinking to a whisper. "That's not all. I told Mr. Norwood an untruth."

"You told him you'd produce half of a new Clovercote novel in a fortnight's time. If it takes longer than that, he'll have to wait."

When she opened those green eyes of hers, shimmering with unshed tears, he had to stop himself from moving his hand from her shoulder to caress the curve of her cheek, be at the ready to brush her tears away.

"I told him that I had a titled fiancé of ancient lineage. I made up a story about having to wait to announce our engagement because of his family's objections."

Dex cocked his head. "Why would you tell him that?"

"Because he was belittling and disparaging. He implied that a single lady with no connections, living in poverty, could never achieve the exalted heights of literary publication with his hallowed imprint. I said whatever I had to say to make myself a desirable author."

"Ana. You didn't."

"It was beyond foolish. I've always had this tendency to exaggerate, to embroider the truth . . . let's be honest, to tell outrageous lies. Now I'll pay the price. I have no fiancé, no manuscript, and a scandalous past."

"Damn." Dex dropped his hand. He needed a drink. "Is there any brandy in this library?"

"Brandy won't solve this problem."

"No, I'll solve it. I'll go have a talk with Mr. Norwood."

"That's your solution to everything, isn't it? Brute force, threats, bribery."

"Do you have another solution?"

"Not presently, but I only need time to think. That's what I was doing when you interrupted me."

"You can't write your way out of this one, I'm afraid. My way will be best. I'll take him into the gardens and while we're gone you'll find Aunt Glynis and tell her you have a headache and must leave."

"I can't think of anything better." She stared into the fire, her eyes troubled. "It's an ignoble end to my first ball. Running away with my tail between my legs."

"There will be other balls. At least you danced with several eligible suitors."

"And you didn't dance at all."

"I'm not looking for a wife. And when I do, I'll simply allow Aunt Glynis to prepare a list of candidates for a marriage of convenience. Sensible ladies of some years. I know my visage is frightening to some ladies. You fled from me the moment you saw me."

"Because I thought you were attempting to purchase me."

"You don't find the sight of my scars gruesome?"

"It's only startling upon first acquaintance. It didn't deter Lady Lydia. She was eager to dance with you."

"She's eager to be a duchess and mistress of Drakefell Castle."

"Don't be so cynical. You have an allure all your own. This dark brooding air about you that makes people, ladies in particular, want to solve your mysteries, unlock the key to your heart."

"Who told you that I have a heart?"

"You've been quite kind to me, in spite of all the bluster and commandments."

"Enough about me. You danced with eligible gentlemen, what think you of Patrick?"

"He's very handsome, obviously, and he was flirting with me, I think . . . although I don't have much experience with that. He has a young son who needs a mother. There's something very sad behind his eyes—it must have to do with his wife's death. He's a fine figure of a man but . . . I felt nothing other than friendship."

He hid a pleased smile that threatened to betray how happy her words made him. "Then what of Lord Chetwynd-Ellerton? He's scandal free and very well set up."

"He's bland, like a meal where the cook forgot the salt. If I were looking for a match, I certainly wouldn't settle for bland. I'd want someone who challenged me, who gave me the frissons."

"The what?"

"I've been searching for words to describe the pleasurable sensation of attraction for my novel. I could call it the tingles, the shivers . . . I like the French word *frisson,* it sounds better, think you not? It has those soft *s*'s in it. My heroine, Miss Adora Dansey, will have the frissons when Lord Fortescue kisses her for the first time. It's difficult to describe something I've never felt."

"The Season has only just begun."

"Yes, but I was expecting to have my first kiss this evening. I wanted to feel the frissons to describe them in my novel."

"You're not kissing anyone tonight. You're begging a headache and going straight home."

"Or perhaps I'll take a detour first. I'll allow Lord Somersby to lure me behind a curtain for my very first kiss."

"I forbid it."

She stuck out her chin. "What would happen if I defied you?"

"You don't want to find out," he growled.

"Lock me up in the tower of your castle? Feed me bread and water?"

"You're provoking me deliberately."

"Is it working? I love to see you lose your temper. It's such fun."

"You haven't seen me lose control because I never do."

"Never?"

"Even if I provoked you further?"

"You're playing with fire, Ana. Tempting the devil."

"Do you find me tempting?" She drew closer. "Do you find this provoking?" She touched her chest to his, standing on her tiptoes. "What if I kissed Lord Somersby? What if I slipped into the garden with him. What if it was dark and shadows striped his face and he had a hunger in his eyes that was thrilling. What if I wanted a handsome, dangerous man to kiss me in the garden of my very first society ball?"

He had to admire her bravery. She was a guileless novice, yet single-minded in her seduction, willing to explore whole new worlds in pursuit of artistic truth. She had no idea how effective the combination was. She wanted him to lose control, and he was precariously close.

"I forbid you to dance with him, tryst with him, and most especially to kiss him."

"You're always barking orders at me."

"I was an army commander."

"One could interpret your short sentences to mean any number of things. And the looks you give me. Something so wild and unbridled, the way you look at me something so fierce in your eyes. It's giving me the frissons, I do believe."

"I look at you protectively." And lustfully if he was being honest. "I promised to protect your honor, not sully it."

She moved closer. "Do you want to kiss me?"

Don't answer that, just leave. March out of this library and fix this tangle.

"I'll only ask someone else to kiss me if you don't. It's for my book. I've never been kissed and I want to experience it."

"No." He was fighting a losing battle. How did she have all the right words to say, the right way to look at him, to touch him?

She cocked her head, examining his face. "I want to savor this. I want to provoke you into losing that famous control of yours. The way you're staring at me. You're angry but there's something else there. Desire. Desire flickering in your eyes, turning them from gray to glittering silver."

He backed up until he hit the wall and still she advanced with that fire burning in her eyes. "I want to write the best kiss ever. I want my readers to feel the frissons, too. I want them turning pages, feeling as I'm feeling right now. This breathlessness."

She rose onto her tiptoes, steadied herself with a palm against his chest. "If you won't kiss me . . ." She kissed his lips and twined her small hands around his neck. He stayed absolutely still. Set her away from him. Jump on his horse and ride away fast, anywhere far away from this enchantment. Anywhere but here in this firelit room with this tempting innocent.

"You're made of granite, just like the walls of this room. Nothing moves you. Nothing sways you. You're immovable."

He was made of granite. Yes. His body, his cock so hard she couldn't fail to feel it.

"Enough."

"Not enough," she said stubbornly. "When I was in the ballroom I was at a remove. The scene was happening around me and I was viewing it with an eye to writing it all down. But when I'm with you . . . it's simply impossible to remain at a distance. When I'm with you, I feel these violent emotions and there's no way I could stay at a remove from you. You have to be experienced. You make me so angry and you make me want . . . I don't know how to explain what I want."

He knew how to explain it. The flush on her cheeks. The light, questing brush of her fingers on his bicep. Patrick had been right. She was attracted to him.

Despite his scars, despite the cold way he treated her. He tried to be glacial because he needed to keep her at arm's length. There was an undeniable pull between them he felt too, and now it had been confirmed.

"You want to kiss me, I know you do." She leaned against his chest, her soft breasts brushing against him. "Do it . . ."

"I can't. We can't." Let her tease him, let her test her power, let her provoke him. He'd never succumb. Never lose control.

She lifted her lips again, brushing them against his.

Something broke, some tenuous thread of decency that had been holding him back. And then, suddenly, his iron control shattered. He took her into his arms, crushed her against him, held her hands behind her back and kissed her. Hard. Not a gentlemanly peck on her rosy lips. He kissed her with intent to thrill. To seduce.

She'd slipped beneath his barriers and he had to taste her. He lowered his lips to hers, taking her into his arms in a fierce embrace. He wasn't thinking anymore, or holding back. He crushed her lips to his and slipped his tongue inside. She tasted sweeter than spun sugar, sweeter than any dessert he'd ever had.

She moaned softly, surrendering to him, throwing her head back to give him better access to her lips. He slipped one hand behind her neck, closing his fingers around her slim neck. The other hand roamed inside her bodice, cupping the silken skin of one breast.

"Oh, that feels good," she whispered, her eyes widening as she glanced down at his huge hand covering her breast.

He resumed the kiss, deeper now, claiming her, giving her a kiss to write about, to dream about.

"Warburton?" The voice, female, piercing, intruded in some dim region of his brain that still had the capacity to translate words into sentences.

He stopped the kiss. Fuck. Someone had entered the library. Aunt Glynis, and a strange man.

They were well and truly caught.

Chapter Seventeen

As she slid down the dragon's back, she felt the rumble of his voice. "I have given you what you desire, Amsonia. I am taking you home. But steel yourself for what awaits! I have seen the Evil that has taken root. You will find things much changed."

—*The Dragon and the Blue Star* by Analise Crewe

Dex pulled back. Ana stood there all dewy-eyed, rosy cheeked, her lips stained red, bodice askew, breasts heaving.

Cursing inwardly, he turned to face the intruders, shielding Ana from their view. "Aunt Glynis."

Was it too late to say she'd had some dust in her eye? He'd lost control. He should have been stronger.

"Warburton." His aunt nodded coldly. "This is Mr. Norwood. He and I have been having rather an interesting conversation about Miss Crewe. And now we find you here engaged in what can only be described as—"

"Research!" Ana interjected. "Research for my Clovercote novel. I wasn't able to complete the scene when Falconer steals a kiss from Adora and so I asked the duke to help me fill in some details. I'm absolutely safe because he's my guardian and would never actually importune me or—"

"I kissed her," Dex said bluntly. There was no bending the truth or fabricating a new reality.

"No, you didn't," Ana insisted, desperately attempting to salvage the situation. "You weren't really kissing me. You were pretending to be the villainous Falconer and I was pretending to be innocent Adora and it was all in the name of research."

Aunt Glynis snorted, nostrils flaring with disapproval. "Mr. Norwood informed me that Miss Crewe was found living in a disreputable boarding house and that she is purported to have a fiancé. Is this true, Miss Crewe?"

The look on Ana's face was nearly comical. He could see the gears whirring in that sharp mind of hers, searching for an explanation, a fantastical story to explain this infernal tangle. She opened her mouth to speak but he cut her off.

"Indeed, Aunt. I rescued her from an unfortunate choice of lodgings." He took a swift breath to gird himself for what was to come. "And she does have a fiancé. Me."

"You?" Ana, Aunt Glynis, and Mr. Norwood spoke in unison, gawping at him.

He took Ana's hand and addressed her tenderly. "We don't have to maintain the charade anymore, darling. We can tell the world we're engaged to be married."

Ana's jaw dropped. "*Darling*?"

Perhaps that had been laying it on too thick, but he wasn't accustomed to telling lies. It was against his code. He was swimming in a dark ocean, bleeding out, and there were hungry sharks closing in all around him.

Mr. Norwood blinked rapidly. "Your Grace, do you mean to

say that you are the secret fiancé of whom Miss Crewe spoke when we met in my office?"

"That's exactly what I mean, Mr. Norwood."

Ana was frozen, her mouth slightly open as if she wanted to speak but couldn't find words for once in her life.

"Then why would you go through this charade of asking me to chaperone her, my boy?" asked Aunt Glynis, shaking her head so that the feathers stuck into her hair quivered indignantly. "None of this makes any sense."

"Because I wanted to wait for an appropriate time before announcing our engagement. I wanted to introduce her to society and make my triumphant return. I didn't want there to be any rumors of a hasty engagement. Isn't that right, dear?" He turned to Ana, who was looking a little green about the gills.

She searched his face, nonplussed. "I . . . suppose so."

"When Miss Crewe visited you, Mr. Norwood, she didn't feel at liberty to reveal our connection. I believe you promised to publish her manuscript?"

"I . . . that is, er, there were certain stipulations attached to any offer of publication. I haven't read the manuscript as yet."

"You have read it."

"I beg your pardon?"

"*The Dragon and the Blue Star.*"

"Your Grace, that is . . . Warburton." Ana lay a hand on his arm. "Mr. Norwood wishes to publish a new Clovercote novel, not my fantastical tale."

"Then he is gravely mistaken, for I have read excerpts from *The Dragon and the Blue Star* and it is a work of astounding imagination. I predict it will be a bestseller for Norwood & Pennington."

Mr. Norwood cleared his throat. "If Miss Crewe gives me Lady Claridge's novel outline, then I promise I won't mention to a soul where she was living or the truly outrageous depths to which she'd fallen."

Ana drew herself as tall as she could. "Are you threatening me, Mr. Norwood? That would be ill-advised."

Dex moved her slightly behind him. He could fight this battle for her with one hand tied behind his back. "Surely," he said, slowly and distinctly, "you aren't attempting to extort *my* fiancée, Mr. Norwood? I must not be understanding you correctly."

"Nothing of the sort, Your Grace. You misunderstand me." The man blanched, his face going whiter than his collar. He sensed that he'd taken a giant step too far and was backtracking as quickly as his faculties would allow. "It's only that we are *very* selective about which authors and works we publish, naturally, and we feel that Miss Crewe's fantastical novel wouldn't fit within our list of titles."

Dex took a casual step toward the publisher and Mr. Norwood backed away, the tips of his ears turning fiery red. He smiled blandly. "I think you'll take a chance on her book. New and different isn't always a bad thing. Aren't you tired of publishing the same books over and over?"

"We give the public what they clamor for," he responded faintly.

"They don't know what they want until you force-feed it to them. It's time to expand your hallowed list."

"Warburton," Ana said urgently. "May I speak with you in private? This matter doesn't need to be decided hastily."

"It's already been decided, isn't that right, Mr. Norwood?"

"Er, of course, Your Grace. Norwood & Pennington would be delighted to publish *The Dragon and the Blue Stone*."

"The Blue *Star*," Dex corrected. "You'll attend me at my house tomorrow at precisely noon to discuss the terms of the contract."

Mr. Norwood bowed. "With pleasure, Your Grace."

"Aunt, escort Mr. Norwood back to the ballroom."

Aunt Glynis clicked her tongue against her teeth. "I hope you know what you're doing, my boy."

"What in the hell was that?" Ana asked after Lady Glynis and Mr. Norwood had left the library, closing the door behind them. She placed her hands on her hips. "You shout orders and expect everyone to do your bidding."

"It worked, didn't it?" he asked smugly.

"You made everything worse. Mr. Norwood will never believe that we were engaged. And you can't bribe him to publish my novel, I want to publish it on its own merits."

"It's good, Ana. Truly, it is."

"That doesn't matter if no one wants to read it."

"*I* want to read it. Will you give me the second half to read?"

"The only existing copy is at Norwood & Pennington. I thought it would be buried there forever. It's the Clovercote novel he wants."

"Then write it and publish them both."

"Why don't you write a bloody novel! You're so good at creating fantastical fictions such as our false engagement. You can't marry me. We'll . . . we'll wait a few weeks and then break it off. No harm done."

"You've been out of society too long. Within the hour this story will spread the entire length and breadth of Mayfair, and then beyond to the newspapers. You are my fiancée in truth. We were caught kissing in the library. Your hair was mussed, your lips were swollen, we were in each other's arms."

"You don't have to ruin your life just because they saw us kissing. If you'd only backed me up on the research explanation, we could have avoided this situation altogether."

"We are marrying by special license within the week."

"Don't be silly! You can't marry a common little hellion like me."

"There's nothing common about you. You're a firebrand that burned through my life, permanently altering its landscape. You may be small of stature, but your impact is monumental."

"You know that you were meant to choose a noble bride, raised to be a duchess, like any number of those alluring ladies back there who were dying to dance with you."

"It doesn't matter whom I was meant to marry. This happened, and that's the end of it."

"It's not the end of anything! I refuse to believe this is our only solution. I'm not the lady you would have chosen to wed."

"And I'm not the handsome, laughing gentleman you dreamed of in your letters to your father."

"That was a foolish schoolgirl's dream. And you are handsome. Too handsome, damn you, or none of this would have happened."

"Neither here nor there. We will marry. You will bear me an heir. Then you will be free to spend your life as you will. You won't be bothered by me."

"Because marriage is solely about an heir for you."

"Well . . . yes. I always knew I'd have to marry someday. I'd been putting it off, but now I must do my duty."

"Duty, honor . . . is that all you ever talk about?"

"There is an aggrieved tone to your voice."

"Because . . ." She lifted her shoulders and set them back down again with a huff. "No young lady likes to think that she's merely convenient. That she's interchangeable with any number of other women. That it's only her womb that holds any real value in this relationship."

"I didn't say any of that."

"That's the problem. You don't say enough. You hide behind these monosyllabic responses and short, terse sentences. I'm always searching for precisely the right words to express emotions or to describe the world as I see it. You're always biting back words, swallowing your feelings. I want to know what you're thinking, what you're feeling."

"I'm feeling remorse. I lost control. I never should have kissed you."

"We kissed each other."

"And now your reputation will be ruined if we don't marry swiftly."

She set her jaw. "I won't marry you."

"You will."

"You're trying to do the honorable thing, but I release you from any obligation my father placed upon you."

"That's not your choice."

"You're the most cold, unyielding, domineering, frustrating man in the world."

"The cold, domineering man you're going to marry. I made a promise and I never go back on my promises."

"Stop saying that!" She massaged her temples. "Let me think."

"There's nothing to think about. I understand that you don't wish to marry me, but what's done is done. Your reputation was harmed. It's the honorable thing."

"And you're so honorable that you'll marry me even though you don't care for me at all? My father didn't mean for you to wed me."

"He wouldn't approve of this union but he would understand it because he was a military man and he understood codes of honor."

Her shoulders sagged. "Is this really happening?"

"I know you would rather have found someone else to marry," he said stiffly. "I know you believe in finding your true love. I'm sorry, but our actions have consequences."

"It was only one kiss."

"Your life will be your own. You will have all the money, prestige, and diversions you could want. You will live at Drakefell Castle. I'll make sure you have the writing desk of your dreams with a magnificent view."

"I must stay in London to find news of my father. I was going to begin interviewing the surviving members of his . . . of your company."

Dex winced. "There are only two."

"I was also going to place an advertisement in the paper, as soon as I have the funds, offering a reward for any news of his whereabouts."

"I will help with that."

"What if we announced our engagement and then broke it off after a month?"

"You already suggested that and I shot it down. A swift and binding marriage is the only way to save your reputation and ensure your book contract."

"It sounds like you're trying to help me but you're forcing me to marry you. I'll run away."

"I'll track you down."

She knew what he was saying made sense, but it was still infuriating. "It's war, then."

"It's marriage."

"Much the same thing, in our case, Your Grace," she huffed, spinning on her heel and forcing Dex to run after her.

He saw her safely into the carriage with a very grim and silent Aunt Glynis and then turned his steps to the Thunderbolt Club. He needed a drink in the worst way.

"WHY SUCH HASTE to marry?" Dalton asked Dex after he arrived at the club and told the startling news to his old friend.

"We were caught kissing in the library at Lady Chetwynd-Ellerton's ball. And now she's marrying a ruin of a man." He swiped a hand in the direction of his scars.

"Don't be so dramatic. You're still a handsome devil, and you know it."

"Half a handsome devil."

"Sounds as though she was eager enough to kiss you."

"For research purposes."

"Come again?" Dalton asked, his brow wrinkling. "Oh, yes. I remember. Patrick told me about the novel Miss Crewe is writing. He said she'd chosen him as a model for the hero of her story. Guess she decided to go with the villain instead."

"She'll never be published if she doesn't salvage her reputation by marrying me."

"So that's why she agreed to marry a bounder like you," said Dalton with a smirk.

"She didn't agree. I forced her to for her own good."

"And what did she have to say about that?"

"A hell of a lot."

Dalton laughed and punched him lightly on the shoulder. "I like her. She'll lead you a merry chase."

"She'll be the death of me."

"Then she'll be a wealthy widow," Dalton said, pouring more whiskey into his glass. "To wedding nights."

The wedding night. It was all Dex had been thinking about since that kiss in the library. Good God. If one kiss made him lose control like that . . . he'd have to be more careful in future.

"Give me some of that." Dex swiped for the bottle but Dalton held it out of reach.

"Not until you confess that you're in love with the girl."

"Love has nothing to do with it." Dex grabbed the whiskey bottle from Dalton with one fluid movement. He swallowed a healthy amount and wiped his mouth with his sleeve.

Dalton chuckled. "Miss Crewe may have more to say on that subject. She'll make a romantic of you yet."

"Don't hold your breath," Dex muttered. The situation was complicated enough. At least theirs would be a marriage of convenience. A mutually beneficial partnership, and nothing more.

Chapter Eighteen

She had seen enough. She turned back toward Qavox, face hidden in her hands. The empty, echoing streets. The red river winding around the castle. The face of a man, horribly familiar to Amsonia and clad in her father's crown, painted on a giant banner over the entrance.

"Look upon it and know the truth! Your uncle succumbed to dark forces. It is he who vanished your father into the Red Mist, he who now rules over the lands of Vyranthrall. You must be brave, Amsonia. If you hope to vanquish this evil, you must first open your eyes."

—*The Dragon and the Blue Star* by Analise Crewe

Tessie, why is your mistress still abed?"

"I'll rouse her immediately, Your Grace."

Ana nestled her head deeper into the pillow, her mind blurred from sleep. Surely the duke wasn't there in her bedchamber? What a bizarre dream.

"Get up, Ana." His deep voice, coming from somewhere alarmingly close by. She cautiously opened one eye. He was there. In the formidable flesh. Standing over her in a dark claw hammer jacket, the high cropped front displaying the full power of his muscular thighs encased in buff-colored leather riding breeches. Feet clad in high black boots tapping impatiently on the floor as Tessie began to bustle about the room, drawing the curtains and readying her mistress's toilet.

An unwelcome ray of sunshine fell across her eyelids. "Go away!" She rolled over and buried her face back in the pillow. "I'm hiding."

"You can't hide in here all week until the wedding."

"I absolutely intend to." She wanted to keep as many doors as possible between herself and reality. She felt a potent mix of dread, anxiety, and a kind of chagrin—she had, after all, brought this unthinkable situation on herself. It was she who had pressed forward with her research, she who had instigated the incendiary physical contact that had changed everything in one moment. She had nobody else to blame, not even the duke. Now she was officially part of a bona fide full-size scandal, and the reality of it was much more stomach-churning than her imagination could have possibly warned her.

Hiding was the only answer.

"I'm taking you riding."

"Riding?" She sputtered and sat up. That didn't make any sense. *I'm taking you riding.* The words immediately conjured Princess Amsonia, clinging to the dragon's scaly back, sailing underneath night stars with the wind whistling in her ears. Riding was motion, freedom—exposure, contact with the outside world. She shook her head vehemently.

"On Rotten Row, just as you asked."

Well, there was an interesting thought. The infamous Rotten

Row, sure to provide a fascinating look into the ton, everyone parading up and down the bridle path on their best horses. She was sure to observe a million details that would help her flesh out the bonier parts of her book. But she would be observed in turn, used as fodder for idle gossips to chew up and spit back at each other. Researching real life was a dangerous game. She wanted none of it.

"I don't want to go out in public."

"But Rotten Row is on your list of things to do."

"I'm not writing the novel anymore."

A sigh of exasperation. "Yes. You are writing the damn book. You talk about it incessantly. Let's help it along."

"Won't people be whispering about us?"

"Most likely. That's the routine on the Row. But the best way to quell rumors is to face them head on."

"Or stay in bed until they die down on their own," she whispered, sensing that she was losing the battle.

"Ana, you are coming riding with me. As my future duchess, with a soon-to-be burgeoning literary career of her own, this is a logical and necessary step. We must be seen in public together."

She cocked an ear. Half of that statement filled her with dread, the other with excitement. "A literary career?" Since that extraordinary kiss had turned her world topsy-turvy, she had scarcely dared imagine what life post-marriage might be like. It was a daunting gray area. But this sounded . . . intriguing. Something to consider.

"Yes, of course. As my wife, you'll have nothing but time in which to write all the countless books your fertile imagination can conjure. Now, Tessie, stuff her into a habit and have her downstairs within the hour."

Tessie dropped a curtsy. "Yes, Your Grace."

When he'd gone, Tessie folded the covers away from her body. "You heard His Grace. Up you get."

Ana groaned. "I can't believe this is happening. I never meant for any of it to happen."

"Perhaps not, but you were caught kissing and that's the way of the world now, isn't it?"

As Tessie helped her into her finely tailored navy riding habit, arranging the shirred epaulets just so over her shoulders and fluffing the jaunty peplum, Ana's gaze found the window with its partial view of the square. She hadn't seen Cygnette at Lady Chetwynd-Ellerton's ball. Perhaps she'd been wrong about her making her debut. Maybe Cygnette was an independent young lady who had decided never to marry and to pursue her farfetched dream of becoming a physician, or an archaeologist, or even an author.

Was marriage really a cage that kept one from fulfilling one's dreams?

What if her marriage to the duke actually enabled hers? He seemed to be fine with the idea of having an author for a wife, someone with her own career independent of their union. She shook her head, denying the possibility. He would want all her attention on the heirs she would be forced to produce, like a broodmare cooped up in a stable. Surely a loveless marriage would crush her creativity, stifle her spirit.

"Hold still!" Tessie shoved several hat pins into her backswept coiffure, attempting to afix the pert bonnet. "What's got you sighing so? It's a lovely day for a ride!"

"Tessie, life is already too much of a ride for me at this particular point. It's moving far too quickly into uncharted territories, and I'm having a hard time hanging on."

Tessie smiled behind her mistress's dramatic head. "You're to be a duchess, Ana. A duchess. You'll never have to worry about anything again for as long as you live!"

Ana didn't bother to contradict her as she gathered up her gloves and crop. She knew that from her friend's perspective she had indeed stumbled into a spot of luck. But the prospect of a lifetime of luxury didn't hold the same allure for her. She had never felt quite so beset by uncertainties, not even when she'd been destitute and desperate in her tiny room at Miss Flanagan's. At least then she'd known her missions: find her father, publish her book.

Life had become complicated and mysterious since then. The duke had made it so. And now he was making her face her fears, forcing her out into the stark light of the public stage. She'd thought that observing society was what she wanted. But today, it would be society observing and judging her. Let them.

She set her chin and marched down the stairs.

LATER, DISMOUNTING FROM the horse with her fingers tucked into the duke's strong hand, she had to admit she'd been wrong, utterly and completely. He'd engineered an almost perfect afternoon, something from a dream belonging to someone else. Someone in an affectionate relationship with a well-dressed lover who nodded reassuringly at her from his horse at intervals and pointed out interesting sights along the sandy gravel road. The inquisitive looks from passersby, so daunting at first, had faded into a harmless blur as the magic of the sunny, stimulating scene took hold.

The duke had provided what amounted to, for him, a steady

stream of comforting commentary. For someone else it might have been more of a brook, she allowed, a trickle really, but for him it had been volubility itself. He'd provided the names of the more outrageously dressed riders, noting their titles and marital statuses, even tossing in a line or two about their unique peccadillos or peculiarities.

"That's Sir Alexander Howell, in the frothy cravat," he said, nodding his chin at a gentleman wearing two clashing waistcoats from which a fountain of lace erupted. "He spends the bulk of his leisure time in the company of elderly women of means."

"Countess Bettina Davencourt, on the braided mare. Never seen out with her husband, the earl, who is always seen *in* with her lady's maid."

Short, to the point, but ever so provocative—she peered at the people in question and marveled at how ordinary they appeared under their finery. Was absolutely everyone hiding a secret or two? It would seem so. It was satisfying fare.

They'd run into a number of his friends along the road, who struck Ana as a surprisingly pleasant and lively group. They were sculptors and barristers and viscounts and merchants, from a motley assortment of professions and stations, united by high intelligence and an obvious zest for life. Not a single one of them looked askance at her; rather, they'd all smiled directly into her eyes and exclaimed warmly at the pleasure of meeting her.

She was struck, too, by the genuine regard they seemed to have for the duke. Hearty congratulations were offered, gentle jokes made about the duke's good fortune at finding her. It was obvious that these good-seeming people thought very highly of him.

Toward the end they'd crossed paths with Thea and Lulu, riding in a gaily painted phaeton, Thea holding the reins and Lulu cradling a sketchbook in her lap. The women had cried gladly at the sight of Ana, and Warburton had directed his and Ana's horses to the side of their carriage so they could move forward together.

Thea had made her promise to meet them after the ride at her favorite teahouse, and Ana had eagerly obliged. Thea and Lulu had ridden off directly, while Ana and the duke concluded their saunter down the Row. A quarter of an hour later, they'd arrived in front of Gunter's. She was ready for some mousse and sweet meats, being unaccustomed to riding for such a length of time, but the hunger itself was enjoyable. She felt like she'd accomplished something and deserved a reward.

"Did you enjoy your long-awaited ramble on Rotten Row?"

"I did! Thoroughly. Thank you." She beamed up at him unguardedly. "I've ever so much fodder for my work now. It was every bit as full of scandal as I'd dreamed it would be. I feel positively ordinary! All I've ever done is kiss a duke in a library."

"That's hardly all you've done, Ana," he said, his face suddenly serious. "Never undervalue yourself and never let other people's opinions undermine you." She watched a cloud fall over his face, blotting out the unexpected warmth she'd basked in all afternoon. He dropped her hand abruptly. "I'll see you at the house."

"You're not coming in?" She couldn't keep a forlorn note of surprise from her voice. He had been such a good companion on the ride, she was loath to end the afternoon. She had been looking forward to pumping him for more information about the figures they'd encountered, hearing more of his succinct character assassinations.

"No," he said, already turning away. "I'll send someone for your horse. Thea can drop you home." His terseness stung her.

What had happened? Who had she just spent the afternoon with? Surely not this cold figure, remote and forbidding, shutting down her attempt at continued camaraderie. He swung his long leg over the saddle and rode off at a brisk pace. She watched until she couldn't see his hat above the crowd anymore, then entered the shining facade of Gunter's.

Thea and Lulu were already seated at a small table near a window, strategically situated so that they had a splendid view of the teahouse clientele. They waved her over, pulling out a chair for her and pushing a silver tray of flavored ices in her direction.

"We ordered without you—couldn't wait! The Rotten air gives one such an appetite," Lulu said, biting into one of the many pastries crowding the china in front of them. "Hope you like sinfully delicious things, we've loads to share."

Thea grabbed Ana's hand and gave it a squeeze, pouring tea into her cup with the other. "Well, well. Glad to have the chance to talk with you, just us girls. Much seems to have changed since we last met." She laughed. Ana blushed.

"You've heard . . . everything?"

"I've heard rumors but wanted to hear all about it in your own words. Gossip can be insidious in this fishbowl of a city."

"It's all happening so fast. We shared a kiss. Now we're getting married."

"Polite society has such a way about it. No kisses and you're in danger of spinsterhood. One kiss and you're ruined," Lulu said with a sage air, undermined by the delicate tongue she stuck out to lick the crumbs from one corner of her mouth.

"I kissed Dalton before we wed," Thea said confidingly.

Ana gave a sigh of relief. "Really?"

"Indeed. And we did far more than kiss, to be completely honest. But I was luckier, in that there was nobody there to observe."

Ana perked up. "Might I interview you on the subject for my novel?"

"I think you'll be having plenty of experiences of that sort yourself in short order," Thea said, smiling gently. "Now tell us all about it—if you'd like. We're dying to hear, but only if you're comfortable sharing."

"Oh. Yes. It was—well, it was . . ." Ana shivered, gooseflesh rising on her arms as she remembered the kiss. How she'd melted into him and acted in such an unguarded manner.

"Are you picturing your wedding night?" Lulu laughed, touching one of Ana's radiant cheeks. "I wish I could paint you right now! Such a glow . . ."

Ana blushed harder. "About that . . . I'm afraid I don't know precisely what goes on? I mean, I know the logistics of the act, of course: what is what, and where it goes. But . . . how, and for how long, and will he expect me to do it more than once in one night? I have questions."

"If you're lucky, it'll be more than once a night. Possibly much more," Thea said with a throaty chuckle. "You'll understand all very soon. It's normal to feel a bit nervous."

"It's only that he's so very . . . large . . . and I'm so small of stature and I honestly don't know how it would even work?" She'd been running through the matter in her mind for days now. Surely it would be painful. It struck her suddenly as comical; she'd only just sat down, and here they were, talking about the most intimate of intimacies in a very public setting. She liked these women, who were so free and so freeing.

Thea laughed with her. "If this wasn't such a rushed affair, I would take you aside and explain certain things. Yet, every woman's experience is different. I will say this—Warburton is a man of experience and I would hope that he ensures you are well-pleasured first before he . . . before you consummate the marriage."

"Does that make it easier?"

"Yes. Precisely. Oh my dear." Thea took her hands. "It truly is wonderful with the right person."

"Is he the right person, though?"

"He's the satyr from my painting that you admired," said Lulu emphatically. "And you're the wood nymph. You were fated to be together."

"I don't think fate had anything to do with it. I was carried away by the frissons I was experiencing. I had no idea where it would land me."

Thea placed an arm around her shoulders and gave her a hug. "I understand what you mean. Sometimes desire makes us behave in uncharacteristic ways. Marriage is a serious undertaking. You should be certain about spending the rest of your life with the duke."

Ana took a bite of her rapidly melting ice. "And that's the thing. Certainty escapes me. It's been so sudden—one minute, he was my guardian, and the boundaries were clear enough. The next, this mysterious man whom I know next to nothing about is my betrothed, and I'm to give him my body, and some heirs, and all the rest of my days, 'til death do us part."

Lulu's sympathetic eyes met Thea's. "Given the circumstances it's very natural for you to be a little trepidatious. But surely you and the duke have feelings for each other, however sudden? I've observed that he has a certain regard for you, and he isn't one to simply bow to convention for convention's sake."

"He says it's a marriage of convenience, a means to an end, and that I may have my freedom, spending my time at Drakefell Castle while he lives in London."

"Sometimes people say things they think the other person wants to hear," Lulu said.

"But how will I know what he's thinking? What he's feeling?"

"If you don't wish to marry him, you shouldn't," Thea said matter-of-factly. "I was in a similar situation once. Standing at an altar with a man I had no desire to marry. I'm so very glad I extricated myself. He was in love with another woman—Lulu's sister, and my half-sister, Charlene. You'll meet her soon, I hope."

"I've been searching my heart, and I honestly don't know whether we will suit. He's so silent all the time."

"He didn't used to be quite so silent, Dalton says. The war made him lose the gift for easy speech."

"He's so cryptic, nothing but closed doors and mysteries." She thought back to her first moments in his house, the impersonality of his décor, the terse list, the locked room. "Do the names Kitty, Janet, and Laurel mean anything to you? I found them written down in his handwriting."

Thea shook her head. "No, I can't say that I recognize any of them."

"Could they be his . . . mistresses?" Ana felt herself hesitant to voice the thought, and strangely fearful of Thea's response.

"I highly doubt that. As far as I know, he was considered a rake before the war but after returning he's been mostly solitary. That is, until you arrived."

Ana felt relief wash over her. Thea wasn't offering her any

substantive help solving the mystery of the names, but at least she was eliminating an objectionable explanation.

"Perhaps Dex has been waiting for a vivacious, well-spoken companion to draw him out of his solitude," Lulu said dreamily, ready to believe the best for her new friend.

"But I seem to be failing completely at drawing him out. He's immovable. I can't imagine a life with him . . . long evenings, totally silent after I exhaust my own chatter. He said that once I bore an heir he would leave me alone. I could live my own life." To her consternation, she felt tears pricking the insides of her eyes. She thought of the fun she'd had, riding in the sun at his side. The fresh air and gentle pace of the horses and his steady attentiveness lulling her into a deep sense of security. She'd felt . . . at home, in a way she could hardly describe.

"Ana." Thea took her hands and gave them a small shake. "We could talk about this all day, but you'd only be hearing our side of things. If you have this much doubt clouding your mind, the person you should be talking to is your fiancé."

Chapter Nineteen

Amsonia's face crumpled. "I can't believe . . . my own family . . ."

The sight of her tears made him want to kill for her, made him want to comfort her. He longed to touch her. He could not. He must not.

These cruel talons would rip her to shreds. The only thing he had to offer was his protection.

—*The Dragon and the Blue Star* by Analise Crewe

Ana paced the long hallway, steeling her nerves. She'd arrived home to a silent house. She was to eat supper alone, again, McArdle informed her. His Grace had barricaded himself in his study with a visitor. No other information was given.

Enough. She'd had enough with the whole situation.

She must force Warburton, Deckard . . . what was she supposed to call him now? She must force him to speak his mind, answer her questions. His actions that afternoon had obviously been an act designed to stave off gossip, and while she appreciated the gesture, it left her feeling hollow inside. She couldn't marry someone who had no genuine affection for her. She thought too highly of herself for that.

She paused outside the parlor door, hearing loud voices from inside. The duke and . . . Lady Glynis? What was she doing here? Ana lingered outside the door, not wanting to interrupt their conversation.

"Have you seen the scandal sheets?" she heard Lady Glynis ask. "They're having a feast off this: *A Marriage Made in Haste. To Wed a Winsome Ward*. It's humiliating!"

"I don't read the scandal sheets," was the cool reply.

"Well, you should. Then you might reconsider your rash promise to marry."

"You were there, Aunt, you saw us in a compromising position. Is there any other possible outcome?"

"It was only myself and Mr. Norwood who saw you. And you extracted a promise from him not to tell anyone, as well as making a most sizeable donation to his publishing company, I understand. I'm certainly not going to tell anyone. So why must you marry the girl in such haste? Tongues are wagging."

"If I don't marry her, the possibility of ruin will always be around the corner. I will remain unscathed, and she could pay the price if the truth came out. I won't stand for it."

"You're too honorable by half. And I always thought you such a heedless young buck, arrogant and cocksure."

"You thought rightly. I was that man, Aunt. I thought the world should bend to my every whim. I was heedless and even cruel. The war changed me."

"Still, you can't possibly be considering going through with this unsuitable marriage."

"We marry by week's end by special license."

"Care you nothing for this family's reputation?"

"I made a promise to see her future secured."

"That damned battlefield honor of yours. Surely a dead man can't force you to throw your life away."

"It's my duty."

"You'll be saddled with an inferior bride forever."

Ana could bear to hear no more. She rushed down the hall, tears blinding her eyes. She couldn't marry him! He thought she was inferior and he was only marrying her because it was his honorable duty.

She ran down the stairs and was halfway across the entrance hallway when a booming voice halted her progress.

"Just where do you think you're going?"

Keep running, or turn and face the dragon? Running was a coward's way out. She should be able to face him, to tell him her feelings and see the truth or lies on his face when he responded.

She turned around. "I'm leaving, Your Grace. I can't marry you."

"And why is that?"

"Any number of reasons, the chief among them being that I just now overheard you and your aunt speaking about me in the most demeaning of terms. I will not be your burden, an inferior bride you only marry out of a misguided sense of duty."

He reached her side. "Come, let's not speak out in the open. Allow me a moment to explain everything." He held open the door to a sitting room. "Please, Ana?"

Drawing a deep breath, she followed him into the room.

"Am I just another war for you to win?" she asked, after he'd closed the door.

"I'll admit that marrying you was not the plan. But any good general will adapt his strategy when confronted with new intelligence, fresh challenges."

"You're only tied to me by your own decision; your honor isn't at stake. Can you possibly want this? I'm not some duty for you to dispatch."

"Are you not? I may not be the partner your father or you would have chosen, but now that we're bound by circumstances and mutual benefit, we'll win this together."

"Bound! Like a chain around both of our waists. What of . . . free will? Spontaneity? What of affection? Marrying me is like some military campaign you're under orders to complete. You're approaching this in the same way I imagine that you approached an enemy skirmish. You prepare your defenses, you look for weaknesses to exploit, you fix on a strategy, and you never waver, you just steadfastly see the thing through. At whatever cost."

He winced. "That's not true. I care about your welfare and your reputation."

"I'm nothing but an obligation to you."

He took her hands in his. "Ana. I understand your misgivings. A beautiful young lady could do far better than a wounded, scarred man like me."

"That's not it." She shook her head impatiently, but something about the clasp of his hands was making her head spin and her thoughts scramble. "There's another thing: I'm still angry at the way you bribed Mr. Norwood to publish my novel."

"Your novel is excellent. Once it's in print, it will be up to the book to find its audience. It's going to be an instant success. You'll see. I'm fully confident in this matter."

"I wish I shared your confidence."

"You don't require me, or any reader, to tell you that your book is good. You must know it in your heart. Believe it."

She paused. This wasn't the way she'd envisioned their conversation going. She'd expected him to be his usual abrasive self, to bark orders and push her away. Then she would have been justified in leaving. Instead, he was encouraging her to believe in her writing. It was almost . . . sweet. A word she'd never thought of using to describe the duke.

"Even though I'm not the match you would have chosen," he continued, "I swear to you that you shall want for nothing, you shall finish dozens of novels and become a celebrated authoress. I will help you achieve your dreams, Ana."

"That's all well and good"—she attempted to keep the sternness in her voice, even though he was softening her resolve to leave—"but I would set some rules of engagement if we are to go through with this."

"Such as . . . ?"

"You can't be so silent all the time. You must promise to speak in fuller sentences and to allow me to know your thoughts from time to time. I don't even know what to call you. Am I to use Warburton, or Deckard, or do you want me to go around calling you Your Grace?"

"Dex. That's what my friends call me."

"I would also ask for your help in placing an advertisement in the papers, asking for information about my father. With a generous reward. Something to catch people's eye and increase my chance of finding him."

Was that pity in his eyes? "It will be done, I swear."

"And I want to know about your past, what you were like as a young boy, things like that."

"I was a right little imp. Anyone will tell you. I bossed my younger brother about and turned my nursemaid's hair gray."

"Did you always play with toy soldiers and dream of being a military commander?"

"You ask a lot of questions."

"You're a mystery for me to solve. The mystery of the duke who lost his smile. I want to know what you're thinking and feeling. What made you the way you are."

"Men don't talk about their childhoods or divulge their innermost feelings."

"That's a shame."

"We have unspoken communication."

"In other words, silence. Do you know that my father described you in his letters as a handsome, charismatic, and fearless commander?"

"I was those things, at least that's what everyone told me. I was coddled and flattered. It made me heedless and selfish." He stroked his fingers over the back of her hands, making her knees go weak.

"Ana, you think there might be glimmers left of the man I used to be somewhere buried inside me. I'm telling you that man wasn't worth saving. I thought I was invincible. I never considered that my actions might put others in danger. And the man I became after the war? Well, that man isn't handsome anymore, certainly not charming or charismatic. And as for your father, he was a better man by far. A true friend. We played cards together most evenings. Whist. Piquet, when we couldn't find enough players."

"And who won?"

"Mostly he did, Ana." He sighed. "It's not good for you to dwell so much on this mad hope that he's still alive."

"I keep him alive in my mind. It's what he did for me."

"What do you mean?"

"My mother died in childbirth, and he kept her alive for me by telling me memories, stories about her. I miss him so terribly. If only he were here. He would give me advice about my novel. We would share all the dear familiar jokes, laugh until we cried."

"I'm sorry, Ana." He touched her cheek, wiping away a tear.

Her name said in his deep, rough voice felt right, somehow.

"He was a wonderful man, a friend and a stalwart soldier. The world is darker for his loss. I know your hope for his survival springs from a pure and loving place. And I also know that he would have been very proud of the woman you've become—inquisitive, talented, bright."

She blinked. She was dangerously near to crying. Instead, she launched back into the subject of their marital bargain. "If we are to marry, you can't keep so many secrets from me. Everything about you is locked up in compartments, like that wardrobe in the forbidden room I'm not supposed to open. Everywhere I turn, more mysteries. I found a list you made, women's names. Kitty, Tessie, Janet, Laurel. Who are they?"

He dropped her hands, a shadow passing over his face. "Ana, you must let me keep certain parts of my life in the past. Please trust me, there is nothing in that room or written on that paper that is a threat to you."

She wanted to know his secrets. He couldn't give her that. But he could keep her safe. Make sure no man ever threatened her again. No woman tried to sell her body into servitude. He'd be her protector, her lover, her guardian. Pledge to guard her body, her spirit.

While keeping his heart locked tightly.

"Ana, I will attempt to fulfill your requirements for more communication, and less secrets moving forward. And, for my part, I pledge that this marriage will ensure your safety, nurture your writing ambition, and that you will not lack for pleasure."

"Pleasure . . ." She bit her lower lip. "Of the carnal variety."

"Just so. You'll be well-pleasured in our marital bed. If you're a good girl."

"What does that mean?"

"If you obey my rules, my commands." He cradled her cheek in one of his large hands. "Do you know where I always express myself eloquently?"

She shook her head, her breathing ragged.

"In the bedchamber. I'll give you instructions, encouragement. I'll tell you how beautiful you are, how much you please me." He closed the slight distance between them, leaning down to whisper in her ear. "And if you're naughty, I'll take you over my knee and spank you. And you'll like it. You'll beg me for more."

He moved his hands around to squeeze her bottom, bringing her hips flush against his hardness. With his hands still cupping her bottom, he kissed her deeply, expertly. Tasting her sweetness, reveling in the silken heat of her mouth, the soft sighs that escaped her lips. The way she twined her arms around his neck to pull him even closer.

This wasn't just the frissons . . . this was an all-out riot inside her body. Hot and cold at the same time, melting and languid and yet so exquisitely aware of every movement he made.

The way his tongue filled her mouth made unfamiliar muscles inside her clench and unclench.

So deliciously good. She wanted more. She lifted her lips and he complied, kissing her again, his hands roaming to her waist, gripping her tightly.

When the kiss ended, Ana felt dazed, as though she'd stared at the sun for too long. He released her gently, a serious look on his face.

"Our marriage will be full of physical pleasure, Ana. And friendship. We will be a team, nothing more. Nothing deeper than that. I am what and who I am for a reason. That won't change. Please don't expect any magical transformation, or a rake's redemption, like the ones you might write in your novels. There is no charming prince hiding behind these scars, just more scars, in layers all the way to my core. The sooner you accept this, the more content we will be."

Ana took in this uncharacteristically long speech, the blazing flush caused by his touch fading quickly. He obviously meant all he was saying—or thought he meant it. She wasn't sure which.

"And you can live like that? Never being truly intimate with anyone, never giving your heart or accepting someone else's heart in return?"

He gave a short laugh. "I have learned that hearts are given and accepted far too lightly for my taste. I'm better off without one, mine or someone else's."

So he had loved someone once, maybe. Perhaps he'd been ill-used. The thought was a kernel of comfort in the wash of confusion caused by his words. A broken heart was still a heart. And broken hearts could be mended.

His was well enough to show her kindness, to take care of her, to promise her the career of her dreams. To set her on horseback and ride straight into the maw of the ton with her, just to show her that there was strength in simply being oneself. This was a heart worth saving.

And save it she would.

Chapter Twenty

By the next evening Amsonia had, in her usual indomitable fashion, absorbed and reconciled herself to the situation. Now the only thing left was for them to return—she armed with a small sword she'd found in a pile of jeweled armor, the Dragon with his fire and claws.

Brandishing the blade, its emerald-studded hilt gleaming, she stood resolutely in front of Qavox. "Let us make haste back to Vyranthrall!" Amsonia cried. "My father needs me!"

Was there nothing that truly scared her? he wondered.

—*The Dragon and the Blue Star* by Analise Crewe

The first thing that went awry on the day of their wedding was easily explained. Ana, of course, had no time to have a special wedding dress made for herself, no lovely dollops of Belgian lace or exquisitely embroidered netting over champagne silk (these being integral elements of the Clovercote wedding costume she'd just designed).

She was to wear a simply cut gown of pale lemon-yellow silk, its only affectation a cunning border of seed pearl scallops around the bodice. Tessie dressed her hair in an equally simple style, drawing it upward into a Grecian top knot, letting her natural curls dictate the fall of the swoops on either side of her brow.

It was when Tessie attempted to insert the only fancy flourish she'd opted for, a tall spray of blossoms made out of silver wire and matching seed pearls, onto the top of said knot that the unraveling began. The tips of the ornament hadn't been properly finished, and the poor thing was no match for the vigorous thickness of Ana's curly hair. The seeds began to pour off the unfastened ends, lodging themselves in her bun and streaming down her jaw, a whole host of them losing themselves in her cleavage. She could feel them rolling around under her breasts, captured at last by the empire waist of the dress.

"There's no time!" she said, waving Tessie away as she attempted to loosen her dress. "They'll roll out eventually . . ." and off she went, shedding little dots of pearlescent white as she went.

The second thing that went wrong was slightly more ominous. She'd joined Dex in the drawing room, where McArdle and the curate were waiting in front of the giant trio of Palladian windows.

"Here are the contracts for you to sign," Dex said, handing her a pen. His face was unreadable, the lines of his jaw as terse as his words. She put nervous fingers to her mother's necklace and touched the matching ear drops quickly in succession, letting the familiar feel and familial connection soothe her rattled senses. Rain beat against the paned glass, the world outside a grim sea of gray and brown shapes, nearly impossible to distinguish.

She bent over the table and put quill to paper, feeling a pearl roll to the center of her chest and down toward her legs, and at that moment a large bird smashed into the window, gazed at them all with a stunned and protruding eye, then slid to the ground, trailing blood and feathers as it went.

"Good lord!" said McArdle.

"Heavens!" cried the curate.

"Bugger it all," muttered the duke. Ana closed her eyes, counted to ten, then continued signing the documents. The words swam before her eyes.

> *. . . which holy estate Christ adorned and beautified with his presence, and first miracle that he wrought . . .*

Some miracle, this! She glanced desperately toward the door. As if reading her thoughts, McArdle edged toward it, lodging himself firmly between her and any possibility of escape.

"Ana," Dex said, "I can't have you looking like I'm dragging you to the guillotine. Is this really such a devastating prospect for you?"

The curate's mouth dropped into a comical *O* of shock. Ana smiled despite herself. "It's only . . ." she began. How to explain? That she had seed pearls clicking around her undergarments, that she had always thought her wedding day might be one of light, joy, and romance?

"I had only just finished writing a wedding scene, did I tell you? A grand affair, Adora and Lord Fortescue's union. I'd jumped ahead to the end, because writing their wedding was ever so much more attractive than slogging through the impediments that tear them apart in the middle. The wedding wrote itself—a stately chapel, light flowing in through the stained glass, a host of good friends standing in attendance. There were glowing banns published in the papers, detailing the glory of their union. Rose petals sprinkled down the aisle. A wedding cake reaching almost to the ceiling, covered in candied fruits and topped with the sugared likenesses of Romeo and Juliet. I'd only *just* finished writing it, Dex." She wrinkled her brow at him, hoping he'd understand without any more guidance from her.

Dex looked at the red smudge running down the middle of the window and grimaced. "And this . . . suffers by comparison. Emphasis on 'suffer.'" She nodded, unable to contradict him.

"Never mind. I'm being a bit silly, the real world so seldom matches the written one. I do know that for every reason we spoke of, this marriage is the best course of action. I've been compromised, and we must marry quickly." She finished signing the marriage documents. "There. We may proceed, Your Grace."

The curate couldn't have looked more scandalized if they'd all been in their naturally born state of bareness. He grabbed the papers from them, eyes conveying a deep and abiding moral disappointment, and the ceremony commenced.

The third, fourth, and fifth things that went wrong were really just the icing on the nonexistent wedding cake. McArdle, having eaten his breakfast too quickly as a result of obsessively checking and rechecking the list of things he had to accomplish to facilitate the ceremony, emitted a belch when the curate beseeched anyone knowing of any impediments to their union, "Ye are to declare it!" Mortified, McArdle turned purple and snapped his mouth shut, keeping it that way for the rest of the day.

"Doesn't count as a real impediment, I wager," murmured the duke to Ana, and she caused further affront to the scandalized curate by giggling nervously.

The ring didn't fit. It simply wouldn't pass over her knuckle, which wasn't a large knuckle and shouldn't have presented such a problem. Dex glowered at the offending finger and left the plain gold band sitting awkwardly just at the joint. Which accounted for it slipping off her finger at the first possible opportunity and rolling far away, requiring an immediate cessation of the ceremony until such time as the reluctant ring could be found and forced over that same, equally reluctant knuckle.

By the sixth disaster, Ana had mentally thrown her hands up and cast herself upon the mercies of the universe. Whatever cosmic force was attempting to give them pause was overplaying its hand; she felt almost giddy with the horror and hilarity of it all. They were almost done with it when the chimney backed up, and the fireplace began to choke out thick black clouds into the room. Coughing prodigiously, Ana ran to the side windows to push them open and thought longingly of the Clovercote nuptials. So neat, so sweet, and so free of smoke!

"Dex," Ana couldn't help croaking, lungs filling with smoke. "Do you think the universe is attempting to tell us something?"

"Too late now," he said grimly. "We're married, and there's nothing the universe can do about that."

Chapter Twenty-One

"Now is the time to sleep, Princess. You need your rest. Tomorrow I will take you to someone who can help you. There is a faery queen known as Gaethryn, whose magic can match that of your uncle the Red Wizard."

"You refuse to help yourself? Aren't dragons supposed to be bloodthirsty? We must strike! Together we can avenge my father!" There was no response. She was saddled with a very poor excuse for a dragon, she fumed to herself.

He responded by extending one wing, and gently, inexorably, drawing her into the fold of his body.

—*The Dragon and the Blue Star* by Analise Crewe

Dex watched Ana closely as they exited the carriage in front of the crouching stone beast of Drakefell Castle. She'd been strangely quiet during the journey. At first he'd been glad of the silence, then he'd begun to wonder what was wrong with her. Was she ill? Or just having pangs of remorse for marrying him, discomfited by the mishaps and ill portents. Probably the latter.

When he helped her down, she felt so fragile and light in his grasp. He made a flourishing bow. "Your new house, milady."

"House?" Her eyes widened in what looked like abject terror. "I don't see a house. This is a fortress. There's a portcullis. A moat with a drawbridge. Battlements."

"Those are the usual elements of a castle."

Her eyes shone with what looked like tears. Was she about to weep in front of the long line of staff assembled in front of the house with military precision? He sincerely hoped not. They kept their gazes pointed forward, but were obviously straining to catch a glimpse of their new mistress. It wouldn't be right to have that first impression be one of weakness.

"Ana. Are you all right? Do you need a moment before we greet the staff?"

"I . . ." She clutched her hands together at her throat, staring up at the time-darkened stone battlements.

She hated it. She was sorry she married him. She was going to run away the first chance she got. He shouldn't have talked her into this marriage.

"It's . . ." She took a shaky breath. "It's . . . absolutely magical! Like something from a fairy tale." A delighted smile played over her lips. "Can't you just imagine Qavox the dragon crouching there?" She pointed up at the high walls surrounding the castle. "I can see him launching off the wall, wings spread wide, blocking the sun over the village below."

"Ah . . ." Dex attempted to picture such a fanciful occurrence with no luck. "I'm told during one siege the castle employed the use of a trebuchet, so there have been large projectiles launched from the walls."

"Is that right? I'll wager this castle has many tales to tell. I want to know all of them! I never in my wildest dreams imagined that

I'd be living in something as grand, as wild and magical as this castle."

"Then you like it?"

"Like it? I love it!" Late afternoon sunshine found the shades of apricot in her hair as she danced to the carriage where her maid was disembarking. "Tessie! Tessie, we're going to live in a castle!"

"Yes, Your Grace. It's majestic."

"Don't be too excited," Dex said as the two women approached. "It's terribly drafty and the towers have bats."

"Ooh. Bats!" Ana clapped her hands. "Do the stairs creak most mysteriously? Are there suits of armor that move to inexplicable new locations during the dead of night?"

Dex shook his head. "Not that I've observed. But there are cracks in the walls that let in vast amounts of icy wind. You may prefer to live in London after experiencing a winter here."

"I shan't. I have a feeling that this castle and I are going to become fast friends. When I write the sequel to *The Dragon and the Blue Star*, I'll set it in just such a castle. In fact, the castle will be a character in the novel."

Dex smiled despite the stretching pain of the scars on his cheeks. He'd been worried that she would hate the castle and here she was already making it a character in a future novel. She constantly surprised and disarmed him.

She turned to him with shining eyes. "Are you smiling?"

"Never."

"I think you were smiling. Come, my duke, show me my new abode." She took his hand and led him forward.

McArdle, who had reached the castle ahead of them, glanced askance at the slip of a girl who had brought such merry chaos to the house in London. He made the introductions and Ana had a kind word for each member of the staff, from Mrs. Hedges, the jolly housekeeper, to the youngest scullery maid.

It was too much. She was too much. He was in grave danger of being charmed out of his customary malaise.

"I must visit my ailing steward," he said gruffly as they entered the great hall. "I'll see you for a light supper later this evening."

As the duke strode back out the door without a backward glance, only one thought ricocheted round Ana's mind: and after supper . . . the wedding night.

They'd slept in separate rooms in the inn on the journey from London to Surrey. Travel-weary, Ana had been only too happy to snuggle up on a comfortable bed and fall into an immediate slumber. But tonight . . . tonight there would be no peaceful slumber.

Tonight she faced the dragon in his castle. He might eat her whole.

The castle staff had stood stiffly, awaiting his inspection, like the ranks of an army. But she hadn't detected any fear on their faces. Rather, she'd seen admiration, respect. There was something compelling about him. Warburton against the world. A man who needed no one, showed no weakness, a man who was comfortable with silence and needed no society except his horses. How would she fit into his world?

She wanted to crack that stern facade, wanted to see him smile, or show some sign of softness. Everyone jumped to his orders. Well, she wouldn't give him the satisfaction. He'd known he was marrying a redheaded spitfire. She'd show him that he couldn't treat her like a foot soldier. She'd find a way under his skin, she'd find the cracks in his defenses, like the cracks in the stone castle walls.

"Aren't you the prettiest wisp of a thing?" a maid asked, bustling into Ana's cavernous new bedchamber and curtsying.

"Doesn't have any meat on her bones," another maid added, following close behind. They looked like twins wearing identical uniforms.

"You're . . . Cloris and Agnes, are you not?" She'd tried to make a mental association with each name she'd learned today. Cloris had pale green eyes, matching the color her name described, which was convenient. Agnes had a dour expression and deeply etched frown lines, which Ana had decided to remember by thinking she must be agonizing over some slight from her past.

"Bless you, what a memory," Cloris said, clapping her hands with a gleeful smile.

"Lucky guess, I'm sure," Agnes said.

"Are you sisters?"

"We are," they spoke in unison.

"I'm one year older," said Agnes heavily, as though the year she'd waited for her sister to be born had been interminable. She wore her thick chestnut hair pulled back and fastened severely at the nape of her neck, while her cheerful sister wore hers in a coronet of braids with tendrils framing her face.

"You've met my lady's maid, Tessie?" Ana asked, as Tessie entered the room.

"Pleased to meet you," the sisters said in unison.

"Thank you, kindly." Tessie seemed a little awed by the two older maids. She ducked her head shyly. "I'm not really a lady's maid."

"You are," Ana said.

"The truth will out," Tessie insisted. "I was a scullery maid before milady, that is Her Grace, promoted me."

"You don't say," Agnes said with a baleful expression.

"You're doing a wonderful job," Ana enthused. Tessie had been her only friend at the London townhouse when she'd arrived and the two of them had grown close.

"We've been waiting for this day ever so long. A bride at Drakefell Castle!" Cloris wiped at her eyes with her apron. "It makes me weep tears of joy. This castle has been silent and lonely for far too long."

"Don't be maudlin, Cloris, we've much work left to do," Agnes said grimly.

"Do you think I might be assigned a smaller chamber?" Ana asked. "I might get lost in this cathedral of a room."

"Oh no, this is your chamber, Your Grace, it adjoins that of His Grace. When it's time, he'll visit you here tonight." Cloris pointed and spoke in hushed tones. "Through those doors."

Ana studied the wooden doors, carved with twining vines. She said it so matter-of-factly but Ana's imagination had run wild. Dex, opening the doors, wearing nothing but his black silk dressing gown that could be opened with one swift tug on the sash . . .

She gulped. "I . . . I hope I shall be ready."

"Never you worry, Your Grace, we'll prepare you, won't we, Agnes? We'll give you a nice hot bath to wash the travel grime away."

Tessie began unpacking Ana's clothing while Cloris and Agnes undressed Ana in preparation for her bath, which was being poured into an enormous bathing tub by a brigade of maids.

"Ow, what was that?" Ana twisted around. It felt as though someone had pinched her.

"Just me, Your Grace." Cloris grinned. "Making sure you're real. We've been longing for the duke to take a wife for so long, it feels like a dream."

"Cloris!" Agnes remonstrated. "Behave yourself."

"We didn't think you'd be so young, though," Cloris said, with a note of uncertainty.

Agnes helped Ana into a green silk dressing gown and tied the sash, a bit too tightly. "Is she up to the task, I wonder?" she muttered.

"Which task?" Ana asked.

"Why, winning the duke's heart and restoring his good humor!" said Cloris. "He's entirely too grave and taciturn. Ever since he came back from the war, he thunders around the countryside dressed all in black, frightening ladies and children alike with that scarred visage and his glowering looks."

Ana nearly tripped over the hem of her overlong dressing gown as she walked with the maids toward the tub. "Seems a tall order."

"I'll say," Agnes agreed.

"Don't you worry, Your Grace. We'll help you." Cloris untied her sash, slipped off the robe, and both sisters helped Ana into the tub.

She sank into the steaming water gratefully. "This smells divine."

"We scented it with orange flowers and oil of roses. After I wash your hair, I'll scent you with the oil as well. We're going to make you delectable and irresistible, never you fear."

"He's made it very clear that this is a marriage of convenience."

"And yet we all remarked on the way he looked at you so tenderly when he handed you down from the carriage. Wouldn't let anyone else touch your hand, oh no," Cloris said.

"And you . . ." Agnes appraised her shrewdly. "You might already be in love with him. I saw the light in your eyes, as well."

Ana ducked her head under the water. She did have strong feelings for Dex. There was attraction, frustration, curiosity . . . she was always so on edge around him, her emotions like a tightly wound ball of yarn. This talk of falling in love felt dangerous, as though someone had begun to tug at her heartstrings, and she might unravel completely. How could she love him when he withheld himself from her? He wouldn't give her what she craved, and so she craved it even more.

When she emerged, Cloris began washing her hair. It felt lovely to have strong fingers massaging her scalp, releasing the tension born of travel and these tangled thoughts. "I don't think he wants to be won. He's very set in his ways, isn't he? I've only known him a short time but I can already tell that he's as immovable as the stone walls of this castle."

"You shall chip away at his fortress with smiles and laughter and soft touches," Cloris said.

"Or she'll go mad, like so many of the ladies who lived in this cold heap of stones."

"Agnes! Now who's misbehaving? Please forgive our frankness, Your Grace. We've been so long without society as the duke never invites anyone to the castle."

"No one? Not even a dinner party every now and then?"

"Not even his friends from London visit us. And certainly, no family. His brother so close and all, and they're estranged."

"It's very sad to have family living close by and to have no contact with them."

"I know," Cloris said with a sigh. "But you'll change all that, I have a very good feeling."

"Perhaps," Ana said softly, "he's buried himself too deeply."

Cloris continued her gentle ministrations. "You'll find a way, dear lady. You must."

It wasn't very subtle. His staff were obviously delighted by the fact that he'd brought a wife to the castle. They wanted it to be a love match. They were hoping she would transform him. They served the meal with foolish grins on their faces, conspiring to make this a romantic occasion.

It wasn't a romantic occasion. This was a convenient arrangement to save her reputation. Nothing more.

Ana was seated far away across the long dining room table, though her scent wafted toward him, like rain-soaked roses and meadowgrass. There was about her some subtle change that he couldn't place.

"Why do you look different?" he asked, tilting his head.

She took a bite of pheasant. "Because Cloris and Agnes spent fully two hours bathing me in rose petals, drying my hair by the fire, arranging it into this elaborate style, and choosing this gauzy gown for your pleasure, Your Grace."

First he pictured her naked, steam rising up around her as she idly trailed a hand through the water, trapping a rose petal with one finger and bringing it first to her lips, then trailing it down her chin, her neck, and between her breasts.

Then he noticed the mocking way she'd said *Your Grace*.

"I bid you call me Dex." He set down his fork. "Is something the matter?"

"Well." She blew the word out on an exasperated gust of air.

"We have been sitting at this monstrosity of a dining table for half an hour and you have not said more than ten words to me! Didn't we make an agreement?"

"Oh. That." He'd completely forgotten. He'd been too busy licking rose petals off her naked flesh in his imagination. "Yes, of course. I promised to speak in fuller sentences. Very well. What are your first impressions of the castle?"

"My first impression is that the castle is much like its owner . . . gloomy and guarding untold secrets."

"I thought you said it was magical."

"It is magical, but to find the magic, one must unlock its secrets."

"I'm told there is a network of tunnels beneath the castle and within the nearby cliffs that served as barracks for armies during invasions. There's a hedge maze so complicated that it claimed the life of one of the former dukes when he entered it inebriated and couldn't find his way back out. The local farmers often turn up bits and pieces of history, such as pottery and coins believed to be from sometime between the fifth and seventh centuries. Some of the armor and weaponry hanging on the walls in the great hall date back to William the Conquerer. There. That was at least six sentences in quick succession."

"I call that a history lesson."

"You didn't specify what I was to speak about."

"I'd like to talk about the war. My father wrote and said that the men admired you and they were willing to keep going, to keep fighting because of you."

Dex gripped his wine glass, willing her to stop talking.

"Did I say something wrong? I meant it as a compliment."

"They followed me. And they died." *Full sentences*. "I don't give a damn about my own wounds, the scars on my body. What kills me is that I can't bring them back. Your father, the other men from my company, their names are a litany that keeps me up at night. I led them into death."

"For your country. For peace."

"War can't be easily justified, I've come to understand. When you're inside a war, there is no philosophy, no stirring patriotic music, no making sense of any of it. Flesh ripped apart by mortar and bullets. Blood flowing like water. Suffering. Pain. Lives ended, snuffed out like candles. Young lads. I've come to believe that this bloodlust, this desire for power, for dominion over man, over cities and countries, is wrong. The men who want to own, to subjugate, to benefit from the pain of others—those men are demons, they are not to be deified or looked up to. The shiny gold medals and the crisp uniform don't tell the whole story. They only tell the acceptable part of the story that people find palatable. Gloss it over, give it a good shine. Sometimes I wish I had died in your father's place."

"Don't say that," she said in an anguished tone that sliced through the fog that had descended in his mind.

"I apologize. I shouldn't speak of such dark things. It's your wedding night. There should be . . ." Tenderness. Love. Laughter. He had none of those things to give her. "Wine."

He motioned for a footman to fill her wine glass. He resumed eating, washing the excellent meal down with a good French wine from the cellars. He was happy to see that she ate heartily as well, though she hadn't touched the wine yet.

"You don't care for wine?"

"I only like brandy."

"At least try a few sips."

She sipped delicately, her expression changing. "This is actually quite delicious."

"Isn't it? A good wine paired with the right meal is a pleasure not to be missed."

Other pleasures not to be missed: watching Ana smile as she tasted his excellent wine for the first time. The candlelight wavering over her oval face, teasing the green from her eyes. The way her tongue darted out to capture an errant drop of wine.

He wanted to kiss those plump lips of hers. Taste her like wine.

He wanted to learn the shape of her with his tongue. Was her navel a swirling indentation or a concave pearl? He'd rip the pale green silk of her gown instead of unbuttoning it. Then he'd slide it down, slipping over her upper arms, the fabric caught now, held up only by her nipples.

He'd take the silk in his fingers, brush it over her nipples, watch a flush rise in her cheeks, her breathing rapid, watch the languor in her eyes as she watched him watching her.

Then he would tongue her through the silk, shape her nipples with his lips, wet the silk, wanting to prolong the pleasure of seeing her for the first time, seeing her wearing nothing but a smile. For he would make her smile. He would make her laugh. He would make her sigh and moan with pleasure. He imagined these gentle, breathless, teasing explorations.

"What are you thinking about?" she asked. "You promised to let me know your thoughts."

"I'm thinking about what I'm going to do to you tonight," he said roughly, unable to keep the raw, pulsing need out of his voice.

Pink rose in her cheeks and her eyes went wide. "Oh." She took a big gulp of wine.

"Shall I elaborate?"

"No," she squeaked, adorably flustered.

"You don't want to know my thoughts?"

"I . . ." She glanced at the footmen standing stiffly along the wall. "It's not appropriate dinner conversation."

"Then let's finish this meal quickly and I'll show you what I was thinking instead of telling you. Dessert," he called.

The footmen jumped to attention, racing for the kitchens.

"Better yet, let's have dessert delivered to your room," Dex said. He had no appetite for anything other than Ana.

"Come." He threw his serviette down on the table and rose, holding out his hand. "It's time."

Chapter Twenty-Two

When the storm of her anger had passed, she realized she was curled within the length of Qavox's forearm. It was hard, and warm, like the slate hearth under a winter's fire. She could feel the coiled strength of it beneath her own soft flesh. She lay still, reveling in this new sensation of being utterly helpless, yet totally protected from the outside world.

"Don't think anymore, Princess," he whispered, the reverberations echoing and reechoing through her body. "Plenty of time for that tomorrow . . ."

—*The Dragon and the Blue Star* by Analise Crewe

Dex led Ana into her bedchamber and extinguished the candles the servants had lit on the bedside tables.

"Here are the rules. Tonight is about you discovering the pleasure your body is capable of. I'll do nothing you don't explicitly consent to. If I give you an order that you don't wish to comply with, simply refuse. I will honor your wishes. Though I believe you'll find you want to obey. You may not touch me unless given express permission."

"I can't touch you?"

"Not yet. Another rule: we never spend the night together." He couldn't risk it. When he had nightmares about the war, he thrashed about, sometimes even waking in a cold sweat, his fists bruised from punching the headboard. He never wanted to hurt her.

"So many rules."

"It's the way it must be. Now stand there, by the fire, and let me look at you."

She walked to the fireplace and stared at him defiantly. "Is this precisely the right spot?"

"Stand with your hands at your side and your feet slightly apart."

She was a vision of sensuality. The wine had given her cheeks a healthy glow. Her freckles stood out like the kiss of bee pollen on a rose. The gown rippled like sea foam over her body. He sipped from a tumbler of brandy as he viewed her from every angle, knowing that the heat of his gaze would increase her anticipation.

He walked toward her, stopping an arm's length away. He caught the end of the silk sash tied about her waist between his thumb and forefinger, stroking the soft silk. Her gaze dropped, watching the movement, her mouth unconsciously parting.

"Now I'm going to untie your sash and use it to secure your wrists to remind you that you can't touch me. I won't bind you too tightly. You'll be able to slip free should you so choose. But I don't think you will. There's a freedom that comes with surrendering control. If you're good, and you allow me to tie you, and you don't attempt to touch me, I'll reward you."

When her wrists were tied behind her back, he left one of his hands on the silk bow, taking a lingering satisfaction in the way the position thrust her breasts forward.

Her breathing was shallow and erratic, her pupils dilated. She was under his spell.

“God, you’re beautiful, Ana,” he whispered in her ear. He tugged on the silk tie and her wrists lifted farther. “I’m going to devour you. I’m going to make you scream my name. You’re going to lose yourself and demand to touch me and then I’ll have to take you over my knee and spank you for such naughty behavior.”

“S-spank me?” she said breathily.

He ran his free hand over the contours of her lush bottom. “Yes. You need discipline in the worst way.” He showed her what he meant by slapping one bum cheek lightly.

“Oh,” she cried softly.

Keeping hold of her wrist tie, he cupped her bottom, bringing her flush against his erection. She glanced down at where their bodies met, wriggling softly against him, her thighs parting.

“Do you feel that? That’s what you’ve done to me. I was hard all through dinner watching you eat, watching you drink that wine. I was thinking about ravishing you. I wanted to tousle that careful coiffure.” He removed the silk bandeau holding up her hair and waves of red gold tumbled over her shoulders.

“I imagined ripping your gown.” He caught the silk in both hands and ripped it easily, exposing her small, perfect breasts. “Most of all I wanted to taste you.”

He lowered his head and sucked on each of her nipples in turn, flicking them with his tongue until they were hard peaks and she was panting, her head thrown back, knees buckling. In one swift movement he caught her up into his arms and carried her to the bed. Removing her gown, he made short work of her petticoats, stays, and shift, leaving only her white stockings and pale green garters.

He placed her bound wrists over her head. She kept her thighs clenched tightly.

"Open your legs," he commanded.

THE WAY HE ordered her about gave her the frissons. Up and down her spine. Between her shoulder blades. Inside her belly. Between her thighs.

He'd told her that he spoke freely in the bedchamber, but she hadn't truly believed him, hadn't imagined this steady stream of commands and praise. She'd complied thus far, but really . . . exposing herself on top of the bedcovers . . . it was too much.

She kept her thighs closed. "Mightn't I go beneath the sheets?"

"I want to see you. It's half the pleasure for me. Looking at you, watching you obey my commands. Open your thighs, Ana. Show yourself to me."

She closed her eyes tightly, as if that would make her feel less exposed, and inched her thighs apart.

"Good. Now wider." She heard his breathing grow heavier, sensuality lowering his voice to a husky growl. "Wider.

"Fuck. Ana."

Those filthy words he used. She hadn't expected that. The low growl in his throat as his fingers traced the line of her inner thighs. She peeped through her eyelashes and he was staring intently at her body. He brushed his thumb over a place that made her hips buck.

"Easy, Ana. I'm not going to hurt you. Quite the opposite." She closed her eyes again, collapsing against the pillows.

She felt the bed move as he lowered his weight onto it, felt his huge hands slide underneath her bottom to lift her for his . . . what was that wet sensation? She opened her eyes. His head was between her thighs. He was . . . licking her. Good God. It was so unexpected and at first it felt so strange that she cried out. He stilled, lifting his head. "You don't like it?"

"It's so strange. I don't know if I like it or not."

"Relax into it. Try not to think too hard. I'll stop if you don't like it, but give it a chance."

"All right," she said shakily. She lay back and he resumed his position. He applied a gentle, soft pressure with his tongue in the same way he'd kissed her lips in the library. After a few moments it began to feel good. Then it began to feel exquisite.

She shifted her hips, wanting him to move a fraction to the right. He complied, listening to her body's demands. "Oh . . . yes, there."

Dex was silent once more, this time because his mouth was occupied with the business of bringing her bliss. A melting, pleasurable sensation began undulating inside her.

For the first time in her life Ana couldn't find words to describe what was happening. She didn't even want to imagine an alternate version of this moment. Her imagination completely shut down. She was a body, made of hair, skin, bones, sinew, blood. A body filled with one objective: pleasure.

Her abdomen shook and her inner thigh muscles clenched. Her face flushed with heat and her breasts felt heavy and sensitive. He took little breaks every now and then, stopping for a moment. When she lifted her hips, he resumed. In that way she knew that she controlled his movements. Even though her wrists were tied over her head, she was in control.

"I think . . . I think I'm going to . . ."

His tongue moved faster, just in the right location, and her focus was on the place beneath his tongue that pulsed with need. Only a few moments more . . . there . . .

"Yes," she cried. "Yes, yes."

When the pleasure had ebbed and he'd moved up her body to rest next to her, lazily tracing circles on her belly with his fingers, she released a long sigh. "That was starry," she said. "Tiny little white stars, sparkling through my body."

He untied her wrists, moving her hands to her belly. "The next one will be like the sun, burning through you swiftly."

He slid down her body, intent on his mission to make her his.

"Wait—"

"You don't want another climax?"

"I want to see you. You still have your clothing on."

"Easily remedied." He jumped off the bed and shrugged out of his coat. He unknotted his cravat with one brutal tug that for some reason made the waves of pleasure resume in her belly. She noticed that he kept the scarred side of his face turned away from her while he undressed. His profile was all powerful lines drawn with a bold hand. His dark chestnut hair was wavy, and it gleamed in the firelight. His eyes were the cold color of frost on steel.

He removed his shirt and stood with his arms at his sides.

"Are all of those bulging muscles from bareknuckle boxing?"

"Among other rugged pursuits. I like to chop my own firewood. Build my own carriages."

When he stepped out of his trousers and smallclothes, she gaped at what had been revealed. Thick thighs, as big around as tree trunks, and between them . . . "Um . . . I think I've changed my mind about the consummation. I don't want to marry you, after all."

"It's a little late for that." He stood proudly, hands on his narrow hips, thick thighs and long limbs planted on the carpet, his enormous, erect male member pointed directly at her.

"This will never work."

His lips quirked. "It will work. Trust me. But not yet. I don't think you've achieved the heights that you're capable of."

He lay down on the bed next to her. "Roll over so that you are face down."

Every time she obeyed one of his commands, Dex experienced a bone-deep thrill. His bride was so beautiful. She trusted him enough to roll over and bury her face in the pillow, her body quivering slightly.

He'd reward that trust, that sweet compliance.

He moved into position over her, parting her legs slightly to allow his cock to slot into place inside the soft, smooth heat of her thighs.

She tensed beneath him.

"I'm not going to take you, yet. This is a position that will give you pleasure."

She made a soft sound, a moan, of protest? But this was his night, his rules. He wouldn't take her, not yet. She turned her head to the side, her curly red hair like fire licking the white pillowcase.

He slid between her thighs and when he found the wetness lubricating his way he groaned, kissing her cheek, the back of her neck, while he moved slowly, angling upward to stroke over her core.

She understood the aim soon enough, moving with him, finding her pleasure.

Damn. It was all he could do to hold himself in check. He longed to bury his cock in her to the hilt but not before she orgasmed again. Not until she cried out his name and begged him to take her.

"Please." She rubbed against him, angling her hips up so that he nearly slipped inside her.

"Not yet." He held her wrists against the bed, controlling their movements. She whimpered, but complied, going still under him. He let go of one of her wrists and moved his hand beneath her, using his fingers and his cock to pleasure her.

She began to shudder, her breathing coming in gasps. She was close now.

"Come for me, Ana. I know you can do it."

"I . . . can't," she moaned.

"You can. Don't try so hard. Let yourself float into it."

"Oh . . . Dex. That feels so good."

The sound of her voice speaking his name made his heart stop for a few beats.

Finally, he felt her body tense and then loosen as she moaned her release. He continued stroking her with whisper-soft movements, drawing the final little twitches and gasps from her until she lay still, panting. "You're my good girl," he whispered in her ear.

He rolled her over, notching himself into position.

She stiffened, her whole body tensing.

"It may hurt," he said. "I'll go slowly." He eased into her a mere inch.

She gasped, cried out with pain.

He stopped, holding himself in check.

"Why did you stop?" she asked, her voice sounding strained.

He stared into her eyes. They were wide, frightened.

"Just get it over with."

He rolled off of her. Those weren't the words he wanted to hear.

Take me, Dex. I'm yours.

Those were the right words. And he could wait to consummate this marriage until he heard them.

"Is something wrong?" she asked softly.

"It's late. You've had your lessons in pleasure for the evening. I'll leave you now."

He grabbed his clothes and boots and left her there.

His bed was cold. Ana-less.

Sleep, when it finally came, was filled with dreams of flame-licked hair, pleasure-hazed green eyes, and his name spoken on a breathy moan.

Chapter Twenty-Three

She kneeled in awe at Gaethryn's feet, which hovered above the mossy banks and twinkled in the darkness.

"Amsonia. A name that means Blue Star. Come closer, my dear. I want to look at you."

Though she was struck nearly dumb by the Faery Queen's starry beauty and frightened by her protective cadre of unicorn guards, it was imperative that she receive an answer to the burning question at hand. She crept closer.

"O my queen! However does one turn a dragon to one's bidding?"

—*The Dragon and the Blue Star* by Analise Crewe

Ana awoke in her bed. Alone. He'd said he'd never spend the night with her, that it was against the rules.

She'd work on that—find a way to make him stay. She'd just have to make him so exhausted that he fell asleep. Her whole body hummed with aftershocks of pleasure. They hadn't consummated the marriage, but surely they'd done everything else. Or at least he'd done everything else to her. She hadn't been allowed to touch him.

Why hadn't he consummated the marriage last night? She'd gotten the impression that his experience had been less pleasurable than hers, in terms of . . . what had he called it? Climax. She'd had several . . . he'd had none.

He held himself so firmly in check. Preferring to always be in control. He was a wounded warrior, wrapped up in his codes of honor, wearing his rules like a badge, his silence like a shield. Giving orders instead of conversing, as if he were still on the battlefield. Perhaps he was, in his mind. Maybe he'd never left his position as cavalry commander.

All the rules he'd made—she couldn't touch him, he visited her only in darkness, he would never sleep the night with her in her bed.

She had agreed to the terms of this marriage of convenience. She had agreed that it wasn't a love match. He had pretended to be her invented fiancé to save her reputation and gain her the publishing contract she'd wanted for so long. And she'd agreed to attempt to give him an heir.

She wasn't a sophisticated, beautiful society lady born and bred to be his duchess. She was unpolished, brash of speech, all clashing freckles and red hair. She never moderated her speech. She wasn't the least bit diplomatic. She should be hosting balls and foreign dignitaries and being a duchess. She should be grateful that he wasn't demanding she be someone she wasn't. She was luckier than many.

And yet . . . the love matches. The true love matches. His friends the Duke and Duchess of Osborne—Dalton and Thea. The way they smiled at each other, the way they argued with such laughing familiarity.

His rules were a challenge flag thrown down. And she was not one to back down from a challenge.

"Good morning, Your Grace," Tessie said, pulling the bed-curtains aside.

"I told you not to call me that," Ana said with a yawn. "I've never been graceful in my life. You called me Ana in London, please continue to do so here."

"I'll try to remember, Your . . . Ana. I suppose it's the castle, so grand a setting! I can hardly believe we're here. And how are you this morning?" Her question was laced with other questions, about how she'd fared during the wedding night, about why the duke wasn't still in her bed.

"I could use some chocolate."

"It's a good thing I brought a pot with me then." She helped Ana out of bed and into a silk robe and cozy slippers.

Ana sipped the chocolate, sweetened with sugar and frothy with milk, remembering how she'd used to think that drinking chocolate must be one of the most satisfying pleasures available to a girl.

Now she knew otherwise. It was still delicious . . . but it paled in comparison to the secrets she'd learned last night. Some things in life were actually better than chocolate.

"Warburton knows the man who makes this chocolate, did you know that, Tessie? We could even tour his factory together."

"Could we swim in a pool made of chocolate?"

"I can imagine us swimming around with our mouths open like fishes . . ."

They both giggled, picturing the scene. Then Tessie sobered. "He shouldn't have left you alone on the morning after your wedding night."

"He's very busy, though. Off riding the estate, in the absence of his steward."

"Of course he is, I'm sorry, it wasn't my place to comment."

"I'll stay busy, too. Mrs. Hedges is giving me a tour of the kitchens. Mustn't start off on the wrong foot with the staff."

"They are all disposed to be kindly toward you. I think the staff view you as their best hope of restoring His Grace to his former self. He was greatly changed during the war."

"Yes, Cloris and Agnes mentioned as much. How are you getting on with them and the other staff?"

Tessie dimpled involuntarily into her cup of chocolate. "There's one footman that I find rather agreeable."

"Tessie! Do you have an amour already?"

"Not yet, it's so soon. We hardly know each other. But when his eyes fall on me—oh! It's thrilling."

"Which one? Tom? Or the other young handsome one . . . what was his name?"

"George. George Armstrong," she said dreamily. "Isn't that a wonderful name? Armstrong—so powerful!"

Ana laughed. "Most definitely."

"He's a local lad, born not far from the castle. He's been working here for a few years. He's promised to take me under his wing, show me the ropes."

"I'm sure he has. Just be careful, Tessie. Make sure he's a good and honest fellow."

"I have a feeling about him. You just know, don't you? He's not like that Tom, who knows he's handsome and uses it to tease all the maids and put them in a flurry. My George is modest and hardworking."

"'My George,' is it?"

Tessie's smile widened. "I shouldn't put the cart before the horse, eh? It's only been one day. But Ana, just think! If we were to marry, I'd be Theresa Armstrong. No more Tessie Alcox."

"Do you mind your family name so very much?" teased Ana, enjoying this window into her friend's life.

"Oh, I loved my family, of course I did!" Tessie said reproachfully. "I miss them every day. But you can't imagine how much I was teased by those vile village louts growing up! 'Tessie Alcox, will you test all our—'" She blushed. "You can imagine the rest."

Ana laughed in sympathy. "Children can be cruel, boys disgustingly so."

Tessie took her leave, and Ana was left alone with her thoughts and the pot of rapidly cooling chocolate. Theresa Alcox. The name had lodged itself in her mind. She'd never known Tessie's surname before. *Theresa Alcox*. Something about it nudged her, not hard enough to dislodge any particular memory, just enough to annoy. She shook her head. What she needed was fresh air and physical activity that was not accomplished in bed.

"I think I'll take a walk around the grounds after my tour of the kitchens," she announced to Cloris and Agnes, as they helped her into a sage green muslin day dress.

"Very good, Your Grace," Cloris replied. "We'll have your cloak and bonnet readied."

The late autumn breeze was blissfully brisk and bracing. Ana breathed deeply, filling her lungs. Her bonnet, gloves, and thick cashmere shawl kept her warm enough.

He'd left her alone all day, after doing those things to her.

She shivered, remembering the things he'd said to her, the things she'd done willingly, asking for more. Why couldn't they lie abed together of a morning? Perhaps eat breakfast together in bed from a tray. Honeymooning couples did that sort of thing, did they not?

To stave off the loneliness seeping into her mind, she'd asked Cloris and Agnes along. They flanked her in their great black bonnets like two kindly crows, answering her questions and matching her pace.

The grounds were gorgeous, well-kept and pristinely ordered. She'd expected nothing less of the duke's estate. From the edge of its orchards on the farthest side, the hill sloped downward toward a peaceful-looking valley. In the distance, atop a pleasant purple field of heather, there was a comfortable-looking estate, not terribly large but perfectly situated, with attractive grounds and a river snaking along one side.

"Who are our neighbors in the valley?" she asked.

"Why, that's the duke's brother Rupert, it is!" they responded, in almost perfect unison. "But we never see him, there's no love lost between the two," Cloris added. The women shot stern looks at each other, a tacit agreement to speak no further hanging in the air.

"How terrible. What was their falling out regarding?"

"They have their reasons and are right stubborn about reinforcing them, as men always are! But it's none of our affair, really."

"*He's* our affair!"

"Yes, but *his* affairs are *his own*." They nodded wisely on either side of Ana.

"Does the duke ever host visitors here?"

"Never," Cloris replied. "Not even his closest friends from London. That's why you could have knocked me over with a feather when I saw you emerge from that carriage. A sweet young thing like you. He'd sworn never to marry until he absolutely had to. Swore it up and down. And now here you are. You'll bring life to this gloomy old castle. Life and love and . . ."

The two sisters glanced at each other.

"Babies," Agnes finished her sister's sentence.

"Yes, adorable sweet fat cooing babies," Cloris enthused. "We want babies to cuddle and babies to sing to, and babies to rock in the cradle."

"Now, let's not get ahead of ourselves," Agnes warned.

"When the duke was a little lad, he had such a ready laugh. Now he rarely even smiles. That's why we're so happy that you're here. Just look at you. You can't go ten minutes without smiling. You're determined to be joyful and that's just what he needs."

"He'll probably leave me here and return to London," Ana said. "Do you know what he does there? I was unable to ascertain his whereabouts most of the time. I did visit his club, however, and observed him bareknuckle boxing."

"Then you know as much as we do, dearie," said Cloris. "He boxes, he trains horses, repairs and builds carriages, that sort of thing."

Ana considered these manly pursuits. A dead end. She thought of another dead end she'd encountered in unraveling the mystery of the duke. "Does the duke know anyone named Janet? Or Laurel? Or Kitty? Have you ever heard him mention anyone by those names?"

"Can't say as we have, Your Grace," Cloris said. Agnes clucked in agreement.

So much for the list of names. Who the devil were these women? Ana had thought about them enough to give them personalities, like characters in one of her books. Kitty was a coquette, Laurel was a busybody. Janet was the worst, a real hard-headed tyrant, ordering an uncharacteristically docile Dex about the bedchamber.

She had to get a handle on her imagination. Thinking about Dex in another woman's bed, giving her those whispered commands, made her stomach lurch. He'd explicitly told her to forget about the list of names, warning that it held no meaning that concerned her.

After a stretch of silence, the maids stopped alongside her and bobbed curtsies. "We must be running along, Your Grace, with your permission," said Agnes.

"We're delivering baskets of food and sundries to the widow Miller, in Darbyton, to the east," continued Cloris, picking up the thread. "She's feeling poorly again, and the duke says we are to look after her."

Another good deed. Add it to the pile of mysteries. "He must have a fondness for her. What is the connection?"

"His Grace doesn't say and we haven't asked. He just says run along and tend to her whenever she's ailing. She gets the nervous headaches, she does. Hasn't been the same since she lost her husband in the war. Almost lost her house, too, until she came into some money unexpectedly."

"Ah!" cried Agnes. "I just thought of something, Cloris, we are silly old things. We do know a Kitty, indeed we do. I'm a fool not to think of it sooner."

Ana felt her legs go numb, rooted to the ground. "Who is she?"

"Why, it must be the widow Miller. Katherine's her Christian name, but she was Kitty to her husband, sure enough, I heard her say it, and must be so to the duke as well. How droll! You ask about a Kitty and we are off to see the very one. Would you like us to pass along a message?"

Ana thought quickly. She was dying to know more about the woman. But what could she say that didn't sound dreadfully awkward and upsetting? *Are you or have you ever been my husband's mistress? Why is he lavishing baskets of food on you?* By all accounts, the woman was unwell and pining for a departed spouse. She would think about it and revisit the subject later, Ana decided, perhaps pay the widow a visit on her own. "No, that's fine. Goodbye! Have a pleasant journey."

"Goodbye. Mind you don't get lost in the hedge maze!" And they took their leave, sensible black cloaks flapping in the breeze.

Ana continued along, lost in thought. She reached the hedge maze, with its neat springy green walls, and entered, taking turns at random. Kitty Miller. The same sensation of being elbowed in the ribs by a distant memory she'd felt earlier in the day nagged at her again. Miller. There had been a Miller in her father's company! In Dex's company. She'd written him a letter, addressed somewhere . . . she couldn't remember, would have to check. Was it Darbyton? Could it have been? Kitty Miller. Widowed in the war. It must be.

She pictured the list she'd copied out at the War Office, a handful of names and titles, addresses flung across the countryside. Miller, Merrick, Harrison . . . Alcox! There had also been an Alcox in the company. Tessie, Kitty. Alcox, Miller. The lists hung side by side in the air in front of her mind's eye. Her handwriting, cramped with grief, the duke's dark scrawl. They were the same list, seen from different angles.

The duke had hired Tessie at some point not so long ago. Her father must have been in his company, and he was obviously taking care of Sergeant Miller's widow, too. Janet and Laurel—they must be surviving family members of other compatriots he'd lost. Probably experiencing generous strokes of good fortune by the duke's machinations, their financial concerns taken care of, no longer alone in the world.

She could place herself on that list as well.

Another good deed, or five, for the pile. At this rate, he'd achieve sainthood before too long. The thought brought a smile to her lips, Dex in martyr's robes, a halo crowning his dark head. She'd solved one of the enigmas of this man she was married to. She'd find the perfect time to tell him she'd solved one of his mysteries. He couldn't hide his kind deeds from her. She'd won a minor battle in the war, he would have to acknowledge it. And maybe, seeing how futile it was to remain so opaque in the face of her determination, open up about other things.

She was at this point rather lost in the maze, she realized. She'd reached a dead end somewhere close-ish to the center, was surrounded by unyielding green. She took a seat on a low stone bench facing the farthest wall and listened to a thrush trill a thrilling song from somewhere nearby. Fitting, she mused, to be contemplating Dex's closed-off nature in the setting of a maze. She let the wall of green hedge fill her vision, quieting her mind.

Suddenly, fantastically, a rabbit leapt from seemingly thin air onto the grass in front of her. Where had it come from? One minute, greenery. The next, a gray, flop-eared little ball of fluff, regarding her calmly over its twitching nose. She stayed still. It stayed where it was for a long minute, then turned and hopped back toward the wall. Then disappeared. Into the wall. *Around* the wall. A false dead end! She could just make out the cleverly concealed threshold if she squinted her eyes.

She leapt to her feet and followed, squeezing through the narrow gap that allowed entrance into a brief grassy corridor—then out into the heart of the maze.

It was a lovely spot. Quiet, still, forgotten by time and humanity. Overgrown rosebushes ran riot in every direction, mixing with sweet-smelling banks of lavender, thyme, and rosemary. A multi-tiered fountain with sweet cherubim frolicking at its sides held court over several stone lovers' benches.

She walked on the cobblestones to its edge and ran her hands over the mossy marble. The barest trickle of water flowed from spouts set at intervals, and its various drains were choked with weeds. There was a statue at the center, an impossibly beautiful and stately goddess, barely discernible under a patina of moss, with stars carved in her hair and long flowing robes that sank into the stagnant water. A greening copper plaque lay at her feet.

For my Celestia
The stars be always thine

The date beneath was just before Dex had left for the war. Ana started, feeling as if she'd been shoved by invisible hands. All the air was gone from her lungs. She felt it in her bones, the deep importance of this forgotten place. This neglected shrine to someone named Celestia. Who was she? More importantly, who had she been to Dex? The woman he had loved, obviously. If so, why had they never married if he'd seen fit to gift her with such a grand gesture of his devotion?

The statue's blank eyes seemed to lock onto Ana's. She backed away, skirts catching on the wild herb tendrils that reached out to her. The only corner of the duke's estate not militantly groomed and managed. The wildness terrified her. What could it mean? She hurried back around the false wall and began to laboriously find her way out of the maze, hindered by a swarm of questions nipping at her like gnats.

Solve one mystery, uncover nine more. It was a hydra-headed conundrum. Open a door only to discover a hall full of closed ones. It took her twice as long to find her way out of the maze as it had to reach its center, but she persisted, grimly forging forward, doubling back as necessary. She emerged finally, breathless and panting.

She would persevere. And win this war. She wouldn't stop until she'd opened every last lock and thrown wide all the doors in her way. *I will solve this*, she thought. The inaccessible duke *would* open up to her. Failure was not an option.

Chapter Twenty-Four

"You do have need of my Magic," spake the Faery Queen. She drew from her breast a glittering amethyst pendant. "The dragon must offer his help willingly; to that end I have no power. But take you thou this amulet, and keep it on your person. You will then have everything you need to vanquish evil and realize your heart's desires! Just remember: trust in thine own Self, and let the magic follow . . ."

—*The Dragon and the Blue Star* by Analise Crewe

Ana stared up at the pink silk canopy above her bed, attempting to catch her breath. He'd done it again. Made her come apart into a million pieces, made her scream his name and clutch the bedsheets while she cried out in ecstasy.

He held such power over her. She wasn't making much progress on her mission to win this tug-of-war between them. He kept himself separate from her, played by his own rules.

During the day he was occupied with restoring order to the estate in the absence of his estate manager. At night he came to her bed. And then he left her. Replete with pleasure, but their marriage unconsummated. His heart still a locked room mystery.

She could feel him readying to leave even now, the tense of his muscles, the air growing colder.

"Dex." She rolled onto her side and nestled into him. "You touch me and I feel as though you're trying to communicate something that you won't allow your lips to say. You won't allow yourself to open to me and tell me what you want. You will only control, and I like that. I like to surrender, I also want to know you, not only your body, but you. What makes you, you?"

"Very well." He sat up. "Let's talk. You introduce a subject and I shall converse upon it for an acceptable length of time. And then we shall resume our bedsport."

"That's not how this works. You make the rules for our meeting of bodies. I shall make the rules for our conversations. And they are very, very simple. No lies. No half-truths. Full honesty in all things. And . . . a striving for honesty, for something deeper than a perfunctory conversation about the weather, or horses, or houses or household staff. I want you to talk to me about what's in your mind. What you're thinking."

"I'm thinking you are lovely by firelight. That I want to be the flame flickering and casting shadows across you. I want to lick you with fire, and make you burn. I'm thinking that this desire I feel for you is rare and something to be treasured. I'm thinking that I'm lucky. To be in this bed with you. To be allowed to touch you."

"You seduce me with words. And you think I'll forget about our bargain."

"Our bargain was open to interpretation."

"Then I won't allow myself to surrender to seduction. A true feeling, one true feeling or one thought about life, and your place in it, for one kiss."

"You don't want to know my true thoughts. War left me with

a darkness, a wound that will never heal, and you're always so cheerful. Learning my thoughts might infect you, like a wound not properly washed. You might become morose by association."

"We'll have to take that chance. Don't you understand? Hearing about the war brings me closer to my father, makes me understand what he experienced and perhaps potentially will help me find him."

"I can't talk about it. I dream about it often enough. Horrible nightmares. Sometimes I lash out in my sleep, punch the pillows or the headboard."

She could tell it took a great effort for him to say the words. "Is that why you don't want to stay the night with me?"

He nodded.

She reached for his face, lightly touching his scars.

He flinched. Pulled away.

Her hand on his scars. Too much.

"Did I say you could touch me?" he asked in a low, warning voice.

She snatched her hand away. "I was only trying to—"

"Comfort me? I don't require comfort. I require you to follow my rules. You don't touch me, remember." He caught her hands behind her back. "I'll have to discipline you now."

He pulled her toward him, arranging her over his knees with her head over the side of the bed, her hair tumbling down nearly to the floor. She squirmed against him, her soft belly sliding over his erection.

"I'll release you if you don't like it." He tested the smooth skin of her bottom with his palm, gliding over her curves, before bringing his palm down in exactly the right way to sting but not hurt, to draw the blood to her lower regions. She squirmed harder but stayed silent. He spanked her again, and again.

"Shall I stop?" he asked.

She shook her head no.

He smiled. He reached around to lightly squeeze her nipples with one hand as he spanked her again.

"Have you learned your lesson?" he asked on a low growl.

"No," she whispered, her thighs clenching and unclenching. "Spank me again."

The firm smack and bounce of his palm against her flesh brought all the blood rushing there, and made her squirm, clenching her thighs together.

"Open your thighs," he ordered.

She complied, lost to everything but the promise of pleasure. He rewarded her by sliding two fingers inside her, gently working them in and out at a pace and depth that soon had her moaning.

"Do you like that?" he asked.

"Yes. Keep going. A little deeper."

"You're such a good, brave girl, asking for what you want. What you need." His fingers sank deeper and her thighs moved to meet his thrusts. "Soon I'll be inside you with more than my fingers."

"When?" she asked shakily.

"Soon. When you're ready."

She shuddered her release, thinking about taking him deep inside her, wrapping her legs around his hips.

It had taken every ounce of his tattered control to leave Ana's bed tonight. They were separated by only a door. So easy to open it, go back to her bed, be with her completely. Make her his.

Why was he torturing himself? He couldn't stop the thoughts spilling out like water overflowing a dam. He couldn't stop wanting her, longing for her. He woke up hard from dreams about her. He went to sleep with the phantom indention of her body next to his, fiercely wrapped in his arms. He woke hugging a pillow, not her. Not warm, sleepy her.

His life had been devoid of laughter, lightness, happiness, sunshine for so long and, like a man dying of thirst, she was his imaginary oasis, a cool wellspring of thirst-quenching happiness.

She was everything he'd denied himself for so long.

The delicate fragile bones beneath her skin, the smallness of her next to his enormous frame. This fragility coupled with the outsize enormous fierceness of her concentration when she orgasmed. She was going to get this right. She attacked bedsport with the same singularity of focus, the same drive for perfection, that she attacked a blank page with a quill dipped in ink.

She would write her pleasure in bold prose, make it sing, make it memorable. And he loved that about her. It was a gift. A lover who wasn't worried about posing, and making sure that she was always attractive, a woman who let herself feel in a raw, present way, who carried her heart on her negligee, who met him more than halfway and was eager and wholly present.

It drove him toward a dangerous tenderness, a desire to unburden his heart to her, gift her his cold, charred heart and ask her to breathe life into it. An insane notion that she could protect him from himself, that she was a haven, a place to lay his head, to lay down his burden.

And it was thoughts like those that stopped him from consummating the marriage. He told himself that he was waiting for her to be ready . . . but really he was the one who needed more time. It had something to do with the idea that physical consummation with this extraordinary woman might force him to confront his buried emotions, that he might lose the iron control that had sustained him for so long.

What had always been an act of measured control for him—giving pleasure freely but never giving his heart.

But it was Ana. And this was different. Her smile, her incessant questions, the joy with which she attacked life, it disarmed him.

Waiting gave her more power over him. He would consummate this marriage tomorrow.

He'd make sure she was so thoroughly pleasured that she begged him to take her. Picturing her surrender filled his mind with desire and stiffened his cock. He'd give her instructions and feel the thrill of having her obey. Rough, gruff instructions. The dark needy things he would do to her. Stroking himself, body tensed to the point of pain, moaning into his pillow, close now . . .

"Dex?"

Fuck. He threw the coverlet hastily over his throbbing erection.

"Is this what you do when you leave my room? You pleasure yourself with your own hand."

"Yes," he ground out. "This is what I do."

Her gaze traveled from his lips down his torso to where his cock stood upright, tenting the coverlet. "Could I give you the same pleasure?"

"Go to bed, Ana," he growled.

"No. I won't. I'm cold and I want you to warm me." She slid the covers back and crawled in beside him. It was all he could do to keep from groaning aloud when she curled her body up against his, laying her head on his shoulder and her arm across his chest.

"Now then, as you were, soldier."

"What?" He bit back a laugh. The cheeky baggage.

"As you were. Keep doing it. I want to watch." She lifted the covers and stuck her head inside.

No way he could refuse that request. He was too far gone, and her warm, womanly curves pressed against him were only making matters worse.

She wasn't looking at his face, intent instead on his hand and his cock. He resumed stroking himself, driven nearly mad by the knowledge that she was watching. Then . . . dear God—then her hand slid down his chest, over his naval, and joined his, tentatively circling his cock with her small fingers. "May I?"

He grunted.

"Is that a yes?" When he didn't answer, she lifted her head a little, searching his face in the darkness. "I know you said that I can't touch you . . . but this isn't the same situation, is it? You were already touching yourself, I'll just add another set of hands . . ."

He grunted again, unable to find the words to tell her to go away.

"Say it, Dex."

He couldn't refuse. He was too far gone now. He wanted her too much. In the darkness, her soft hand questing, sliding gently over him.

He lay back with a moan. "Please. Touch me."

She fit her hand around him, her fingers barely clasping together. "Like this?" She moved tentatively up and down. Not hard enough. Not fast enough. But it was enough, more than enough. To feel her touch, her hair silk and feathers, brushing his chest.

Her eyes glowing in the dark as she concentrated on her task.

"Perhaps . . . two hands," he said through gritted teeth.

She understood, wrapping both her hands around his cock, her grip tighter now. But still so inexpert. The need was growing, he must find release.

"I'm not doing it right . . . show me."

It was sweet torture, her fingers on him, the pressure so light and soft . . . he had to finish this. He wrapped his hand around hers, showing her the way of it . . . the firmness of the pressure.

Then he lifted his hand and prayed she'd continue. She did. She was nothing if not a quick study. She kissed his neck as she worked her hand up and down. He'd spill soon. He took her other hand and guided it to his ballocks, showed her what he liked.

"I'm nearly there," he said jerkily, "don't stop."

She doubled her efforts and the muscles of his abdomen bunched and tensed until finally he found a shattering release. He flopped back on the bed, panting, riding the last waves of surging sensation. "Ana. That was incredible."

She handed him a handkerchief after wiping her own hands.

"Good duke," she said.

He smiled into the darkness. He liked it when she took control, he thought sleepily. Then jolted awake. What were these errant thoughts?

Dangerous. That's what they were. "Go back to your bed now, Ana."

"You said you wouldn't sleep in my bed, but you didn't tell me not to sleep in yours," Ana said, trying to make light of his command for her to leave.

"It's the same thing. I told you why I made that rule. It's for your protection, so that if I have a night terror, I won't accidentally harm you."

"I think it's for *your* protection. You're too comfortable in your silence, in your solitude. You refuse to change or compromise even the slightest bit."

She'd come to his room to tell him that she'd solved the mystery of the list of names, that she knew he was a good person at heart, but when he said things like that, when he pushed her away, it hurt.

"Good night, Ana."

Back in her room she lay awake, reliving the evening in her mind.

There was a lingering afterprint from his touch, like a page accidentally printed twice, a ghost script underneath the real words. It didn't matter what she said during the day, she was really living for the night, when he was all hers. His focus completely on her pleasure. On bringing her to ever steeper heights.

Then he became distant again. She touched him but he didn't reciprocate. He was preoccupied. But tonight she'd commanded him. She'd made him groan and call out her name.

Perhaps this was the key to his heart. Remove the barriers between their bodies, and she might be able to reach his heart.

Chapter Twenty-Five

"Redeem yourself, Qavox! Fight this evil with me."

"Princess," he growled, "my mind hasn't changed. I must leave you here. There is no redemption for a dragon." He bowed his neck, and she slid down to the ground in front of the castle gates.

She placed a hand against the warm column of his foreleg. This beast had been her sole companion lo these many months, and in that time he had frightened her, disappointed her, maddened her with his implacability. Yet he believed in her in a way that nobody ever had, made her feel as if she could indeed take on a castle full of evil and be excited for whatever came next. Tears sprang into her eyes. "Goodbye, my Dragon."

—*The Dragon and the Blue Star* by Analise Crewe

Tonight was the night.

Tonight they would consummate this marriage.

Dex stood at the tall windows looking out on the garden path. It wasn't the early autumn foliage, or the late summer roses, resplendent golds and fuchsias and magentas harmoniously blending in the hazy late afternoon sun that caught his gaze. It was the woman walking up the path, her slight form in a butter-yellow gown, bending gracefully from time to time to smell a random bloom, then straightening and staring off dreamily into the distance, no doubt composing a description of their scent to be written down immediately once inside.

He was supposed to be back in London by now. He'd finally located Harrison's sister, Laurel, and the situation was worse than he'd feared. She'd been forced out of the family home after the war, where she'd been set up as Harrison's housekeeper, and had subsequently disappeared into a succession of increasingly menial jobs, until finally his solicitor had found her selling meager posies in St. Giles, sleeping in a shanty with dozens of other down-on-their-luck sorts.

She was currently waiting for word from his solicitor at a respectable boarding house he'd secured for her, but she was half-blind from a fever and badly needed a companion to aid her in her daily tasks. He had a list of potential candidates and had meant to be in London to interview them all personally.

He had work to do, the work that had occupied him since he'd recovered from his injuries. Doing his part to ease the lives of others who had been devastated by the war. He shouldn't be lingering here like a lovesick schoolboy, staring out the window at Ana, dreaming about what he would do to her tonight.

He'd promoted one of his staff to serve as temporary steward, a man he trusted. He should be on his way back to London. Fulfill his duty and resume the life he'd built for himself. Ana would stay here where everyone doted on her.

The house hummed with new life. Christ, he'd seen McArdle smile at her earlier today. McArdle, whose name should really be McCurdle, because he had a constant expression of judgmental distaste, as though life and society had disappointed him so thoroughly that his lips had forgotten how to do anything but frown.

He looked out the window again, noting the now empty path. Where was she? Somewhere in the house working her magic, maybe heading to her writing desk? Bringing to life the denizens of Clovercote in the same way she'd created an entire new world out of thin air, one crawling with dragons and steeped in enchantment. He wanted to return to Vyranthrall. He wanted to know how the story ended, true, but he also wanted to escape its creator, dive into a reality where she wasn't always so tantalizingly at hand.

Or right behind him.

"Whatever are you looking at, Dex?" Her voice danced across his senses. "I see nothing outside to glare at with such consternation."

He'd been caught thinking about her, yearning for her. And here she was, the sunshine of her gown and her teasing smile breaking through the clouds in his mind.

She was a crackling fire on a cold damp night. All he wanted to do was stretch toward her, warm himself in her smile. His capacity for joy had atrophied, his smile was out of practice, stiff with unuse, like cold fingers, aching joints.

"I thought I saw a deer at the edge of the woods."

"A deer? How magical. I adore the woods on your grounds."

"Our grounds," he reminded her automatically.

"Ah, yes! I suppose so. Our grounds." She'd plucked a yellow rose on her walk through the garden. Now she traced its petals with one finger, looking at the rose and not at him.

An awkward silence fell. Normally, she would fill that silence with chatter but she chose to remain silent, as though she believed him capable of finding the perfect topic of conversation. He cleared his throat. "Are you making any progress on the Clovercote novel?"

"Some, although I confess I've been a bit distracted. I've had several letters in response to the advertisement we put in the papers for news of Papa. None of them with any ring of veracity. People wanting the reward, pretending to have knowledge. But it's all false." She sighed. "Maybe nothing will come of it."

He'd known nothing would come of it, but he'd been willing to go along for her sake. She'd have to come to terms with her father's loss at some point. "I'll renew the advertisement for another month while I'm in London, shall I?"

"Then you'll be going again soon?"

"Yes. I've much to attend to. Taking care of business, tenants . . . business things." He realized how lame he sounded, and he was glad that she chose to ignore it. She looked a little vexed, with a pout forming on that kissable mouth.

"Well, it must be frighteningly fascinating to keep you so long away from home. While you've been visiting your tenants, I've been getting to know the household staff. There's a whole world happening here, right under our noses, every bit as exciting as the London ton. McArdle's quest to squash the more creative tendencies of the cooks, Cloris and Agnes antagonizing the gardener with their criticisms of his vegetable plot. My Tessie has even developed feelings for one of your footmen."

"Which one?"

"George."

"The strapping lad from the village?"

"That's the one."

"He's a good fellow. They should be very happy together."

"They've only known each other a matter of weeks."

"You and I married after a month."

"We were forced to marry."

"Indeed." He cupped her cheek with his palm, stroking his thumb over her plump lower lip. "We are married. Therefore, we must do something before I depart for London. Can you guess what that is?"

"Er . . ." A fetching flush rose in her cheeks. She surely knew what he was going to say. She was thinking about consummating, as much as he was. "You must throw a dazzling dinner party for all of the neighboring gentry, including your brother, Rupert?"

He froze, her words throwing ice water on his erotic imaginings. "What do you know of Rupert?"

"The household staff pointed out his house. You can see it from your grounds and yet you've never invited him to meet me. It's extremely vexing."

"You're extremely vexing."

"I'm just getting started. I also discovered that—"

"Enough." He stilled her with a finger over her lips. "I'm not talking about dinner parties, or discovering buried familial secrets. I speak of making this a marriage in truth."

He leaned closer, brushing his lips against the soft skin of her neck. "I speak of consummation," he said huskily.

"Oh." Her eyes closed and she swayed against him. "I was wondering why . . . that is, I don't know why we haven't achieved that state before now."

"Because I've been biding my time, waiting for you to be ready, to bloom for me like this rose you hold." Gently, he took the rose from her fingers, smelling the lemony-sweet scent. "I've been dying to take you, Ana." He slid the soft rose petals down her neck, into her decolletage. Her breathing quickened. He trailed kisses down the same path, slipping her bodice lower to kiss her breasts, finding one nipple with his tongue. She arched backward, offering herself to him. He sucked greedily, supporting her weight with an arm around her waist, splaying his hand over her belly.

"Dex," she said breathily. "We're not in private."

"Are you ready for me, sweet Ana?" The sheer force of his need made his voice low, nearly a growl. She must say yes. She must be his.

"Y-yes," she said shakily. "I'm ready."

He gathered her up easily into his arms. "Then it's time I took you to bed."

SHE STUDIED HIS face, the firelight sending shadows over his scars, his eyes holding hers, waiting for her response. The room seemed to be holding its breath.

It was as though her mind had decided there was no use in attempting to fathom what was happening to her and had just decided to allow her body to steer the ship.

He kissed her forehead, her lips, her neck. "Your skin is like silk. Are you really mine to touch? To smell. To taste?" He moved lower, trailing kisses over her breasts, down her belly, and lower still.

She wound her fingers into his hair as his head moved and his tongue pleasured her. He didn't stop her from touching him. The allowed intimacy warmed her insides as though she'd drunk a glass of wine. He slipped his fingers inside her as his tongue continued teasing her, coaxing her toward climax. She sighed dreamily as ripples of pleasure played through her body.

He raised his head and licked his fingers slowly, savoring the flavor of her, making her watch. "Salt-honey on my tongue. Are you mine for the taking, Ana?"

"I'm yours," she breathed. "Take me, Dex."

He reared up above her, bracing his arms on either side of her body.

There was no strategy to her words, no thought of making him lose control. She was the one who was lost. Her head spinning from this feeling of closeness, from being so thoroughly pleasured.

He spread her with his fingers, readying her for his penetration. And then he was nudging his way inside her, and it stretched, and stung and she couldn't help tensing up.

He stopped immediately. "Is it too much?"

"It's a lot," she said truthfully.

"Relax your muscles," he instructed. "Breathe deeply. I'll take it slowly, allow you time to adjust to my girth."

She nodded, biting her lip. "All right," she said shakily.

He began moving again, slow and steady, filling her inch by inch. She spread her thighs wider, finding a more comfortable angle.

"Yes, that's right. Find what feels right, Ana."

When he was all the way inside, he stopped moving. She could feel him, a stirring, a pulse buried inside her, like a heartbeat.

"Ana. I want you to know pleasure as you've never known it before."

"I already have. Tonight was beautiful, it was melting and urgent . . . I want more of that pleasure. I want more of you, Dex."

"I'll give you everything. Everything, Ana." He held her gaze and began moving gently inside her, a rolling sensation, as though she were a ship riding a wave. "Let me love you."

The familiar beginning, undulations deep within her belly. "More. I want more."

He moved faster, thrust deeper inside her. Her body expanded to fit him; her thighs spread wider. She lay her head back on the pillow, surrendering completely. He knew what to do. He knew how to take her to that place that existed outside of time. A place where the only thing that existed was ecstasy.

"If I touch you while I move inside you, I may be able to give you another climax."

Waves of pleasure beginning to flow inside her, his body above her, braced on his wrists, looking down at her with a hungry expression. It was dark, he'd blown out the candles, but she could see the hard lines of him, the jaw, the dark eyes. The enormous muscles of his arms bulging as he supported his weight above her, moving slowly, slowly. Deliciously.

"Wrap your legs around my hips. Cross your ankles."

She did as she was told.

"Good, Ana. That's so good. Now, move with me."

She didn't know what he meant intellectually. He was the one moving, thrusting, pulling out and going back in.

Move with him. Move her hips up when he moved his, ankles crossed over his body. She could control him. She understood that suddenly. With little movements of her body, she could control his rhythm, the depth of his thrusts.

"That's right," he praised her. "You're in control now. Show me what you want."

Wordless felt good. It felt like just letting go of the constant struggle to make the world understand her, to impose her will, to assert control. Here, in this bed, she didn't have to struggle. She was understood. She was cherished.

He understood that she wanted him to stop for a moment, so she could catch her breath. She didn't have to tell him. He listened so carefully, his breathing going harsh and ragged from the effort of controlling himself but wanting to do what she needed. And then . . . the need building.

His fingers finding her sex, gently massaging her as he slid in and out. The friction making her gasp. And then he angled deeper, rising above her, the root of him hitting the place where his fingers had been. Every stroke, every slide of him against her bringing her closer to that wordless place.

"That's it, sweetheart. That's it, you're getting closer. You're going to come hard. It will last longer this time. You're sweating, your hair is damp. You're so beautiful. Your lips are swollen because I've been kissing you for hours, biting you. Your lower lips are swollen around my cock. Gripping me, kissing me, begging for me. You want me to fuck you. You're going to beg me for more again and again."

She still never expected this torrent of words from this silent man. In the dark, surrounded by velvet, the taste of brandy on his tongue, the lingering scent of his musk and citrus cologne. His gruff commands. The instructions he gave her. The endearments.

"Come for me, sweet Ana. Beautiful Ana."

It was the endearments that undid her. That made her lose control. Hearing her name in that deep, throaty growl. Hearing him say such tender things. The contrast of his sweet words and the iron of his grip holding her arms above her head, the total control he had over her body.

"Dex . . . Dex, I'm . . ."

"Yes, you're coming. You're going to come. You can let go. I've got you. I'm here inside you. I'm all around you. Your body is mine, Ana. You're mine to pleasure. Let go, let me take you there."

And she did. And it was glorious.

And then as she was still floating, still dancing with pleasure, his movements became more frenzied, he groaned and dropped his full weight onto her body.

"I'm . . . going to come," he growled. He pushed into her so hard and fast, her body lifted off the bed. He pumped fast, faster, until she thought she couldn't take anymore and then he shuddered, groaning, sweat dripping from his face, and collapsed against her, his hips jerking.

"Fucking hell, Ana. I've never . . . that was . . ."

"It was beautiful," she whispered, the words demolishing a wall inside her chest, some piece of herself that she'd been keeping separate. This was no convenient arrangement. This feeling of wanting to own him more completely, give everything to him, body, heart, soul. This loss of control and this needing.

In this moment, limp from pleasure, replete with the warmth of him wrapped around her, the sound of his ragged breathing in her ear, his breath on her cheek. How close he was holding her as if he would never ever let her go. As if he couldn't get enough of her in the same needy way she felt about him.

Was this enough? If this was all she could have of him, his body, his whispered commands, was it enough?

Her mouth filled with words she couldn't say. *I love the way you hold me. I think I could love you. If you let me. I want to melt into you and never be separate again.*

Instead, she blurted out what she'd been wanting to tell him for days: "I know your secret."

He rolled over, his eyes shadowy in the firelit room. "Back to that, are we?" His voice was quieter. She stirred, a bit uneasily.

"I've discovered, despite your best efforts to hide it from me, that I'm not the only damsel in distress negatively affected by the war that you've rescued. You're a regular Sir Gawain."

"I don't know what you mean."

He had become, if possible, even more motionless. Like a statue in the dim light next to her. She reached for one of his hands.

"Dex, it's nothing to be ashamed of. You're a good person. That's something to aspire to, to be proud of! Agnes and Cloris told me about Katherine Miller, and I made the connection to that list of yours I found—she's Kitty, isn't she? And she's the widow of one of your men who died? And you're making sure she's fed and cared for, and it was probably you who provided her with the funds to keep her house, wasn't it?"

"I am not a good person. It was my fault they died. The least I can do is provide for their families."

"Then you're admitting it!" she cried triumphantly. "Aren't I clever, Dex? I've figured you out. Why you would want to keep your generosity a secret from me is beyond comprehension. But you can't hide from me. Like it or not, I'm intimately connected to you now. I'll find out every little heroic attribute about you and force you to confront the fact that you, the Duke of Warburton, are changing people's lives for the better."

"After robbing them of the best parts, forcing them into poverty, illness, darkness. Stop it, Ana. Stop talking about this. You can't understand what it's been like, all this time, knowing I'd ruined so many lives. Not just the lives of the enemy, but the lives of men I cared for, and the lives of those they cared for."

Ana heard the rawness of his voice, and it broke her heart. For the first time she could see clearly the magnitude of the burden he carried. The same burden that had introduced him to her, that had brought them into this marriage together. She understood, at least that part of him. It was a large piece to his puzzle, but the solving brought her no joy. Not when he was so obviously anguished.

She touched his arm. "I won't mention it again, Dex. I thought you might like to hear good things about yourself, most people do. But you aren't a bit like most people, are you?"

"No." He turned his head to her, searching her face with unreadable eyes.

She shivered. "Well, I'm glad for that. Most people, it turns out, are predictable. The more I learn about the world, the more I find that to be true."

"I can think of one thing you might learn tonight that won't be predictable," he said, a glint of fire sparking in his steady eyes.

An answering spark lit a fire deep in her belly. She allowed him to roll her over until she was face down on the bed and couldn't ask him any more questions or confront him with secrets. She allowed her body to take over again.

"Take me again," she whispered. "Harder this time."

He held her by the waist as he took her from behind with long, sure strokes. She felt depraved. Desired. Cherished.

It was enough. But only for now.

Chapter Twenty-Six

"You always were an annoying child, Amsonia!" sneered her uncle in his sinister voice, folding his hands into his garnet sleeves. "When I learned you'd escaped, I sent my men after you, but that cursed Qavox thwarted them! I do wish he hadn't, could have saved me from this annoying little confrontation you've contrived . . ."

"Enough!" she cried, tears of rage and fear coursing to her troubled breast. "Uncle, you do disturb me mightily! Have you no heart? Take me to my father at once!"

—*The Dragon and the Blue Star* by Analise Crewe

You look uncommonly well this morning," Tessie observed.

"I feel uncommonly hungry." Ana attacked her bacon and eggs with voracious intent.

Tessie smiled knowingly. "I'm glad you have such an appetite."

And not only for bacon. She hungered for Dex. Their lovemaking hummed in her veins, sang her a song about freedom. The freedom to seek pleasure, to give pleasure. It wasn't only those hours in bed. The glow spread through her body and lasted the whole next day. Pleasant little after-ripples when she walked, crossed her legs, bathed.

Her body reminding her that she was something wholly new, a woman well-pleasured. A woman who had cried out her release not caring who heard, wanting the world to know how happy she was.

Let me love you. He'd said that to her last night. That was clear progress. Even if he only meant love her with his body, she'd heard the subtext, the silent message.

He was afraid to relinquish the armor he'd pieced together over his heart like dragon's scales.

Take me again. Harder this time. Words she never thought she'd say. This secret pleasure-haze, this darkness that filled her with a need so sharp it felt like she was still subsisting on bread and butter . . . that he was the only thing that could fill her, satiate her.

Each morsel of him that she consumed made her want more. Not only his body, his confident commands. She wanted him to talk to her, tell her the dark secrets he held in his heart. She wanted to understand him.

She wanted more. She wanted everything. She wanted him wholly, not just during the nighttime. How could she make him see that it wasn't enough? That as beautiful and feverish and ecstatic as it was, it wasn't enough?

While he was away, she spent her days in Clovercote with the familiar characters living out their complicated lives through her pen, and completing the light edits she'd received on her fantastical novel from Mr. Norwood. She threw herself into the work, welcoming the distraction. She'd be finished very soon, then she would travel to London to submit the manuscript. It never ceased to give her a thrill when she thought about holding her book in her hands.

She'd stopped being upset with Dex for giving the publisher a donation. It was exactly as he'd said, her book would have to stand on its own merits upon publication. He couldn't very well purchase the entire British public. The critics might hate her book, or they might ignore it completely. Or, just maybe, someone out there might read it and fall in love with it.

Someone other than her husband, of course.

Oh Papa, she thought. *I wish you could be here to see me achieving my dream.*

He would be very proud. She had written the dedication to her father. Only appropriate for a book about a girl who lost her father and found him again with the help of a great and terrible dragon. She hadn't given up hope of finding him yet, even though she hadn't received any credible information about his whereabouts.

She'd been sitting at the breakfast table for nearly an hour, lingering over her mostly empty plate. Her stomach was full, yet she felt . . . hungry. Restless. One thing she had learned about herself in the hard years following her father's disappearance, was that inactivity rubbed her the wrong way.

She wasn't one to mope, to swan about, to wallow in self-pity. She needed to take solid steps toward her goals, although she admittedly preferred taking wild fantastical leaps. The crumbs of progress she felt she'd made, as meager as the remains of her breakfast, the subtle shifts in his manner with her, the passionate language he used during their lovemaking—none of it was enough. Further action was required.

She'd spent a few hours the day before wrestling with a particularly tricky detail of Lady Claridge's plot outline—the heroine, unsure of her paramour's fidelity, had invited all members of the ton to a masquerade, the invitation instructing guests to "wear your feelings," the goal being to force all unsaid emotions out into the open.

She'd had a devilish time designing the correct costumes for the corresponding players in the novel but had finally landed on the perfect costumes for the protagonists to wear to signal their true colors, so that all the intricacies of the plot could be neatly resolved by the conclusion of the ball.

It was a big scene, rather farfetched, but full of satisfying drama and meaty confrontations and by the end of it (or so she had felt, throwing down her minuscule pencil nub triumphantly on the desk) the characters had all learned something about themselves and each other, enough to enable the much sought-after happy ending her readers would require.

She was jealous of her heroine, who had forced her lover's feelings out into the open quite easily. Real life didn't afford such neat endings. Dex would never don Romeo's doublet and proclaim that her beauty was "too rich for use, for earth too dear!" She smiled at the thought. Besides, if she threw a ball, who would come? They were certainly very isolated here at the castle, their only neighbor the estranged brother, Rupert.

She could speak to Rupert. She gasped, feeling an echo of the excitement she'd experienced finishing the masquerade scene. Inspiration was striking again.

She could talk with this important figure from Dex's past. He was possibly the only person who could shine some light on the dark corners that made up her husband. Why not? At the very worst, he would reject her advance or have no insights to offer. Maybe he was as closed and unyielding as Dex, and that was why they were locked into this enmity. Maybe it had all started over something very silly in their childhood, a coveted pony being gifted to the wrong brother, something trivial that had grown hard layers of meaning over time. Shells that slowed each brother down and kept them from seeing each other clearly.

She could peel off the layers, get to the heart of it. And maybe get to the heart of Dex in the process.

Ana arrived at the door of the neighboring estate in a sorry state. She'd charged out of the castle with the barest of goodbyes to Tessie and the rest of the staff, fastening her coat as she went. She didn't want to tell anyone where she was going, lest they try to stop her, give her some logical reason not to undertake this quest. Logic be damned today. She was giving her intuition free rein.

It had led her to this doorstep, out of breath and windswept, raising the heavy knocker with a shaky hand. In the moment before the door opened, she had enough time to conjure up a thousand potential forms her new brother-in-law might take, none of them pleasant. A dastardly cad, a pompous imbecile. A bitter man, jealous of Dex's birthright, plotting his downfall from just down the hill.

The attractive brown-haired gentleman with the ready grin and friendly crinkles around his eyes was wholly unexpected.

"Hullo! You'll have to excuse me for opening the door myself—Mallard's been taken ill and our footmen are helping the stable-master with a breached foal's birth. I'm Rupert. You must be Analise, the authoress? Come in, please! Come in."

"How did you know it was me? How do you know my name?" Confusion contributed to her overall ruffled state, as she slid her arms out of her coat and passed it into Rupert's helpfully outstretched arms. He was taking her in with interested and approving gray eyes, the mirror of Dex's but with warmth tempering the steel.

"I like to keep abreast of my brother's doings, as much as he would rather I didn't. We'd heard he'd brought a young bride to the castle, and you fit the description. I hope you aren't terribly shocked by my lack of propriety, I've just been hoping to meet you but unsure how to make it happen, and here you are, on our doorstep. Astonishing!"

She could hardly help smiling back at him—his easy manner was contagious. "You know more about me than I know of you! I'm so pleased to be received like this, I felt positively gauche arriving unannounced."

"Did my brother—are you here with his blessing? Does he know you've come?"

"Your brother is in London on urgent business. I haven't had a chance to write him," she said, neatly evading his first question. "I wanted to invite you over for dinner so that we could all spend time together as a family. I never had a large family; it was always just me and Papa. So, I thought—wouldn't it be better to deliver the invitation in person? So that we could dispense with the awkwardness of first introductions?" She looked at him hopefully, willing him to let her gloss over Dex's participation, or lack thereof, in the scheme. He seemed relieved and pleased to do so.

"Quite right! Admirably so. Firmly believe in avoiding awkwardness at all costs. My wife will be overjoyed to meet you. Come into the drawing room."

He ushered her through the hall and into a brightly lit, warm room, full of harmonious colors and big bowls of flowers. She had an overall impression of domestic bliss, such that it tugged at her heart poignantly. This was a house full of love, she had just time enough to think, when the raven-haired woman at its center arose from the comfortably stuffed chair she'd been sitting on, embroidery materials falling to her feet.

"Celestia. Look who's come. It's Analise!"

Celestia. The periphery of the room blurred. All Ana could see was the woman. Tall, statuesque. An oval face, deep brown eyes, fine features—a face of stunning, ethereal beauty surrounded by a bounty of glossy black hair. A match to the figure in the maze's fountain, although the sculptor had scarcely done her justice.

Ana was suddenly aware of her own curls, blown willy-nilly by the autumn wind, and her walking clothes, damp with perspiration and hanging heavily about her. Celestia was walking toward her with open arms, a timid expression of pleasure brightening her eyes and tinting her cheeks pink.

"Your Grace, it's wonderful to meet you."

Ana clasped hands with Celestia, one hundred questions bubbling behind her lips. She sensed that the goddess in front of her had just as many questions, if the quizzical narrowing of her delicately veined eyelids was any indication.

"I—" she hesitated. "Forgive me, I am woefully uneducated on family matters. I didn't know that Rupert was married? I didn't—well, I don't know much of anything."

Celestia nodded, understanding dawning on her face. "Rupert, will you ring for tea? Her Grace must be exhausted after undertaking the journey by foot, and in this blustery weather! Shall we sit and attempt to clear out some familial cobwebs?"

Ana sank into the proffered chair with relief. "Oh yes, please! You don't know how much I've longed to learn a little bit more about Dex. He is rather a closed book to me."

"To us all. But with good reason," Celestia said enigmatically.

Rupert pushed a large armchair toward them and the trio sat for a moment looking at one another, as a maid entered with the tea service. Ana decided that she liked them both very much, whatever Dex's reasons for not feeling the same. She was conscious of a fierce jealousy toward Celestia, but the woman's kind demeanor and readiness to divulge information were immediately endearing. She had meant something to Dex, that much was obvious. Ana thought of the wild, abandoned fountain, its motion stilled by neglect, its surfaces fallen victim to nature's design. The sightless statue had filled her with foreboding. The real Celestia radiated a calm warmth. They were as different as night and day.

Rupert and Celestia exchanged glances. "I take it," began Rupert, "that my brother didn't tell you the nature of our quarrel? If you didn't know that I was married, that is. He could hardly have told the tale while leaving that bit out."

"No, he won't talk about it. And those around him are forbidden to speak of it. Myself included."

Celestia sighed. "I'm afraid I'm the cause of it all. I have spent so much time going back over the whole story, hoping to find some way to set it all right, but it all comes down to this—I tore the two brothers apart, quite without meaning to. But there it is."

Ana held her breath, leaning forward eagerly in her seat. She had the dizzying feeling of standing at a cliff's edge, transfixed by the distant landscape below. Whatever painful truth she learned here would change her forever, but turning away from it felt physically impossible.

"I've known Dex and Rupert my whole life, the three of us were childhood friends. Oh, I was never very interested in their games of war and endless talk of horses, but whenever they needed a damsel in distress to rescue, or a regal queen to send them out on a new quest, I would fill the role. I suppose it fit me well, because as we grew up, they both seemed to feel that I was destined to be in their lives always."

"She's painting too faint a picture! We were both madly in love with her," Rupert interjected, beaming devoted eyes at his wife.

"I liked them both well enough, but it was Rupert that I was always most drawn to, if I am being fully honest. Dex was so commanding, a born leader. I was a little in awe of him. He orchestrated our make-believe vignettes, told me where to stand and what to say. Rupert had a softer way about him, a gentleness I found more appealing. He would leave funny little bouquets and trinkets for me in my favorite haunts and peep at me with these adoring eyes."

"Come, come. You make me out to be something of a ninny!" Rupert laughed, slapping his knee in mock consternation. "I suppose I was, at that. Utterly besotted, I was."

Ana smiled, picturing the trio as youths. A smaller version of Dex, every bit as tyrannical as the adult version, directing the show. Rupert and Celestia, falling in love in the wings.

"I knew at a young age that my father and theirs had decided that I was the most suitable candidate to be Dex's wife. It was something I just grew up with, my future being planned for me. The current of life was bearing me in that direction. I floated along with it. I don't like conflict. It wasn't a disagreeable prospect. It was just that I would have much preferred it to be Rupert. I was so young . . ." She took a sip of tea.

"We became betrothed shortly before the war. Dex showed up one day asking to speak with my father, and then he marched out to the garden, where I was daydreaming in the sun, and said,

'It's time for us to be married. I love you, and you love me.' What could I do? I could hardly say no."

"It damn near wrecked me!" cried Rupert. "My dearest love, and my older brother. I'd known it was bound to happen, but I'd had fantasies of whisking her away for myself, even dueling Dex for her hand. Nothing at all realistic, boyhood passions run amok and all that, but real enough to me. I was desolate."

"When Dex knew he was to go abroad with his regiment, our engagement became prolonged. I didn't mind that, in fact, I encouraged it to be so. He would have preferred to be married beforehand, but I insisted on a grand, elaborate wedding, something that would require months of preparation and the attendance of absolutely anyone of importance to society. Dex acquiesced, because he could deny me nothing. He had grown rather ardent during the engagement, perhaps because I often withdrew into my own head. He must have found me aloof, more alluring in that way. You've seen the fountain he had made for me?"

"Yes." Ana nodded into her teacup, raptly watching the drama unfold in her mind's eye. Poor Dex. Poor Rupert. Poor Celestia!

"I never told Rupert my misgivings about the marriage. I purposefully avoided him leading up to Dex's deployment. It should have been Rupert who went to war—since their father had died and Dex was the duke, but Dex insisted on riding off to battle, leaving Rupert to remain at home for the duration, to manage the estate."

Celestia's hand trembled slightly as she brought her teacup to her full, crimson lips. "Before Dex left, he installed me at his London townhouse. The wedding preparations were to proceed apace while he was away. I was fitted for a beautiful wedding gown fit for a princess."

"I've seen it," said Ana. "In the forbidden room."

"The forbidden room?" Celestia asked, her face puzzled.

"When I first arrived at the duke's townhouse, he told me I might choose my own chamber. I unlocked the door to a room that had an expansive view of the square and a wardrobe filled with fine and expensive ladies' clothing. It caused quite the argument. He forbade me to have that room. It seems his memories of you were to be kept preserved like a fossil in amber, locked away tightly."

"Oh. I had no idea. I thought he would have been rid of all the wedding trappings."

A charged look passed between Rupert and Celestia.

"It seems my brother never found a way to move on after . . ."

"You're racing ahead of me, Rupert," Celestia chided. "Let me finish my story."

"Of course, my love."

"While I was in London, Rupert visited frequently. We would talk about Dex and the war, and when that topic grew tired (which it did rather quickly), we would spend hours upon hours just talking about stupid, trivial things. Caricatures in the papers that made us laugh, favorite foods, architecture we both admired. Meeting as adults for the first time, truly getting to know each other. We had such a comfortable rapport, so very much to talk about! Before I knew it, I was hopelessly in love."

"The state I had always been in. You finally joined me there." Rupert and Celestia gazed at each other, obviously forgetting their visitor for a moment in the happy memories.

Celestia turned back to Ana.

"Those years flew by. We never spoke words of love out loud, but much was simply *understood* between us. We were best friends, existing in our own little world of happiness. When Dex was injured and transferred to a hospital in London, that illusion was shattered. I'll never forget visiting him there, half his face turned from me in shame, a terrible haunted air emanating from his every pore. He was surrounded by ghosts. The natural brevity of his conversation had degraded into a silence that terrified me. I knew in that instant that it was all wrong. That I finally had to do an unthinkable thing, for both of our sakes. But I couldn't speak the words aloud. I couldn't break our engagement. I simply left. And then I . . . and then Rupert and I were married, in secret."

"But he'd suffered so much during the war!" Heat rose in Ana's chest, making her feel like she had a sudden fever. "How could you do that to him, especially after he'd just come back?" Her heart broke for him, imagining the agony of his existence in that moment. Body wounded, heart broken by his brother and his fiancée's betrayal.

Celestia bowed her head. "Nothing you can say to me is worse than the recriminations I have told myself over the years. I know that I dealt him a terrible blow when he was at his weakest, but I didn't know what else to do. I gave it weeks, but things went from bad to horrible. I didn't want to ruin three lives, when two of them could be salvaged. I was naïve enough to think that it might eventually be all right. That he'd realize, as I honestly suspect to be true, that he'd never really loved me for me. He loved the queen in the castle, seen from afar. He loved the roles he'd made me play in our youth. But he didn't really know me, not really. It was Rupert who knew me, inside and out."

Ana's outrage calmed somewhat, tempered by empathy and understanding. "It was a terrible choice you had to make."

"Yes. And I . . . we paid the consequences most dearly. Dex

vowed never to speak to either of us again. And because he's Dex, and his will is stronger than any other force on earth, he made it so and has never broken his word."

"I miss my brother," Rupert said quietly. "You can't imagine what it's like knowing you deserve the hatred of someone you love. I worshipped the ground he walked on. I was overjoyed when I heard he'd taken a wife, because surely that meant things were shifting?"

"*We* were overjoyed," Celestia amended. "And we are so happy to meet you. We deserve for you to judge us harshly, I won't deny that. I couldn't help observing how quick you were to defend him, and I applaud you for that. You must love him, which is what he badly needs. I hope hearing the circumstances surrounding the event has brought a tiny bit of understanding. And maybe you'll be able to forgive us. Even if he can't."

Ana looked at the two of them, considering all they'd told her. She could see it from all three perspectives, the author's curse. Their narratives entwined in this relentless, inexorable spiral. Her imagination filled in the details, painting the scene as richly as if she'd lived it herself. And she was living it, was also a character in their story. Dex was who he was in part because of these two people, people who hurt him but loved him still, pain begetting pain begetting more pain.

She must attempt to put an end to the cycle. Even if he hated her for it. There was no other way forward. It was time to write a scene of reconciliation. Of redemption.

Her brother- and sister-in-law sat still as stone, staring at her with anticipation, Celestia for the first time truly resembling her marble counterpart in the fountain. Ana took a deep breath.

"Would the two of you care to dine with us at the castle in two days' time? How do you feel about flummery?"

Chapter Twenty-Seven

"Behold!" her uncle said, throwing open the dungeon doors. "Your father awaits."

Red, red, red was the terrible light that barely illuminated that woebegotten room. His dear features, so still behind the thick vermilion. His eyes open, yet dull. His mouth frozen in an awful rictus of disbelief. Her beloved father, immobilized in an impossible coffin constructed of purest ruby . . .

—*The Dragon and the Blue Star* by Analise Crewe

Drakefell Castle smelled divine. Cook had outdone himself, preparing what seemed to Ana's nervously assessing eyes to be an absolute masterpiece of culinary achievement. There were to be ten palate-stimulating courses, and the crowning moment, the pièce de résistance, was a towering, tiered flummery, prepared by Ana herself.

She'd labored intensely over the blanched almonds, vigorously mashing them in a mortar with careful drops of rosewater, as if she were pounding some sense into Dex's head with each jab of the pestle. The boiling and straining had been a whole other set of painstaking maneuvers. At one point, it appeared as if the calf's foot stock had not helped the dish set properly, and despair almost overwhelmed her. The kitchen staff, breath bated, watched her gently, bravely, lift the conical mold away from the jelly, and to everyone's amazement and pride the dish held. It sat, quivering slightly, upon a magnificent platter surrounded by a festive garland of flowers and foliage, on a sideboard, ready to be served once the meal had been consumed.

She hoped they'd all be hungry.

She hoped Dex would like it.

She hoped Dex would not skewer her or her guests on the points of the rapiers that hung upon the dining hall walls.

Tessie, with Cloris and Agnes as backup, had put as much care into dressing Ana as she'd put into the flummery, sensing that this was a Very Important Occasion. The woman looking back at her from the mirror was quite pretty in her wild rose–colored silk, the deep pink hue pairing unusually well with her ruddy curls. But she was pale, oh so pale. She'd bitten her lips, a nervous habit from childhood that had reappeared with a vengeance, until they were as rosy as her dress. A small crease of worry that she'd never seen before had taken up residence between her brows.

Do you know what you're doing? Ana asked her reflection. *Will this end in disaster?* There was no answer forthcoming, so she turned away in a flurry of pink skirts. Her guests were due any minute, Dex likely to be not far behind.

She was at the door when they arrived and ushered them in herself. Celestia was looking calm and ethereal in indigo taffeta, Rupert a bit disheveled, cravat askew and waistcoat rumpled. His brown hair was standing high off his head, as if he'd raked nervous fingers through it many, many times. They repaired to the drawing room for a fortifying beverage, all ears cocked for the sound of Dex in the front hall.

Polite conversation was blessedly easy with Rupert around. He was a fount of ready observations; they flowed from his lips and required very little in the way of thought. Ana strove to match him, and soon they were volleying observations on the weather, road conditions between the estate and the castle, and the fate of the new foal in Rupert's stables (it had lived, reported Rupert triumphantly) back and forth, while Celestia nodded and smiled as required.

Ana was grateful for their willingness to be there, to indulge her possibly ill-fated experiment. They wanted this dinner to be a success even more than she, and she was grateful for the solidarity. She wished with all her heart that she might be able to keep these amiable and friendly people in her life, add them to her tiny list of family.

If only Dex would be reasonable . . . She caught Rupert's eye and knew he was thinking the same thought. He gave her a reassuring grin and a shrug, as if to say, *It's out of our hands now.* As she returned the grin, she heard McArdle hurrying to the front door, the large metal hinges of which groaned laboriously as it opened and admitted the duke. His deep voice greeting McArdle, McArdle's officious answer. Heavy footsteps growing nearer.

Ana stood up.

Dex walked into the room.

His eyes flew first to Ana, with that hungry look she couldn't help but reciprocate, her insides melting instantaneously. He started across the room toward her, stopping abruptly as he noticed the other two figures in the room. He stood still. Stared. Swung his head back to Ana, nostrils flaring.

"Your doing, I suppose?"

"Dex! Welcome home. I thought we'd have a drink before we dine? Cook's prepared a feast. And I've made flummery! Haven't lost my touch after all these years, although I admit I was terrified it wouldn't come out of the mold. Looked a bit sticky on the sides. But it did, it slid right out, and it's glorious." *I'm babbling*, she thought.

Rupert chimed in. "Dex, I hope you'll allow us to stay. Perhaps we might converse as a family for a while. We only want to get acquainted with your bride, who is as charming as we could have wished for. Would that be all right with you, just a conversation? And then, of course, maybe some of the famous flummery?"

Ana shot him a grateful look. "Yes, Dex, please! I went to so much trouble—I only want to become acquainted with my new sister- and brother-in-law. And I thought . . . I thought you might—"

"Rupert." Dex cut through the chatter with the broadsword of his voice. "You were banned from Drakefell. I haven't changed my mind since. You will do me the service of leaving at once."

Rupert's face blanched.

Ana realized she was clenching her fists so tightly that her nails were carving little crescents into her palms. "Dex, no! You can't. For me."

"For you," Dex said through a clenched jaw, "I will not throw him out bodily. Just for you. Is that enough, Ana? Am I reformed enough for your taste?"

Ana's heart sank. The wounds were too deep. His heart clenched as fiercely as his fists. What had she been thinking? She should have talked to him first. Eased him into the idea. Chipped away at his resistance until he allowed her to invite his brother to dinner if only to silence her. But no, she'd forged ahead, straight into the maw of danger, as she always did.

And now both she and her newly found family would pay the price.

"Deckard." Celestia rose. There was a ring of authority in her usually mellow voice. The queen was speaking. She walked slowly toward the duke, the dark blue of her skirt like a column of night sky. Ana held her breath; she sensed Rupert doing the same. Dex appeared to be frozen to the spot, a wince of pain etched on his face.

"Deckard, enough. You are justified in your anger. We made a mistake by coming here. We hoped, as we will always continue to hope, that the hurt and betrayal you feel might lessen over time, enough for you to allow us back into your life. In whatever capacity you are comfortable with, to whatever degree you are able. But you are still living in the past. You became stuck in time on that battlefield, and have never managed to become unstuck, and I grieve for you."

"Enough. Celestia, stop." Dex's eyes were hollow pits.

"Yes. I grieve for the lack of you, in my life and in the life of your brother. Look at me. I am not the person you thought I was. I was not the right woman for you. You've always been wrong about me. It wasn't your physical scars that daunted me, it was your mental ones. Scars that possibly, if I were a better person, stronger and more patient, I could have helped to heal. But I am not that person. And now I can see that you have that person in your life—Ana. She is a treasure. So strong, so caring and capable. She is fighting for you. She was brave enough to seek us out, to invite us to your home, to risk your good will toward her on a chance for healing, for all of us. Isn't that a beautiful thing, Deckard? Can't you at least acknowledge that?"

"She does whatever she wants. She's incorrigible." The hint of a tortured smile, quirking one corner of his mouth.

"And that's what you want. What you need. A fighter. We'll leave Drakefell, Dex. We won't push any further. But we want to know Ana, if she wants to know us. And we will always be waiting, just down the hill, ready to welcome our brother back to us. When you are ready. Which I think may be sooner than any one of us imagine, if my intuition is correct." And with that enigmatic pronunciation, Celestia glided to Rupert's side, linked her arm through his, and led him out of the room.

Ana watched them go, tears filling her eyes so that the whole room swam. "Dex." Her voice sounded tiny and vulnerable to her own ears. "I only wanted to help."

"And I have told you so many times there's no helping me. Some things are broken forever."

Even as he spoke the words, his heart yearned to take them back. He watched shadows stripe her face, obscuring the green fire that usually lit her eyes.

"You're still angry with them for betraying you," she whispered. "After all this time."

"I'm not angry, Ana. I don't . . ." he continued, dragging the words out, as if feeling them out for accuracy. ". . . hate or . . . blame them anymore, in any way. I see that what Celestia did was right. I was an arrogant, entitled, cold duke. I was raised to be that way. My brother was the kind and humble one. I always saw it as a weakness in him. She made the right choice."

"How difficult that must have been—to have lost so much in the war, and then to lose your betrothed as well." Compassion covered her face.

"I'm still alive, aren't I? Others aren't, and all because of my arrogance."

"Oh, Dex. That's . . ." She rushed toward him and folded her arms around him, laying her head on his chest. He bent down to touch his cheek to her cheek.

For the briefest of moments he felt safe, loved, warm, understood . . . forgiven.

Never forgiven. He pulled himself upright and gently removed her arms. "I don't need your sympathy. I don't deserve it."

"I don't care if you want or deserve it. You have it. Nobody can change the past, Dex! That's an accepted truth of life, one you seem to ignore. You attack the world with that chip on your shoulders. As if swinging away wildly at it will make the past disappear."

"I'm not stupid. How can I make it disappear? I'm forever scarred by it physically."

"*I* forget about your scars, Dex. I don't even see them anymore."

"Please don't." He winced. "Don't insult me with lies. Next you'll say it's the character of a man that makes him worthy of love. Platitudes don't remove scars, Ana."

"And scars don't obscure or prevent love! They are evidence in themselves of new life, of the body protecting itself. Your scars are proof that your body wants you to be whole, to live. Your mind yearns for love, it must."

Love. Warmth. Her warmth, her love.

"You've gone silent, Dex. Do I have to stand here and watch you retreat back into your cave, time after time? What is it like in there? Why do you stay?"

The chaos of war. Cannons detonating in his eardrums, waves swamping a boat. The screams of people he'd sat with, played cards with, just the night before, writhing in the dirt. Their blood, their limbs, littering the ground. He sat down on the nearest chair, without feeling it under him.

"It's dark. Chaotic. Empty."

"Surely not empty, Dex. Tell me what you see. Let me in. Say the words out loud. I can help, by listening, by lightening your load. Please let me carry some of your burden, Dex."

"No."

"Speak, damn you!"

"Is this what you want to hear?" His voice a razor-sharp bitterness, an ocean of emptiness. "Do you like knowing that my hands are soaked with blood? The hands that touch you have strangled, have murdered in the name of King and country. Do you like knowing that I hate what I've done? That I wish I'd been born in an era of peace. That the only thing that stopped me from running away and taking a coward's way out was my sense of honor and duty and that's all I have. Do you understand that? All I have is my duty. And I am the reason for your father's death."

"I cling to the hope that he may still be alive."

"He's not, Ana. Stop saying that!"

"But how do you *know*? Because my heart tells me otherwise."

"I know because I held him in my arms as he bled. He's buried in a shallow grave somewhere, along with a heap of other bodies. Ana, I'm speaking plainly because I believe it's best for you. You wanted to hear my truth, and this is part of it. Your father is dead."

She started weeping softly. "You don't know that for certain."

"I do."

"You're saying it because I forced you to relive the hurt of having your heart broken—you're saying it to wound me, to bring me down to your level. I won't come down there with you, Dex. I can't. I believe in living life."

"Then you must live it alone. Because I can't. And I never will."

Her breathing quieted, and he saw a familiar look of concentration form on her tearstained face. It was a look he knew well, one that vexed him, but filled him with so much pride that his heart threatened to push out of his rib cage whenever it appeared.

She was quickly analyzing all the information in front of her, her writer's brain busily plotting possible moves. Her instincts for self-preservation were remarkable, her knack for thinking her way out of situations part of what made her so formidable, so unforgettable.

"But I have seen you live, watched you come alive. I have lived with you. Nobody is perfectly divided into separate boxes. The passion you share with me in bed, the pleasure you take in sparring with me—yes, pleasure! That's life. Your honesty and directness would make you a terrible actor. It's not an act. I *see* the warmth in your eyes and *hear* the amusement in your voice when we talk."

She paced toward the fireplace and back to him, her voice as agitated as her walk. "And as for your brother and Celestia—you've forgiven them, and you don't even know it. You didn't look at her with any love, but there wasn't any hatred there either. Just habit. You've made this way of being your habitual mode. And I've discovered the truth. At last, Dex. The truth is that you're already alive and healing, you just won't admit it yet."

The pink-clad woman in front of him, eyes snapping, certainty ringing in her voice, angered him in a way he couldn't explain. Had she struck the main nerve, the heart of the thing? Was that why he felt his fists clenching? His fury mounting, that dependable weapon—or crutch, perhaps—something strong enough to lean on.

"I am telling you for the last time. And you must mark my words, Ana." He drew himself up, towering over her. "I can't be redeemed. This is our last battle on this front. You cannot win."

"I've already won, you're just too cowardly to admit it!"

"Then I am a coward. One who doesn't require or seek deep emotional connections. I don't need romance, I need an heir. A tranquil home life. You need the comfort and security I can give you, the space in which to pursue your writing. It's a good and sensible arrangement. It's the arrangement we both agreed upon."

She shook her head, sadness filling her eyes. "I've changed since we made our arrangement."

"And I remain the same. This isn't a fairy tale, Ana. This fire-breathing dragon will never transform into a doting, handsome prince."

"Then leave me alone, Dex!" she cried wildly. "Slink back into your cave and live your cold, solitary existence. I'll honor our arrangement, but I'll continue to live my life on my own terms. I'll build a relationship with Rupert and Celestia, I'll wrestle the joy out of living. I need life—beautiful, awful, messy, heartbreaking life! And I'll have it with or without you."

The challenge of her words rang in the air. An opportunity for him to bend to her will, take her into his arms. Kiss her and tell her that he wanted to live life with her.

The old darkness dragging him down, stealing the words from his lips. Filling his mouth with soil. Sending him back to the grave that should have been his.

"As you will." He squared his shoulders, feeling a hundred years older than when he'd entered the room. "I'm headed to London at daybreak. Be well, Ana."

He left behind a heap of rose-colored silk on the divan, shoulders shaking with the effort to contain her sobs.

Nobody had won the war.

There were no survivors this time.

The castle staff tiptoed past the open door, hastily removing the evidence of the ill-fated dinner from the dining room. The heated conversation had floated out into the rest of the house, the anger and hurt in their master's and mistress's voices unmistakable. McArdle was the last to pass by. If he lingered a bit too long outside of the room, or if maybe a tear or two gleamed in his eyes, one could never tell for sure, hidden as he was behind the gelatinous conical splendor of the flummery, destined to go untasted into the dark recesses of Drakefell's rubbish bin.

Another casualty of their irreconcilable clash.

Chapter Twenty-Eight

It was time to end this evil. She uncorked the amulet and raised it above her head. "Restore my father to me!" Nothing happened.

She waved it in front of her, sending a spray of glittering blue drops into the air like tiny stars. "Reverse this evil, o amulet of enchantment!"

The droplets settled onto the stone floor in front of her uncle, who was grinning a nasty grin, completely unharmed by Gaethryn's enchantment.

"Oh foolish Amsonia. Was that trinket supposed to transfix me with its prettiness? How quaint!"

—*The Dragon and the Blue Star* by Analise Crewe

Dear Duchess,

I am writing in response to your advertisement in the Morning Post. I believe I know the whereabouts of your Father, having met a Gentleman that matches your description of him while traveling to see relatives in Dorcester. The Gentleman in question was granted passage from Belgium to Dover by a kindly merchant and has been wandering the countryside in a westerly manner ever since. He suffers from a near total Amnesia and is in a greatly weakened state. Seeing him will be a matter of some delicacy, due to the poor quality of his health. I fear the shock of learning his own identity might cause irreparable damage to his heart.

He has been taken in by a family in Littlebredy, of which I am well acquainted. They are Good People and were moved by his piteous state. They found him by the side of a road outside the village, asking anyone he encountered if they knew his little girl, but could give only the name "Anna," no surname or other details that might help determine his or his daughter's identity. I was much Moved by his sad tale, which has remained present in my mind ever since. Imagine my surprise in reading your advertisement, and my Great Joy at the possibility of reuniting father and daughter!

I would speak with you further on this matter and beg you to travel quickly to London. I am staying at the Rose & Crown for another two days, then must return to the countryside myself. I would be happy to accompany you there to ascertain whether this man is truly your own Father. I would also ask that when you meet me, you don't bring your husband, the Duke, lest the man who might be your Father be overwhelmed and succumb to his injuries. He exhibits a mortal fear of all Men, especially those of Military Bearing, but is soothed greatly by the presence of Womenfolk.

I will be waiting at the Rose & Crown. Haste is Essential!

Respectfully yours,
Margerie Dunnock

The lone sheet of paper and the envelope it had been delivered in fell from Ana's grasp and floated to the ground. Since Dex had departed, she'd been alone in the castle, albeit surrounded by staff and the kind attentions of Tessie and the sisters, who all seemed to know that something devastating had happened and were solicitousness itself. She had felt herself floating around ghostlike, the spark she'd always carried within her snuffed out by a great darkness. What had caused her light to be extinguished, like a candle under a douter? What had happened to change the makeup of her being?

Dex had happened. She made herself think the thought through, absorb its meaning.

She'd lain her heart at his feet and he'd crushed it under his boot heel.

Since he'd left, she hadn't been herself. She was a phantom living a one-sided life, with no outlet for her vitality, no oxygen to keep her inner fire alight. She was by turns anguished and angry, as if she were being frozen in ice, then roasted over a fire, again and again.

But these written words felt like a slap to her face, a bracing one, administered by fate.

". . . *wandering the countryside . . . asking if they knew his little girl . . .*"

Could it be? Her father, alive. If it was true, it would be the answer to her prayers. She would have her father back, and with him life wouldn't feel empty at all.

She found Tessie back upstairs in her bedchamber, polishing the contents of her jewelry box. Ana held the letter aloft. "Tessie, I've had word from London. A woman who claims to have met my father."

Tessie lifted her head. "That's wonderful news."

"We'll leave for London immediately."

"Oh . . . Ana." Tessie's voice trailed off; her face was pale and the hand that held the polishing cloth quivered.

"Tessie." Ana rushed to her friend's side. "Are you ill?"

"I . . . I've had a dreadful headache all morning. And now it's gone much worse. I feel quite dizzy. I do suffer from the megrims from time to time. Nothing helps except a dark room, and time."

"Then what are you doing sitting here in my room in the sunlight? Come. Off to bed with you." She helped Tessie stand and threw an arm around her shoulders. "I'll help you to your room."

Ana saw her settled into bed and drew the curtains. "I'll have George bring you water and a cold cloth for your eyes."

"Thank you," Tessie said weakly. "Ana . . . you mustn't go to London alone. It could be an unscrupulous person attempting to prey upon your good and trusting nature."

"I've thought of that. I will exercise the utmost caution. I'm to meet an elderly lady in a public house. I don't see how harm could come to me there."

"Take one of the duke's footmen with you. Or, better yet, His Grace."

Ana promised, even though she had no intention of bringing Dex. The letter had explicitly forbidden it and she meant to ascertain the veracity of the woman's claim herself, before involving others.

She had ample time on the long ride to somewhat collect her thoughts, which had grown tumultuous and impossible to wrangle in the aftermath of Dex's departure. She didn't wish to see him in person again, not yet. To do so would break her heart afresh, and she needed time and sufficient distance in which to let it mend—if doing so was possible.

But she also knew that she owed him some explanation, some courtesy to answer the kindness he'd shown her, the goodness in him that drove him to help those in need.

She scrawled out a note on parchment paper perched on her knees, the carriage's lurching gait making her handwriting as wild and scattered as her feelings. It was short and to the point, outlining the contents of the letter she'd received and her intention to travel to Littlebredy to find out the truth for herself.

She couldn't help the tears that fell, smudging the penciled words here and there. Let him read between the lines and know how badly he'd hurt her. She doubted he would care. He was too far gone, locked back up in the dungeon of his chosen existence.

The coachman, spurred on by her flushed and tear-stained face, had heeded her instruction to make haste, and she arrived outside of Dex's townhouse a full half day sooner than she'd expected. She looked furtively out the window for any activity that might signify Dex's presence inside, but the house seemed still.

She didn't knock on the front door, just slipped inside in the hopes that nobody would be alerted to her visit. The folded piece of paper with its blunt penciled lines could be left on the side table in the lofty foyer, where McArdle, who had accompanied the duke to London, would surely spot it and fulfill his duty (as always), delivering it to his master immediately upon receipt.

She almost fulfilled this mission. The missive was delivered to the glossy inlaid surface of the table and she was turning away, hood drawn low over her brow, when an imperious voice sounded from a nearby doorway.

"Analise? Is that you? Whatever are you doing creeping about in your own home?"

It was Lady Glynis.

Ana turned slowly. "Why, Lady Glynis, what a surprise. What are you doing here?"

The lady snorted, looking down her patrician nose at the intruder. "Didn't I ask that very question of you first? I can see that time and marriage have not improved your manners. I am staying here at Warburton's behest while my London apartments are remodeled. Did he not mention this to you?" She subjected Ana to a particularly searching gaze.

Ana bristled impatiently. "No, Lady Glynis, he did not. But we haven't been in contact in the last few days. I have only just arrived."

"How unusual. Did you truly travel to London without prior communication? He never mentioned you would be joining him. He's been in the most frightful of moods since his own arrival."

"His moods are his own concern," Ana snapped. This final barrier between herself and her quest to find her father felt unbearable. And she was terrified of seeing Dex. If Lady Glynis delayed her long enough that he intercepted them . . . "If you'll excuse me, I must be on my way."

"Not staying?" Disapproval dripped from Lady Glynis's voice. "A lover's quarrel? I swear, I will never understand the peculiar nature of your relationship with my nephew. He has been completely changed by you."

"Not completely," Ana said quietly. "But I really must take my leave, Lady Glynis. Please forgive my lack of manners." She glanced involuntarily at her note, sitting on the side table, and then gave the surrounding hall one last regretful look.

"I have always done so before," sniffed the lady. "Why should I stop now?" But Ana was already gone, the door closing behind her. If Ana had glanced back, she might have seen Lady Glynis looking perplexedly after her, then turning her formidable gaze to the rectangle of paper Ana had left behind.

The Rose & Crown had been surprisingly easy to find, with the help of several strangers, happy to give direction to a young lady with excitement and hope filling her heart and eyes, and a determined air. It almost felt as if London itself wanted to help her on her way and was exhibiting its kindest side to her. She pushed down the doubts when they slithered through her mind, spreading shadows and despair.

My father is waiting for me, she thought to herself. *He needs me*, repeated like a prayer. She arrived out of breath, from anticipation as much as exercise, and darted inside the tavern before she lost her nerve.

It took a moment for her eyes to adjust to the low lights inside. The pipe smoke and the thick odors of steak and kidney pie combined to form a greasy haze that obscured the occupants of the busy tavern. She fought her way to the bar, evading elbows making busy work of steaming plates and men leaning back in their chairs, roaring with laughter and shouting rowdy boasts and toasts at each other.

"Pardon me," she asked the barkeep, an affable-looking man with a cauliflower ear. "I'm looking for a Margerie Dunnock, who has taken a room here."

"Eh?" He cupped his free hand to his good ear, leaning across the bar top.

"I'm looking for—" but Ana got no further. A hand fell on her shoulder. She turned around and saw, swimming before her in the smoke and murk, a middle-aged woman with a nondescript dun-colored cloak fastened about her, bulky and shapeless. She had on a pair of round spectacles under the brim of a straw bonnet with sad little brown feathers emerging from its brim.

"Your Grace?" asked the woman in a soft, breathy voice that Ana could barely hear.

"Mrs. Dunnock?" Ana asked, leaning in eagerly. "I'm happy to make your acquaintance. May we speak in private?"

"Certainly," said the woman, a small smile quickly flickering over her face. She drew Ana by the elbow to a table in the corner, waited for her to sit, staring intently at her through the thick rings of her eyeglasses, then sat opposite her. "I'm so pleased that you received my letter and came. I've been very curious to meet you."

"And I you!" Ana felt a strange nervousness flood her, unrelated to the nervous energy she'd been swimming in since she'd received the letter. She felt quite sure she'd never seen the woman before, but there was about her a vague familiarity, as if she were someone Ana had met in a dream, or another life. "Can you tell me more about this gentleman, this man you think might be my father?"

"I'm happy to, but I really must caution you—we haven't much time to waste! The doctor said he was suffering from shock in addition to multiple wounds on his body, likely incurred in the war. They are mostly healed but have taken much from him. If he doesn't reorient himself through the loving care of those dear to him, he may be lost. And his heart is very delicate—you came unaccompanied by your husband, as I asked?" The woman looked toward the door, squinting through the crowd.

"I did. I'm prepared to journey with you—but please, one moment." She closed her eyes and thought. What would Dex, with his steady practicality and cutting logic, require of the moment? What would he do to strike to the heart of the matter? "Can you give me any more details that might make me certain it is my own father? I imagine there are many veterans of the war with daughters named Anne or Anna . . ."

There was that small smile again, almost furtive. There and then gone.

The woman ducked her head, nodding solemnly. "So wise, you are, to ask. One can't be too cautious. A noble lady like yourself would naturally need further proof before venturing on such a quest. There are evil characters in this world that would drag a blossom like yourself through filth if they had half a chance! Here—this was the only possession he had on his person the day my friends encountered him. He passed it along willingly, understanding that it might help reunite him with his beloved Anna."

She reached inside the capacious coat, and for a second, Ana caught a jarring glimpse of purple silk inside, incongruously bright against the sensible brown wool, and then it was gone. The woman's hand emerged, holding out a thin gold chain with something round at the end of it that caught the low light and flashed green fire into the tavern gloom.

The ring her father had worn always on a chain around his neck. Her mother's small gold ring with one emerald set in the middle. A match to the set she owned.

She took the ring from Margerie, running her thumb wonderingly over the sparkling green stone, holding it to the light to read the initials etched on the inside. The woman watched her, unblinking, from beneath her bonnet, the sparrow feathers puffing slightly into the air with each controlled breath she made.

"This is my mother's ring, that my father wore always about his neck. It's truly him." This woman was an honest Good Samaritan. She'd handed over the ring readily, when she could have kept it for herself and never contacted Ana at all. Heart pounding a joyful rhythm, she slipped the chain over her head, nestling the ring inside her bodice. "I'm ready to go to him. I'm ready to find my father."

The woman was on her feet before she finished, urging her up from the table. She conducted Ana through the room, paused to pass a sum of money to the barkeep with a nod, moving with a purposeful swiftness that was at odds with her meek demeanor.

She fairly pushed Ana out into the daylight and propelled her down the street, turning several times, exhorting Ana to move quickly, to make haste. Ana felt as if she were floating, borne along by a strong current in an ocean. It was happening so quickly. She barely had time to think of Dex and wish he were here, after all, before the woman practically shoved her into a low carriage, crowded in behind her, and shut the door.

Darkness. In the momentary stillness that followed, before the handkerchief with its achingly oversweet smell was pressed to her nose, Ana was struck by a sudden memory.

"That necklace was a beauty!" Miss Flanagan's voice from far away, a lifetime ago. Miss Flanagan, who had a key to her room. Miss Flanagan, who had seen the emerald necklace, who could have read the letters from her father and heard tell of the matching ring he wore around his neck. Miss Flanagan, who had greedy fingers. And a sister, Maggie.

"Pleased to finally make your acquaintance, Ana," said the woman, with a wide, voracious grin, as Ana collapsed onto the hard cushions of the carriage. "Maggie Flanagan's my name. You deserve what's finally coming to you, make no mistake."

Chapter Twenty-Nine

"You! Aren't you done meddling in my life?" Qavox fixed his whirling eyes on the ephemeral image of Gaethryn, floating in the air in front of him in the gloom of the cave. "What do you mean Amsonia needs my help? She needs help from no one. She has your magic."

"There are some things that mere magic cannot fix. Amsonia needs your fire, Qavox. You were her captor and protector, now go to her and do what a dragon does best!"

—*The Dragon and the Blue Star* by Analise Crewe

The Thunderbolt Club was quiet that afternoon, and Dex was enormously grateful. He'd arrived with a bundle under his arms, having made a quick stop at Norwood & Pennington, and meant to find a solitary nook in which to examine his prize.

He was hailed by several acquaintances, forced into a few conversations. He'd made, he hoped, the appropriate sounds. He'd swallowed the libations offered him, shook the hands proffered.

He'd hoped, as he'd been hoping since he'd left Drakefell, that contact with his old life, his solitary Ana-less life, would shake him back into place, make him feel like himself again.

It hadn't happened yet. The numbness that he craved never arrived. Nor could he silence her lively voice ringing in his ears.

I need life—beautiful, awful, messy, heartbreaking life! And I'll have it with or without you.

He couldn't bury the memory of the tears shining in her eyes. He'd left her crying. Turned his back when he wanted to sweep her into his arms and never let her go.

Since the war, he'd been alone by choice. Now it was devastating, the loneliness. A deep, dark cavern from the bottom of which he could just barely make out the faces of those around him. He saw now that his life before Ana had been a barren, solitary existence with no one to challenge him, no one to tease him, and no one to . . . love him.

He tossed back a tumbler of brandy. Love. Something he'd sworn didn't truly exist. He'd thought he loved Celestia and she'd cast his heart aside easily and chosen his brother. Her words had rung true, though. Perhaps he'd never truly known her. She'd been his childhood love, and then the beautiful shining beacon he'd fought for during the war. An icon purely of his own creation.

Here. He laid his palm against the thick stack of pages crammed with words that had flowed from Ana's passionate and imaginative mind. Here was something solid to hold on to, a chance to see inside the dreams of the woman he'd married. In this deep leather chair partially obscured by an enormous potted fern, with just enough light coming in from the window behind it to illuminate the manuscript, he would read *The Dragon and the Blue Star*. It was the only piece of Ana accessible to him in London.

Hours later, the light had faded to the point where he had to bend over and piece the words together. He was nearly to the end. It was good. It was better than good. It was strange, lyrical, dark, at times hilarious. It called to his dormant imagination, long put to bed because it persisted in conjuring battlefield scenes, and bade it to soar with hers, to see the mythical land of Vyranthrall beneath him.

The castles, the forests, the mountain cave. The creatures—ogres, talking hedgehogs, mages, that dragon! The dragon fascinated him. He felt a kinship with it; the obvious similarity between its literal cave and his metaphorical one pleased him. Dex and Qavox. They could be twins. Scars and scales. Similar protective layers.

He was racing toward the end against his own will, the pages dwindling too quickly. The threads were all coming together in a gratifying tapestry. The characters were being dispatched to their just desserts—the evil, vanquished. The princess reunited with her father. The dragon—he turned the final page and stared at the blankness of the page behind it. He smiled. It was all becoming clear to him now.

"What are you smiling about back here in your dark corner, Warburton?" asked Somersby, sauntering over with a drink in his hand and picking up a few pages of the book. "You're reading fiction? Never knew you to read instead of box, or ride."

Dex reclaimed the pages, placing them carefully back where they belonged. "This book was written by my wife."

Somersby raised both of his dark eyebrows. "Erm . . . what are you doing here reading a book written by your fetching young bride, when you could be with her in the marital bed? Aren't you still on your honeymoon?"

"Events . . . happened."

"So you had a quarrel. A fiery lady like that is sure to cause conflagrations from time to time. Stop reading her book and go back to her bed, man! I know I would."

Dex decided to ignore Somersby's lewd suggestive wink. That was just Somersby. Always a bawdy joke. But his words held the power of an earthquake.

Stop reading her book, searching for her in the pages. Go and find her. Beg her forgiveness. Tell her what he'd found at the end of the novel.

Himself. A dragon transformed.

"You know what, Somersby?" Dex leapt from his chair and slapped his friend on the back so hard he nearly dropped his drink. "For once in your life you're absolutely right!"

He was leaving the club, leading Odysseus by the reins, when a familiar yet incongruous figure alighted from a carriage.

"Aunt Glynis?"

She looked uncharacteristically excited—there was an almost animated quality to her face, and her gray hair was ever so slightly loose at the crown, as if it were preparing to spring away from her stern head and run off.

"Nephew." She spoke in ringing tones, waving something white in her hand. "I must have a word with you. Your wife arrived at the townhouse earlier." She advanced a step toward him, her words cutting into the air between them. "She left a note."

Dex felt every muscle in his body tense. "A note?"

She passed him a sheet of paper, unfolded and obviously preread. He scanned it, jaw clenching. It took a few moments for the contents to assemble into some sort of logical order. Ana's father, alive?

Aunt Glynis folded her arms over the rigidly contained shelf of her breast. "Well, nephew? What say you to the foolishness your impetuous wife is caught up in this time?"

His heart thudded in his chest, the world tilting off its axis. "She actually left the house alone? To meet this person?"

"It would appear so. I had half a mind to call for the constable and take care of it in my own way, but I decided you would want to rescue her yourself, being the war hero and all." She fixed him with a withering glare. "Your wife (the future mother to your heirs, lest we forget that fact!) receives a letter made up of the most *absurd* fantasies, with details anyone could have gleaned from *anywhere*, written by an *absolute* stranger who bids her to—my boy, please attend this part, if you have retained any amount of sensibility at all—*travel without you to meet them*?"

"You're right. It's a damned trap. I'm going after her." He placed Ana's manuscript carefully into his saddlebag and swung into the saddle. "Thank you, Aunt," he shouted over his shoulder as he urged Odysseus to a gallop.

Lieutenant Crewe was dead. It was only Ana's obstinate will that had kept her father alive, and he only lived in her imagination. Whoever had written the letter somehow had intimate details of the man. But blast it all, who? And why?

They hadn't clamored for the reward but were attempting to draw her away from the city by herself. A kidnapping, the chance to raise the stakes and ask for more money? If so, he'd be hot on their heels.

When he arrived at the public house, he paid a groom to hold Odysseus's bridle in anticipation of his return. The crowded room parted easily for him, his height and breadth cutting a straight path to the bar. As he moved, he scanned the throng with eager eyes that yielded nothing of interest. The barkeep, all obsequiousness, spread his hands wide on the bar and asked, "How can I be of service, my lord?"

"I'm looking for a young lady. She's small and has red curls, and she may have met with a woman who was already waiting for her here."

"Small with red what'd you say?" The man leaned his good ear toward Dex.

Dex repeated himself at top volume. To his relief, the barkeep grinned immediately and nodded. "I know the very one! I said to myself, it's not often we have such a vision o' loveliness round these parts, is it. Fresher than springtime. An' she did, she met with a woman, just as you says."

"Are they still here?" Dex yelled. "Did you recognize the woman?"

"They left not an hour ago, m'lord. I remember because the older of the two was in a real hurry to take her leave, most anxious, she was! Left a large sum and dropping feathers the whole way, like a bird flying the coop."

"Did you say feathers?" Dex said, suddenly still. An odd detail. Some memory began to beat a tense rhythm at the back of his mind.

"Aye, feathers it was. Hat covered in 'em. You know how ladies are with their fashions. I said to myself, this is a strange bird, though. Made a special note, I did. Me hearings not s'good, but my mind is sharp as a penknife. Sorta makes up for it." He nodded wisely and winked at Dex.

Dex slid several coins across the bar. He masked the impatience threatening to erupt within his breast and fixed the garrulous barkeep with a glare of pure steel. "What made her so strange, may I ask?"

"Well, you see, it's like this: that older woman weren't much to look at, plain as anything, like a little wren. But under her coat she wore purple feathers, like some tropical bird. Seen 'em when she reached inside her cloak to pay me, I did. Purple feathers, on the inside, brown on the out. What kind o' bird do you think that is?"

"A dangerous one," Dex growled. His fists clenched at his side. The memory was unfurling quickly in his mind's eye: the hard gaze, the gaudy affectations, and the undulating marabou of Madame D'Oiseaux, neé Flanagan. "Let's hope she flew back to her coop. For her sake. And mine."

Out of the Rose & Crown, and back onto Odysseus. Driving his horse as fast as he dared on the crowded street. Ana, trapped in the talons of that monster. Ana, without an ounce of artifice in her entire being, caught up in the machinations of that imposter, with her faux French and feathered finery. He hoped he was wrong, but he feared he was right.

La Maison de Mme D'Oiseaux, gaudy as ever, was singularly empty and quiet. No muscle at the door to greet him, no impediment to slow him down as he stormed through the salon. The place looked in a sorry state, dirty and neglected, the garish trappings finally failing to conceal its ugly innards.

"Where is your mistress?" he bellowed at the handful of women peeping out of alcoves and hallways at the noisy intruder. They skittered away from him fearfully as he approached. He tore open door after door, calling for the Madame. A belligerent customer, pulling trousers over his hips, hurried out of one room to protest, caught sight of his glowering face and beat an expeditious retreat.

"She ain't here," a small voice volunteered from behind. He

wheeled around, fear and rage making his scars a livid red. The owner of the voice, cowering a bit, examined his face and nodded with recognition. "Not many are these days. You're the duke as helped Daisy and t' others escape, ain't you?"

"I am," he said, biting down on the insides of his cheeks to keep from yelling. "Where is the Madame?"

"We're not supposed to say, Your Grace. Could get in real trouble." She screwed up her face in a grimace of indecision.

"I promise no harm will come to you," he got out through gritted teeth. "I swear to God I will shut this place down and find good stations for all of you—just tell me, where is the Madame?"

She pursed her lips. "I'm not sure, to be honest. She rode off with Burt and Figgleston, told us to keep the house running and not to talk to any strangers that came looking for her. That's all."

"Did she say anything else? Anything at all. Please think carefully."

The poor girl searched her own recollection for a long minute, far too long for Dex to be at all optimistic about the outcome, before emerging triumphantly with a memory in hand.

"I did hear Burt say something about visiting 'the sister'! His sister, maybe? Or Figgleston's? Or—a nun? D'you suppose they went t' church?" She trailed off in confusion.

Dex had a momentary feverish vision, a phalanx of sisters in dark habits surrounding Ana, carrying her aloft and away from him. But his logical brain was still working and had already made the necessary leap to the truth.

"You've been very helpful. Thank you." He gave her a coin. "Please don't worry about the Madame. I will take care of you. And her, as well."

To his horse again. Galloping around carriages on the street, causing people crossing the streets to spring backward or throw themselves forward, anything to stay out of this madman's way.

One thought in his mind: Ana was in danger. This was beyond the simple kidnapping he'd at first assumed it to be. It wasn't just money at stake. Maggie Flanagan was no ordinary criminal, spotting an opportunity for some quick coin in the form of a ransom. Not she. Maggie was made of hatred. And she had a reason to hate him, to want to hurt him. Hurting Ana would accomplish this. Thoroughly.

It didn't matter how many ill-used girls he aided, how many families of the fallen he helped. His own salvation lay in the well-being of a small, stubborn, sweet woman named Ana. And he'd put her in danger.

Running up the steep front stairs of Miss Flanagan's boarding house, his thoughts chasing each other around like howling wolves circling a campfire. The dilapidated rowhouse standing tall in front of him, the windows lifeless and forbidding. He raised his hand to the door, and in that moment, memories flooded him.

Lieutenant Crewe clutching at the lapel of his uniform. *Promise me you'll find Analise . . . protect her . . .*

Ana's bright face, the first time he'd seen her, opening this same door.

The oval of her face again, on their wedding day, turned up toward him, her green eyes full of challenge.

The sweetness of her body under his, her musical sighs and moans.

He'd been letting a legion of dead men stand between himself and living. Nothing could erase the past, but she—she wanted to help him build a new future. He was the luckiest man in the world. He would revel in this gift she was offering. He would cherish her until his dying day.

As long as he could save her from harm first.

He tried the door. Locked. He braced himself against the low railing of the porch and kicked with all his strength. Once, twice.

On the third kick, the lower half of the doorframe splintered inward.

He was in.

The house was dark. Quiet. If anyone were here, the demise of the doorframe would have alerted them to his presence, but there was no answering din, nobody rushing to meet him. He moved quickly through the rooms in the front of the main floor. Nothing.

And then he heard it. A muffled cry, footsteps scuffling at a distance. Not from the ground floor or the basement floor below, but farther away, overhead. He ran back to the foyer and took the stairs three at a time.

The third floor was one long hallway stretching from front to back, with rooms opening off to either side. He paused. What was his strategy? *Think quickly.* Opening each door one by one would give whoever was behind them ample time to plan an ambush, to hide. He made himself go still, slowed his breathing. Concentrated on the stillness. *Listen.*

There it was again, a muted murmur, even higher up. The garret. Its door ajar, the glow of lamplight spilling down the narrow stairs and casting deep shadows on either side of the landing.

He crept forward, thankful for the carpet, however ugly and worn it was. Up the creaking stairs, hand out to grasp the doorknob, eyes adjusting to the shift in light. The door swung wide at his touch. Without thinking, he crossed its threshold and moved into the room, drawn inexorably toward the evil sight framed within.

There, by the window, stood Maggie Flanagan, in a violet robe over a blazingly orange silk dress, lamplight glittering in her dark eyes, slim white hand holding a knife to the throat of his very own redheaded hellion of an Ana.

Chapter Thirty

With a tremendous boom, the head of Qavox came crashing through the wall, shattering the stones. He drew in a mighty breath, then expelled it in a jet of white flame at the Red Wizard, who caught fire instantly. In seconds all that was left was a pile of ash. Then the dragon turned his head and blew a gentler stream of flame that licked and danced around the nightmarish red encasing her father. She watched in wonder as the ruby faded from his face.

"Father!" Amsonia cried, hastening to his side.

—*The Dragon and the Blue Star* by Analise Crewe

You're just in time for the soiree, Your Grace!" purred Maggie, French accent made notable by its absence. She threw back her head and laughed throatily, and Dex felt the back of his own head explode as something very hard and very solid made a meaningful connection with his skull.

As he fell to his knees, his head bounced in a violent circle, showing him the rest of the room. Miss Flanagan, leaning on the bed to his left, a cross-eyed look of confusion covering her face. Two large bodies just behind him emerging from the shadows of the alcove.

"Burt? Or is it Figgleston?" he inquired, when the stars stopped imploding behind his eyes long enough to let him speak.

"Figgleston," grunted the one roughly dragging him back to his feet and restraining him with meaty arms. "That's Burt." Burt was crossing the room toward Ana.

"And you've met my sister, Carol," Maggie simpered. "There! We've all been introduced. We're delighted you could join us. Aren't we, dear? We're going to have such fun." She ran the tip of her knife along the front of Ana's dress and winked at her.

Cold dread seized Dex and he struggled against his captor, partially breaking free before receiving another staggering blow to his solar plexus that knocked the wind from his sails.

"Maggie!" slurred Miss Flanagan. "Put that knife away. You said you weren't goin' to hurt 'er, remember?"

"Oh, I remember, sister mine. I remember quite a lot of things. I remember all the years of hard work and sacrifice it took to set my business up, the men I had to satisfy, the palms I had to grease with my hard-earned coin. I remember having a full house at the brothel, a line of gents in the parlor waiting to meet my birds. I remember money fairly pouring in. Do you know what happens to a bawdy house that suddenly loses five of its most precious wares? Dead of night, very sudden? It has a strange effect on morale, it turns out. The other girls start misbehaving. Don't do as they're told, find other work. And the clientele—well, it hears rumors about a certain duke putting his seal of disapproval on the place, and business dries right up."

Dex, finally finding his breath again, saw Ana's eyes fly wide. She gazed at him approvingly, smiling, despite the knife pressed to her throat.

He'd made her proud. The glow of it was enough to restore his reserves of strength. He'd bide his time. Find precisely the right moment to escape Figgleston and take out Burt and Maggie. He didn't think Carol Flanagan would be much of a threat. She appeared to be half in cups.

She wove to her feet, one hand holding a bottle loosely at her side. "But that weren't all 'is fault, were it? And it certainly wasn't 'ers," she said, gesturing at Ana. "And we won't miss it much, once we get him to pay us the ransom. All is business, sister, and business is all! Isn't that what you always say?"

"You idiot, there will be no ransom!" said Maggie angrily, waving a hand at the whole scene. "We can't let them go after this! His High and Mighty will never let this die, look at him. He's besotted by his tiny little Ana. So we'll let him watch Burt and Figgleston take away his future, like he took away mine. Then we'll kill him, too."

Ana's face went parchment white as Burt grabbed her roughly by the arm, to stop her sudden squirming. Dex stared into her eyes, willing her to be calm, to conserve her energy for what lay ahead.

"But—but the money!" wailed Miss Flanagan. "You said I'd be swimming in champagne and riches, enough to leave this rubbish cart behind for good! 'at's why I told you about the necklace and told you about her father's ring so you could have a copy made. What kind of money can we get outta killing 'im? You said we'd be rich!"

"So?" Maggie tapped her feet impatiently, waiting for her inebriated sister to catch up. "I say a lot of things. Just like I remember a lot of things. Like his lordship here lying to my face, stealing my belongings, ruining my hard-earned business."

Dex turned his head slightly to look at Ana again. She

was flushed and intent. Her brow was furrowed and her eyes narrowed—but he knew with innate certainty that she wasn't frightened. She was listening, she was thinking. She was *scheming*. The glorious machinery of her nimble intellect was whirring, he could almost hear it. He held his breath.

Ana raised her head. "It's really too unfortunate you've antagonized my husband so badly," she proclaimed, dramatically. "He'll never give you the jewels from the family vault, like we discussed before I came. A reward it was to be, for reuniting me with Papa. The diamond diadem fit for a queen. That was to be your reward."

"A diadomd—diamem—jewels!" breathed Carol Flanagan, beginning to mist over as she imagined the sight. She refocused on her sister. "Maggie! Cain't we just let bygones be bygones?"

"Bygone! But it was *by* his hand that it's all *gone*, sister. There's no solution to that. All my hard work, vanished."

"My hard work, too, and I ain't complained," returned her sister. "Bedded my share o' strangers, worked my poor fingers to the bone running that boarding 'ouse, all's so I could send you more girls, while you swanned around a parlor eating bonbons and rubbing elbows with the nobs!"

"Worked your fingers to the bones," spat Maggie. "Drank your bony ass into a stupor, more like! Chirping the whole time about how 'respectable' you were, how *proud* you were of yourself. A whore, just like the girls you sold me."

"A wh-whore," Carol sputtered, her face turning vermilion. "You name your own sister a whore. 'Ow do you like that?"

Dex saw an opening to heap more fuel on the fire. "There would have been such a handsome reward for you, Miss Flanagan, knowing how steadfastly you worked toward providing those young women with respectable lodging and guidance. I could have overlooked everything else. Why, you gave my Ana a home when nobody else would have her. Surely that's worth a healthy fortune in gold?"

"Gold! Maggie." Carol wheeled on her sister. "Let them go! Do y'hear? Do the right thing for once in your goddamned life!"

"You imbecile!" Maggie shouted, her eyes widened in a frightening glare. "If your brain wasn't so pickled in booze, you'd hear how stupid the words coming out of your slatternly mouth actually are. I raised you up with me out of the muck. I gave you everything you have! And I'll ruin you, too!"

"Ruin me? I'll ruin you!" shrieked Carol, raising the bottle over her head, ready to advance on Maggie, who was backing away with her knife outstretched.

Ana met Dex's intense gaze for the briefest of seconds and gave a brief nod. Now was the moment. Burt and Figgleston were staring raptly at the screaming sisters, engrossed in their fighting.

Now, Ana mouthed.

As he wrenched his torso out of Figgleston's beefy grasp and brought his elbow up and back in pursuit of the man's jaw, he saw Ana's arm raise, lightning fast, something slim and cylindrical clutched within it. The pencil connected with Burt's eye. He went down with a yell. Figgleston followed.

Dex supplemented his initial blow with some well-aimed kicks to the kidneys, then vaulted over the body to aid Ana in subduing Burt, who was swinging his head around blindly, the pencil stub still sticking out of his eye, blood spurting from the wound.

As Dex and Ana conquered the hired muscle, Carol thudded headfirst into Maggie's chest, driving her forcefully back, slamming her against the windowsill. The rickety frame of the window was no match for the weight of the two feuding Flanagans. With a *thwack* and the sudden crystalline *crack* of shattering glass, the sisters crashed through, Maggie on bottom. The violet marabou of her robe billowed around them both, fluttering in the night air, as they disappeared from Dex's sight, flying down to the street below.

Dex tied Figgleston's and Burt's hands together with his neck-cloth, while Ana grabbed the knife with shaking fingers, so they couldn't use it to free themselves.

"She stabbed me, that witch," Burt moaned. "I can't see anything."

"Told you we should never 'ave taken this job. Those sisters are Bedlamites, they are," Figgleston said, wincing from the beating Dex had administered.

"You'll live," Dex said. "More's the pity. Don't try to look through your good eye. Keep them both closed." He tore a length of cloth from a shirt hanging in the wardrobe and wrapped it around the pencil.

"Ow!" Burt roared. "Wot you doing?"

"Saving you," Dex said. "You don't want anyone but a physician to dislodge that pencil. We'll call for one."

Ana leaned out the window, mindful of the broken glass. "They both survived," she reported. "Their fall was broken by a passing flower vendor's cart. Carol landed on top of her sister and is already standing up with the help of bystanders. Maggie is . . . well, she's alive, it appears, but still hasn't been able to stand."

"And you?" Dex asked, dread gripping his throat. "Are you injured?"

"Less so than you, I'd say." She walked toward him and touched the bruise rising on his cheek.

"Nothing new," he growled, though it did hurt like hell and there were probably a few cracked ribs as well.

"Come," he said, holding out his hand. Ana placed her small hand inside of his. "Let's go home."

In the distance, a constable's whistle sounded.

Chapter Thirty-One

Embracing her father, happy tears flooding her face, Amsonia turned toward Qavox. "You came back! What changed your mind?"

"You remind me of someone I used to be long ago. Someone I want to be again, if possible. And I think I know who can help me."

"I don't know what you mean! There is much I do not understand," said the princess. "Why didn't the amulet work? What was it all for?"

"Let us go to Gaethryn. She holds the answers . . ."

—*The Dragon and the Blue Star* by Analise Crewe

Ana hadn't stopped shivering since they'd arrived home. Dex had fed her hot beef broth, given her a generous pour of brandy, wrapped her in blankets, and now they sat together in front of a blazing fire.

There was a dullness to her eyes, a listlessness to her posture. "How did you know where to find me?"

"Aunt Glynis came to the club waving the letter you wrote and telling me that my foolish bride had put herself in danger. It was quite remarkable. I honestly think that she's rather fond of you, though she'd never admit it."

"That's . . . unexpected." Ana's head drooped. "I'm so . . . tired."

"Are you certain you didn't sustain an injury?"

"Only to my heart. He's gone, Dex. Papa is dead. I must let him go." She choked back a sob, her body quivering.

"Shhh," he said soothingly, wrapping his arm tighter around her slender shoulders. "You don't have to do anything tonight but rest."

"You were right all along."

"I didn't want to be right. I'll help you grieve him. I have experience in that area."

"Does the pain dull?"

"The pain . . . lessens. With time, with friendship, with . . ." Love. He wanted to tell her everything in his heart but she was grieving, lost in a dark place. He knew what that was like. He must give her time.

"We made a good team facing down those villains, did we not? I almost feel sorry for old Burt, having narrowly escaped a similar fate the first day I met you."

His attempt at humor fell flat. Only a brief nod. Not even the glimmer of a smile.

The tables were turned and he didn't like it. Was this what living with him was like? She was always teasing him, always trying to make him smile. And now he couldn't do the same for her.

"Ana, talk to me. Tell me what you're feeling. It will ease your pain."

She shook her head. "How could I have been so stupid? I trusted the letter because I followed my heart and not my head.

Maybe I've finally learned my lesson. Maybe I'm with you in the cave. Lost in the darkness."

"You can't be. You're the brightest light I know, filled with hope and optimism. They preyed upon that."

She sighed. "I've always told myself that even in the darkest of times, the sun will return. Now I'm not so sure."

"I don't want you to lose that belief that the sun is waiting to shine again. You make me want to believe it, too."

"It's too much, Dex," she sobbed, collapsing against him.

He held her tightly. "We'll feel it together, shall we? It's never going to disappear. The pain of losing him will always be there, like a hard knot of scar tissue on your heart. I'm willing to flay myself open for you, Ana. I would die to ease your way in life."

He was desperate to lighten her heart, hungry for the sweet curve of her lips, the answering gleam in her eyes.

"Ana, do you know what I was doing at the Thunderbolt Club tonight?"

"Talking to Odysseus . . . carousing with your rakish friends . . . getting pummeled in the boxing ring."

"I brought a book with me and I sat quietly reading in a corner the whole evening."

She quirked her head. "I find that unlikely."

"Believe it. And do you know what book I was reading?"

"A scintillating tome on the bloodlines of Yorkshire Trotters?"

"Ha. There were no horses in this book, only hedgehogs and dragons."

She lifted her head. "What do you mean, dragons?"

"I went to Norwood & Pennington and retrieved your manuscript. They'd already had a copy made. I started where I'd left off and read straight through to the end, hardly pausing to breathe or relieve the call of nature."

"Dex." Her lips twitched. "Why on earth did you do that?"

"Because I wanted to see how the story ended. Whether Amsonia's father was saved. Whether her dreaded dragon became a hero in the end."

"You were right," she said, her voice low and raspy. "Life isn't a fairy tale. Fathers are lost forever. Curses can't be lifted."

She was lower than he'd ever seen her, lost in the despair of saying goodbye to the blind hope she'd nurtured for so long.

"He's dead. He's really dead." She hung her head, tears falling on the blanket. "And nothing I say or do, no matter how fiercely I believe, nothing will bring him back."

"He's dead," Dex agreed. There was no use denying it.

The anguish on her face slayed him. "But you're alive, Ana. So vibrantly alive, you have so much light and love to gift to the world. Your book will bring joy to so many."

"I hope . . . you're right," she spoke through her tears.

"I know I am."

She lay her head on his shoulder. He let her cry, not trying to stop her, handing her a handkerchief and holding her damp hair away from her face.

When the sobs subsided, he offered her water. A little bit more brandy. Her head dropped back to his shoulder. He rocked her gently back and forth.

"I liked the ending of your book. When the curse was lifted."

"Mmm," she said sleepily.

"In fact, I believe that dragons can change. They can learn to shed their solitude, learn to . . . love. I saw myself in your story.

I saw how my stubborn refusal to open my heart to giving and receiving love hurts everyone around me."

He glanced down. Her eyes were closed. Her breathing even.

"Ana?" he whispered, but there was no response.

She'd fallen asleep. Exhausted from their perilous evening and from grief.

His leg was beginning to cramp. The fire was dying. But he couldn't move. He didn't want to disturb her. She was too beautiful, too sweet and vulnerable nestled into him, trusting his shoulder to cradle her, his arms to warm her.

She slept so soundly, the soft rustling noise of her breathing like leaves ruffled by a breeze. This was what it would be like to sleep with her at night, to listen to her breathing beside him. He wouldn't be alone anymore.

Her hand in his, so small and trusting. He'd been given a great responsibility: her welfare, her happiness, her pleasure. He wanted to wake her with kisses, take her to his bed and truly warm her, until they were both sweaty and hot and gasping for more.

He wanted things he'd never longed for before. He'd thought of himself as a grumbly, scarred, and dark-hearted man who was past redemption. She was silken sunshine poured onto him, warming him. It gave him this stubborn little flicker of hope. Hope that he might deserve to win her heart. That she could be his.

Hope that he hadn't succeeded in pushing her away.

That she could love him still.

God, he missed her smile. Wide and carefree. Lifting the freckles around her lips, making his heart light up. He missed her laughter, the sly way she looked at him with heat in her green eyes that seared his heart.

What could he say to make her understand that her smile was precious to him, that he'd do anything to bring it back?

He had to find a way. He had to show her what was in his heart. How she'd transformed him. How he'd strive to be worthy of her love from this night forth.

Chapter Thirty-Two

The mists parted, and the Faery Queen drifted across the river toward them. "Welcome, friends, and well done! We will celebrate the end of the Red Wizard's reign. Have you the amulet?"

"I have, but what—" Amsonia stopped. Qavox was approaching Gaethryn, bowing his great head at her feet.

"I repent for my arrogant youth, the harm I did your people. If you deem me worthy, o Queen, I beg you to reverse what you set in motion those long centuries ago."

"Qavox, you are indeed worthy! Your love is your redemption. I have been but waiting to hear you say those words. Amsonia, the amulet . . ."

—*The Dragon and the Blue Star* by Analise Crewe

Ana watched the familiar landscape roll by, thinking how dear it all seemed to her now. A few weeks ago it had seemed strange, a world not entirely belonging to her, but now she watched for every milestone that brought her closer to the castle.

Dex sat with an arm flung protectively around her. He'd insisted that going back to Drakefell would help ease her mind, since she'd be with Tessie, and among her familiar possessions, and the Clovercote manuscript that she'd left unfinished.

Now, she was glad she'd agreed. After days of doing nothing but sleep, and cry, and sleep some more, her eyes craved greenery and sunshine. That tree—that meant they were a quarter hour away. The low stone fence—ten minutes to go.

Just outside the tree-shaded drive, Dex slipped something out of his pocket and brought it to her eyes. She felt the cool silk of a handkerchief as he placed it around her head and turned her face blindly toward him.

"What's this?"

"I want this to be a surprise."

When the carriage rolled to a stop, he lifted her down gently, strong hands encircling her waist.

"What's that heavenly smell?" Her nose wrinkled appreciatively beneath the blindfold.

"You should ask me what it isn't, first."

"You're being very enigmatic. Very well—what *isn't* that heavenly smell?"

"It *isn't* smoke from a backed-up chimney."

"I should say not! It smells more like . . . cake! A delicious cake."

"Do you remember our wedding, Ana? The smoke that made our eyes water, the mind-numbingly boring address of the curate, the interminable documents to sign . . ."

She shuddered. "Don't remind me."

"It's a day best forgotten. And I aim to drive it from your memory. No peeking, please," he said, as he tucked her arm under his and began walking.

"I was tempted! But I decided not to."

"Good girl."

"We're not going into the house?"

"Not yet. Come, down this pathway."

She had no idea where he was taking her, the pleasant sun shining on her upturned face and the sway of their bodies moving in tandem were hypnotizing. She guessed they were somewhere near the gardens, moving along the cobblestone path that led to the chapel. He walked her up one step, then another, and cooler air washed over her.

Dex's knuckles lightly rested on the nape of her sensitive neck as he undid the blindfold and slid it off. She blinked, letting her eyes adjust.

They were in the chapel.

And it was full of people. Friends. She saw Thea, and Lulu. Celestia and Rupert: Rupert crying without shame, Celestia nodding serenely. Cloris, Agnes, McArdle, even Lady Glynis, all standing as one, turning toward her with smiles full of love and approval. They were bathed in beautiful light from the arched stained-glass window of the apse, emerald green, ruby red, cerulean blue, and a gentle gold turning them into enchanted creatures from one of her stories.

A string quartet, somewhere to the side, began to play. Softly. Something by Haydn, a gentle swell of joyful notes.

Rose petals covered the aisle between the rows of chairs.

"I . . . what . . . Dex! Please, explain to me what I'm seeing? Did I fall asleep in the carriage, and this is all a dream?"

"No," laughed Dex. "You are very much awake." She turned to look at him, just as he sank to one knee, his hand outstretched to clasp her own.

"If you can love this wounded, scarred man, then anything is possible. Any dream can come true. Ana, I lay my armor at your feet. You have utterly conquered the dragon in me. You've driven the nightmares away and filled my heart with hope. With love."

"Dex." She began to cry softly.

"I want nothing more than to make you happy. Your smile is the only reward I require in life. I can't explain how you unknotted the scars, how you found the last slim remaining pathway to my heart. I don't need to understand it. I only need to know, do you still feel the same way? Is it too late? Can you still love me?"

She was dimly aware of the crowd holding a collective breath.

"I never stopped loving you, Dex."

Audible sighs from their audience. A smattering of applause.

"Then Analise, before this gathered congregation of friends and family, will you do me the honor of becoming my bride?"

"We're already married, Dex," she responded with a tremulous laugh.

"Then will you do me the honor of allowing me to re-create our wedding in a manner more befitting a clever, imaginative, inquisitive, passionate whirlwind of a redheaded hellion?"

"That might be the longest rambling sentence I've ever heard you speak."

"There's more where that came from. Though this floor is damnably hard."

"Yes. Oh Dex, yes." Tears filled her eyes. He'd done all of this for her.

"Well, then." Dex leapt to his feet. "Let's let that good news tide us all over for a bit while Cloris and Agnes dress you!"

Through a veil of happy tears, she saw the two maids approaching and let them sweep her quickly into the house. She started toward the stairs.

"No, Your Grace! We don't have time," said Cloris, pulling her toward the drawing room.

"Yes, Your Grace! We mustn't keep them waiting," said Agnes, agreeably.

Ana followed them in, and saw, lying on the divan, the dress to put an end to all other dresses—lashes of delicate lace at the hem, intricately embroidered roses dotting the mesh overlay, a delicate underdress of fine champagne-colored silk. It was the Clovercote costume, pulled from the pages and brought to glorious life. She clapped her hands at the sight of it.

"No time for a rose petal bath," said Cloris.

"No time to tame those curls," Agnes said.

"But he likes her untamed, now, doesn't he?" They winked at each other.

Ana allowed them to quickly undress and redress her in the finery.

The whole thing felt like a dream. *The best kind of dream you can possibly have*, thought Ana, as she glided back to the chapel, a dream she never had to wake from.

Tessie met her at the door and placed a wreath of blushing roses on her head. She was crying softly, with a beatific grin.

"When did all of this happen?" Ana whispered quickly to her friend.

"His Grace sent us very clear instructions, from the rose petals to the dress. You should see the cake!"

And see the cake she did, once the dream of a wedding was over, and the dream of a party commenced. Once she'd been clasped to the bosom of old friends and new and made to feel as welcome as any orphan had ever felt in any setting, ever. Her new family, her new life. Her new husband, sending her looks of adoration that took her breath away.

The cake was, itself, equally breathtaking. She'd never seen a cake like it, although she'd described its every tier in her novel. Frosted within an inch of its sure-to-be-short life, stuffed full of frangipane, studded with sugared fruits of all kinds, and reaching to the heavens.

And on the tiny tier at the top, a miniature candy princess, standing side by side with a miniature candy dragon, its tail wound protectively around the princess's sugar skirts.

"I took a liberty," Dex said apologetically, as she stared in wonder at the cake. "It isn't authentic to Lady Claridge's intent—I hope you don't mind?"

"Mind?" his newly remarried bride laughed into his ear, grabbing him in a ferocious hug. "It's brilliant! Such an imagination, my love. Clovercote meets Vyranthrall. I couldn't be happier."

He laughed with her, and they served the perfect cake to everyone assembled.

LATER, WHEN THE guests had been shown to their rooms, slightly inebriated and picking candied fruit out of their teeth, Dex and Ana were finally alone.

"Are you happy?" Dex asked his bride.

Wavering firelight caught in her hair and played over her curves. "I am," she said simply.

"You're too beautiful," he said worshipfully, drinking in the sight of her.

"So are you," she answered, her gaze raking him, lingering on his scars, his chest, and then resting on the visible bulge in his wedding trousers. "Dangerously so. Stop talking and kiss me now."

He laughed. "I never thought I'd hear you say those words." He kissed her, pouring his love and gratitude into the dance of their lips, their tongues.

"Now, here are the rules," she said, pulling back, a wicked light flickering in her eyes. "You will take me now, and we'll stare into each other's eyes, and I'll wrap my arms around your neck, and my ankles around your hips and we'll ride together until we're both flying high above the earth, until we're 'thrilling to the glittering stars above.'"

He smiled, recognizing the passage from her book. "I'm yours to command, Ana."

"Good duke," she said playfully, reaching for his scarred cheek with a touch so whisper-soft that he didn't even flinch.

"You've given me a reason to live, Ana. I understand now that life can hold both darkness and light. That day and night can exist together inside my heart. That I can feel the pain simultaneously with the love. You are a fierce and strong warrior princess. I will become worthy of your love, I swear it to you."

"You are worthy, Dex."

"I don't need my legacy to be reparations for that evil day on the battlefield. I want my legacy to be that I loved you. That's the legacy I want carved on my headstone. That he loved faithfully, and fiercely. That he was felled by a redheaded hellion and he never recovered his footing."

She laughed, and he laughed along with her. Even if it was a bit rusty, that laugh, it spoke volumes. And then they weren't laughing any longer. They were kissing.

Discarding clothing at breakneck pace. Wild for the feel of her skin on his skin. Soft strands of her hair flung across his chest. There was no longer any need for rules. Everything was allowed. Every sigh, every moan, rang with love. Every kiss held untapped depths of emotion.

She climbed on top of him and eased her body down, down, until he was buried in her wet heat, like returning home after a long war, where he belonged.

She rode him with intense concentration, learning how to make him gasp with a clench of her thighs, the brush of her fingers through his chest hair.

Her eyes had gone smoky and languid.

The love in their depths shook him to the core.

She rode him until they were flying . . . reaching for those stars she'd written about so eloquently, swallowing them whole.

Several hours later, after an exhausted sleep, Dex woke in the middle of the night to find that they were sleeping entwined on his bed, her head on his chest, his arms around her and his leg stretched across her thighs. This was a new kind of contentment. A hard-won joy claiming victory over the darkness. He folded Ana closer against his chest.

"I love you, Dex," she whispered, still half-asleep. "My fire-breathing dragon."

"I love you, Ana. My brave princess, the star that guides me. Slayer of darkness. Bringer of joy."

"I knew you had a poetic soul all along."

"You bring it out in me."

"I'll keep challenging you, Dex, for the rest of our lives. The battle's not over just yet." She nestled in closer, rubbing her cheek against his chest.

"I wouldn't have it any other way," he breathed into her hair, feeling his whole being relax into hers. "The rest of our lives . . . what a magical thought."

Epilogue

One year later . . .

Ana pushed her shoulders back, took a deep breath, and walked to the lectern in front of the small crowd of book lovers.

Rupert and Celestia were in attendance. Ana had become fast friends with her sister-in-law, who, after reading her book, had become her biggest supporter. It was she who had organized a group of ladies into a book club. They'd read *The Dragon and the Blue Star* and sent her a long list of surprisingly detailed questions to answer.

The book club ladies were in attendance, sitting in the first row. One was garbed as Princess Amsonia with a sapphire diadem circling her brow. Another had chosen to come as the Faery Queen, holding her young child in her lap, plump and adorable in a cleverly constructed hedgehog costume. Still another was wearing a golden horn atop her head, portraying one of the queen's unicorn guards.

And Qavox was there, of course. Standing at the back of the room against the wall, arms crossed over his muscular chest, glaring at everyone most fiercely as if to say: *This authoress is under my protection, heckle her at your peril.*

Tessie sat with her George by her side, who had been so moved by Ana and Dex's second wedding that he'd proposed to Tessie that very evening.

McArdle was there, wearing a sour expression, but clutching his cherished copy of *The Dragon and the Blue Star* that Ana had already signed for him.

Mr. Norwood had organized a series of book readings for her at London's premier bookshops. And he'd sent her one of the coveted velvet bags when the first printing of the novel had sold out. She wasn't certain but she was beginning to suspect that her little novel was outselling most of his list. He didn't want to admit it to her, of course, though he had shown her the dubious of honor of insisting on attending today.

"This book is dedicated to my father, Lieutenant John Crewe. He read the first pages I wrote but, sadly, never read the last. I miss you every day, dear Papa." She took a steadying breath. She felt her father's beaming presence, as well as Lady Claridge's, giving her strength and confidence.

She held the weighty book, reveling in the feel of the royal blue cloth binding, the smoothness of the paper's gilded edges. Lulu's drawing of the dragon never failed to thrill Ana. Her friend was much in demand as a literary illustrator now that the book was a success.

She began reading from the final chapter, amusement tickling her throat as she saw several members of the audience mouthing the words along with her, as though they had memorized her words by heart.

When she reached the last paragraph, her eyes misted over. She loved this part the most.

Chanting a strange incantation, Gaethryn drew a rune in the air. The figures glowed with an unearthly blue fire, then drifted away like smoke across the still waters.

Amsonia was suddenly conscious of the dragon's massive figure to her right, rippling, shifting, dwindling. She turned, and then she saw him for the first time: Prince Qavox reborn. A tall man, broad of shoulder and stern of face.

"My dragon," she murmured, pressing herself to him.

"My princess," he replied, his arms encircling her.

And then, for long minutes, the only sound was the clamor of their hearts.

The Faery Queen looked on with a benevolent smile.

Qavox the Dragon had been conquered by the brave Princess Amsonia, and all was right with the world.

As the last words lingered in the air, and enthusiastic applause erupted, Mr. Norwood rose from his seat and moved to stand beside her.

"Ladies and gentlemen, before the question and answer, I have an announcement to make."

Ana tilted her head, mystified.

"Because of the popularity of Her Grace's novel, beloved by yourselves and so many others across the realm, it is my great honor to announce that Norwood & Pennington will be publishing more novels by her esteemed ladyship."

"A sequel to *The Dragon and the Blue Star*?" asked the lady dressed as Amsonia.

"Perhaps, in due time. No, what I speak of is something new. Something very, very exciting. You see, I have just finished reading the manuscript and I can assure you it is certain to be a great success. Her Grace will be taking up the mantle of that most beloved authoress, Lady Claridge, and publishing a brand-new Clovercote novel."

There were gasps from the crowd and murmurs of approval.

"This talented authoress is more than capable of writing in two genres. She moves hearts with her dragons . . . and her dukes."

"Thank you, Mr. Norwood." Ana had delivered the manuscript to him only last week. My, how fast he must have flown through her pages.

She opened the floor to questions and was asked most of the usual things: how did she come up with her ideas, what was her writing process, could she give any advice to aspiring writers.

And then the Faery Queen raised her hand.

"Yes?"

"Did His Grace inspire the character of Qavox the Dragon?" she asked with a sly smile.

Ana grinned. "I rather think it was the other way around. The Dread Dragon inspired His Grace."

Dex caught her gaze from the back of the room and held it tightly.

The look that passed between them spoke of whispered midnight commands. Long, lazy conversations wrapped in each other's arms on sun-dappled mornings.

The man he was becoming . . . more open, more trusting. The slow unfurling of a deep, enduring love that had the power to transform the darkest night, the strongest curse, into the sunniest of hopeful mornings.

I love you. I'm yours, he mouthed, for only her eyes to see.

And the words filled her heart to overflowing.

And all was right with the world.

Acknowledgments

A wholehearted thank-you to my dear agent, Alexandra Machinist, and to my fantastic editor, Laura Schreiber. Many thanks to the wonderful team at Avon, especially Catherine Hay. All my gratitude to my critique partners and beta readers—Charis, Maire, Rachel, and Neile. I couldn't have finished this book without my brilliant sister Amelia. All my love to my partner, Brian, and my extended family in Alaska and Wisconsin. I wouldn't be publishing my eleventh novel without the unflagging support and exuberant enthusiasm of all the historical romance fans, reviewers, librarians, and booksellers around the world. Thank you so much!

About the Author

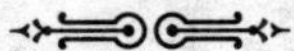

LENORA BELL is a *USA Today* bestselling, award-winning romance author. A teacher with an MFA in creative writing, Lenora has lived and worked on five continents. She currently lives in Colombia with her partner and two tiger-striped rescue kitties. She loves hearing from readers! Sign up for her mailing list to hear about new books, sales, and giveaways.

Read more from *USA Today* bestselling author

LENORA BELL

The Thunderbolt Club

Wallflowers vs. Rogues

School for Dukes

The Disgraceful Dukes